Living Tissue. 10 x 10

Emilian Galaicu-Păun

LIVING TISSUE. 10 X 10
A NOVEL

Translated from the Romanian by Alistair Ian Blyth

DALKEY ARCHIVE PRESS
McLean, IL / Dublin

Originally published by Editura Cartier as *Țesut viu. 10 x 10* in 2014.

Copyright © by Editura Cartier in 2014.

Translation copyright © by Alistair Ian Blyth, 2019.

First Dalkey Archive edition, 2019.

Library of Congress Cataloging Number 2019952211

www.dalkeyarchive.com
McLean, IL / Dublin

Printed on permanent/durable acid-free paper.

In memory of Gheorghe Crăciun (1950-2007),
who would have been the first to want to read this book

He who was living is now dead.
We who were living are now dying.
With a little patience.

T.S. Eliot, *The Wasteland*

I carry with me a silent baggage.
So deeply and for so long did I pack myself in silence
that I can in nowise unpack myself in words.

Herta Müller, *The Cradle of Breath*

Brief Guide to Reading

THIS BOOK OUGHT NEVER to have been written, if only in order not to prolong the agony of its characters and the post-mortem of those who inspired them; although on the other hand, to leave it unwritten would have been tantamount to a confession that was false by omission. But now that it has—often despite inner resistance—it is appropriate that I make clear that reading it will be impossible unless the following authorial warning is heeded: "ANY RESEMBLANCE TO ANY REAL PERSON IS THE PRODUCT OF THAT PERSON'S OWN IMAGINATION," which means that although no circumstance is autobiographical, there is no event that does not find its equivalent—be it directly or indirectly—in the life of the author, and therefore the latter feels entitled to exclaim, à la Flaubert: "The father (but also F., ---n, et al.), *c'est moi!*"

Of the itineraries for reading, one might follow the chronological, in which case, the reader ought to start at Chapter 8, continue with Chapter 1, Chapter 9, Chapter 2 and so on, ending with Chapter 4. Another two patterns—the "hopscotch" (leaping from square to square: Chapter 1—Chapter 5; Chapter 9—Chapter 2; Chapter 3—Chapter 6; Chapter 7—Chapter 8; Chapter 10—Chapter 4) and the "roulette wheel" (where the sequence of chapters is aleatory)—are closer to the inner structure of the text, which, above all else, is labyrinthine and kaleidoscopic. But since the novel has been fleshed onto the skeletal frame of the *Decalogue*, nor is the normal numerical sequence (from Chapter 1 to Chapter 10) to be disregarded. But one

might equally well read each chapter as a rewriting of the previous chapter(s), so similar is the present text to a palimpsest.

Internally a funeral train, with ten sleeping cars for eternal
slumber, a rollercoaster, or *montagnes russes*, in its external load-
bearing structure, *Living Tissue. 10 x 10* should ultimately be
read as a simple railway novel: "Astapovo Station!" "Astapovo
Station!" "Astapovo Station!" "Astapovo Station!" "Astapovo
Station!" "Astapovo Station!" "Astapovo Station!" "Astapovo
Station!" "Astapovo Station!" "Astapovo Station!" [1]

---

[1] The station where Leo Tolstoy died — *Translator's note*

Contents

Summary [dressed]

THE SLANT OF THE WRITING—the way you might pluck the eyebrows of a beautiful woman, from the majuscules of the strands at the bridge of the nose to the *petit* of the wispy hairs at the outer corners of the eyes—due not to the calligraphy lessons that once were but to the reading that has always been, is of primordial importance in the work of fleshing out a character: before this character opens her eyes, the left eyebrow—at the point where it joins the partly plucked right eyebrow, allowing the one and the other to look like indented paragraphs—expresses someone's astonishment at having drawn the attention of the viewer, and simultaneously her own embodiment's horizon of expectation, now revealed on her face by the barely perceptible flutter of her eyelashes, still sugared with sleep, like quivering reeds, but impatient to view themselves in the mirror of the page; the Sleeping Beauty awakens to life, exhales through her every pore, takes control of her body; see how she tunes her senses; by the way in which she studies her reflection it's obvious that at any moment she will cease to be content with self-contemplation, but will seek confirmation in another's eyes—man or woman, but let's hope for her sake it's a man—who will undress

(. . . when she ties her hair in a bun (as if she were rolling up her sleeves) on the top of her head, *das Ewig-Weibliche* shows itself in effigy like a French treble clef

whose sweet curve runs down the length of the spine to the sacrum

her with his eyes, and who in turn (*"Au suivant! Au suivant!"* the Jacques Brel song sounds in his ears) will do his utmost to make of her if not a Miss World then at least a Miss Text ("Ah, let me see you naked!" from the final screen test, the *Scriptease*), but now is now, a woman happens / a man occurs, her body of supreme joy / his joy between the sheets, and after she gave herself to him / he had her, *repetez encore une fois*, and after countless other times when they woke up in each other's arms, the Lover's best wishes—"you deserve the best in the world! . . ."—heralding the moment of imminent parting, I turned the page; further pages, further couplings; original documents / notarized copies; the game of analogies acquiring new expressions: *I give what I haven't got* (her), *give me some of what you've got* (him), each vaguer than the last, the way you might bunglingly translate *hardcore as cœur lourd*, in a Frenglish that limped with both legs (with the same *L'Origine du monde* between them) and so on, and so forth—"alphabets burgeon with sylvan wildness between girls' thighs at puberty—some curly, some smooth, as nature dictates"—, and this, that, and the other—"if it's written across the forehead, why read it in the palm, with the hand *sous les jupes des filles*?! . . ."—, the metaphysics of sex now [and forever and ever, amen] avenged by genetic engyneering, and then, *игра в одно касание*[2] reverts to *toucher et jouer*, and auto-writing—in the feminine: *l'écriture de soi(e)*, alias *belle écriture*, put simply: *belles lettres*—reverts to prayer:

"Be your benevolence over us, Lord God! And strengthen the work of our hands, yes, strengthen the work of our hands!"

The lesson of modesty having been learned—whenever she goes on a first date, let her put on "passion-killer" *dessous*, so that she won't be tempted to capitulate that very same night—, the derogations from the law of decency were as numerous as they were *ad libitum*. The canon that she herself had laid down—so that she wouldn't end up in anybody's bed unless, during dinner, which had to be romantic, at a chic restaurant, she managed to

---

[2] The one-touch game

take off her knickers under the table without anybody noticing—transformed the "dexterity" test into brain surgery: you
had to scratch the back of your neck vigorously in order to quell
the itch between your legs. Thus, whereas before she used to
wear only jeans & checked shirts, now she found herself with a
wardrobe of evening gowns, to each of which she gave a name—
Marilyn Monroe, Gina Lollobrigida, Kim Basinger etc. (how was
she supposed to know that the famous owners, of the names,
not the dresses, would have been happy to exchange, *in corpore*,
their fame & (some of them) their posthumous glory for her
living body, that of a thirty-year-old woman, to exchange it for
her *Trentes Glorieux*, as it were)—a name that betrayed not only
its design, but also its sex appeal. The fact that over her bloomers
from grandmother's dowry chest she wore a white *Romy Schneider*
signified that she was ready to fall in love again, the same as her
wearing a *Monica Vitti* unfailingly signaled that she wanted to be
loved, and a *Madonna* that she wanted to be f—ked. Her private
sartorial code made plain what the code of good manners had
tried to conceal—desire, passion, temperament—but without
making it any more accessible, since she obeyed only the call of
her hands; it was only in the naked flesh that she answered to
the name Helga. Those who celebrated her name day could be
counted on the fingers ("of one hand," as each believed, although
only she knew each hand's ordinal number); as far as she was concerned, before entering her radius of action, every man revealed
himself to her from the viewpoint of either "He wants me, can't
get enough!" or "He wants me, can't get it up . . ."—since it
was impossible not to want her!—, but, even after being sorted,
the latter were not struck from the list, but went on to demon-
strate the opposite to her, under the banner: "*Liberté. Helgalité.
Fraternité.*" Once she was in the arms of one or another, she
had one overriding demand: "Never just once!"—, which was
in keeping with the more than natural desire of her partner: "A
woman means something for one night. / And if she was beautiful, for the next one too!" (Gottfried Benn); but as a student she
had won the Miss Alma Mater competition—with her, not to be
beautiful was quite simply out of the question. The combination

of beauty and pleasure—"The beautiful is not what is beautiful, but what I like!"—came of themselves in the man's case, as did the orgasm, whereas the woman had to make herself beautiful for the sake of his pleasure and, with a little luck & much imagination, hers too, but rarely both. This lack of harmony between his guaranteed satisfaction and her difficult-to-satisfy desire was at the very foundation of the inequality between the sexes, whence too the different perception in the case of an *homme à femmes*, who is sooner admired, and in the case of a woman buzzing like a fly from one partner to the next (why merely a fly?!—her buzz is sometimes that of an industrious bee, sometimes that of a swarm of wasps), who is always viewed as a whore. To attain, even in passing, the goal of perfection—it would have been like the *Elizabeth Taylor* gala dress encountering the natty *Paul Newman* suit in the cloakroom of some provincial theatre for just one performance. "*A Cat in Heat on the Tin Roof*. . . You what! . . . *The Cat on the Hot Tin Roof.*" The way things had been going for her lately, she ought to have fired her tailor. Not the tailor, the tailoring! (Or to have taken a correspondence course, *postrestante*, with Jacqueline Kennedy; they say that whenever she wanted a new dress, the first lady used to go and stand naked in front of her husband and ask: "John, darling, do you think I can go to the reception for the President of France looking like this?" The 35th would look at her carefully, utter a determined "No!" and then sign a blank check for an evening gown from Chanel or Yves Saint Laurent, in honor of his distinguished guest.) She had been told so many times that she was cut out for it that even she had started asking herself why it was that she hadn't yet founded her own fashion label, or at least a line of off the peg clothing, and then she would climb down from the catwalk of empty praise with her tail between her legs. Alone with her buttonhole, through which a suitable button had not passed for quite some time, and now ready to hang up her craving on the peg.

She lacked neither the opportunities, nor the skill—she had practiced for the last few weeks, evening after evening, when putting on her nightdress and taking off her panties, by shaking her bottom rather than using her hands, timing herself against

the clock—, rather she lacked the man for whose sake she would
have been prepared to embarrass herself in front of everybody,
in the event of failure. Now and then she let herself be taken
out on the town, so as not to get out of practice. But fearful she
might lack the courage to go all the way, she would slip inside
her handbag a lacy little number, in reserve—in the event that
she liked the young man enough to follow him into the night,
but not enough for her to torture herself taking off her "passion-
killers" in public. Watching her vanish into the bathroom "to do
her make-up," nobody would have suspected that in fact she was
readying for complete surrender; but it was enough to catch a
glimpse of her returning to the table waving a white smile to realize that a transfiguration had occurred (in fact, that's inside out;
in the end, who hasn't put on an item of clothing back to front,
at least once in life?!), one that was obvious to anybody, but
which wasn't on show. How red she had flushed, like a poppy,
one evening, when her beau, taking the initiative, had conspira-
torially remarked to her over the table before going to the bathroom: "I'm off to shake hands with a close friend, whom I hope
you'll be meeting very shortly . . ."! Exactly like in the joke with
the beard—the billy goat's beard. What if she had said, as she
headed toward the ladies' cubicles: "I'm just off on an expedition
to find the golden fleece, I'll be right back via the silk road"?! Or,
less roundaboutly: "I'll be right back with the blank accreditation
papers for desire—would you like to put your name down, on
receipt?" Stubble-field version: "Take me!"?! . . . But the morals
of refined society, in general, and her sentimental education, in
particular, demand that potential partners engage, for the sake of
appearances, in a dance of *qui-perd-gagne*, with set moves, a kind
of compulsory quadrille that transforms reciprocal desire into a
web of intersecting lines. (A word out of place, a wrong move—
and the threads get tangled, snap, the strings are yanked etc., etc.,
whence the meaning of the game is that their legs should inter-
twine, in bed.) *"Par delicatesse, j'ai perdu . . . mes dessous,"* let her
whisper to her husband in pleasure (in the Shiite tradition—it
wasn't for nothing that she had taken Arabic as her second foreign language at university!—, after uttering the set phrase: "I

marry thee for pleasure, in accordance with the Book of God and the tradition of the Prophet, without any inheritance, but only for a limited number of days"), paraphrasing Rimbaud, and he shall reply to her: "Ну ты и *perdu*-нья!"[3] Ultimately, who decides how far speech can go in designating the organs/ actions that the other's hand have touched, once acts have been concluded, as is known, in consummate conviviality?! Which is more shameful, to lift your skirt up or to ask your partner, looking him straight in the eye, like in the final scene of *Eyes Wide Shut*, when Nicole Kidman says to Tome Cruise: "F—k me!"?! She had met guys who had mustered all their awkward words & lewd expressions in order to lure a woman into bed and who—having got her there—had gone out of their way to heap choicely phrased praises on her; and the other way around, too, chaps whose lips had dripped honey beforehand and who afterward sullied her from head to toe and crotch betwixt. There are more things in heaven and earth! Banished from heaven, the Garden of (earthly) Pleasure.

She would now be unable to say who had been first to suggest they go to the *Délice d'Ange*; what is for sure is that by their second or third date they already had their own little table, by the window, separated from the next, also a table for three, by a beige curtain, at the back of the dining room for families with small children. They have so many words to tell each other, about lives they have spent with someone else, whomever and wherever they could, that they risk never progressing to action; but it's enough that they retire in silence, like two bodies abruptly exposed in their post-peccant nakedness—*Eve asking Adam after he beds her for the first time: What was that? And he says: It's called f—king. And she says: I want more, it is good!*—that seek to dissimulate their natural urge for reciprocal closeness. "Reci-*porc*-al," since they're hiding behind words, *our brother the pig* being not only a gratuitous expression, but also evidence of anatomical kinship, so much so that "medicine (…) from Antiquity to the fourteenth

---

[3] Pun: "You are lost (French)/flatulent (Russian)!" —*Translator's note*

century, and sometimes as late as the sixteenth century, studied the anatomy of the human body by dissecting pigs" (Michel Pastoureau, *A Symbolic History of the Western Middle Ages*). And that's right: "if life is piggish, better never to have cast it before swine; give us this day our eternal life, / like a sow-shaped piggy bank—that we may break it open day and night!" he recites by heart from a poet with a spotted past: Rac Mozgov. She a bona fide unpaired woman; he a "peerless artist" ("with a past record of illicit pairing," as his wife used to say, busting his pair, when she was mad at him)—there was no question of there not being a conjunction of suitable halves, and this was what attracted them. And this quite apart from the fact that she is exceptionally attractive, and he is simply exceptional. There is nothing between them, not even the words the young woman transcribed in his notebook: "I'm giving you the opportunity to destroy me, fully convinced you won't"—as a sample of her handwriting, supposedly similar to his—, a motto as declaration of war, containing *in nuce* also the request for a truce. She has a pared-down hand, with feminine curves undulating beneath the taut skin of the ink, which wholly suit her; his hand, is just skin and bone— more bone than skin!—, creaking at the joints, syncopated, like his highly consonantal speech. But so long as they get along, who is affected by the fact that the man articulates as if he were cracking pebbles in his mouth, whereas her vowels fall like dew and dissolve as easily?! . . . "Where was I?" he realizes he has lost the thread, and also that in fact he ought to have begun by asking her where she was headed and whether they were going in the same direction. She comes to meet him halfway, ready to toss him a lifebelt: "You were talking about the script for a program . . ." but looking in her eyes, he instantly remembers: "*Beautiful & Best!* It's a TV project I was forced to drop last year after two abortive attempts, because I didn't have a presenter: the first girl wasn't photogenic, what with her owl-like glasses, which lent her the air of a woman *mal baisée* (and God knows, she wasn't!); the second let it all hang out on screen, baring pistil and stamens . . ." "Stamens are the male organ of the flower . . ." "That's what I'm saying, stamens—she used to arrive for filming as if she just been

part of a gang bang; you couldn't look at her without catching
on . . . her *černá hodinka*, melting masterfully like in a Salvador
Dali painting . . . How can I put it: she was *like a fly-covered
flypaper*, 1.88 meters long, laid out horizontally, that's how las-
civiously flyblown she looked! And sure, she couldn't even be
bothered to open the script, preferring to read her lines off a
prompter, not even by the syl-la-ble, but by the l e t t e r!" And
after a pause, during which the man closed the parenthesis, letting himself be ushered into her open brackets: "When we met,
at Noël, at the *Crème de la crème*, after losing sight of you in the
last few years, I knew from the very first moment that you were
the one, the presenter I lacked!" "What is it I've got that the
others haven't? . . ." the woman sooner states than asks. "A physical presence which, merely by appearing on screen, proves presence of spirit." There's no need for him to undress her with his
eyes—his words slide under her skin, they're tingling throughout
her body. Now let's see what she'll come out with first. (How can
he know that even if she does come out with something, *hic et
nunc*, she'll do it in such a way that nobody will see?!) "How
physical does presence of spirit have to be?" she can't be caught
out as easily as that, but his gesture of leaning across the table
and fastening a button of her blouse, which is buttoned almost
to her throat as it is, bowls her over. No doubt about it, it's an
unexpected move, to which, were she to respond, she ought to
lift her skirt a palm's width, under the table, the skirt that barely
covers her knees as it is. "In her place," he can't suppress the pleasure of applying a narrative treatment to her, "I would have pretended to stretch my legs a little—enough for limbs momentarily
to touch, as if by accident;" but in fact that's a completely different story, not out of a book, but one he really experienced—how
long can it have been since then?—, when, invited by a young
couple to dinner, during the meal, the young lady uninhibitedly
ran her bare sole up and down his legs, an endless touch, finally
letting her foot be caught between their vise in order thereby to
measure his erection, which was all but bursting out of his trousers. Now it's her turn to delineate a timid *pas de deux*: "So, I take
it the rôles have been written, and you are . . . Beau or Beast?"

"Wrong," he says, wrongfooting her. "It all happens to the rhythm of a *pas de trois*, the Beast—it's obvious who the Beauty is; I'm content with the '&' of dangerous liaisons!—being the Guest of honor, alias the best actor, director, musician etc., etc., depending on the theme of the show." "I've never done it with two at once," she titters, but since it occurs to her that she's jumped the gun, she makes a point of adding: "I've never even two-timed!" "It's a game for four hands," he says, allowing the girl's confessions to pass his ears unheard, "like *Cat's Cradle* in childhood. Except the one you'll be twisting around your fingers will be none other than our guest; like the man on the cross said: *hold on tight!*—as many lines as there are faces; all we have to do is capture each, the way the lads in that band *Trigon* do in that song of theirs, *Dodă*, when their bows freeze in mid-air, punctuating the pauses." She has to bite her own tongue not to tell him—for a time, her lover had been an older man who zealously practiced *coitus interruptus*; he'd driven her out of her mind by always pulling it out at the worst possible moment and then starting all over again just when she'd cooled down. "Have no fear," he says, seeming to read her thoughts, "the show is taped and, in any case, the two of us will be there when they edit it, and so, there won't be any void intervals." Their conversational back and forth resembles a rubber band which now one, now the other stretches before suddenly letting go and waiting for the other to guess which hand it's in; but when they let go of the end of what they're saying, they have to be careful lest it sting their hands. Before verbal prestidigitation gives way to the first actual touches, each adjusts his or her words to make an offer impossible to refuse: "Be with me!" after which they learn not to demand the impossible: "Be mine!" precisely because it might happen. He prefers her in the rôle of the Young Maybe—"maybe yes," "maybe no"—, as long as he has before him a mere reader and hasn't yet decided whether it's worth penning her, transforming her into a character, or leaving himself in her hands, making her his co-author. And so, whereas the narrative promised to be a love story, its mind still ends up on tales of matters lewder. But, again and again: the tale is a long and winding road, and there's still a long way to go! "What can I tell you, it's like in that play by Rac Mozgov"—he pronounces it in the French manner: *Mozgoff*—, in which the characters, Right Curtain and Left Curtain, are merely the *mise-en-scène* for the great absence, Naked Transcendence, the stripper from Germany. With one by no means negligible difference, that it is incumbent upon us to *mettre en valeur* a local presence!" The girl's intuition perfects the picture: "In other words, it's you wearing pajamas and me a *négligé?* . . ." "Not quite like that!" in his imagination, it all ought to look like in the *Dejeuner sur l'herbe*, and so he instantly corrects himself, looking her straight in the eye, unblinking: "Men dressed to the nines and the presenter in her *négligé.*" He passes over in silence the fact that the project's original title was *Dessous chics* and that the opening credits were a stylized reproduction of Sharon Stone's leg play in *Basic Instinct*; only later was it agreed that—the gospel according to Roland Barthes: "Is not a body's most erotic spot *where the clothing gapes?*"—the naked flesh should not be exposed, but merely glimpsed. Unexpectedly, she bursts into laughter, baring her teeth *like a flock of shorn sheep, emerging from a ford, all of them heavy with twins, not one of them barren*: "I was picturing a young woman in a magnificent evening dress talking to two men in pajamas . . ." "*Her Majesty the Queen Mother, setting an example to the war wounded . . .* Except that nowadays, the small screen looks more and more like a nudist beach . . ." And then, after a pause to allow the switchman to change the points: "In short, I want a presenter whose mere appearance on screen would seem to say:

> *Pull down my knickers.*
> *What for?*
> *So my snatch can smile*"[4]

All smiles, she pulls out her tablet, without which she wouldn't have left the house, not even to go to the grocer's on the corner, and a moment later, she shows him a video on youtube, http://www.220.ro/emisiuni-tv/Jurnalista-Fara-Chiloti-In-Fata-Premierului-Sarb-Ivita-Dacici/yhT1FxPXnZ/

---

[4] Poem by Katalin Ladik

As for him, as Mallarmé once put it very well: "I read whole libraries that I might f—k you." It's therefore no wonder that he liked well-read girls (*Elle lit* in his language translates as: She [in] bed; which is also how the author and reader of Italo Calvino's *If on a winter's night a traveler* end up at the end of the novel, each with a book in his/her hand), but never well-read enough to deny him, the "book cupboard," as the author of *The Enamored Cupboard*[5] once nicknamed him in a broadcast for Radio Free Europe, room to show off. He cultivated batches of female readers the way others cultivate fields of cannabis or plots of poppies, and, like any other grower of narcotics—literature is *une drogue douce, n'est pas?*—, he never got high on his own supply, for fear of addiction. He was not content merely to recommend books, he also lent them out—if instead of giving back the books, each girl had given herself to him, today he would have been the proprietor of one of the most extensive f—kotheques in Ch—ău. How groovy they would have looked lined up on his shelves like a flock of swallows on a high-voltage wire, minge next to minge, brunettes and blondes, curly and slick, cropped and shaven, one emitting a tweet, another an elaborate trill, each in her own idiom and all of them in his head. What a delight to run his fingers over the skin bindings! To insert your c—k by way of a bookmark between pages opened at random, after you have read and reread them all from front to back, what greater professional satisfaction could you wish for?! *Au pied de la lettre*, font size X. *Lire en fête*, literally and figuratively. All well and good, if in his madness he had not decided to produce his own book of books, which line by line was to contain all the women he had ever desired—numerous when compared with the few he had possessed—, consisting of God knows what: an unusual gesture, a stray glance, a snarled word, an indelible touch. Ranging from an event of his student years—in the U.S.S.R., the same as everywhere else in the communist prison camp, the university year began with the students having to perform agricultural labor; in the autumn of eighty-two, they spent the day picking grapes on the hills and the evening dancing in the village club,

---

[5] Emil Brumaru (1938-2019), Romanian oneirist poet. — *Translator's note*

where he picked up a quite presentable young peasant woman, whom he offered to initiate in the mysteries of love, talking to her all the way home about how they were going to have sex, until she lost patience and said: "Yes, all right, but after we have sex, are we going to f—k or what?!!"—to the confessions of one of his students—she'd won a week's holiday at the seaside, and her insanely jealous husband had made sure to provide her with a more than decent two-piece bathing costume, telling her when she left that he could hardly wait to see her suntan; but on her return, hastened, it was true, by a sudden drop in the outside temperature, she had caught him in bed with another woman, and so she had left the house without unpacking and with a single thought: "How am I going to pay him back?" after she had gone around looking like a nun, wearing that stupid bathing costume on Mamaia beach (and here she took off her dress and slip, revealing to his gaze uniformly tanned skin, less the breasts and bottom); she could have "avenged" herself on the spot, but in any case, her husband would never have found out, and that was when the saving idea came to him: "Go to a beauty salon right away and tan yourself all over, as if you'd just come back from a nudist beach!"—, he had raw material aplenty. But it had to be purged of the anecdotal, stripped down to pure fact—the boundless amazement of the husband on discovering the wife's "sea-bronzed flesh that walked around / naked from head to toe" (Gottfried Benn) after he with his own hand had garbed her in a white chastity belt in the form of a two-piece bathing suit—, sublimated to the point of the divine, intangible in its ultimate perfection. Writing it was reminiscent of that childhood game with a piece of string, in which one player would lift from another's fingers all kinds of "patterns"—running tracks, suspension bridges, rhombuses etc., etc.—, and then change them according to an implacable logic, and which was called: *Cat's Cradle* (an undeniably inspired name, evoking the grace of feline plasticity, but also the fragility of a game of transformations, always held in suspense). Even so long ago as childhood, he had intuited—and a lifetime's practice had confirmed it with each new experience lived to the full—that our world wasn't an arm-wrestling bout

between God and the Evil One, but rather a living tissue that
was renewed by the Supreme Prestidigitator and the Entangler as
they played the *threads*, moment by moment, in a predetermined
series which (even so!) left room for free will. (In the meantime,
the Parcae, also known as the Spinners, take care that there always
be threads of life in abundance—it's enough to stroke a cat to set
the spinning wheel of its purr in rasping motion.) To feel yourself an integral part of the Great Game, thinking of what figure
you will make at the will of the hands that play on your fingers,
and even to dare to take the initiative, first by imitation, then
by weaving your own design: nothing could be more beautiful
in this world. But since the number of possible combinations
stretched to infinity, the game began with his discovering the
number of his own life, which had to be conjugated using the
numbers belonging to his family, who in turn were caught up in
a genetic/elective web, and then there were *ces gens-là*, the poor
relations & acquaintances, further complicating the sum to the
power of. Now that he was up to his elbows in the *living tissue.
10 x 10*, all that remained was the final move, the extraction of
the root, after which he could start the game all over again and
fold his arms across his chest. All with a view to the fact that "the
artist must make posterity believe he never lived" (Flaubert to
Louise Colet, March 27, 1852). Only when devoid of any trace
of materiality could the work of his hands—they too reduced
to the votive image of the edifying act—be appropriated *tel quel*
by another, at the end of a long process of communication that
sinks back into communion, and not even then is it known
whether the prayer will be granted or whether it will be answered
with a f—k you. Like Him who said:

she dances on a sphere he sits on a cube

and when she does the splits it's like the horizon
the rope that she too skips

and when he moves his palms together it's as if
he grasped the newborn lifted her: "it's a girl!" as if he played

cat's cradle on ten fingers in childhood, careful
not to spoil the pattern—*the same one*
let another take her, the same as

his fingers might lift the lifeline from his palm

He would have deserved a slap, he was expecting her palm to
engage with his face at the least, but he was rewarded with a
radiant smile. "Now is now!" the young woman abruptly
decided, twisting around in her chair sufficiently to feel her
knickers ride up the cleft of her bottom and thereby accentuate
the curve of her buttocks, like two clinking champagne glasses:
"Happy Birthday!" It was barely four p.m., their five-o'clock tea
having been put back an hour because of her busy schedule, they
were in a café that was bursting at the seams and she had less
than forty-five minutes to perform her act, in premiere. The idea
seemed all the more amusing to her since it left no room for any
promises; and in any case, the first attempt ought to be for art's
sake. Nor did the man sitting opposite her seem interested in
mounting her whatever the price, and his way of looking at her,
gauging her price with his eyes, was that of the gambler who has
bet on the thoroughbred and is now in the stands about to watch
the race that might bring him, besides money, aesthetic satisfaction at the most: he doesn't own the stables, nor is he the jockey
that will ride the frothing Helga. This being the way things
stood, she could move at will, her first gesture released from all
constraint was to adjust her *brassière*, through her blouse, as if
trying to bring her breasts into equilibrium. The casualness with
which she raised her hand to her collarbone, as if to make the
sign of the cross, momentarily put him out of sorts—couldn't
she look on him as a man, rather than just a man of letters?!—,
but straightway he realized that it might equally signify a first
move, on the part of the white pieces, in a chess match about to
begin. He imagined how in his turn he might adjust his "neck-
tie," thrusting his hand inside the flies of his jeans; he knew, and
not only by hearsay, that *if you want to possess a woman, make her
laugh*. Although he wouldn't have liked the sort of woman who

laughed at anything at all—to top it all, he was more of a one for doing than possessing, and it wasn't for nothing that when she was angry at him as a child, his grandmother used to call him, "You done deed!" "It's impossible for you never to have done it in the open air, exposed, on the verge of being caught in flagrante at any moment, but still taking advantage of other people's inattention . . ." he started saying, distantly, and after a pause in which he watched through half-closed eyelashes as his words took effect, he hurriedly concluded: "On screen, it's just the opposite—you're the object of every gaze and it's none of your business what they all do to you in their imagination." But the girl had already left the studio, before even setting foot there, and invited him to follow her: "The last time I did that was with my ex, it was the middle of the afternoon, on a third-floor balcony. My parents and his were inside, trying one last time to get us back together, over our heads, and we had gone outside, into the open air, to cool down. After a while, I threatened to jump off the balcony and had even parted my legs to step up onto the balustrade"—she rose from her chair a little, stretching one leg to the side—, "I was leaning against the cupboard of empty pickle jars, as if about to push off against it. He entered me unexpectedly, like a knife through hot butter, and the surprise was so great that it never even crossed my mind to put up any resistance. My only thought was for my parents not to catch us, at least not before we finished, because I couldn't have cared less about the neighbors . . . Not even on the rollercoaster had I ever squealed with so much pleasure, although this time it was with my mouth closed!" And this time he didn't know how to react to the girl's confession—you don't say such things to the man with whom, at least in theory, you think you might be about to start a relationship: such things are to be savored only by lovers once they get to know each other well enough to compare their past experiences. You don't get anywhere if you become the confidante of a beautiful woman—this he knew like none other: after she had let her dress and other items of attire fall to the floor, his former student had not given herself to him, as one might have expected, but rather told him about how she had cheated on her husband twice in their very first year of marriage, once because she had been a virgin when she married a man she didn't love, for her parents' sake, and the second time because she had wanted a child that would be like anybody except her husband, on the grounds of rhesus incompatibility. "Now that you've thrown down the gauntlet . . ." and he placed before her the ring-bound proofs of a book, open at page 328: "read from here to here." Watching her hop from one word to the next, as if stepping on little chunks of wobbling ice during the thaw, in a desperate hurry to reach the other bank, he tried to divine from her facial expression which part she had reached in her reading: "Three girls renting a one-room apartment. Even if she's managed to get rid of the Russian, telling her to go out and see a movie, the Gagauz girl has just come home, complaining of a headache, and so our heroine has to conduct her gentleman caller to the kitchen, and you can kiss all thought of the bedroom goodbye (. . .) Now they're like two animals in heat, sharing the confined space of the same cage, two and a half paces from gas stove to fridge, one pace from table to crockery cupboard, with the air growing hotter and hotter (. . .) The partitioning curtain becomes what it presumably has been all along: an eardrum; the main thing is to know whether only the two of them are preventatively listening in on the adjacent room or whether the Gagauz girl is also discreetly spying on them. On that side of the curtain, the only sound is the television blaring, and on this side, only their teaspoons stirring their tea (. . .) The way the girl sits in his lap, lifting her skirt so that the gentleman caller can feel her bare buttocks—the knickers riding up her cleft are as thin as the string for slicing a dollop of maize porridge—, smacks of a declaration of war; from where he is sitting, the man keeps an eye on the front door, while his hands advance on two fronts, seeking her breasts under her T-shirt with his right, and climbing the inner flank of her thigh with his left (. . .) It is the watershed moment, when the gods laugh at mortals: either they stop halfway, regretfully signing a shameful truce; or they shamelessly get down to it, right under her roommate's nose, with the risk of being caught in flagrante. His head votes *pro*, which is to say, the

dumb head now poking above the elastic waistband of his underpants; she twists around toward the front door one last time and
then takes off her knickers (. . .) And then he makes the cleverest
possible move in the given situation—he doesn't pull her toward
him, as he sits on the chair by the window, but holding her up,
he steps toward the middle of the kitchen, whence he can see the
Gagauz girl reflected in the windowpane of the half-open door
as she dozes in front of the television. With a sure hand, he twists
his partner around, she is attentive to his movements, which are
peremptory and tender at the same time, she is firmly convinced
he knows what he is doing and that whatever happens, he's going
to pleasure her. Letting her hang forward, holding her arms to
form a suspension bridge above the void, the two are now a system of *poids-contrepoids*, whose equilibrium resides in his ability
to guide the assembly work. When finally he penetrates her from
behind, he feels his wand engulfed by a pot for smelting gold
(. . .); the sacs pump scorching air from both sides; the *bielle-
manivelle*—'the beast with two backs'—'*and he pulled and he
pulled, and he pushed and he pushed*'! A herd of horsepower galloping from one body to the other, the engines racing until they
reach a hundred miles an hour in just a few seconds, the combustion of desire achieves an explosion readied by mutual agreement, love is a Formula 1 race down the wrong side of the road,
a hurtling fireball eating up the asphalt. They both finish simultaneously, all in one breath, one of those (few) cases where haste
(or rather speed!) doesn't make waste, but rather makes the head
spin." There is nothing in the world more indiscreet than watching from close by as a beautiful woman reads a titillating text—
bodily necessities, sexual congress and the solitary vice pale
beside such a revelation of her basic *bovarisme*, comparable only
with his authorial *donquixotism*, the first of which comes within
a hair's breadth of death, the second of which within a hair's
breadth of madness. "Lend me it overnight," was her first reaction, lifting her eyes from the book. "Who's it by?" "I'll let you
have it after I finish writing it!" "How will you know when
you've finished it? . . ." "From the taste of rat poison in my
mouth, Madame!"

In the minutes that follow—too few in order to go back, plenty enough to change your mind a hundred times—they each open their own books, far too absorbed in the combinations that can be glimpsed therein to sneak a peak at the other's. Now, their game is each to act out his or her number to the very end: he, impatient to clothe his reader in his words, thereby incorporating her into his *living tissue*. *10 x 10* in the final hundred metres before the finishing line; she, straining to take off her knickers, which are more decorative than useful—with or without them, she'd still be bare-arsed!—without anybody noticing, now that she's allowed herself to rise to the challenge. With her back to the window, with the protective screen of the beige curtain to her left, separating them from the next table, and to the right another table at which two business ladies are talking animatedly, each with her nose in her laptop, and with the man sitting right opposite her talking to her—what is he getting at?!—about Beria's supposed mistress, who was imprisoned in the same cell as Polina Zhemchuzhina, whom he claimed to have met in Moscow in eighty-seven (". . . All of a sudden the 'bad NKVD cop' stopped beating her—but now he started telling her in copious detail about everything he did in the Lubyanka cellars during the course of a day; no sooner had he finished his confession than the 'good torturer' started wheedling her, begging her amid increasingly voluptuous sighs not to tell anybody, for her own good, as well as theirs, and just to make sure, threatening to cut her tongue out. They weren't empty words, an empty threat—the man had half a razor blade hidden behind his teeth, which he was trying to push inside her mouth with his tongue, in a passionate kiss. But she realized what was going on, and what might have seemed from one side a long kiss à la Paolo and Francesca, was in fact nothing but a life-and-death struggle of tongues, each trying to wield the same weapon. Rarely did it end without bloodshed!"), the woman twisted around in her chair, almost imperceptibly, as if she wanted to get up and go to the bathroom but was too polite to interrupt him. But he had eyes only for the girl's face, and her leg-play as she danced the *zook*—*"une danse qui à la base est faite pour faire jouir l'homme; le couple doit s'arrêter de danser uniquement lorsque l'homme a éjaculé*—with an invisible partner was beyond his ken. In the meantime, she was all eyes and ears, simultaneously adjusting her brassiere, through her blouse, cupping her hands around her cup of jasmine and green tea, lifting it to her mouth, straightening the skirt over her thighs under the table, or whatever it was she was doing down there, it was as if—three in one, said the Parcae—she had grown an extra pair of arms, so industrious was she. Arms, schmarms, her legs looked like two cobras with flaring hoods (white ones or black ones, he couldn't remember . . .) moving to the rhythm of an enchanted flute, which they themselves had aroused—suddenly the man realized that he had got an unexpected hard-on, not even he knew since when, probably while he was narrating the episode with the razor-blade kiss—, and now she exults as her legs manage to rid themselves of the silk bond that held them pressed together. In parallel with the subtle horizontal movement hidden from the gaze, on the vertical plane the narrative thread has openly swapped hands—the hand that writes for the hand lifted to the mouth, as it were—, with the girl proving to be an excellent storyteller: "I'd gone to sign up for modern dance classes, I was standing in front of the door of the dance classroom, eavesdropping, still undecided, before opening it. Then I heard a voice—the voice of the dance teacher, from the way it was giving orders: 'Бедра вперед, я сказал . . . ну прижми ж ее . . . между ног . . . да крепче же!!! вперед . . . мееееееедленно . . . быстро-быстро . . . . мееееедлено . . . быстро-быстро . . .'" [6] I couldn't tell what was going on in there, but I felt so embarrassed the ground could have swallowed me up! Afterward, I found out that it was the basic dance steps for the tango, slow, quick, quick slow." He looks at her meaningfully—perhaps now isn't the time to recite to her from Katalin Ladik, but rather from Lala Lallded: "The wise man told me a single word: / Go from being exterior to being interior. / I then stripped and danced naked," since she was once a dancer . . . "I want to read your thoughts . . ." says

---

[6] Thighs forward, I said . . . grip it already . . . between the legs . . . harder!!! forward . . . slowly . . . quick-quick . . . slowly . . . quick-quick.

the middle-aged man, taking the cup from her hand and raising it to his lips, as if to mark the transition from the tea ceremony to—although for that he would have to move farther around the circle; but at the *Délice d'Ange*, the tables don't communicate among themselves, and at a closer look, oftentimes nor do those seated at the same table—Plato's *Banquet*, that too almost at an end. But he can move back around the circle, doing like a tea master does—in other words, smashing the cup from which he has just drunk, "that it might never again be used by any other human being," having been "sullied by the lips of misfortune" (Okakura Kakuzo, *The Book of Tea*)—, but he might just as well drain the cup and have done with it. If there is one thing he lacks right now in order to preserve *à jamais* this afternoon in the memory of the flesh, it is Georges Bataille's *Story of the Eye*, from which he might read—borrowing the tender and yet virile voice of Radu Benea from Radio Free Europe—, also right now, on the spot:

"In the hall there was a saucer of milk for the cat.

"'Saucers are made for sitting on,' said Simone. 'Want to bet I won't sit on a saucer?'

"'I bet you won't,' I replied breathlessly.

"It was hot. Simone put the saucer on a stool, walked in front of me and, without taking her eyes off me, sat down, wetting her bottom in the milk. For a time I remained stock-still—the blood had rushed to my face and I was trembling—, and she watched as my sex made my trousers bulge. I lay down at her feet. She sat still; for the first time, I saw 'the pink and black flesh' soaked in white milk. For a long time we remained motionless, both of us blushing"; as for her, she is now all nerves and muscles, tensing herself for the final leap, in her mind she repeats for the hundredth time that, ultimately, taking off one's *dessous* can't be more complicated than taking a single skip of the rope; and back in the day, nobody could beat her at skipping a rope. She was a big girl by then but still she sometimes hopped in the schoolyard, to the delight of the lads in her class, who watched in enchantment as her chest jiggled like in a Maasai marital dance, but most of all they looked at her legs, bared all the way to the top, as if she were trying to leap out of her school uniform straight into her first evening dress: "Undress me!" and now she was assiduously preparing the decisive step. In the instant when she decides, she drops her teaspoon next to her chair, and, pretending to grope for it under the table—without taking her eyes off the man sitting opposite her—, she quickly pulls off her knickers; but the man is what might be called "a gentleman of the tea," and so he quickly leaps to her assistance, finding himself at the girl's feet. Their hands meet on top of a scrap of white silk—too small to be a handkerchief, too delicate for shoelaces —, and then he seeks the answer in her eyes, but incapable of reciting the sentence she prepared in advance: "My knickers fell down," all she can utter is a drawling "Meow . . ."; in other words, *Cat's cradle*—blessed is he who whose fingers have lifted off the name:

"A heptagon with equal points,
Seven signs, placed cyclically:

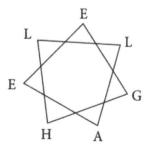

Seeing she is about to lose the thread, even though she was the one who pushed the game into extra time, and intuiting more than realizing what exactly their hands are touching, he replies in jest: "Are you playing *Băsmăluța*? . . ."—as if she were the queen of the ball fluttering her monogrammed handkerchief to signal the start of the quadrille—and without waiting for an answer, he repeated the dirty version of the childhood rhyme:
"Cine joacă *Băsmăluța*
Îi dator s-arate puța."

[He who plays the game of *Shawl* / Must show his winkle small]

Living Tissue. 10 x 10

Emilian Galaicu-Păun

Cap. 1
Rhesus-incompatibility

The tone: "... *for love is as strong as death*"

The Song of Songs, 8:6

A CHECKED HANDKERCHIEF—*échiqueté*, in heraldic terms—
which the stranger pulls from the pocket of his blue jeans to
hand to the girl, thinking of Georges Bataille's Simone, from
The Story of the Eye, and she wipes the pearly liquid dribbling
down her thighs after dipping her bare bottom in the cat's saucer of milk; the ancestral, natural gesture with which she wipes
up there—"Is that blood?!"—as if she had been making love in
the open air since the world began; the raw wound, having now
died of pleasure and been resurrected by the presentiment of
fresh desire, yawning open to overflow its edges like an eye astonished at what is happening to it; the perfume imbues the fabric,
the perfume of an orange stuffed with cloves, that cuneiform
script—deriving from cunnus, obviously, as follows: "*Peter, quid
est cunnus? Locus pessimus atque profundus*"—the fabric folded
in four, so that once unfolded its axial symmetry can be read
plainly. "Watch your mouth!" The sentence barely having formed
on his lips abruptly emerges feet-first. "After all, you're hardly a
seedbed of maidenheads, nor I a *Hymen*gway!" "*Old Maid Inc.*
Special orders for traditional weddings & one-night brides," her
riposte, sharper than might have been expected, causes him to

rue his words. "*Laisse tomber*," he capitulates. "Instead let me tell you about how I lost my innocence. Blood for blood, as it were. But bear with me." The girl darts him a glance, one of those swift looks that hit their target no matter how hard you try to fend them off. He ought to look like a mammoth from the cave at Altamira, given how many times he has been struck right in the face, were it not that, in its phylogenesis, the flesh has transformed the darts into as many pores, each with a delicate strand of hair on top, through which his entire being is exhaled. "And do you know with whom?" A theatrical pause, long enough to read on his lips: "Because I hardly kept a candle burning for you . . ." The question makes her burst into complicit laughter, in memory of the Night of Perfumed Candles, their first—their unforgettable. But now it is his turn to emit a warlike whoop: "With Lenin!" And without giving her time for an answer apposite: "You, whatever you were called at the time, what were you doing in 1971?"

. . . no earlier, since it wasn't until '70 that they struck the commemorative one-ruble coin with the face of I. V. Lenin (1870-1924). He had two of them, brand new, and wouldn't have parted with them for anything in the world, had not a man and a woman crossed their threshold one spring afternoon, soaked from head to foot, each with a knapsack on their shoulders. They were roaming the villages of the Soroca plain, begging, after the Dniester burst its banks and washed away their house and chattels. They looked so wretched that the child hid behind the oven in fear, whence at irregular intervals he heard the voice of his grandfather asking them one thing and another—peasants born and bred, authentic to the soles of their feet, they recognized each other by their smell, like farmyard animals; if the gypsies came to their door, they would have slammed it without a word!—before placing in their sack "what God has given." Old rags, a handful of flour, runner beans. They were about to leave, they had even exhausted their stream of "God bless you! God bless you!" when Grandma called him by name—a name same as hers, except in the diminutive—to come to her and give her what he had in his little pouch. Thitherto he had never heard

the saying, "money is the devil's eyes," but that was all his grandmother said to him as she took his two rubles, the way you might
snip off the balls of a male piglet. He never forgave her and when
warmer weather came and his grandmother set about repairing
her stove (which is to say, sealing all its cracks by plastering it
with horse flop, after trailing along behind the arse of "Năstică's"
horse for a whole week—Năstică, the village carter, was a kind of
relative, who got his nickname from the rhyming insults that his
wife used to fling at him, such as: "Năstică, Năstică / tu nu ştii
pe lume nică!" [Năstică you stupid lout / you don't know nowt],
until her nastiness finally drove him to suicide a few years later),
he told her to her face: "Grandma, you're a cow with boots on!"
Days unnumbered—excepting those when Grandpa dated his
letters to his son, an officer in the Soviet Army on the point of
finishing his service, with the invariable closing words, penned in
capital letters, in his preschooler's hand: ". . . AND A RETURN
SAFE AND SOUND"—days in which he did nothing but grow.
22nd of the 6th. 7 years. First birthday celebrated at home.
Taste of cheap wine on the tongue. Slight dizziness—"Lordy,
the world's spinning 'round! . . ."—and the inexpressible feeling
that everything was just beginning, if it hadn't ended already.
Anyway, the cock crowing on the threshold to announce guests,
its blood chasing around the yard after Grandma perfunctorily
lopped its head from its body, and the bird managed to wrest
itself from her gnarled hands, filling the yard with Pollock paint-
ings. "It's running away from death," his voice burst out of the
blue, somehow against his will, as if an angel had blown on a
silver trumpet, "but he still won't get away!" Another time, he
was supposed to have chased after the bird, who knows whether
he even managed to catch it, but this time, after an angel came
out of his mouth—as Grandma would have put it—you might
say it dogged death's every step. Later—the cock was simmering
in the pot over a low flame, lest the flesh fall from the bones;
the soil outside had wiped its mouth clean, that was that; the
notch of another soul was added to the cherry tree stump in
the middle of the yard—his parents made their entrance, arriving "from Rossiya" via Ch—ău, his father dressed militarily, his

mother dressed maternally. He realized they had arrived from
the commotion out in the yard, and here he is running from
the bottom of the garden with his short trousers still around his
ankles—the moment, so long awaited, had caught him doing
his business—so that he almost fell and broke his head, shouting
at the top of his voice: "Mama and Dada! Mama and Dada!"
Of that afternoon he will still recollect Grandma's gesture as she
raised her hand to her mouth, as if he of all people ought not to
hear what he had always known: "Blood is thicker than water . .
." All of a sudden, amid the festiveness, he vaguely sensed a bar-
racks-like atmosphere: Dada was giving clipped orders, starting
with hand-washing—he may also have uttered the word "chol-
era," unless some other, subsequent memory has not overlaid the
events of that day, a memory from when Grandpa was admitted
to the county hospital with a simple case of diarrhoea—and also
supervising the orderly progress of operations to ensure collective hygiene. Oh! with what zeal did he soap them, as far as the
elbows, as if pulling on a pair of long bridal gloves, so that they
would be to his father's liking before he presented them: "Lenin's
hands!" Nobody had taught him to call them that, he hadn't even
been as far as the next village, C—ii de Sus, where, inside a special glass display case at the heart of the settlement, there was a
miniature replica of the Kremlin office, with Ilyich busily writing
by the light of a lamp with a green shade that burned all night
long; on the contrary, Grandma immediately muttered: "To hell
with him, the Yid!" which drew the prompt admonishment of
her son: "Mama, don't talk like that in front of the bairn!" But as
for the bairn, the child was no longer a child. Without it being
known, he had just repudiated the grandmother whose name he
bore and knowingly devoted himself to belief in the Father in
whose basilica he knelt. "Thou shalt have no other gods before
Me." Here yawns a hiatus of a few weeks, during which time he
was taken to the city, berated with parade-ground yelling till he
didn't know what day of the week it was, scrubbed, dressed up
smartly, and sent to school.

    Whereas one in ten of the little girls of his age was called
Rodica, and their parents (*la perduta gente* on the construction

sites of the unwelcoming city, on whose streets was spoken
a different language, the same "от Москвы до самых до
Окраин"[7])—without exception, the first generation ever to
wear shoes—barely were they able to find a room in a hostel for
married citizens (his parents had a corner room, which meant
that their balcony made a right angle along two outside walls),
not before bringing into the world two or three babies, the first
out of love, the rest out of curiosity or by mistake rather than
by a father legitimate or unknown—, barely did the sun set at
one end of the motherland than it rose in the other. How exactly
that miracle happened and whether the country actually had
two suns, his first schoolteacher did not bother to explain in the
patriotic education lesson named, unsurprisingly, "ленинский
урок",[8] the first lesson in the lives of "Ilyich's little grandchildren." Seated at their desks—little girl next to little boy, and
when there weren't enough little boys to go around, little girl
next to little girl—they were an idyllic sight against the backdrop of a cherub that looked as if it had come straight out of a
Raphael fresco—chubby, with golden curls, interlacing its fingers
in a well-painted gesture of candor—and set in a *fer-blanc* frame
painted black and hung from the back wall of the classroom.
The same smiling face took up two thirds of the opening page
of the ABC, above a poem in which the return of the migratory
birds & the rebirth of nature were ascribed to the fact that "in
April, in April / was Ilyich born." That the kiddies had not even
begun to learn to read and write and therefore had no way of
comprehending the message of the Annunciation announced on
the threshold by Grigore Vieru[9] did not seem to have occurred to
the officials at the ministry, just as—two and a bit months later,
on the eve of the Great October, celebrated on 7 November—
neither sluggish learning nor unsatisfactory behavior was any
impediment to the whole class *in corpore* being received into

---

[7] From Moscow to the farthest margins. Line from a Soviet popular song.

[8] Lenin lesson.

[9] Grigore Vieru (1935-2009), Moldovan children's poet of the communist period and
nationalist poet and politician of the post-communist period. — *Translator's note*

the ranks of the Little Octobrists, after both the former and the latter had been threatened for weeks on end that they would never in a million years wear on their chests the little star emblazoned with the face of Lenin. Even more inexplicable was the manner in which the little Volodya Ulyanov on the October badge managed in less than three years (between the first and the third grade) to have aged on the pioneer badge, now depicted in profile, bald, his goatee trimmed short, peering into mankind's luminous future through the Mongoloid slits of his eyes and crowned with unleashed flames. He had not seen people burning like a torch; but the image of them made him think of "the man above the treasure" in his grandmother's stories, it being a known fact that above hidden treasures flicker the scarlet tongues of hell. That is, unless God Himself showed himself as a burning bush. His first schoolteacher chuntered on interminably, but it was enough for her to ask a question—"Children, which of you knows who Vladimir Ilyich Lenin was?"—for a forest of hands to sprout automatically. Why she picked him in particular—he was the only son of "intellectuals" from a class of children that had become city-dwellers by virtue of Ch—ău expanding across the surrounding villages, whose parents had exchanged spades for trowels and now labored on the capital's countless construction sites. And then, in the silence that made the moment's solemnity vibrate, his squeaky voice, as if issuing from a pioneer's bugle, filled the classroom: "A Yid!" The blast of the explosion (of laughter!) devastating the class; his first schoolteacher bursting into tears; the door slamming behind her so loudly that at the other end of the corridor the headteacher came out to see what the hell was going on in that school of his; and his father's voice on the evening of the same day, berating his mother, who had taken his side ("What does a child know?"), passing the final sentence: "He did it on purpose!" Twofold were the consequences of that first term at school: 1) Whatever the lad did, he did it deliberately and therefore, 2) nobody had the right to take his side. All that was lacking was for the covenant to be sealed with blood, and then no angel would have been able to stop him: "Don't lift your hand to the lad, don't hurt him . . ." As for him, he had sworn to bite his own tongue whenever it was about to get carried away; it wouldn't be hard for him to keep his word: when he was little, he had learned to talk to himself, in two voices, his own and all the others—he knew them by heart—in his head there was room for everybody. The only voice he couldn't do, not because of its timbre, but because of what it said, was his father's. As authoritative as if it were speaking from Mount Sinai!

One day, coming home from school, he discovered above the little table at which he did his homework a portrait of V.I. Lenin, in half-profile, A4, printed on a card of eye-catching whiteness. Done in *pointe-seche*, Ilyich emanated a power that could only be spoken of in the infinitive—to take an axe to God! (By comparison—since we've opened up a breach in time, why not force it to the utmost?—Raskolnikov's axe is a mere bagatelle, albeit a bloody one. One for the ears of every old woman for whom the blah-blah-blah bells . . .) Above all you couldn't avoid the gaze that riveted you, with the painting giving the impression that it wasn't pinned to the wall, but rather hovered in mid-air by sheer force of the unusually vivid, penetrating eyes. (Might the "harmonious bilingualism" zealously cultivated by the Michurins and Lysenkos of the national cadre policy be to blame for the adjective *vii* (vivid) having to take a deferential step back when faced with the terrifying character from the Gogol tale of the same name: *Viy?* See *Мифы народов мира*, Издательство "Советская энциклопедия," Moscow, 1980, vol. 1, p. 235: "Вий, в восточнославянской мифологии персонаж, чей смертоносный взгляд скрыт под огромными веками или ресницами (. . .) По русским и белорусским сказам, веки, ресницы или брови Вия поднимиали вилами—for spite, he would have written, *В.И.Л.*-ами!—его помощники отчего человек, не выдержавший взгляда Вия, умирал"[10]) You might say he now had someone to keep him company when

---

10 In the mythology of the eastern Slavs, *Viy* is a character whose lethal eyes are hidden beneath gigantic eyelids or eyelashes (. . .) In Russian and Byelorussian fairy tales, Viy's helpers held up his eyelids, eyelashes or eyebrows using hayforks [Russian: *vily*, which makes the narrator think of Lenin's initials: V.I.L. — *Translator's note*], after which the man, not being able to resist Viy's gaze, would perish.

he did his handwriting exercises, and not even his father had
to keep a close eye on him anymore. (Not that he would have
been able to anyway, since he was at work all day long, but
he would rather cheat than admit to not being omnipotent!
Omniscient, his deeds were examples, and his examples were
tablets of law. And even if the father were caught putting a foot
wrong—and woe unto him who caught him!—his voice would
thunder: "On my word as a communist!!!" God might just as
well have said: "On My word." Father and God were one and
the same, up till the moment when the former declared himself
a Communist.) In imitation of him, the son was to get nothing
but good marks at school, to grow up—and here everybody from
the countryside employed the sacrosanct phrase imprinted on
the genetic makeup of this nation—"with the fear of his parents,"
to become a grownup, and at the end of his life, having forged
an exemplary biography for himself, to be buried with military
honors in the wall of the Kremlin, alongside the urn housing the
ashes of Yuri Gagarin (when asked what he wanted to be when
he grew up, he had a readymade reply—"a cosmonaut!!!"—the
same as most of his other classmates, regardless of sex, given
that Valentina Tereshkova, the first woman in space, had added
to that locally manufactured neologism, intended to be distinct
from the American *astronaut*, not a suffix to denote gender, but
another substantive, prefixing it, in order to declare her status
as *woman-cosmonaut*): "Stand to attention at the mausoleum!"
Childhood as a stick with two ends, his father and Lenin, to prod
him from behind. Days in which the little hooks of his handwriting exercises transformed into letters, and the letters into syllables. His handwriting personalizing the printed words. The slight
rightward slant, as if each letter wished to lay its loops on the
shoulder of the next. Finally, the right to write his name on his
exercise book calligraphically, *manu propria*. The presence of his
father, unexpected at that hour—usually it was his mother who
fixed his lunch on his return from school—must have amplified
the effect the portrait made on him. The two of them ate their
meal together, in an atmosphere that transformed communication into communion, after which he was sent off to play. He

even had the feeling that his father was in a hurry to get rid of him—in the meantime, his mother had made her appearance on the threshold, drawn as if by an invisible magnet—maybe also because of the free time he had granted him so generously. Not a soul to be seen in front of the hostel. He had done a circuit of the building, against the clock, once, twice, when, all of a sudden, he saw glinting in the sky a small silver butterfly, which landed at his feet. It was a razor blade—a "Sputnik" (in the USSR the latest conquests of space were one by one turned into the brand names of consumer products)—barely used, the first he had seen in his life. Never had he held in his palm so delicate an object. Weightless, each edge the mirror image of the other, incorporating between its two blades, each the size of an eyelid daubed with silver makeup, an aperture through which the world was shown in transversal section, the razorblade weighed as much as all his toys put together. He turned it on every side, he even tried to turn it inside out, without success, before finding for it a practical use. It was able to cut, with both edges, and this discovery filled him with the happiness in splitting a thing asunder that he was to discover at university between the legs of his first woman. Not a woman, but a girl. The blood spurted in a gout, he did not even manage to make the connection between the double cutting edge and the burning sensation in his right thumb. He licked the wound, nonetheless too deep for him to be able to stop the bleeding. He then tried using a plantain leaf, as he had seen his grandmother do whenever she cut herself when hoeing. In vain. He ran to the men's washroom on the ground floor, deserted at that hour. He did not lose his sangfroid even when the water continued to flow reddish under the tap. Without tears. Without regrets. With great difficulty, he managed to bandage his thumb with his handkerchief, thitherto a purely decorative checked object. As for the razor blade, there was no question of him throwing it away: Its sharpness had entered his blood. He could not hide it in the chest pocket of the shirt from which he had just extracted the handkerchief—it would have been seen. Even less so in his sandals. How could he tread on the embodiment of perfection? He carefully examined himself in the mirror—for better or worse, he had not spotted his clothes—seeking a hiding place. The reflection of his child's face revealed no great difference from that of other children, although he stubbornly rejected his not being any different, of which his parents constantly reminded him. He angrily stuck out his tongue. Just as he was about to turn around, the action having overcome the resistance of his flesh, it struck him in a flash: from head to toe, he himself was a hiding place, with a mouth under lock and key.

At the end of his hour's play, he knocked on the door of their room. His father, alone in the house, opened the door, wearing a suit and tie. Without a word, the boy sidled along the wall, with the manifest intention of going to do his homework. About to go out, his father cast a final interrogative look over his shoulder— for form's sake—curious as to whether the boy would manage on his own. By way of reply, his first-born waved his left hand in front of him and turned on his heel. "What have you got in your other hand?" asked the man, suspicious. The boy's shrug ought to have conveyed "nothing," but not to him: "Show me it! Right now." Sticky with blood, the handkerchief looked more like a blotter soaked with the red ink for marking exercise books. The boy wiggled his hand, as if wishing to dismiss it as a mere trifle, and then . . . the handkerchief . . . plop! . . . on the floor (the kerchief wrapping the dragon's tongues must have dropped at the feet of the Red Emperor in similar wise). At the sight of the blood, his father turned white in the face. "This hurts me more than it does you," he declared furiously, clouting him across the back of the head. "You asked for it! . . ." It drove him out of his wits the way the boy said nothing, clenching his jaw and enduring every correctional beating with a stoicism worthy of a better cause. Without so much as blinking. His only tears, which were of impotence, were not shed for others. And they too were numbered. The clout failed to set his head ringing; suddenly he saw his father helpless—he was incapable even of bandaging his finger. All the better, he would send him to the first-aid room on the ground floor. But it would have been too wonderful for him to get away with as little as that. "Say something. Why do you keep your mouth shut?" His father's intuition was infallible: "Open your mouth!" Lying on his tongue, at one with the fibres of the muscular tissue, the razor blade answered the question that had not been asked—he sensed his father's blood freeze in his veins, despite his military training—something of the following sort: "Just look at what the lad's capable of!" Thus, the cut finger was just a ruse to get the razor blade into the house. So that he could cut his throat in the night. He's not a child, he's a . . . he's a . . . "Are you bleeding, lad?" the words reached the ears of "Bleeder," as he would call himself henceforth, without anybody knowing it. With infinite care, the man removed the dangerous object from his mouth, the way you would extract the venomous fang of a viper. "What's this?!!" Submissively, the boy followed the trajectory of the silver butterfly, flung out of a window for the second time during the course of that afternoon. "Sputnik," a satellite, in other words. He had got away with it, this time too. Albeit not in the eyes of his father; but since he could not find a fitting punishment, it would have been the height of stupidity to squander his rightful rage with two spanks on the boy's bottom. In the end, he bandaged the thumb with a strip of lint, inwardly proud of the lad, who didn't cry even when he poured a phial of iodine over the open wound. "I'll make him a cosmonaut," the words flashed through his mind, "as long as he doesn't get out of control!"

His father's precipitous departure ought not to have signified a commutation of the punishment. At most, it could keep its specter at a distance. The days when the boy was well-behaved; the weeks when he brought home only good marks; his parent's joy at having both a male heir and a girl in the house, in the person of one and the same child; no doubt about it, rather than keep him on a short leash, better they entrusted him with the care of his baby brother, the little shopping to be done, in short, the house key. It was enough that he turn the baby over on its side at regular intervals. And sometimes, that he read to him: "Feeling his scalp, he came across a little key on the top of his head. He took it and feeling some more, he came across a keyhole in his bellybutton and when he looked through the keyhole, he saw a large, beautiful town, where all were working for the child that was to be born." The first seven years of his life, spent at home before starting school, did the rest. His first teacher lauded him at all the parents' meetings, although out of caution (once bitten twice shy!), she hadn't made him Red Star chief when he was received into the ranks of the Little Octobrists. On November 7, he saw—live, with the rest of his family—the military parade in Victory Square. When they got home, they all watched (the black-and-white set with just two channels, one broadcast from Moscow, the other from Ch—ău) another parade on television, in Red Square, the repeat, followed by the march-ing ranks of people of labor spilling in endless human seas over all the other squares of all the other cities of the USSR & satellite countries, broadcast live (and featuring the meteoric appearance/ disappearance of a hero of labor, his chest full of medals, who was straining to recite a text learned by heart—from stage fright, he couldn't find the right words; he probably hadn't slept all night, trying to cram—which he attempted to embellish from his own imagination and in language at the level of the proletariat: ". . . твою мать!"[11]). The words of the slogans, even though mean-ingless, sedimented themselves in your head: "ЛЕНИН ЖИЛ, ЛЕНИН ЖИВ, ЛЕНИН БУДЕТ ЖИТЬ!"[12] For the first time (if not for the First Time) he saw with his own eyes—albeit on the small screen—the omphalos of the world, and in the ompha-los of the world, the mausoleum of him who, having been born/ died (who the hell could understand it?! given that "МОГИЛА ЛЕНИНА — КОЛЫБЕЛЬ ЧЕЛОВЕЧЕСТВА!"[13]), was to transform cities large and beautiful, villages and towns into his name. A country turned inside-out, which exhibited its dead to the whole world, horizontally (the tombs lined up behind the mausoleum, a token of distinction) and vertically (the Kremlin wall, transformed into a dovecote, smacking of a hostel for unmarried workers), the Motherland! What he had not yet dis-

---

[11] ". . . your mother!"

[12] "Lenin lived, Lenin is alive, Lenin will live!"

[13] "Lenin's Tomb – the cradle of mankind!"

covered—everything in its own time—was that the author of
the mausoleum, A.V. Shchusev, was born in Chişinău in 1873,
and that before becoming the undertaker of the eternally living
man, he had designed the church of the Holy Trinity (1913-14)
in C—ii de Sus, his native village. The same hand garbing in
red stone the idea of the deity and—this time in granite—the
throne of the Antichrist . . . Overwhelmed by how many things
he had experienced in a single day, the biggest in the Red calendar, the boy fell asleep in front of the television, he didn't
even manage to watch the bedtime story. He woke up in bed,
in the dark, having had a bad dream: a great illusionist, the
greatest of all time, had wagered he could walk through the wall
of the Kremlin. No sooner did he appear in the dream than his
technicians assembled the set, the television vans were ready to
broadcast the show live, and the crowd thronging Red Square
frenziedly applauded the state & party rulers in the viewing
stand of the mausoleum—some had even managed to reserve
themselves a place in the red dovecote—even they had come to
see the marvel. Two lady assistants flanked by four plainclothes
optimists took the transatlantic illusionist by each arm and led
him to the wall. A drumroll, then the first notes of the *Funeral
March*—only the music of Chopin enters the Kremlin walls!
. . .—transformed Red Square into the world's biggest open-
air concert hall. With his face to the wall, pressed against the
bricks from which—*dixit* Democritus the materialist—our uni-
verse is made, the illusionist took a determined step into the
wall, at the very last moment turning in half-profile, as if setting
himself in bas-relief for all eternity, just in case he never came
back. Then he vanished, along with his name. Since they could
not follow him, the television cameras roved along the marble
plaques engraved with illustrious names: Ordjonikidze, Klara
Zetkin, Zhukov, Gagarin, Komarov, Dobrovolsky, Volkov, Patsayev
. . . The docile crowd froze in Kremlinated silence, awaiting the
second coming, on the other—inner—side of the battlements.
The clock of the Spasski Tower wound time around its fingers,
thumb and index, the golden pointers scissored into the raw
flesh of the authorities' iron patience, but the illusionist still

did not show himself. at a signal from Leonid Ilyich, the head
of the KGB issued a curt order to the emergency squad, who
evacuated Red Square as quick as you could say "Разойдись!"[14]
Dozens of plainclothes officers surrounded the wall, on both the
one side and the other, painstakingly tapping it in search of the
intruder. The live broadcast was abruptly interrupted and, after
a brief news bulletin, in which was reported how many liters of
milk Stakhanovite dairy worker Anastasia Ivanovna Zatychkina
had milked from a fodder-fed cow to mark the fifty-fourth anniversary of Great October, on the small screen there appeared
the opening balletic motions of *Swan Lake*. Just as alarmed are
the great illusionist's technicians; after everything else, it seems
that they have not taken into account the fact that since 1925
the mortar of the wall has been reinforced with the ashes of
professional revolutionaries, Soviet and foreign, all convinced
Communists, members of the Comintern and the CC of the
CPUS, commanders of the Red Army, etc., etc. Nothing slips
past them! In his sleep, the boy senses the illusionist's cracking
joints; his flesh quivering like aspic falls away from his bones; he
wants to scream uncontrollably, but a red brick stays his tongue
. . . Once awake, he did not close his eyes till daybreak. To pass
the time, he recalled all the exploits of his little life: how he had
inscribed in ink pencil his name on his grandparent's funeral
memorial because he hadn't found his own name on the page in
question; how he had trodden barefoot on the thorn of a robinia;
how he had fallen from up in a cherry tree; finally, how he had
said, not even he knew why, "the hands of Lenin" . . . He would
never open his mouth again unless he was spoken to, he decided,
or even if he was spoken to; there was nothing for it, in order to
stifle any urge to talk, he would imagine the razor blade lying on
his tongue, the sense of danger combined with the exquisitely
pleasant and, precisely because of that, the unconfessed sensation
of the forbidden thing.

Waking up at the same time every day; four lessons a day,
from Monday to Saturday; the signature of one of his parents in

---

[14] "Disperse!"

his marks book, at the end of each week. The passing of time—imperceptibly, as if somebody on high had ordered: "Stand at ease!"—if one fine day he had not decided to replace violet with blue ink. His fountain pen now flowed, now pointedly refused to write, so that he would have to shake it a number of times before he was able to do his homework. A jerk of his right arm, from the shoulder joint. Air sliced slantwise. He didn't even notice when he splattered the portrait of Lenin; in any case, nobody ever looked at it. It was past the gloaming when his father appeared out of the blue to inspect his son's exercise books. He appeared content. He examined the textbooks stacked on the table. He raised his eyes. All of a sudden, he turned whiter in the face than the boy had ever seen him thitherto. The eyes he turned toward his son expressed horror, that mixture of fear and panic that self-combusts. All in sepulchral silence. Each waiting for the other to break the silence. For the boy to ask the question. For the father to provide the answer. The father's patience was a timebomb: the longer it was allowed to tick, the more devastatingly it would explode. But he required witnesses. Through clenched lips, he sent him to fetch his mother, a childminder in that very hostel: "Don't you come back without her!" And here he is, running from floor to floor, knocking on doors and pressing his ear to them, searching without any hope of finding, a search from which he will never return. His cry fuzzes in his throat. The mere thought of how his mother will react on seeing him so scared makes him ill. It's not that he is the unwitting bearer of bad news. In fact, he is precisely that; he is the bad news; you only have to see how everybody leaps out of the way as he pelts down the corridors. He senses he is about to burst into tears. And what will he tell her?! . . . When he finally finds her, he pours out his soul. Luckily, his mother asks him no question. Straight-backed, she rises from her chair, she says something to the tenants of no. 78 and turns on her heel. The clack of her high-heels can barely keep pace with the racing of her heart. At their front door, she lets him enter first. On the threshold, no sooner does she close the door behind her than his father flings in her face: "Did he tell you what he did to me?"—a jerk of the head in the boy's direction replaces the proper name (in a sentence with three pronouns, one for the mother, one for the father, one for the perpetrator)—"or did he play dead in the maize field?!!" All of a sudden, his mother's eyes fill the room. Endlessly blue. She doesn't know what has happened, but even so, she will ask only after her husband's acoustic signal: "Good God, what did I do to you to deserve this?!" But still she does not ask, lest she offend the as yet un-disburdened Rage with a capital R by hastening to find out what a mother's heart already knows. "What is to be done? What is to be done?!" cries her husband, clutching his head in his hands, but since he can hear only his own voice, he finds himself forced to drag the others into his chorus. "He did it on purpose!" he exclaims, his finger pointing at the portrait of Lenin slashed with a slanting splatter of blue ink. A streak as fine as a cicatrix furrows Ilyich's cheek, and that's about all. But since the penny has still not dropped, her husband switches to Russian, so that the child won't understand: "Голубой Lenin!!!"[15] Now she sees the small nebula of drops, a freckled Lenin at most. But from this to the crime of *lèse majesté* . . . Obviously, the nuances elude her—she doesn't know anything about politics!—but in the USSR, as is well known, every little mistake has consequences (entire editorial offices, from the editor-in-chief down to the lowliest proofreader, shot *in corpore* for high treason during the Great War to Defend the Homeland, for the sake of a missing letter: Сталингад[16] or гавнокомандующий[17] . . .) The threat hovers overhead, but the question is not even voiced, the question as old as the world: "Who is to blame?" The main thing is to channel her husband's rage in a different direction. As far away from her child as possible. She is prepared to lie; ultimately, she is the one who refuels his tank, morning and night, but precisely at this moment, she hears the boy's little voice: "The pen wouldn't write . . ." Wrong! The father still refuses to acknowledge his presence in the house,

---

[15] Light blue, but also slang for gay.

[16] Without the *r* Stalingrad translates as Stalinsod.

[17] Shit (*gavno-*) leader for Supreme (*glavno-*) leader.

even if does accord him the status of pronoun: "Did I ask him a question?!" It is as if he had shoved him outside the door, but leaving it open a crack, wide enough for him not to miss any of the drama he was acting out. But his mother hastens to pick up the hot coal using her own mouth: "I'll wipe it . . . with a rag . . ." but she realizes she has made a blunder and instantly attempts to rectify it: "With cotton wool and oh-dee-cologne . . ." She does not manage to finish making this suggestion before her husband erupts: "They'll throw me in prison, on my word as a Communist!" All three are now caught in the gearwheels of criticism; it would have been superfluous to say what wiping Lenin's face with a rag meant. Even the child appreciates the gravity of the situation. Usually, after the sacrosanct oath—"On my word as a Communist!"—there unfailingly followed amendment No. 1, whack! and the scolding voice of the mother: "When your dad hits you, it's for your own good . . ." But the flat of his hand is late in coming, and the waiting becomes unbearable. "Maybe you could take it down . . ." perseveres the mother. "And just how will I explain to people who come to our house *why* I took it off the wall?" And even if he hid it in a drawer, he for one would not tolerate keeping a blemished Lenin in the house! Even now, the man can see himself having to hand in his Party membership card. He turns his eyes, which are as bloodshot as if after a sleepless night, from the portrait to the child: "I can't even throw it in the dustbin. Lord, forgive me for my sins!" A brutal blow—not so much its force as the effect of its surprise—restores the banished lad to the bosom of his family, a sign that the theoretical prelude has come to an end. Now, yes, there is space for an exchange of opinions. *En famille.* A clout, a question. An answer, a wallop. Each smack has the weight of a commandment; but since the boy has not stolen, has not committed adultery, has not borne false witness, the commandments are reduced to two—"Thou shalt have no other Gods before me" and "Honor thy father . . ."—which are drummed into him repeatedly, lest he forget. When the father teaches the "*mater studiorum*" it is advisable you do not flunk the class. But nor does he feel like "pissing his eyes out," even if he knows that is what is expected of him. On the contrary, he grits his teeth and bears it. How else is he going to grow up?! His imagination races ahead of him, fueled by the expressions he has heard in the country, from the neighbors ("I'll skin you alive!" and "I'll wind your skin round a stick" and "Your blood'll spurt as high as the roof!"), which in a way makes him immune to actual pain; if his mother were not there, turned to stone in her powerlessness to leap to his defense . . . In the lull between two smacks, the man catches his breath: "Now do you understand?" But the son guesses that the father won't believe him and will therefore have to prove he has understood; or else, since the solution is late in coming ("What do you understand?!"), neither is he prepared to talk nor is his father prepared to listen. The game of cat-and-mouse continued, but nobody was in a hurry to give a round of applause—the overture had finished, at best, and the first violin was showing signs of impatience, keen to start the next movement. Start again, from the top: "What was it you said? Who is Vladimir Ilyich Lenin?" The fact that he'd been through it before taught him a lesson; he had no idea what "*goluboy*" meant, but even so, he wouldn't turn the word back on his father. By means of a mental operation, he tries to replace his tongue with the razorblade, the most wonderful thing that has ever left his mouth. Unutterably wonderful. With two cutting edges and no handle. With its slit serving as its heart. "Get undressed!" The father's order is not to be questioned, but better he pierce his skin with every sharp object in the house or scour him with a curette than ask such a thing of him! The child felt his tears about to burst forth like a boxer's blindly flailing punches. He does not hit his target: 7,479 years after God's creation of the World, the father had just put on stage, in a deluxe production (Fiat lux!), the banishment from paradise. Nakedness—the awareness thereof: "and I was frightened, because I was naked . . ."—is part of the show, a sign that part of the genitor's right is *potestas vitae necisque*. It is the turn of the mother to interrupt, but the glare of the paterfamilias—"Who do you think you're protecting him from? From me?!!"—refers her back to *l'origine du monde*: ". . . and thy desire shall be to thy husband, and he shall rule over thee." What does the fact that she brought him into the world have to do with it, when the child is written in the father's name? Like him who said: Little does it matter what gate you come out of, the main thing is in which yard you were unloaded. With every item he takes off, the child becomes yet smaller; once he has taken off his underpants, he is nothing more than the naked form of nothingness. His blood rushes to his cheeks; a pity his grandmother was not there to see that shame had vanished only in nature—in the country, the old woman sometimes lamented, looking meaningfully at a plant with a white umbelliferous inflorescence in the middle of which could be espied a tiny red spot: "There's no shame left! . . ."—but not among mankind. But something else was demanded of him: that he admit his guilt, through a voluntary outburst of self-criticism, a practice that would serve him well later in life. It's one thing to fart under the bedclothes and another to shit your breeches! In both the one case and the other, it stinks, but only in the latter case is washing required. "Is that why I wiped your arse as a bairn, so that you could do this to me?" wails the father genuinely, suddenly stooping over him. "For his sake, I gave up the cosmonaut training center, then he goes and . . ." In the middle of the room, the child shifts his weight from one leg to the other; exposed on every side, he feels like folding in two, like a hinge, but not even axial symmetry can help him there. Not one rustle crinkles the curtain: the show is far from over. But a change has come over the atmosphere, as if the extras had taken a step back, allowing the protagonist the space to get in full swing. All of a sudden, the father adopts the role of victim of some monstrous conspiracy, aimed at taking the bread out of his mouth and the knife out of his hand. And then, *partbilet*[18] adieu! "On my word as a Communist," says he, producing the ace from up his sleeve, "you didn't think of doing it by yourself, did you?!" In that instant, he realizes that a positive answer would scare him to death, but nor is he ready to lay down the whip with which he flagellates himself. "*Mea culpa*, nothing more to say!" he says, bringing it down on his own head, that of

---

[18] Party membership card

the head of the family, meanwhile muttering: "Birthrate decree boy." He's no longer playing to an audience, but only hencefor-ward will his every gesture rebound upon the other two family members. Both mother and child would accept the burden of all the guilt in the world only not to see him suffer. Because it is still they who will pay the final bill. At the first opportunity. But for now, all his majesty is gone, he is but a peasant's son whom the Soviet state raised, educated, made a man—a Communist!—and in whose blood runs the Red Army. "Out of my house!" he barks at the child. "If that's the way it is, I'm leaving too!" the voice of the mother's blood drowns out the young woman's voice of reason. Between the two parents, the final act is consum-mated; the man tries to up the ante—"I'll leave home! . . . I'll throw myself under a train!"—but the wife is undeterred: "Tell him right now to put some clothes on." It's his turn to counter-attack: "How, as a mother, can you let him stand here like that? . . ." Parried: "My only concern is not to let your honor as a father be sullied in his eyes!" All the while, the child has been trembling like a reed; before becoming a cognizant reed, he is the very rod he is sent to fetch and also the one sent to fetch it in order that he, thrice he, might receive the well-deserved pun-ishment. His father gives him a token kick up the backside and then orders: "Dressed! Forty-five seconds." But since he doesn't know what to do with his hands, he picks up one of the child's exercise books, flicks through it and, discovering a crossing-out, he crumples it up, quivering with fury, and tosses it in the bin without further comment. Curtain. But only after the curtain falls does the *coup de théâtre* occur. Somebody knocks on the door. It is a friend of the family, he too an officer in the reserve, with whom the man plays chess in the evening and talks politics. Mama makes herself scarce; at the table, the boy is writing out his homework in a brand-new exercise book when, all of a sud-den—the chess match is in full flow, one of the men is just about to give checkmate—the voice of the son shatters the silence in the room: "Dad, Dad! I wanted to shake the ink off my nib and I splashed . . . Lenin!" And since the stupefaction lingers on the faces of the players, interrupted so inopportunely, the child continues: "It was I who did it, on my word as a Little Octobrist!" "Нечаянно . . ."[19], opines the friend of the family; the father reluctantly accepts the assessment. The match ends in stalemate.

"I still had ten years to go before giving birth . . ." the girl replies, apropos of nothing. "After which, goodbye innocence!" concludes the strange man drily. "I'm a phony." "A forgery," quips the girl, "series A . . . by the way, what serial letter does your passport have?" "And you're a princess. An *editio princeps*, as it were." The fingers of her right hand in his—four pairs clenched in *viparîta maithuna*—the youngest son has a bruised fingernail, one quarter black—"A white dot in a little black number by Coco Chanel?" "No! Just a nail spot . . ."—; Between-the-Legs-Sympathy, when in mid-walk she switches left foot forward for right, to keep in step with him; his lips seeking her ear: "I'd open a shower cubicle in the trunk of every linden for the benefit of those who make love outdoors . . ." But she's the one who draws the line: "*Déjà vu—déjà lu—déjà nu.*"[20] She's all in black, an ESPRIT t-shirt, a miniskirt tight on her hips, leather sandals and knickers riding up her crevice, disappearing the way the night of June 22-23 vanishes between two circumjacent days, it resembles a Latin maxim, with the verb at the end, emerging fresher than ever from the mists of the times. She is such an ingénue that he can barely refrain from teasing her—"Repeat over and over again as fast as you can: *stick dip*" —; she's of two minds whether or not to say it . . . But the strange man cannot shake off the child he used to be: "It was also Dad who took me to visit Lenin's mausoleum, when I was in fourth grade; and even though I felt nothing, absolutely nothing! that one time I didn't let him down—in front of Ilyich's mummy I gave the pioneer salute, and at the exit I read out *à haute voix* the memorial inscription carved in the red brick . . ." What he delays in saying, not even he knows why, is that for years one and the same

---

[19] By accident.

[20] Already seen—already read—already naked

dream has haunted him, that he is lying in a coffin in the church of the Holy Trinity in C—ii de Sus, where he has been laid out overnight, and in the morning, when he is due to be interred, he finds himself lying beneath a glass dome—no candles or funeral banners for you!—exhibited to a crowd of people flanked by soldiers, who file past him endlessly, their eyes to the ground, in token of deep grief. In particular, he is afraid of the moment when they will cotton on to the switcheroo—though all his life he has striven not to step out of line! . . .—not at the Muscovite end of A. Shchusev's work, but at the other end, in some godforsaken village in Bessarabia, where, at any moment, six timeless peasant pallbearers are about to carry forth the man rejected by his native soil and take him to a grave in U—eşti cemetery. How could his grandparents do such a thing, to cast him into the arms of the Unclean One! And how could he remain a captive of the Red Square necropolis, like an insect in a drop of gum—let it be a lesson to the Kremlin dreamers. "I've missed my period," concludes the girl. Between the two of them there is no place for a third—"We can't have children; we've been pretending to each other"—officially, on the grounds of Rhesus incompatibility, unless their suitedness to each other, which is consummate (pending imminent evidence to the contrary), somehow eludes reproductive logic. He remembers, down to the smallest detail, the night he met her; her sex as clean as a steel razor blade on his tongue; the rugose pilosity, like the grass on Mount Cişa, of the mons Veneris (caressing it, he made her laugh till she hiccoughed when he described a deceased schoolmate, Miron I., who in their student years, the glorious eighties, used to dip his index finger in his mouth and draw a Lenin on the belly of each new lover, starting from her pubic triangle, which he made the beard, before inserting himself with the words: "F—k him in the face!"); the copious bleeding, as if after a gang rape, and more than once; her way of crying, from one eye, as if the countless tears—the beads of a bone rosary—moved from one to the other and her question, by no means rhetorical, at the end of a few attempts at penetration ("—n, ooo!!! it hurts!"), once the act proper was consummated: "That's what's called making love, is it?" After which—the shower, both of them in the same cubicle, as big as a student's bed, too small when you're sleeping alone, but so welcoming when you have somebody to lie next to you. Under the powerful jet of water, they kissed with the desperation of shipwrecked sailors giving each other mouth-to-mouth respiration before drowning. Then, as he set some water to boil lengthily, leafing through *Das Kapital* in bed, she came across that *Practical Course on Desire** of his, which she read all in one go. "Whom did you write it for?" asked the girl, looking up from the text. In lieu of an answer—"Ah, so you're jealous?!"—he took the magazine from her hands and flung it under the bed. Willy-nilly, they were thinking of the same thing ("*Un préservatif peut sauver une vie*"), each from a different end—*The First Time*, the girl; *Many returns!*, the man—of the sexual life. "*De gustibus,*" perorated the man as he lifted the boiling kettle from the gas flame, "some drink teabags, 2g a sachet, others make a tisane. How do you like it, with or without?" "You're the one who's the tea expert," replied the girl, "make it as you like it." With the studied gestures of a master of ceremonies, the man poured a little boiling water in the glass vessel, enough to create a bed of steam within the teapot, then emptied a few teaspoons of *Mabroc. 1001 Nights. Pure Ceylon Tea* therein, over which he then poured more boiling water. "Would you like me to show you what's happening under the lid?" She moved the blanket aside, look at (take) me! *Without form and bare*: he could have picked her out from a thousand, to me! give thyself to me! He enwrapped her, whispering her name in her right ear: E—a! E—a!—"candles for the living / for the dead" her ears are called—what else could he say to her, now, as both breathe the same salty perfume that heralds the tide, the salt seeps into their skin, her briar bush spreads its black tealeaves, chemistry gives way to biology, the beast-with-two-backs bolts, in a race against the clock, at the end of which a naked form of the male sex disengages. "The Russians call it жениmь чай,"[21] he says over his shoulder, as he thrice ritually pours the infusion into a teacup and then back into the pot. "The alchemical wedding,

---

[21] Literally "to wed the tea"

as it were." and before that day's page is turned (by whom?), she will have washed the blood out of the sheet, the calendar will have exchanged Sunday red for Monday black, a month ago, a lifetime ago. "I did the test, it's positive," says the girl, bringing him back to reality, "but I can't have children! Do you want me to adopt you?" Their tongues coiling together like the snakes in a famous passage in Le Clézio, before she gives him the apple of the following words: "I was just thinking about placing in your lap the child of seven I used to be . . ." He's verging on fifty, she is the mercy of God; hand in hand, they run all in one breath to the exit of the Botanical Garden, put to flight by the booms of thunder—behind them, the rain hops through the puddles lifting its skirts—all but taking off, leaving the ground, their blood interwoven in four hands & four legs—his A(II)Rh, hers A(II)Rh—flutters in the wind like the two pigtails of a creature unborn, a) and therefore deathless; b) no less mortal for all that (*tertium non datur*). The rain washes away their tracks.

* Practical course on desire

The fiancée (womb as limpid as an aquarium wherein floats the wee golden fish, refracted in each of its 10,000 scales, as many images of the "10,000 things," among corals of blood, expanding/contracting in mensual rhythm) casts a glance in the mirror (the mirror's surface produces concentric ripples) in search of her other half. All she sees, twisted around the clock hands of exactly eight hours (of sleep), are two whirlpools of dark rings as big as the two beds in which "she had had terrible fevers, she had endured the torture of cruel nights when her poor flesh was wrenched, sizzling with desire, she had been ill, she had thought she was going insane, but she had preferred it to any dishonor," the first, and "I sought the night, in my sheets, I sought my heart's beloved; I sought him, but did not find him," the second. All the faces that have ever passed before the mirror now lap over its silvery beach; none resembles his. "What does my fate hold? How will I know him?" she asks—"Your first wish," states the golden fish curtly—; "*Wholly devoid of desire, / you may ponder his hiding places; / wholly consumed by desire, / you may ponder his guises,*" replied the mirror, reflected in the 10,000 faces,

as many scales of the fish that swims within itself—upstream, may
his name be He-without-beginning; downstream, may his name be
He-without-end—over a silvery beach and has neither beginning
nor end. The fiancée—from the outset, the sentence bifurcates, like
Andersen's little mermaid, who, for the love of a mortal, splits her
tail into two endless legs, the Tigris and the Euphrates laving man's
earthly paradise, — a) she looks mindfully into the enchanted mirror "for who is seen therein, be she a girl, she shall become a boy,
and be he a boy, he shall become a girl," in other words . . .; b) she
takes one of the fish scales and puts it on her tongue and is transformed into what she desires, namely . . .— in order to give birth
to a new life, in your image and likeness—she acquires his image.

"Who am I? Where does so much love lead?" asks a man-like-
any-other, sometimes, in the morning, as he shaves in front of
the mirror—"Your second wish," states the golden fish curtly—;
the mirror replies: "*Whoever experiences the male / and preserves the
female . . .*" but the man is in too much of a hurry to listen to it all.
His image sinks into the watery eye of the mirror as if into a bap-
tismal font—". . . *becomes the riverbed of the Subcelestial,*" the reply
finally reaches him—; the shouting of the name (*Adam*) brings it
back to the surface. He looks as though he wants to hide, juggling
the bones of his own skeleton beneath the skin tent of the inner circus—he says: "God, like a surgeon working the night shift, forgot
His rubber gloves in the patient's belly, he forgot His hands in the
first man after he *resealed his flesh*"—the missing rib. In the ivory
luster of that imaginary bone for long years he chisels one and the
same figurine, without form and bare at first, then ever slenderer,
so that finally it is metamorphosed into a stiletto shaped like a
maiden's torso with a blade in the form of legs tightly conjoined to
form the tail of a little mermaid, whose cutting edges shave faces
off the mirror like scales off a flounder. A man of a certain age who,
still in his prime, flips the flesh onto its back, like in a wrestling
match, without shedding it, but not without touching it, he *has a
fluid appearance* when, stripped to the waist, naked Transcendence
cuts a swathe through his moist gaze—where he rocks its reflection to the rhythm of an incantation: "On Monday morn I awoke
/ And set off down the road / Toward the sunrise / Treading the

path / Gathering love / On Monday morn / On Tuesday morn / On Wednesday morn / on Thursday morn / On Friday morn / On Saturday morn / On Sunday morn / The Heavenly Mother did see / She came down the silver ladder / Took me by the right hand / And led me to the Jordan / To Adam's well / Dipped me in the golden trough / Washed me with her hand / My face / My white skin / My mouth . . ."—, and muddied when she is out of her waters. The rainbow of her being arches above him like the goddess Nwt over the body of Geb (see the Egyptian papyrus dating from the first millennium B.C. kept in the British Museum). "*The only coat that fits me is you,*" hums the man, his eyes on the mirror that reveals whom he desires, the beauty that does not reveal itself with a face, arms or other bodily embodiments, the beauty that does not reside in any other being than itself, composing its own image, *Without his knowing / the conjunction of male and female / his organ is roused.*"

"I've taken my coat off, how can I put it back on again?" asks the one-night bride—a borrowed womb, like a condom (remember the French advert: a car brakes suddenly, as if hitting a solid wall of air; in the woman's arms he places an aquarium full to the brim, in which swims a little golden fish; distrait, she crosses the street diagonally, talking to it all the time: "Kiki . . . Kiki . . ."; a car, another car, braking suddenly not two feet from her and which knocks her down; the glass fishbowl shatters; the little fish flaps on the asphalt—"Kiki! . . . Kiki!!!"—then cupped in her sweating palms; a woman rushing inside the nearest pharmacy; the line of men queuing at the counter, like a zipped-up zipper; her cry for help from the doorway: "Je veux un préservatif!"; finally, she walks calmly down the street with a fish floating in a condom that is like an enormous teardrop; and the slogan: "*Un préservatif peut sauver une vie*") in which the goldfish floats belly up—her eyes staring into space (space lowers its eyes) as she sits on the edge of the bed. In the mirror in the bedroom, as if in a cloakroom of all times and all peoples, the Bodiless Beauty preserves her bodies of supreme joy, each body more beautiful than the next. "What does he wish, who loves beautiful things?" the one-night bride asks, getting ready for bed—as she takes off her make-up, the mirror rejects her image, as if in mirroring her it were shedding its own silver—and it is she who answers, She wants to be his." The black dog from the World's Origin, the darkness rubs up against her legs, before beating a retreat when the master appears in that *locus pessimus atque profundus* of all origins; the beast-with-two-backs is born of the grappling of two bodies that wrest their pleasure from each another. "Mightn't it be that what you want is for the two of you to stay together, at each other's side, and for neither night nor day to part you both?" the golden fish asks them. "No!" they reply in unison. "Or maybe," says the golden fish, unrelenting, "you want to reach the point at which *the two will be one, on both the outside and the inside, and the man and woman will be neither man nor woman.*" "Not that either!" reply Birds of a feather flock together. Face to face like two mirrors that take each other's powers and beauty from each other, a) Wholly consumed by desire they seek their other half, in their image and likeness; b) Wholly devoid of desire the "I" composes its own "I"; a) *approaching her, he couldn't see her face, / following her, he couldn't see her back;* b) *and after he gave everything, / he possessed as much again*—between them, the golden fish, cut in two like the flounder in Plato's *Banquet*, each reflecting the other half of a human separated from its whole, offers them now one thing, now another—; "*Neti, Neti!*"[22] cast their mirrors one before the other.

---

[22] Neither this, nor this (Sanskrit).

Cap. 2
Familial house of correction

The tone: "— *the same as in a German romantic fairy tale—*
but rewritten by a Russian (. . .)"

Mircea Ivănescu, *The Birch Forest*

IN THE BEGINNING THERE WAS the silence demanded in and of
itself every evening when—"*at ease!*"—household activities came
to an end, and the children were shoved into their bed, each
with a book in his hand, lest the slightest peep be heard out of
them: You're father's trying to write! It wasn't an issue whether
or not they actually read—one of the two books was a coloring
book—, rather they had to lie in complete silence, each in his
own corner. Rather than bringing the brothers closer together,
the looks they exchanged on the sly would more often than not
end up giving one of them away, when he burst out laughing
for whatever reason, and then the two of them would be punished together. If they got away with just two or three smacks
on the bottom, they would regard it as their lucky day, because
sometimes the father would be so angry, so disappointed that his
words could not match his Law-making will, that he would fling
those words over his shoulder: "I'll annihilate the both of you!"
Given how insignificant their little lives were, the annihilation
promised *à haute voix* exceeded every other measure whereby a
man in his own house might give voice to his legitimate fury

(threats drawn from the language of shepherds & agricultur-
alists: "I'll flay you alive" "I'll tan your hide!" "I'll give you a
threshing (sic)!" and finally, "I'll hang you!") in its abstraction,
its mathematical operation (raising to the cube? determining the
square root?!)—in comparison with which death seemed homely,
always entailing *something nice*, a get-together with fresh flowers
and a brass band, for which you get a taste from an early age,
along with the candies doled out at memorial services. What
with one thing and another, they had been told to their faces so
many times, in school and at home: "Ты никто . . ." now one,
now the other, ". . . и звать тебя никак",[23] that their father's
threat merely potentiated the annihilation. Golden, the silence
weighed heavier and heavier, until leaden sleep laid them low
as they sat up in bed like two teddy bears pretending to read.
More than literature, the father loved politics—a love, it would
seem, whose documents were in order: his Party membership
card, as opposed to his still unrequited advances on the other
front, despite the publication of two slim volumes; therefore
there was no question of him missing the news for the sake of
writing, for which reason, at a quarter to nine, the children, too,
were woken up to watch the evening bulletin and, ever since the
elder boy's teacher complained to his father that his first-born,
the erstwhile *Wunderkind*, stood every chance of ending up an
outsider, the documentary serial "Время", too. Suddenly alarmed
at the prospects of his offspring, the progenitor then tested them,
like in school, genuinely marveling at the scanty interest *his* boys
showed in the arms race, the war in the Sinai desert, and even
all the things that were happening in their own country, that
bastion of peace, but never would it have entered his head actually to check their homework. Their marks book, yes!—with the
impatience of the interested party who has no time to waste on
the cross-examination of witnesses or the presentation of evidence, but who turns up only to hear the final sentence passed.

Mama too had existed from the very beginning, but she
would have to await a special occasion to make her entrance.

---

[23] You're nobody and your name is nothing at all.

She herself had lent her hand—literally, as if her own pupils'
exercise books were enough—to hastening it, and it was she too
who announced it, one Saturday morning, as she was getting
the children ready for school, sternly admonishing them—them!
raised in the father's religion of "fear-of-one's-parents"!—to be
ready that evening. To the younger son's question as to whether
they were to be tested, she replied: "Stop testing me and be more
obedient!" and that was that. Once the countdown had begun,
the way you would enter the ring dance in the game of *Black
Man*, with the only difference that this time the anxiety arises
not from not knowing the when, but from knowing when something was going to happen but not the what, all they had to do
was pass the remaining time somehow. As to the who [as far as
his family was concerned—let it be known from the outset that
he was the *кто ебёт и кормит*[24]], it could be none other than
the father, since he answered to no one; the how was the actions
of the rest of them, which accumulated by virtue of the right to
an education & by virtue of labor and civic duties: cooking—
school, sons; school—grub, Mama. Under the shelter of this
common denominator, it might be said that each performed his
or her own individual number, as best as he or she could, until
evidence arose to the contrary, until there was evidence of "I
can't get my head around it" (from two years previously, when
none other than the better-behaved of the two had suffered a
misfortune; indeed, he had almost lost his head—as you will
see in Cap. 9, whose events are prior to those recounted here),
even though the brothers were in different years at school, and
the mother taught at a different school. But that day they were
not thinking of school; the woman kept asking herself whether
the outing planned for that evening might not be premature,
the outing that she too had unconditionally agreed to, it being
obvious that the father would not be content with just the boys'
obedience; the boys were increasingly worried that they would
have to undergo some ordeal of which they knew nothing. The

---

[24] He who f—ks and puts food on the table; a common expression in the U.S.S.R., expressing the power of the male as husband and paterfamilias.

embarrassed manner in which they had been informed of it, far from cowing them with the sternness of its tone, betrayed a barely disguised lack of conviction. At least it would have if the father had told them in person. In which case he would have been responsible for it. More than anything else, the sons would not have wanted to hear the father flinging, over their heads, the annihilating refrain at the mother: "Rather than have them do this to me, better you had stayed an old maid!"

No sooner had they left the house than Reality greeted them, jumping out in front of them with a friendly wag of the tail. The name of the bitch, who had taken up residence there without asking anybody's permission, encapsulated not only her past, in crooked letters displayed by the entrance to the yard—"ВО ДВОРЕ ЗЛАЯ СОБАКА"[25]—, but also the quantitative seasonal variations in the small pack that accompanied her, four or five dogs in the mating season, two or three pups thereafter. Hard to say why she latched on to them in particular—other children of their age were hurrying to school at that hour—, unless the brothers themselves had made her a playmate appropriate to them. In Ch—ău, purebred dogs answered to commands in Russian, whereas the local strays could be called using the words of the native land. But the native land itself was originally named after a little bitch; the bones of him who gave her to the dogs might not have rotted! From one yard to the next, turning from Armenian Street onto 25 October Street and crossing Kotovski Street just after the "Вина Молдавии"[26] shop, before turning onto Lenin Boulevard via June 28 Street, Reality bolstered the brothers' ranks, so that by the time they reached School No. 1, they had the feeling, engendered by reading *White Fang*, in the case of the elder, that they had just climbed out of a dog-sled, even though the month was May. Obviously, they could have walked all the way down Armenian Street to Lenin Boulevard and thence in a straight line to Pushkin Street, but then they wouldn't have had an escort that rubbed up against their legs and

---

[25] Beware of the Bitch.

[26] Wines of Moldavia.

now bid them farewell. The fact that somebody obeyed them, albeit at the cost of the two sausage sandwiches that they would now not be able to eat at lunchtime, must have boosted their morale, even if more than once they had been addressed with the adage, "Дворняжки, они и есть дворняжки!"[27] It is no less true that nobody else in their class would have been able to set down on the squared paper of Central Sector an entire sentence with a dozen quadrupedal predicates hand in hand with two subjects, one in the fifth year, the other in the third. Had it not been for the reaction of the school's instructor of pioneers, who doubled as the teacher of optional Moldavian language and literature lessons: "Dacă-i mai aduceți o dată, *сдам на живодёрню!*"[28] It was a model of harmonious bilingualism, that threat from the mouth of the comrade teacher: as if the deed committed in the mother tongue demanded punishment in Russian. And were they to say nothing?! "*Союз нерушимый* . . . / cum nu ți-i rușine / c-ai mîncat o coadă de cîine?"[29] At first, they didn't even realize what was happening to them, and whether the instructor of pioneers was yelling at them or barking at the whole world, a world that must have been stone deaf; and it was not till they felt they were suffocating, dragged by their red cravats up the stairs, whither? leaving behind the head teacher's office on the second floor (despite their school's specializing in French, the floors were still numbered *à la russe*!), had they got away with it?! then past the staffroom on the third floor, now they really couldn't believe it, and only when they were shoved into the Pioneers' room on the fourth, Always Prepared! did Reality catch up with them, in the form of Furtună ("Storm", with the femme-fatale first name Elena). The Storm now having been unleashed—even in the staffroom, they called her Tachanka,[30] because she never shut

---

[27] Once a stray always a stray!

[28] If you bring it here again [Romanian], I'll give it to the dogcatcher [Russian]!

[29] "The unshakeable (Soviet) Union [Russian] . . . For shame, didn't you quail / To eat a dog's tail? [Romanian]" The Russian word for "unshakeable", from the anthem of the Soviet Union, is here made to rhyme with the Romanian words for "shame" and "dog" — *Translator's note.*

[30] Light artillery carriage with a machine gun on the back; the most fearsome battle vehicle

up—she was firing long machine-gun bursts of words, more fiercely than Anka Chapayev ever did at the White Guard. Given the rapidity with which she was executing them, methodically and firmly convinced she was giving them a lesson in life, it was impossible to keep up with her. And only when they felt her hands—the same hands that had made them Pioneers—undoing their red cravats, only then did it dawn on them that it was not for bringing a quadruped to the school gates, but for sticking a dog's tail in the State Anthem of the USSR for the sake of rhyming "unshakeable" (*nerushimyj*) with "shame" (*ruşine*), and on the eve of Pioneers' Day of all days. They both blanched, as if all of a sudden, along with the scarlet silk, the comrade instructor had drained them of blood. And they pictured themselves hauled before the rest of the school, like those wretches in the sixth year, whom Tachanka had caught dunshing painted Easter eggs (which had been blessed in church!!!) just as their column of Pioneers was marching down Gogol Street along with the sea of people from Victory Square on their way to the parade past Lenin's statue on May Day. The school's wall newspaper had depicted them to that day, each poking up from half the shell of a painted egg—Russian dolls, nothing short—, with their Pioneer cravats knotted back to front like bibs. The caption said: "'Pioneers, in the name of Lenin's cause and the Great October Socialist Revolution, be prepared!' / '*Really* prepared!'" As was to be expected, the instructor's deed was lauded by the Teaching Board, but afterwards, most of her colleagues, some of whom had children at the same school, turned their backs on her. And now, what would become of her if she publicly denounced the brothers?! In any event, she couldn't be accused of not taking a stance, in the event that the brothers had been overheard in the commotion outside. Besides, somebody must have put the words in their mouths, so it occurred to her, more frightened at what she had deduced than the lads were at what they had said. And before the bell rang for lessons, she found herself scolding them, more for form's sake than anything else: "Is that any way

_____

of the Soviet Civil War.

to tie a cravat?! . . . This is the last time I'm going to show you . . ."
Having re-knotted the cravats, she raised her hand in a brief
salute: "Be prepared!" Each had got back the other's cravat, as if
now they were not only brothers by birth but also blood brothers: "Always prepared!"

Separated by classroom walls—the whole school was an enormous Mendeleev table of reinforced concrete and glass, which
had five floors, and, connected by a corridor the width of a two-
lane highway, a lateral annex, what had once been girls' gymnasium school, now set aside solely for the primary classes—, each
at his own desk (while their mother stood in front of another
class in a different school), on each boy's face could be read latent
guilt, as if before writing out a clean copy of the history of that
day, which looked set to be exceptional, each had, in sympathy
with the other, made an ink blot. Barely had the lesson begun
than, from one end of the school to the other, row after row,
depending not only on the floor, but also on the order of the
classrooms along the corridors, their schoolmates looked at each
other askance and either asked in a whisper: "Ты обосрался?"[31]
or loudly complained to the comrade teacher: "[So and so] has
pooped his pants!" the result in each case being one and the
same—the air stank, and badly too. It wasn't the first time that
somebody had poured a sachet of yeast down a toilet bowl, but
since this time the prank had happened at the end of the week,
when, given how much grey matter went to the latrines every
day, the four cleaning women could barely keep up with it and
the muck spilled thickly over the floor, the feces burst over the
threshold of the cubicles, the dreck turned up uninvited during
the teaching process. "One of you must have done it," said various voices, from class to class. "Nobody is leaving this school
till we find out who it was." They called out the names in the
registers, making a note of those who did not answer—the perpetrator had to be sought in the list of absentees, that was for
sure—but they didn't turn up anything and merely gave (some)
an extra reason to be ashamed of the names their parents gave

---

[31] Have you shit yourself?

them. They were then given a collective moral homily, the ones who were there to smell the reason for it, that is. In a way, it was exactly like in that joke about Vovochka, Bulă's elder brother,[32] who, having been kicked out of class for stinking up the air, wonders indignantly: "Я набздел и меня же выгнали вон из класса. Я на воздухе, а остальные в классе. Я дышу свежим воздухом, а они нюхают . . . Где логика? В чём смысл?"[33] Yet again, the slogan of the day proved true: "One for all and all for one!" particularly the second, disadvantageous part of the statement. Since the memory of the escapade of the brothers Никто-Никак (Nobody-Nohow) from two years ago—when the elder had been summoned during a lesson to come and wipe the younger's arse in front of everybody—, had just been reawakened, in each brother's classroom, the children laughed at their expense (they even laughed out of their arses, as Grandma would have said), but at least the two of them were above all suspicion. The laughter subsided to a muffled titter when the news arrived that the yeast sachets had been tossed down the girls' toilets on the third floor, which were frequented not only by schoolgirls, but also by women teachers, since the staffroom was at the end of the same corridor. Everybody had thought they were pissy, but now look, they were shitty as well! The quotation of the day was to authored by a boy from the tenth year, who, coyly turning to the girl sitting at the next desk—if not the most beautiful girl in the school, then certainly a future contender—, chided her: "I didn't expect a thing like that from you!" Under the circumstances, nobody even thought of asking to be excused during lessons. What angels these children are! . . . A pleasure to listen to them. "Babira, come to the blackboard." "Babără," the boy corrected her for the thousandth time, to which the social sciences teacher, who was also secretary of the school's Party organization,

---

[32] Bulă was the slow-witted butt of a thousand jokes in Romania's communist period. The name means literally "bubble," but with an obvious rhyming reference to *pulă* ("dick"). Vovochka is his Russian equivalent. The name is a diminutive of Vova, itself a diminutive of Vladimir — *Translator's note.*

[33] I broke wind, but I'm the one they kicked out of class. I'm in the air, and they're in the classroom. I'm breathing fresh air, they're gagging. Where's the logic? Where's the reasoning?

curtly rejoined: "Your ma can call you Babără at home, but as far as the State is concerned, you're Babira!" Meaningful in itself, the way in which his name was pronounced—"old-style" or "new-style"—gave away not only him who was called upon to answer, but also the person who called out his name, whether that person pronounced correctly what had been transcribed incorrectly (and besides, the Cyrillic alphabet imposed its own orthoepic rules, although to judge by the impoverishment to which the poor language had been reduced, they might as well have been called orthopedic!), or whether that person balked at the political correctness of names brought up to date by means of a final *-ov, -ski* or *-ko*. Whoever did a roll call had to choose between Ginkulov and Hîncu, Mamalyga and Mămăligă, Kerdevarenko and Pierdevară; the Romanian school did not allow the history teacher to say the Russian name Dikusarov, but since his past in the communist underground must have left conspiracy after conspiracy in his bones, Esther Haselevna called him Decusară and, by way of a joke, Еще-Не-Вечер.[34] Apart from this small-time cross-border traffic—the border being the Dniester or the Prut, depending on which bank of the Bîcul the inhabitants lived—, palatalization was what parted the waters, both territorial and нъеутре (nyeutral). The reek of unblocked drains hung over the waters.

The week's build-up of filth followed its course downstream, bifurcating into as many channels as there were hands to soak, scrub and rinse it, before abruptly taking the shortcut of two past participles: washed for the laundry; bathed—cleansed, you might say—for the people. More easily said than done, however, since most of the houses within the perimeter of Bulgarian, Pushkin, 25 October and M.V. Frunze streets didn't have running water, and the Central Baths were under siege every Saturday afternoon; cleanliness was wanting, the residents of that quarter—mostly of the seed of Israel—went unwashed for weeks on end, in dirty clothes, ponging of *Troinoi* (the men) and *Gvozdika*

---

[34] Dikusarov and Decusară are Russian and Romanian versions of the same name. Decusară sounds like *de cu sară* (not yet evening), which in Russian would be literally *Eščë-Ne-Večer.* — *Translator's note*

(the women) perfume respectively. In folks' yards they hummed: "Если в кране нет воды . . ."[35] and there was not a single doctor, Russian or Moldavian, who did not tell the half-joking, half-serious story of how Rivka (Sarah, Rosa—the names varied, but not the ethnicity) once refused to bare her sound foot for comparison because she had washed only her ailing foot. For the descendants of the shepherd from the Romanian ballad,[36] now city dwellers, "to form a crust of curds", the old expression for getting rich, had been replaced by "to form a crust of grime". As for the residents of apartment 16 at 61, Armenian Street, the curds formed over the course of many weeks, thanks to the assiduous labor of two adults, while the crust of grime was invariably removed on Saturdays, usually before supper, also thanks to the efforts of the mother and father. You would see them, the Holy Family, leaving the yard at four p.m., with the Pioneer brothers striding in front, so that all the world would know they were off to the baths, the same as in the evening, when they would all make a disciplined expedition to the privy at the bottom of the yard, before bedtime, to the malicious delight of the neighbors. "Крепкая семья!"[37] they would say, and the words would sometimes reach the father's ears, without the intonational quotation marks, and he, recently demobilized from the Red Army, in the rank of lieutenant, would turn scarlet with pride at the fact that the strong hand of an officer in the reserve could be felt through the velvet glove of civilized comportment. Having arrived at the Central Baths, the strong and united family separated for an hour into two uneven parts: the mother went to have a shower (not because it was cheaper; by her very nature she was opposed to any form of sitting down, and the fact that once she had passed out in the tub and they had had to break the door down to rescue her was one more argument against it, quite apart from reasons of hygiene: you don't dip yourself in the trough another

---

[35] "If there's no water in the tap"; satirical song popular in the USSR., where the Jews were blamed for all the ills of the world

[36] *Miorița* (*The Ewe Lamb*), in which a Wallachian and a Transylvanian shepherd murder a Moldavian shepherd. — *Translator's note*

[37] A solid family!

woman has just got out of!), while father & sons wallowed in a brimming cast-iron tub, giving each other soap beards and holding their breath underwater against the clock. The hour passed before you knew it, without major incidents, except perhaps for one of the brothers peeing in the tub or the father detonating a subaquatic fart, turning the bath into a jacuzzi; absolute discretion on the mother's part. At five minutes past the hour they met at the entrance, and as a rule, she never had to wait more than two or three minutes for them. But not this time, since the father's impatience meant they were outside waiting a quarter of an hour earlier. "Has something happened?!!" the mother was to exclaim with a start as she laid eyes on her husband, who was red with fury, since the steam had turned him bright pink, as if she had just seen him bursting stark naked out of the cubicle. "Wasn't that what we agreed?" snapped the father, but looking at his watch, he toned it down a bit, although still remonstrating her: "You're five minutes late again . . ." The children burst out laughing, not because they'd caught their father out, but because they remembered the schoolyard rhyme: "Fute, fute / cinci minute!" (f—k, f—k / five minutes), which made them think that something dirty was involved.

For one evening, bread and circuses changed places. Barely had they arrived home, in daylight, still hot after their bath and already burning with desire, than the parents jumped into bed, locking the door from the inside, having first sent the children for a walk, "нагулять аппетит".[38] They worked up an appetite much sooner than when they were finally called inside for their supper; but not for anything in the world would the brothers have tried the door. Not the imminence of punishment, be it undeserved, but the fact that it wouldn't have been opened to them, even though they knew their mother and father were at home, was enough to discourage them from the start; and what were those grownups doing in there anyway that was so dreadful? Even when their father was writing—the most dreaded of all activities—the children were tolerated inside the house! It

---

[38] To work up an appetite.

didn't last long, this time. Soon, knives and forks replaced the hands of the clock, and the four plates showed—like the clock faces in international airports that display local time in various of the world's metropolises—the haste of some to get down to business and the tentative attempts of others to play for time, since the evening's revelation was to follow immediately after supper. Some were able to hold their food down—or rather one of them, but who ate enough for two—while others felt it coming back up, so greasy was it. "It's a good thing, comrades, it's a good thing . . ." the father would sometimes start to recite, and if the mother did not hasten to remind him that other people were eating, he would add, "Folk nowadays eat their fill," and then, "they shit the more heartily for it," a sign of alimentary wellbeing based on quantity—food had to be copious rather than varied or tasty. No question of leaving food on your plate or (God forbid!) bringing it back up: the parents would have taken it as a personal insult. Far more than the long spoon for beating them with (originally used as a shoe horn), the sons feared the ladle, as big as the shovel of an excavator used for digging mass graves, once their father got his hands on it; but that evening, the mother was using it for ladling. After which, she was the one who cleared the table, washed the dishes, swept the small space that served as a dining room, while she chose the words she was about to say to her offspring at any moment, although the speech was late in coming. Nor were the children ready for whatever was in store for them, and the fact that they had been forewarned that morning, the way one would set an alarm clock, made them all the more fearful. One person alone was in his element, bursting with the importance of the moment. "Call the boys," he said to his wife over the boys' heads, at which the mother blanched, but her maternal feelings gave way to her conjugal duty, and so, his spouse stepped forward, addressing herself to them as the true mother-of-his-children, with the stress on the his: "This evening, our father is going to read to you . . . your father is going to read to us . . ." The mother continued to grope for the words to explain to the boys what exactly was demanded of them and at the same time to thank her husband. An arduous ordeal! The

boys couldn't remember the last time their father had listened
to them, but now he was going to read to them?! The man too
was expecting a more enthusiastic invitation, something that did
not escape the woman—before sewing her boys' mouths shut
for an hour, the mother's voice had had to thread not the eye
but the ear of her needling husband. But whereas the lumps in
her throat grated on his ears, the young lads did not dare even
to open their mouths.

Seated stiffly on their bed, in the same places where they sat
motionless all those evenings when ("at ease!") household activities were suspended till further orders, while the father toiled at
his writing desk, it never even entered their heads that they were
prolonging a parenthesis left open for months, by the simple fact
that at any moment they would go from passive spectators to the
first audience of the paternal opus. An unprecedented situation
at both ends: the genitor had never listened to them, cutting out
the middleman in order solely to look at their school reports,
doing so in front of his progeny as they trembled like reeds.
Since nothing could be left to chance, the reading was prefaced
by a brief introductory speech, delivered by the mother, whereby
the wife reminded the children WHO their father was and how
proud they ought to be that they bore his name, and in order
to instill in them an awareness of their belonging to—she spoke
as if reciting—the great brotherhood of Soviet peoples (here the
man nodded approvingly), the writer—and she uttered his full
name—was about to read to them from his own work (not a
felicitous phrase, since every teacher and prize-winning pupil was
always ready! to read from "his own work," officially speaking, of
course), the short story titled . . . Realizing that her mouth had
run ahead of her, the mother tried to catch the man's eye, and
his eyes showed her her first yellow card. It befitted him and him
alone to give voice to his opus, from its title to its very last full
stop. The fact that a clean copy of the text had been transcribed
by the mother of his children (in the inimitable calligraphy of
a teacher of the mother tongue!) did not give her the right to
preempt him, nor to appropriate his Creative work—in the sense
of the process rather than the product—, even if she had lent a

hand in putting it—in the sense of the product—on the page, copying it out all over again rather than make the slightest crossing out. After a brief pause, long enough to convince herself that, for the moment, her unwitting mistake had been forgiven (but not forgotten!), the woman resumed her speech, in a tone of voice sooner suited to a school assembly than to an evening in the bosom of the family. She was now speaking in capital letters, as if she had written the subject of the lesson on the blackboard: *The Image of the Homeland in the Work of* . . ., with the author himself sitting in front of the class. To judge by the way in which the open lesson was unfolding—with pedagogic tact and familial devotion—, it was clear that at the end of it the lads could expect to have to answer questions, without their being forewarned. In any case, the answer was contained in the mother's words, chosen carefully to place in their mouths—it was up to them to anticipate what exactly was expected of them and, if possible, not only to meet expectations, but also to surpass them. The country itself marched to the drum of socialist competition, the slogan of the day sounding like a final sentence: "Догоним и перегоним!"[39] which didn't prevent people from believing—or the official propaganda from claiming—впереди планеты всей.[40] While you could mess with the country, with Father you could only be "at your orders"; even when he told them "At ease!" it meant "Stand to attention!!!"

First of all, Father uttered his own surname—with the Romanian *-ru* ending, as opposed to the Russian *-pь* to be found in his passport—, with his eyes on the sheet of A4, as if only thereby could he take cognizance of the existence of such a writer, and then the title of the work—in a manner so full of pathos that it demanded majuscules: THE GRANITE OF FATE—, after which he made a theatrical pause, long enough to review his troops, and saw that all was well. The first sentence resounded rhythmically, as if the words, having been called to arms—"Volunteers, step forward!"—, all advanced on the attack

---

[39] We will catch them up and overtake them!

[40] Ahead of the whole planet.

in a solid rank. Not a deployment on the battlefield so much as a military parade (not the one on Red Square on 7 November '41, but the one thirty-odd years later, on Piaţa Biruinţei[41]), the words marched and they marched, in dress uniform, for the space of a paragraph. Finally, the opening slogans, even if disguised among the martial banners, transformed the victors' march into a peaceful demonstration of the working class, a May Day, let's say, which at the level of the reading manifested itself as a loss of rhythm: once the ranks had broken, the first hesitations appeared of themselves, filling the gap. What exactly impeded the budding author from reading his text properly was hard to say—it was as if he were in a hurry to get past those sentences in order to see what reaction they would produce in his audience. As for his young listeners, on their faces could be read blind obedience, rather than the pupil-dilating enthusiasm that such a rousing opening ought to have inspired. And then, the father spurred his fiery young steed, which leapt with him over the trenches, his voice reared rather menacingly, his tone became categorical, as if the Brass Horseman himself were about to break into a gallop. It was at this point that he was tossed from the saddle, and the trajectory of his fall marked the next transition. In any event, a pause was demanded, and the mother hastened to fill it: "Why are you straining yourself like that?" An unwarranted remark, for which the woman would have been immediately upbraided had not one of the brothers, the more perspicacious of the two, hastened to ask him in an imploring tone: "And then what? . . ." (In similar wise, Flea the Footman made himself a footstool for Stephen the Great to mount his horse, so that finally his nickname would go down in history as a proper noun . . .) On his high horse once more, the man took it up a notch (to the ninth heaven)—the reading promised to be a bracing gallop.

The final words of the sentence were still treading on the listeners' heels when the man renewed the onslaught. He was now reading at a walking pace, like a man in civvies out for

---

[41] Victory Square, Chișinău — *Translator's note*

his evening constitutional, now looking at his feet, now casting
sweeping glances at those around him, but no matter how hard
he tried to play the guide, it was still the supreme commander
who gave the orders to the brave soldiers in the vanguard (the
future printing-press letters, in the event that his short story
were ever published) dressed up as day trippers. (On the subject
of words, they say one thing and mean another—the settled
grown-up man of today will never in a million years forget the
morning of thirteen or fourteen years ago when, still a student
at the Alecu Russo Pedagogical Institute in Bălţi, he opened
the door of his student hall of residence to find his father, the
war veteran, who had come to take him home: "They said on
the radio that the Romanian army are on their way to Moscow
and they've got off the train in Ch—ău Station!" "What army,
Papa?" asked the son, unimpressed. "A new army," said the old
man, straining to remember what the hell the newsreader had
called it, "I've never heard of an army like that before—*an army
of tourists!*" Since in their beloved country all excursions were "по
местам боевой славы,"[42] they didn't even hear it when the first
metallic notes crept into the commanding voice—notes nonetheless of pacific provenance, like the tap of the chisel against the
block of marble. (—*ru* had an awful soft spot for that poem by
Arhip Ciobotaru: "Emerge, soldiers, from the stone, / Emerge
from the bronze and the granite . . .") Amid the grinding of
the tool and the grating of his teeth, the narrative took shape,
setting itself against the resistance of the matter, as if not only
did the author give voice to his creation, but also the characters
in the text, headed by the sculptor chiseling the visage of the
Homeland, were at his literary beck and call. All those days and
nights when—alone in front of the blank page or in the presence
of his family—he had had to suffer in silence, taking care to fill
their bellies (without voiding their hearts, which had to beat
day and night like this: "pá-pa! pá-pa! pá-pa!") of all those who
cowered beneath his raised hand, now clamored to have their
say. All the more so given that the main character of the tale,

---

[42] To places of military glory

who was to inspire the sculptor—a cross between Pygmalion and Stonebreaker the Giant—the matchless face of the Homeland, was a mute girl from whose lips finally come the words: "The Homeland is Y o u t h emblazoned on the flag." Broadly, the plot resembled that of a Brecht novella, except that the German writer's story was about a blind man who "sees" Lenin by running his hands over a bust of the latter. But since nobody in their house had read the author of *Mutter Courage*, not even the father, the originality of the paternal text was unassailable, even if the message was identical: the thaumaturgic power of the Leader/Party. Since ancestral belief forbade the carving of graven images, idols were at a premium for the new man—wooden, stone, bronze idols, and above all verbal idols fashioned by the pen, which were churned out by the talentless and by countless artists with a calling alike. Fifty years of constant *Leniniana* and—differences goodbye!

For a while, the children followed the voice proper, captivated by the expressiveness of the father's facial expressions as he spoke, and then they realized that what he was saying was a story, one for adults, true (but so what?!), on which they might be questioned. The mother, with her eyes on her sons and her ears on her husband, was conscious of how their listening nourished the author's reading. "Let him be content with that at least," she inwardly implored, "don't let him make them speak!" Even if he had asked her, she wouldn't have known what to answer; but without a doubt, he would be expecting the boys to answer without being asked. But now that he had started reading—quite some time had elapsed since the man had pronounced his own name and then the title of the work—, nobody was allowed to interrupt him. In their house, you didn't speak unless you were spoken to! And even then, you weren't listened to!!! The father read on, and his voice was reminiscent of the red commissars' call to the final battle, a call capable of raising the dead, since behind the rousing words came the dreaded SMERSH: "Ни шагу назад!"[43] Periods as sweeping as troop deployments had long since given way to short sentences, subject—predicate—direct complement,

---

[43] Not one step back.

bayonet charges along the whole front line had given way to hand-to-hand fighting, each new sentence was a vanquished redoubt, and the war correspondents, as if popping up from the ground, were busily immortalizing the fallen in the line of duty. A few lines later, now in close-up, the action abruptly froze, like in a children's game—ever since they moved to the city, all their games had been in Russian: "Море волнуется раз, / Море волнуется два, / Море волнуется три, / Фигура, на месте замри!"[44]—, and behold, the marble-graven visage of the young Homeland is displayed to viewers dumb with admiration, including the girl who had unwittingly served as the sculptor's model and who, recognizing herself in the monumental composition *The Song of the Heart*, does not even realize when she gains the power of speech in front of them all. The silence thereafter, respectful at first, but then, the longer it went on, more and more embarrassing, risked compromising the reading once and for all. But then one of the sons jumps to his feet: "Papa . . . hmmm . . . this story by"—and he clearly pronounced the father's name, the one with the -*ru* at the end—"teaches us to love the Soviet Union!" Not that he wasn't right, the sly-boots, but the father was expecting more than just that; if that had been all, he wouldn't have bothered reading for a whole hour. "Or writing it for that matter!" flashed through his mind, but then he drove away the negative thought—he would have been cut out for a successful career as a "Pachkulya",[45] if he hadn't got it into his head that he could write and also if he hadn't given up smoking when he was in the army!—, and turned his mind back to the matter at hand: "They're philistines, these boys!"

---

[44] The sea heaves once, the sea heaves twice, the sea heaves thrice, freeze-frame, stop where you are!

[45] Legendary figure of Soviet lore. It's said that N. S. Khrushchev, on an official visit to the office of the Party secretary of —sk region, took from the shelf of the magnificent bookcase a volume of the *Complete Works* of V. I. Lenin, and not only was it unread, but its pages were uncut. Consequently, regional Party Committees, Commissariats, large factories etc. started employing, over the head of the cadres sections, persons specially tasked with leaving reader's traces—ink, cigarette ash, coffee and tea stains—in the classics of Maxism-Leninism, readers who answered directly to the organs, alias the KGB. [Pachkulya (Blotty) is a character in the adventures of Neznayka (Dunno) by Soviet children's writer Nikolay Nosov (1908-1976) — *Translator's note*]

The same voices, the same rooms—even the yard of 61, Strada Armenească, with its numerous hideaways, which they were not allowed to leave without permission, was part of the closed world of their short-leashed childhood—; days that differed only by the timetable of the lessons, even if in lessons they did nothing but correct their end-of-year marks, whenever they could; carbon-copy Sundays that drew nearer to the summer vacation, and which were looked forward to mainly for the change of scenery, although that too was predictable; the final bell, strident in comparison with the first; time passed, uniformly, like an earthworm whose rings multiplied insanely, until one of the parents lopped it short: "Run home quick, it's late!" or "Everybody to bed, Mama/Papa has to get up early!" Whereas up until lately they couldn't find anything else to do when they got home from school and so doggedly did their homework, now they had the whole day at their disposal. Given how much free time now opened up in front of them, the space in which they could manifest themselves was no longer large enough; examined in detail, the yard looked bare, drained of all mystery. The games, too, moved out into the street, along with the other children, who were freer in their wanderings, from tossing a purse tied with string under the feet of passers-by to heroic little episodes among the fruit stalls of the Central Market, only a stone's throw from their yard. Frustrated at not taking being able to take part in the other children's punitive expeditions to the stalls of the "speculators"— that's what their parents called all the market vendors, and for this reason they did their shopping at the state food shops, which were cheaper (the quality was also worse, and often they got fiddled at the scales), after hours of queuing—, the brothers one day signed up at a library, not for the sake of reading so much as to expand their domain. It was as if you pulled a handkerchief out of your coat pocket to wipe your hands or mouth, and as you unfolded it, its checks were to transform into as many quarters of Ch—ău. Now they could freely leave the perimeter of the yard; they didn't even need pebbles or breadcrumbs to find their way back, since the library was on the same street, just two districts away, although on the way back the younger of the two would stop in front of every fizzy water machine, asking for a drink, despite the parental ban. You'd have said they were Hansel and Gretel when they left the house, and little Alyonushka and her brother Ivanushka on their way back, if both the one and the other hadn't been boys, even though the first-born was forced to do girl's work around the house and the younger brother gamboled like a kid.

Walking down Lenin Boulevard and back—with books under their arms on the way to the library, with different books on their way home (not that they were dead keen on reading, but it was the first time in their lives when they could choose whatever they liked, which lengthened their sojourn in the reading room, turning it into a game of hide and seek, in which, snug on their shelves, the books waited to be found, even if the two boy didn't really know how to look)—, made them seem well-educated boys in their neighbors' eyes—and no wonder, since "сразу видно, из культурной семьи!"[46]—, when in fact all they were interested in was escaping parental supervision, be it only *in absentia*, so that they could ride the two zebras on either side of Strada Armenească. Thus, hand in hand, they walked to the junction of Lenin Boulevard and Strada Armenească, where their paths parted like in a Russian folk tale—the elder stationed himself by the traffic light on the side that gave onto the Ministry of the Interior, while the younger went to the side that gave onto the "Little Baguette," and on the green light, they both crossed without looking at each other, each on his own zebra, before joining back up on the opposite sidewalk and continuing downhill together. And the same thing on the way back. It was their own little invention, to tot up every zebra crossed, and the total—the net figure weighed in favor of the elder, since he was the one sent to buy milk, bread etc.—, a kind of barcode *avant la lettre*, unstintingly betrayed the worth of each boy's freedom. The younger then altered the rules of the game as they went along: it wasn't the zebras that counted, but the number of pedestrians! Since he invariably crossed on the side of the "Little Baguette"

---

[46] It's immediately obvious they're from a cultured family.

bakery, where there was an endless throng of people on their way to the Central Market or to buy bread, he soon overtook his brother, even though the latter did his utmost to keep up by running every household errand. One day, crossing on his side, the elder bumped into his Russian teacher, and then it was his turn to make the necessary adjustments to the rules: henceforward, they were to collect (that was the word!) the acquaintances each encountered on his zebra. Whereas before, they each crossed their zebras without looking at each other, now they kept their eyes on each other, and the younger knew how to get the better of the elder this time too: he would say hello to people left and right, to the despair of his brother. The man who tipped the scales in favor of the younger brother, once and for all, was no less than Leonid Ilyich Brezhnev, Secretary General of the CC of the CPSU It happened one sunny day. All the inhabitants of Ch—ău had lined up on both sides of Lenin Boulevard as they waited for the official motorcade, and the two brothers caught the moment just as they were coming out of the "Little Baguette." They decided to view Brezhnev from both sides of the street, and so the elder crossed the last zebra they were ever to count, although he did not know it at the time. They stood among the hundreds of gawpers, but since there were still no signs of the motorcade, the elder decided to nip back home, just one district away, to drop off the shopping bag with the bread. He ran back in a flash, since the street was all but deserted, for the first time ever at such a busy hour of day, and when he got back he was barely able to make his way to the front of the crowd. The motorcade had just passed, and the younger was beaming as if Leonid Ilyich had waved to him alone, stopping at the traffic light and inviting him to cross the zebra. Both the one and the other knew, without having to articulate the thought, that that the meeting of their lives had taken place/been missed and that Ilyich—the original in the guise of the boulevard that bisects Ch—ău, and the avatar in his capacity of продолжатель дела великого Ленина[47]— had passed among them.

---

[47] Continuer of the cause of the great Lenin.

With their classmates in the breaks between lessons at school, sometimes even with their teachers during lessons, on the street and in their own backyard, they had come to говоряскэ only по человечески,[48] and now they spoke Russian even at home, under their parents' noses, albeit wary lest their pidgin reach the ears of their father, who, delighted though he may have been to see them coming back from the library with *Рассказы о Ленине* or *Пионеры-герои*[49] tucked under their arms, was wrathful when he heard them mutilating the language of Pushkin. Not that they would have been punished for it, but whenever they were caught in flagrante delicto, the genitor would suddenly be interested in how they were doing at school or would demand to inspect their mark books or would take them to task in some other fashion, and reasons for him to manifest his displeasure would not be long in coming. The fact that two or three years previously, the parents themselves had sometimes used to switch to Russian in the presence of the children, so that they wouldn't be understood, sooner aggravated the situation, probably also because now they felt deprived of a good that once belonged to them alone. But there was also something else behind it: no matter how reluctant he might have been to admit it, the father was raising not only future Soviet citizens in his parish, but also sons who would not break their word. But when he swore: "On my word as a Communist!" the father did so in the true mother tongue, in full harmony with Party doctrine, namely: "National in form, international in content." As for the brothers, they had intuited that the mother tongue was to a great extent a father tongue, since it was the father who was the sole arbiter of that language in his own house. And so, not through fear, but from the obedience inculcated in them from their tender years, the brothers made a pact to talk, at least within their parents' earshot, на мулёвском,[50] they even made efforts to communicate

---

[48] To speak only human language. [The verb here is Romanian, transliterated in Cyrillic, the adverb Russian, creating a kind of pidgin – *Translator's note*]

[49] Tales of Lenin, Pioneer Heroes

[50] In Moldavian (The Russian term for Moldavian here is deprecatory – *Translator's note*)

between themselves in the language, despite their increasingly reduced, tuppenny vocabulary—as if you were to be given a ruble's change for six sixteen-kopeck loaves—, but within minutes they would burst out laughing, a way of making light of a dire situation, after which they would continue in Russian. Which did not prevent them feeling a surge of pride when Felix, peeved at not being able to understand what the brothers were plotting when they played Russians 'n' Germans, would blurt: "все слышали как лают две собаки на своём языке?!"[51] in reply, the brothers called him a "жид пархатый."[52] In that instant, the Averbuch family would turn up *in corpore* at the door of the —*pь* family. The father would then have to swallow "две собаки лают на своём языке" and demonstratively punish the brothers in front of the Averbuchs. But it was also the father who taught the brothers to call Felix in front of his parents: "A*b*wehr-buch," separating the two parts: "Abwehr — buch," strictly forbidding them from divulging who had placed the subversive *b* in their mouths. (It was tantamount to telling, on the eve of the thirtieth anniversary of the Great Victory, the joke about the two war veterans drinking beer and complaining about its poor quality; "You ought to have fought more badly," remarks a young man in passing, "because then we would all have been drinking Bavarian beer!") What the mother and the father, philologists both, stubbornly refused to see, despite all the evidence, was that not only their sons' Russian but also their Moldavian grated on their ears; Cyrillic script—a two-edged blade, if you discount the Russian Ё, Щ, Ъ and the Moldavian Ж—, had corroded their speech from within. The parents' innocence was seriously put to the test when, talking about a war film, one of the sons blithely remarked: "Pulili zburau di pi zdanii pi zdanii."[53] They were punished a few hours later, under some other pretext, and

---

[51] Would you all listen to those two curs yapping in their own language?

[52] Stinky Yid

[53] The bullets were flying off one building onto another. [Pidgin Russian; the verb and prepositions are Romanian, pronounced with a heavy Moldavian accent, the nouns Russian. But shockingly, to a Romanian ear, the Russian for "bullets" sounds like the Romanian for "dicks" – *Translator's note*]

at the end of the week, when she had two days off, the mother took them to the country, much to their delight, so that they could keep their grandparents company.

At the end of the first week of their sojourn in the country, and just a hundred and odd kilometers from Ch—ău, the former "мулы" (mules) became "Russkies" in their very own native village. Whereas in the city they had not taken exception to the nickname generally applied to Moldavians, here, taunts such as "Rus, rus, babarus, / linge curul la harbuz,"[54] which followed them wherever they went, took them by surprise. More unpleasant still was the sudden outburst on the part of their grandmother, who otherwise was all sweetness and light: "What's with all this Russian all the time?!" Not even their father (= the Army) was so blunt with them, albeit for a completely different reason (political correctness and in keeping with the Party's cadre policy). The village didn't welcome them and that was that. Whereas they had expected that they'd never get enough of playing with children of their own age, now they had to invent their own little entertainments, such as riding the pig around its pen, clambering up trees with the goat, and putting the cat in the dog's kennel. But no sooner had they got a chance to enjoy their newfound freedom of movement than they were chased through a maizefield one evening by some lads determined to teach them a lesson; now the only place where they could feel in their element was their grandparents' yard. Out of boredom, one day they went back home in a stew, looked for something to read, but all they could find was an old list of the dead to be mentioned in prayers, a pile of *Moldova Socialistă* newspapers, still unused (i.e. in the outside toilet, where else?), and, in the suitcase of documents, two signed books by Father. All of a sudden, going to the library—as they had done in Ch—ău, before being dumped in this backwater—seemed to them the most beautiful thing in the world, and so they said to themselves it was worth trying the same thing here in the country. A whole week of going to the culture club in the center of the village and back

---

[54] Russkie, Russkie licks the pumpkin's arse – *Translator's note*

again—fruitlessly. Until one fine day, in the shop, they bumped into Grandma and the librarian, who, as eager as anybody else to earn a crust, was working full time hanging up tobacco leaves to dry. They fell to talking and came to an agreement that the woman would open the library every Saturday morning for the sake of the book-loving brothers. Ah! a vacation with the aroma of Alexandre Dumas, Jules Verne and Victor Hugo, all wrapped up in the three local deciduous woods. They were provided with reading matter to their taste. The first time they came to return books and borrow others, the woman was determined to ask them what they were about, as a way of checking whether they had read them from cover to cover; but in the end she didn't, so as not to give herself away—in the umpteen years she had been librarian, she had only ever opened the books to rubber-stamp them, on page 17. From what the grown-ups said, numerous sons of peasants the same age as their parents—the "first shod generation," as they never tired of repeating—had had problems because of that accursed page 17: whereas their parents had accepted, like it or not, that their offspring had to do their homework instead of helping them around the farmyard, reading books borrowed from the library, without anybody forcing you to do it, had seemed a huge waste of time to them. Which is why the more cunning among them had been in the habit of tearing out the page in question, without reading it, hiding it somewhere and then putting it back, still unread, before taking the book back to "school." This (desperate) act smacked of self-mutilation: it was like tearing two teenage years from the book of life—17 and 18 (obviously, you tore out the verso along with the recto)—without even caring; indeed, this was exactly what awaited the boys, at least in theory, at the ages of 18 and 19, when they were drafted into the army. What a monumental work might have been compiled from those dozens and hundreds of pp. 17 sacrificed on the altar of knowledge (nothing in common with Eugenio d'Ors, who was in the habit of burning his most beautiful unpublished page every New Year's Eve!), if somebody had collected them in a single volume, publishing the first edition of *Selected Pages* torn unread from hundreds/thousands of

books. In the books they borrowed, for a few weeks, all the
pages were intact, not even leafed through. A few times, they
even had to lay their hands on their grandfather's razor to open
the uncut pages. Some books had been uncut for two decades,
and now, once opened, the paper emanated a stale, old-maidish
scent. Generous now after long years of neglect, the books gave
of themselves unstintingly—but joyous as she was at first to see
her grandsons so well-behaved, as if by magic, the grandmother
was the first to intuit the peril that wafted from the printed page,
and her dissatisfaction translated as: "What's with all this reading
and reading?!!" But she also burst with pride whenever she was
asked—down by the river, in the lane, at the shop—"Them lads
yours, are they? They're books, not bairns!" Less enchanted were
the other lads from town, who, after excluding the brothers from
their ring dance, now found themselves rejected as outsiders, even
though they were there visiting family. As long as the brothers
ranged the length of the village, along the road that bisected it,
and dished out greetings left and right, there was not much the
other lads could do. But it was enough for them to take the shortcut among the back gardens just once for a gang of unwashed
lads to bar their way, the same age as the brothers and seven in
number, each fiercer than the other. They mostly just threatened
to beat them up, to give them a scare (not that they had a soft
spot for the "Russkies," but they wanted to keep in with their
grandmother, who treated them whenever she took something
out of the oven: a *hulubaș* with raisins, a pumpkin pie, a poppy-
seed cake . . .), and things would have gone no further had not
the village idiot been there. A great big hulk he was, but with the
mind of an infant. He abruptly squatted and made a huge splat
of shite on the path; he was stretching his paw for a burdock leaf
when one of gang snatched the brothers' *Mysterious Island* and
handed it to the mute: "Here you are, have a good wipe the way
city folks do, with paper!" By no means bashful in front of the
others, the village idiot ripped out a wad of pages. A quarter of an
hour later, the brothers burst into their grandparents' yard, yelling in unison: "The idiot boy wiped his bottom with our book!"
Frightened at what might have befallen them, their grandmother

rushed from the garden still carrying a hoe—she had just been weeding the tomatoes—, but on learning the business about the business on the path and seeing that despite the missing pages the book still looked voluminous, she heaved a sigh of relief: "It's only a shitty book! . . . At least you're safe and sound."

The day had got out of hand early that morning: no sooner had it been beheaded on the cherry tree stump in front of the house than the cock wrenched itself from Grandmother's hands and, blindly crossing the yard, passed through the only gap in the fence into the yard next door, where it gave one last spasm before collapsing on the beaten earth. The two neighbors had not been on speaking terms for some time, however, and the fence itself, brazenly impinging one and a half feet into the grandparents' yard, had been the source of discord, that is, if you didn't count the horse stolen in '47, which Grandfather had eventually tracked down at Soroca fair, while —*ski* had gone to prison. But since in the countryside hatred was a family heirloom, the women of the two houses couldn't stand each other either, particularly after Grandmother had on repeated occasions caught the final bearer of the —*ski* name pinching parsley, dill, onions, tomatoes and other comestibles from her garden (in a way it was understandable, since the —*ski* garden was planted to alfalfa). Now she would have to swallow her pride and cross her neighbor's threshold to ask for her headless chicken back. But her neighbor was more cunning and turned up at Grandmother's gate with the chicken as an offering—and thus the host was forced to treat her kindly, regaling her with a cup of wine. On seeing the wife of his enemy pottering around his yard, Grandfather, who had been shaving, slipped with the razor and cut himself. His "Ибиомать!" (f—k it!) woke the brothers, and only then did the day regain, for the space of a few hours (the final hours of a childhood about to end!) its innocence. "May this day bring you good fortune!" the grandfather saluted his grandsons, meanwhile sticking a scrap of *Moldova Socialistă* on his wound, and the printed word thereby received its blood offering. A (twofold!) red letter day, the morning looked set to be festive, despite the fact that he who had first announced it, with a "cock-a-doodle-doo!!!"

that hastened his end and the arrival of the long-awaited guests, was now soaking in a pot of hot water that he might be plucked the more easily. Scenting blood, the cat made her appearance just as the woman was gutting the bird and was almost scalded when she flung out the boiling water, now full of feathers. The dog too received his share of the guts, which he guzzled still full of shit, even though the housewife had taken care not to feed the bird the evening before (the few kernels with which she had lured it at dawn were still in its craw). Now that the cock had been washed and rewashed in hot water and rinsed in cold, milk fresh from the cow was set to boil (the agent of the passive verb is self-evident, and in the meantime, she went to call her grandsons to the breakfast table). And with that, the day settled into its normal rut. Apart from that, there was nothing else worthy of note, except perhaps the waiting, which made time flow twice as slowly: even the sun seemed to stand still, leaning on its shovel. For a time, the hours had elapsed to the rhythm of the buses passing on the main road in front of the house: the three o'clock, the four-thirty, the five o'clock (in the opposite direction). By the time the Ch—ău bus finally appeared from around the corner, all the events of that day had been concluded, and the family reunion now in the offing—the first of that green, waning summer—demanded a fresh page to itself.

The table was laid in such a way that if you sat on the chair by the door, you could see the whole thing reflected in the mirror opposite. There were six people around the table, or twelve, counting their reflections in the mirror. The long-awaited dinner could now commence. The place of the wine—and the bread, if the label on the bottle was to be believed—was taken by Пшеничная (wheat) vodka. "Food is frippery, drink the foundation!" declared Grandfather, his usual pre-prandial grace, and the half-liter passed from his hands to those of the son, the only son left to him, like a scepter; but even without that symbolic transfer of power, Father would still have possessed all the authority and the final word. Pouring the glasses and serving the plates, the male and the female principles were enacted: four fifty-gram shots of Пшеничная from the father (since nobody had thought

to buy soda pop for the children, the grandfather felt obliged
to set the wrong to rights, verbally at least: "Tuck in but don't
wag your chin!"), six dishes brimming with chicken soup from
the grandmother. And while the men knocked back their hundred grams of vodka—the women barely wet their lips with it,
grimacing as if they had tasted poison—, the brothers switched
to autopilot, each with his nose in his plate until further orders.
Nothing foretokened the change in the course of that dinner, not
even the entrance of the grandfather's niece, his sister's daughter,
a childless widow who drank her brains out with the men at the
village tavern, as promiscuous as she was garrulous, whom the
local housewives were loath to have set foot in their houses, and
whom the Party she had lately joined had overnight made a deputy in the Supreme Soviet of the SSRM. Whatever she learned
by chance or heard during a bender would be all over the district
within half an hour, and there wasn't an event at home or abroad
on which she didn't have an opinion. Grandfather couldn't stomach her, although he didn't do anything to get rid of her; but it
was enough for his niece to open her mouth for him to turn his
back on her: "I can't be doing with lies!" The truth is that the
woman's appearance on the threshold, just as the table was being
laid, surprised nobody—their blood relative could sense from
a mile off when drinks were being poured. The second round
of glasses, now with one extra, full to the brim—fortunately,
there was no need to pour her one "штрафной" (as a penalty), since she'd arrived already drunk—, parted the waters: the
men conversed with the heroine of socialist political labor, the
grandmother urged everybody: "Come on, eat!" and the mother
thought about a pretext whereby she might send her sons for a
walk before spirits became too inflamed. The conversation, not
unlike the Party line, kept straying from the subject. At which
the grandfather would call the meeting to order: "Pour another
round, —ică!" After the third round, it was no longer possible
to tell who was berating whom or even what the argument was
about. Luckily, the object of labor was on the table, winking at
them: "Cheers! Have another!" His country cousin's elevation to
the national soviet gave Father no surcease; there he was, a Party

member since the army, and there she was, a Communist for two days, counting today, and where had all his writing got him while his cousin, a member of the "Путю Ильича" (By the Path of Ilyich) collective farm wielded a spade among the furrows of the motherland?! The handsome man seated comfortably at the head of the table was driven out of his wits by the fact that in the case of his slatternly cousin, the words of the *Internationale* had been proven true, but alas, not in the good sense: "Кто был ничем, тот станет всем!"[55] whereas he, a cultured man, with a higher education and aspirations to being a writer, could only cast the Motherland in steely poems, could only hew her as *Laborer and Collective Farm Worker* in the granite of his prose. The bottle of vodka emptied, but another did not yet seem to be forthcoming, at which point the woman remembered why it was she had come—to ask whether they needed anything, because the next day she was going to the regional administrative capital. "Stay a while," said Grandmother, giving the signal for her to leave. No sooner had she left than the deputy returned as a subject of conversation—she hadn't even had time to sneak around the back of the house and, standing up, poking her haunches backward and steadying herself with one hand on the wall, to release a foaming jet of "Veuve Clicquot" de U—eşti. Say whatever you like, but Moldavians talk behind each other's backs after they kiss each other on the cheeks. When it came to his niece, Grandfather had nothing to say except that she put her kinfolk to shame, after which he went outside for a smoke. But Father was in the mood for talking, mostly for the sake of contradicting whatever the others said, although nobody, not even he, was minded to stick up for her, after which he insinuated, looking Mother straight in the eye, that if she arrived uninvited, it meant that somebody made her welcome. Taken by surprise, Grandmother found herself the first to renounce her penurious relative—mostly to please her son. Who let her get carried away, and as soon as her mouth got ahead of her ("You've no idea how she goes round people's houses stirring things up . . .

---

[55] Who was nobody will become all

It's not for nothing that the whole village calls her 'TASSia!'"[56]),
he cut her short: "Mama, I kiss your feet! But don't badmouth
Anastasia—she's one of our own!" "But why would you break
my legs, mammy's darling?!"[57] the candor of the woman, who
suffered dreadfully with rheumatism, had not yet given way to
anger; and, scoldingly: ". . . these legs dandled both you and
your bairns." Now coming through the door, it was Grandfather
who marked the change of tone: "*Yeba yo ti mrtvu matku pod
levym sisom na khladnom grobe!* [an oath he had picked up during
the war and which had clung to him ever since, for better or
worse; here, it served to change the key to a sharp] What's your
mother done to you, daddy's darling, that you should break her
legs?!" At the other end of the table, Father couldn't believe his
ears—thitherto he had been the one to take everybody else to
task, and now here he was obliged to explain himself, in front
of his wife and children, for something he hadn't even said. He
couldn't let such a humiliation pass. His first impulse was to get
up from the table, but then he realized it would be tantamount
to acknowledging his guilt, whereupon he turned to his sons,
taking them as his witness that he had said no such thing. Still
on autopilot, the sons had no idea what was going on or why
the two women had unexpectedly started crying, at different
corners of the table, while the men of the family were glaring
at each other ferociously. The dinner came to an end and with
it everything else. In the silence that descended on those seated
at the table you could sense the juices congealing on the plates.

"*. . . comme on prend l'train / pour plus être seul / pour être
ailleurs . . .*" (Jacques Brel, *J'arrive*) The railroad passed just a
few miles away from the village, and as an irony of fate, U—ești
station was included on the administrative map of the S.S.R.M.,
but not the village of the same name, six miles away. The major
change that this brought to the lives of the villagers could be
summed up in two words: a living for some, the final journey

---

[56] 30 ТАСС (Телетайпное Агенство Советского Союза) the official news agency of
the USSR

[57] The old woman mishears her son's *pup picioarele* (I kiss your feet) as *rup picioarele* (I'll
break your legs), the word for leg and foot being the same in Romanian – *Translator's note*

for others. Not seldom did local men exclaim, when angry: "I'm going to throw myself under the train!" Only a few ever did so, but only the going-there part: no matter how impassioned they may have been, by the time they reached the *zhivaya*,[58] which in any case was strewn with the carrion of domestic animals abandoned there, tethered by the neck till the train came—a few local trains a day and two or three goods trains—, their anger would fade. On the way back, they would stop off at the village tavern, making public the whole adventure, and once home the husbands would beat their wives within an inch of their lives for having driven them to their wits' end. To avenge itself on the villagers who didn't keep their word, every once in a while, the railroad would take a human life, be it a child being hit by a train while herding cows, be it a railroad worker falling victim to an industrial accident. (Animals tied to a rail with a belt didn't count.) "Going to the railroad" meant the die had been cast, and the more experienced housewives would already be thinking whether they ought to spend the night at a relative's or neighbor's house. "We're going to the railroad!" said Father, like a true native son of the village, putting an end to the argument. Which meant: a) as far as his parents were concerned: he was off to kill himself in effigy; b) as far as the mother of his children was concerned, they were going to take the twenty-to-midnight slow train, and therefore she ought to hurry up and get the boys ready; the next day at dawn they would be back in Ch—ău. Nobody bothered to ask the boys whether they wanted to stay or leave: the father didn't ask because it was self-evident that everybody had to obey him; the grandparents because they didn't want to set them at odds with their parents. And so there it was, in the middle of their holidays, with the adults' vacation from work still not over, they all leapt to obey the order and off they went. It was night.

At the end of their strength, after a night journey during which the young brothers made a new beginning, given it was their first train ride, and the parents didn't so much as close their

---

[58] живая изгородь — the strip of trees planted to either side of the railroad tracks

eyelids because of πr^2, the family once more found themselves
alone in the two rooms on Strada Armenească, and more separate
from each other than ever. The fact that they had left without
saying goodbye (although on the porch the grandparents had
managed furtively to hug the grandsons), slamming the door
behind them at an hour when it would have been opened even to
a stranger, while the old folks weren't even able to close the gate
behind them after they'd watched them walk out of sight, meant
a rupture which, if it was not healed in time, would never heal in
a million years. Not even Father had the patience to restore the
status quo of his position as spokesman and head of the family,
the only one to be heeded, and so, at lunch, he laid out his view
of what had happened the previous day: from what he said, it
became plain that the grandparents were at Anastasia's beck and
call, and it was they (without a doubt!) who had invited her to
the meal, solely in order to show off—"And in front of whom?!"
he exclaimed, rolling his eyes—their writer son, who was quite
simply INCAPABLE of saying what had been imputed to him.
Full stop. And so that the boys would commit the lesson to
memory once and for all, they would now write out a letter—as
homework—in which they would explain to their grandparents
the deadly upset they had caused them by putting in their father's
mouth words no normal son would have uttered, let alone a literary man. The haste with which their mother cleared the table
left them speechless ("Can we go outside to play now?" could be
read on their lips); just as they were about to rise from the table,
blank sheets of writing paper were placed before them. Nor did
their mother have any time to lose, since writing to her husband's
dictation, albeit in her own name, proved to be as grueling as a
long-distance steeplechase: as he kept blowing his top, skidding
every few seconds, she had to dodge the obstacles without devi-
ating from the path in order to reach the finishing line. It was
like the Foreign Ministry translating into diplomatic language a
declaration of war. He imagined that beneath his very eyes the
mother of his children was transcribing him on the run, transforming the booted march of his speech into the elegant tip-tap
of lady's shoes; and it was this self-confidence that played him

tricks—after all, it was beneath him to check what she wrote, and in any case, who would have dared to defy his word?! Like Him who said: "This is my opinion and anything else is wrong!" Still oblivious to the importance of the peacemaking mission entrusted to them, "Mammy's little doves" had indited their missives all in one breath, and now they were watching through the half-open door, waiting for the moment to submit their work. "Did you write what I told you?" their father finally asked, and the brothers were quick to nod yes, overjoyed. Instead of putting them in the envelope along with the mother's letter—or rather the father's, in the mother's (loose) transcription—, the father put them to one side: "Let's see!" They had written to their grandparents before—at their parents' insistence, obviously—, but never had their parents read the letters in advance, in no wise; but before they knew what was happening, the mother blanched, sealing the envelope with a deliberately mechanical gesture. As for the father, even a cursory glance at the brothers' letters showed him how different they were, including the way they obeyed him: whereas the younger merely repeated, as best he was able, what he remembered from the speech over lunch, the elder tried to add something of his own; but in both the one case and the other, strength of conviction was lacking. "I don't believe a word!" was the father's response and, after a theatrical pause during which the silence rang in their ears: "Correct what needs correcting, otherwise I'll give you a correction you'll never forget!"

The two monkeys trained not to imitate their master so much as to make manifest his latent desires, with the whole of an August afternoon at their disposal ("Nobody is leaving this house until it's written properly!"), could not help but succeed—at the end of a process comparable to the evolution of the species—in composing the letter demanded by their father, each in his own manner. And in order not to copy each other, the brothers were separated: the younger sat at the kitchen table, the elder at the writing table; the former was supervised by the mother, the latter by the father. Since nothing could be left to chance, they were asked to repeat what had been said over lunch. In a single voice, the boys recited: "Father didn't say what Grandfather said he said!" "Not that he didn't say," the mother hastened to correct, "but that he was INCAPABLE of saying—Father is a writer! . . ." And before they could take the words from her mouth ("Then why doesn't he write it himself?"), she reinforced them, to serve as a lesson to the boys: "He's published!" The change of addressee—even if they were addressing their grandparents, the letters were *to* Father—well and truly inhibited them: now they had to write obliquely. But the same words meant something different depending on whom you were addressing and on whether you were doing it of your own free will or forced by circumstances; it was demanded of them that they convince their grandparents (in other words, that they convice them who had got it into their heads that their son had said what he was quite simply INCAPABLE of saying), while remaining loyal to their father ("Believe and do not question!" as it were). Caught on the wrong foot—as so many times before when they gave an honest answer to the sacramental question: "Whom do you love the most, Mother or Father? . . ."—, they were faced with a choice that was to mark them for life: not content merely to quote them as witnesses for the defense, Father also wanted them (without giving himself away) to be witnesses for the prosecution! No matter how heavily his anger as a man wounded in his own amour-propre might have weighed, in his inner courtroom he knew that the grief of his parents on seeing their son storm out of the door in the middle of the night, with bag and baggage, was infinitely greater, therefore he needed the witness statements of his wife and sons to serve as additional weights in order to restore the upset balance. As for the sons, they sensed their hand was being forced, but how could they have written that their grandparents of all people had kicked them out of the house when they knew like none other how long had been their wait! They had dragged their heels "from home to the station / and from the station to the train," but nor had the grandparents been able to sit still in the meantime; as is well known, it's easier for the one who leaves. In vain had they learned how to write a letter at school—the practical exercise not only beats the grammatical theory, but also dishes out an exemplary correction to make the blood ring in your ears. "Whoever finishes first will help the other one," said the father, casting the apple of discord between the brothers—each was always driven to snatch first place from the other—, which would have been an additional humiliation for the elder, his right-hand son, whom he expected to say things the way he had been trained to, albeit in his own words, whereas for the younger it was enough for him to toss off a few complaisant sentences. He might just have well have told each of them: "Do what you have to do quickly!"

The sun's orange basketball hit the backboard of the west-facing window before dropping through the hoop, and Father had still not cast a glance at the two letters conscientiously submitted early that afternoon. At first, it was a great relief for the boys to see their opuses slipped inside the envelope, but the fact that the envelope had not been sealed meant that was still an opening large enough for the two of them to be put through the grinder once more. In the meantime, they had been taken to the baths, to wash off the country grime, even if it wasn't a Saturday. It had been embarrassing for them crossing the yard on the way there and back because when Felix asked them (old grudges forgotten!) whether they were coming out to play, they had not been authorized to answer, and they didn't have the courage to ask permission. Whereas the night before, on the journey home, they had imagined themselves as Hansel and Gretel, now they felt themselves not even little sister Alyonushka and little brother Ivanushka, but two little kids whom, if need be, their father was going to turn into a single perfect scapegoat. No matter how terrifying had been the episode of the night before, it was the awakening to reality that you had to fear. In the first case, at least you could expect a happy ending, but nobody escaped childhood unscathed. For, of course, there was no way you could leave the Family-Type House of Correction; at best, you would carry it around on your back as a carceral shell for personal use, at worst, you would raise your own progeny in it. Not even twenty-four hours had passed since the dinner, and instead of: "We were good and behaved ourselves—enough to make you wonder, for rhetoric's sake: "Who's ever seen a beautiful old woman or a well-behaved child?"—, their eyes already said: "Why doesn't he leave us in peace?" No anxiety alters your facial expression more abruptly than a question without an answer; but the two boys were summoned to provide an answer not only *to* but also *for* the two-voiced question that had been put to their father and which had remained up in the air ("Why would you break them, mammy's darling?!" and "What has your ma done to you, daddy's darling, for you to want to break her legs?!"), even if *сын за отца не отвечает.*[59] (Years later, one of the brothers was to take as his own Rilke's words in *Letters to a Young Poet*: "Strive to hold the *great questions* dear, like a chamber you cannot enter, like a book written in an unknown language.") And so it was that all unexpectedly, that evening they were summoned to read their letters aloud, in front of Mother and Father, who were all eyes and ears, as if the grandparents themselves were present. No sooner said than done. Well said, on the part of the younger: "The whole family suffers from your absence" (no matter that the sentence was repeated word for word from a school textbook—at least he hadn't been daydreaming in les- sons); overdone, on the part of the elder. Once, twice, n times . . . Writing and rewriting the same letter, for his father, he had had enough practice—but after weeks of tense waiting, the grand- father's reply arrived: apparently, the old folk had been in the wrong; may their unwitting mistake be forgiven. But the child, so good, so well-behaved, couldn't stop writing—always under the father's supervision, a supervision as increasingly impotent as it was increasingly unforgiving, even when the son had long since broken free and made a name (albeit ---*n*) for himself. ("Stand in line! To attention!" are the printed letters to some, the scrum of the handwriting to others, it means that the name of the charac- ter reflects his personality in a direct way, in the event that he is given a name, or obliquely, when that name is abbreviated; but ---*n* is more than just an abbreviation, it is the essence of abbre- viation itself, taken to its furthest limit, it is the circumcision of

---

[59] The son does not answer for the father. I. V. Stalin.

all males, whereby they lay claim to the only thing that cannot be taken from them, their gene, as opposed to their ranking among competing males. In this respect, the placement of the letter that designates him at the end rather than the beginning of the proper noun ought to betray a well-concealed frustration on the part of the author, himself previously marginalized—not the kind of thing you easily forget: lined up in descending order during the physical education lesson, even the boys shorter than him, but who were the friends of the friends of the bigger lads, used to shove him to the end of the row, despite his being five feet nine, and this under the permissive gaze of the P.E. teacher, who was perfectly aware of the balance of strength among his pupils—, and now, since "it isn't a name, but, *expressis verbis, a graffito*" (Şerban Foarţă), he takes his revenge, along the lines of "the last shall be first.") As it says in the book: "---*n* long bore the burden of being a child who made his parents smile, who pleased them (. . .) so much so that now he was left with a dangerous surplus of imagination." (In the meantime, Grandmother broke her legs, once because she hadn't been looking where she was going, the second time because her strength gave out right in front of her son's apartment block, where she had moved in her advanced old age, against her will, as if what she said two decades before had finally caught up with her.) Not thirty-five years had passed since that cruel summer and other adolescents were urged—as part of the National "Let's Carry On the Story" Competition, held by the Latin Union in 2010—to re-knot the narrative thread (snapped after: ". . . a composition on the subject: *I would like to be . . .*") of a text in which, so to say, lies hidden the child that went astray between the hand (that writes) and the mouth (that speaks):

Open lesson on writing
The great cartographer has a light touch: he paints the dandelion globe in watercolor—without snapping the stem, without blowing away the seeds—he paints maps of the world—as the legend shows—, holding his breath lest he unleash the elements, lest he alter the relief—on the physical map—, lest he scatter the

angels—over the celestial map of the clouds—, lest he increase tensions around the world—on the political map—, the countries "being so close that they can see each other, hear each other's dogs barking and cocks crowing." Around him, seated in a circle like the points of the compass, four famous travelers one by one tell of their travels in the North, South, East and West, and the cartographer's hand turns the words of each into (pure) color and (guiding) line. When one of them strays from the path, the map faithfully follows him up to the point where, realizing the storyteller's divagations, the cartographer slips the fantasy map beneath the terrestrial crust of the dandelion globe. Another map slowly sprouts, like a finger-nail, white spots and all, long after the black nail has been shed. In the imperial court there grows a single dandelion; in all the empire there is only a single cartographer. "Your globe is devoid of life; populate it," orders the emperor of the sub-heavenly. In the place of the four famous travelers, so famous that they are synonymous with the points of the compass, the empire's ambassadors take their seats, each telling of the countries to which they have been assigned, and their words are transformed into (local) color and (proper) names. But the moment comes when each attempts to exaggerate the size of the countries where he has represented the empire of the sub-heavenly, to lend them greater importance, to overvalue their material and human resources, not out of love for them so much as from a feeling of self-importance and pride in his native land, so that the cartographer, were he to follow their descriptions to the letter, would require a second, even a third, fourth, fifth, nth dandelion globe. In the imperial courtyard there grows but one . . . One by one, from beneath the cartographer's hand there appear countries that look over the fence into the neighbors' yards and countries that can be seen through the open window when they are getting ready for bed, countries above and countries below, countries like a shadow in the dusk and countries like a shadow in the hearse of afternoon, countries of the rising sun and coun-tries of the eclipse, Siamese countries, brother and sister, dream-ing of coupling with other Siamese countries, sister and brother, 69 countries, countries and countries. "Your globe is devoid of atmosphere," says the sub-heavenly emperor, wrinkling his nose, "give it some!" From beneath the cartographer's hand rises the sun, it climbs the sky like a paper kite, reaches the zenith, dwindles through the evening, turns to shadows, the shadows come to the fore . . . it becomes dark . . . they blend into the night. "Your globe has no sky!" thunders the sub-heavenly emperor. The great cartographer has a light touch: one by one, from the dandelion globe he erases the synoptic map, the political map, and the physical map. "There it is!" The sub-heavenly emperor has nothing in common with the king in Andersen's fairy tale; he does not take him at his word. "The sky, I don't see it." "Because of the clouds." Only now does the child from Andersen's tale appear; it is the sub-heavenly emperor himself, who exclaims: "A Turk!" and blows on the bluish cloud, then watches as they are blown away, the countries with which he was on neighborly terms and the countries with which he was at war, the countries he coveted and the countries he could not get rid of, the countries whither he had sent ambassadors and the countries whence his ambassadors had never returned, probably having died long ago, on their way there or on their way back; he watches as his own empire is destroyed province by province, city by city, neighborhood by neighborhood, until all that remains is a single dandelion seed, which represents the imperial court, in the middle of which an old man—resembling King Lear—holds an umbrella instead of a scepter, beyond whose horizon he has never stepped, and a cartographer—resembling nobody—holds a brush, beyond whose tip he has never travelled. He has a light touch . . .

. . . not lighter than the touch of the executioner, the great carpenter of the block, who takes the head of the carpenter, who is indifferent to what is happening to him or whether it is to him that it is happening and whether he really is who he is—as the tradition goes: "He who makes a head for himself from non-being, a spine for himself from life, and a tail for himself from death has no fear of losing his head, nor of getting his tail caught in the door as he goes out"—, in a single stroke the knife blade divides it from the trunk like a fraction, without remainder. The headsman's dream is the emperor, however; it is him that his eyes imbibe—one blue, one white, like two dandelions, with the three maps laid one on top of the other, the first, and unclothed by all three, the second,

nonetheless before the sub-heavenly emperor scatters the clouds—
which, whenever they blink, behead an imaginary king. Not since
he started plying his trade (a genuine trade, as it says in the books:
"The killing is always done by him tasked with killing; to kill in
the place of him tasked with killing is the same as hewing in the
place of the great carpenter. Among those who hew in the place of
the great carpenter, few are those who do not injure their hands")
has he stained his hands with innocent blood—trickling over the
block, spilling over the concentric annual rings of the trunk, seeping into the meridians of the axe marks, the blood traces the sticky
or almost transparent maps of inner countries, as if to remind him
of his school exercise books, veritable fantasy atlases, in cinnabar
and encre de Chine, of his passion for travel (the measles on the
cheeks of the boy at the desk next to him—of the imperial line,
blue-blooded—were as many continents and archipelagos), which
he gave up forever for literature's sake in the moment when, praising his composition, his teacher put in his hands a book in which
he read: "I saw a headless trunk, and I think / I see it still, and I
alone saw it / walking around like anybody else. / it was holding
its head by the hair, / like you'd hold a lantern in a living hand, /
and the head saw us . . ."—, he never forgot to show due respect to
him who was sentenced to death. From the heads lopped during
all this time he might create his own alphabet, in which, taking
account of the tip of the scales held by blindfolded Themis, the
heads fallen unjustly would be the vowels, and those fallen justly
would be the consonants, or maybe the other way around, in any
case, the script would be one and the same, *Requiescat in pace!* The
exclamation mark resembles Your-head-will-rest-at-your-feet and
can be none other than the king, for whose sake the headsman
chose the trade of headsman, the king's shadow. From beneath the
rim of the umbrella, the sub-heavenly emperor gazes in admiration at the headsman's hands: "Behold the only man in my empire
who does not have to correct his work once done. His movements
are as precise as grammatical rules. The final stroke, as perfect as a
mathematical operation. Intentions fulfilled. The light touch . . ."

. . . not lighter than the child's hand, one of the two—the
cartographer and the headsman—many years before, who wrote,

leaning his whole body over the exercise book, lest the boy at the
desk next to him copy, who was the heir to the throne (for whom
everything was decided from the moment he came into the world,
after they promised him the moon and the stars, without being able
to tempt him, it was only when they plied him with the biggest lie
and he believed them that, as it says in the fairy tale, *he fell silent
and was born*), a composition on the subject, "Who I would like
to be . . ." The future spread before him like a fan: all he had to do
was to be blown away with it in order for the letters to take flight—
dandelion seeds, the vowels; the little umbrellas above them, the
consonants, or perhaps the other way around—in order to for him
to sprout elsewhere, dozens of years distant from the writing lesson
that was to mark his fate. On the walls of the classroom hung por-
traits of the imperial family, in tempera, maps of the world and a
family tree of the (*indecipherable*) dynasty; in the courtyard could
be seen the headsman's block, the pillar of the empire—it was said
that each man sentenced to death added as many rings to the stump
as the years he had lived or, who knows, the years of life that would
have remained to him—, on which, in the intervals between executions, the children used to play leapfrog. The sky is as high as a
paper kite on which somebody has drawn a sun in its zenith. The
clouds form fantastic continents, unattested by any of the world's
atlases. From time to time, the child peeks sideways at the boy
sitting at the desk next to him, the heir to the throne—since from
the very beginning destiny dotted the i in the case of the imperial
scion, the little prince looks like an exclamation mark refracted in
a mirror—, toward the eternal present with whose future he bears
the same relation as shadow to light. "You're writing about me,"
the heir to the throne whispers in his ear, "I would like to be . . ."
The teacher looks up from his book and the final words die on the
lips of the prince before reaching the other boy's ear. The writing
lesson becomes a game of hide and seek, in which, no matter how
far away the boy might burn to nothing, the heir to the throne will
still find him: "a traveler," "a warrior," "a high priest," "an astrolo-
ger," "a poet," "a philosopher," "like you," "not-even-I-know-what-
I-want-to-be" etc. "Wherever you might hide," thinks the heir to
the throne, "writing will give you away: *you seek what you find, you*

become what you already are!" "Yes, but," the boy answers him in
his mind, "in writing *'I' is another."* Without haste—the lesson
has barely begun—, without a care—what is written in your fate
is set on your brow—, the child writes the story of a cartographer
decapitated by an executioner at the command of the sub-heavenly
emperor, once upon a time, all the while having both of them (the
cartographer and the headsman; the king can be one alone and is
to be compared with no one else, as the teachings say: "he has the
form of a man, but not the feelings of a man; having the form of a
man, he is also a man among men; but since he does not have the
feelings of a man, he is beyond good and evil") at his beck and call,
while being neither the one nor the other, up to a point.

P. S. Inevitably, none other than the winner of the contest held
in the Republic of Moldova will have to give up the prize of a
trip to Italy—the palimpsest country of which Stendhal was
to write like none other: "Je voudrais, après avoir vu l'Italie,
trouver à Naples l'eau du Léthé, tout oublier, et puis recom-
mencer le voyage, et passer mes jours ainsi"[60] (*Promenades dans
Rome*)—, namely to Rome, because he didn't have a passport
and his parents categorically forbade him to apply for one, supposedly because of the cursed thirteen-digit personal code, but
in reality, so as not to let him out of their clutches. "What do
your parents do?" Ala Condrov, the director of the Latin Union
in Ch—ău asked him bluntly, and the lad's mumbled reply was
unexpected: "My mother's a housewife — she obeys my father,
and my father . . . Father writes."

---

[60] After seeing Italy, I would like to find the water of Lethe in Naples, to forget everything,
and then recommence my journey and pass my days like thus.

Cap. 3
Авиа Мария

The tone: 'À l'autre bout de la ligne / j'entends ma propre peur'

Bei Dao, *Accents du terroir*

THE CLERK AT the central post office handed him back the form, barely glancing at the text of the telegram: "I don't understand what's written here!" she said. "What language is this?" "Latin," said the young man, turning red. "It reads: *Ave Maria gratia plena.*" "Write it out again in Russian! Next!" And so, thanks to the intransigence of the woman at the counter, and not without the telegraphist lending a hand, it came to pass that a village postwoman in southern Moldova set off to deliver to a Literature student spending the summer holidays at her parents' house the most unusual telegram she had ever handled in all her years of state employment: "Авиа Мария граница плена."[61] Nor did the competent authorities (viz. the KGB) recall ever having intercepted a text so blatant—just a few miles away from the village there was a military air base, and the frontier with the Neighboring Friendly Nation was but a stone's throw distant—but which nonetheless defied decryption: what, for example, might the word "*plena*" mean?[62] Whom were the pair of

---

[61] *Avia Maria granitsa plena—Avia Maria frontier of captivity.*

[62] In Latin, the word means "full" (feminine singular), but in Russian, it is "of captivity" (genitive singular of *plen*) – *Translator's note.*

lovebirds about to take hostage so that they could commandeer
a plane and leave Soviet airspace? The not at all insignificant fact
that the boy's father had been an officer in the parachute corps,
albeit in a political capacity, merely complicated the equation. All
the words looked familiar, but there was only one whose meaning they could be completely sure of: the girl was called Maria.
Her family called her *Musica*. At university, the boy would greet
her with "*de la Moussique avant toute choses*." Not even the girl
herself knew what the telegram was supposed to mean, except
that the lanky youth was thinking of her, as was also proven by
the four letters she had received in the last week and to which
she had yet to reply, and that love was a lofty sentiment. She
didn't love him. She allowed herself to be courted for the sake
of appearances, putting the art of discretion above feelings, that
native version of "what might other people think/say?" cultivated in the family after their return from exile in Siberia. In
any case, the relationship suited her whichever way she looked
at it: on the one hand, like every other girl of her age she had
an "official" admirer, and what is more, one coveted by most of
the other girls, albeit mainly because he was from the city and
of a good family; and on the other hand, the young man was as
bashful as a maid: all the other girls used to talk about how their
boyfriends would ask them for "a f—k" even before they asked
for their hands in marriage, whereas he had not so much as ventured to kiss her. After lectures he would walk her to her hall of
residence and wait for her (she was just popping inside to drop
off her books) a quarter of an hour, half an hour, three quarters
of an hour, during which time the girl would be nattering with
her roommates, testing his patience to the limits, until one of
the other girls would take pity on the lad and say: "Haven't you
left yet? Can't you see he's waiting for you? My boyfriend would
have smoked a whole pack of cigarettes by now." She took some
convincing, but she would have reacted like a scalded cat if some
other girl had tried to make a pass at him. With the telegraph in
her hand, she was still wondering whether she should show it to
her mother when the village militiaman knocked on the gate.
"They're not at home," the girl said, thinking he must be looking

for her parents. "So much the better. In fact, it's you I'm after," and here he jerked his head in the direction of the telegram. "What does it say?" Instinctively, the girl clutched the piece of paper to her chest, but she made no attempt to resist when the man snatched it from her hands. "*Avia Maria granitsa plena*," he read out, shrugging. "We know that," continued the lawman, unimpressed. "But what does it mean?" It was only now that the girl noticed that the telegraph had been sent two days previously (what could have caused the delay?): "They're birthday wishes!" "And what does he wish you?" said her fellow villager, putting the question to himself as much as to her. "What does he want from me, indeed?" she was thinking, somewhat surprised at not having asked herself the question hitherto, when, without waiting to hear the girl's answer ("Nothing!"), the man in uniform rapped out, telegraphically: "You have to give a declaration in writing."

For the length of a whole week she had not found even quarter of an hour to reply to any of his four letters and now here she was being forced to put down on paper a story that had nothing to do with her, although it was precisely through her non-action that she had let herself get caught up in the whole mess. She was not one for writing, and the history of her family, on both her mother's and her father's side, deported to Siberia as a result of denunciations that weren't even signed, was enough in itself for her not to put pen to paper. Apart from the unpleasantness you could expect once a declaration had been filed, the erstwhile prize-winning schoolgirl's fear of being confronted with an unannounced and therefore unprepared-for test paper paralyzed all her senses, and in the minutes that followed all she could do was blink in bewilderment, as if she hoped the letters of the words would patter from her eyelashes. In vain do the world's great poets in fits of inspiration liken the eyelashes of their lovers to quills: hers were like the slats of a fan, as big as palm fronds, shading her face. She couldn't see herself writing either to him or about him—to him from the fear of not having anything to say; about him from the terror she might give away more than she ought to, and willy-nilly in both the one case and in the other. Nor could she see herself in writing, the way she appeared in the young man's poems: not individualized enough for her to be exactly recognizable, but distinct enough to be viewed as such by her girlfriends. Ultimately if she were to describe their relationship, at least from her point of view, it would be fitting to leave a blank, snow-white page, perhaps dating it— January 17, 1983—in the top right-hand corner, the day when he invited her for a walk, during term time, under a pretext that was forgotten as they walked. But the village militiaman had demanded something different from her: to write a declaration disassociating herself from the young man's intention to cross the frontier fraudulently after hijacking a plane, which would have meant openly admitting that the two of them were involved with each other, when in fact she didn't set much store on his words, spoken or written. Her mistrust in beautiful words —and *"Avia Maria granitsa plena"* did indeed sound uplifting, something that should be set to music—a mistrust nurtured in the bosom of the family, found its confirmation in this self-condemnatory-sounding declaration which, *contre cœur*, she now had to complete because of him, if not somehow against him, the man dear to her, for dear he was, although she would not have admitted it for anything in the world. Still delaying the moment for writing the declaration—she had the whole day ahead of her, as the man in uniform was not due back until that evening—she was struck by a premonition: if they were coming down heavily on her, who didn't even know anything, what must they have in store for him right now in Ch—ău?

He knew all too well that the punishment for whatever a person may have done is inscribed within his very manner of being: in a hurry to live the moment, in advance if possible, he was always being made to wait, hours and sometimes days. He had been on tenterhooks for at least a week: not even visits to Nadyusha (as he was fond of calling the N. K. Krupskaya Library of the Soviet Socialist Republic of Moldavia in Ch—ău) could console him. In the first month of the holidays Nadyusha and he had been inseparable. The company of books had become indispensable to him: reading ravenously, he had as many *life-sized experiences* as the literary masterpieces he was able to get his hands on. But now, he would have been capable of abandoning a sentence halfway through—none other than he, who had discovered that "you have no right to open a book unless you commit yourself to reading it to the finish"—if she had given the slightest sign of life. This urge was all the more paradoxical given that when he was with her his mind mostly dwelled on the reading he had interrupted for her sake or the fact that they might have gone to the library together instead. Before he ever imagined himself with her in bed—a conjugal bed, of course, given the girl's upbringing, but also his ecstatic image of her as a Virgin Mary—he dreamed of them sitting together at the same reader's desk in Nadyusha's little foreign literature room. It was there that the woman of his life should seek him, not over land and sea or at the ends of the earth. But the ball of thread he had placed in her hands seemed to have been forgotten and lay untouched in her lap. Ariadne's thread had proven to be a Bickford fuse, lit at one end and about to blow up the explosive charge of silence. And then he would go downstairs to the music room on the ground floor and wearing headphones he would imagine himself as the commander of a supersonic plane, a Tu-144 or Concorde, piloting to arias by Mozart, Beethoven or Chopin. Lacking any musical culture, he would play it by ear, listening to classical "hits," such as the *Fantasy and Fugue in G minor, Symphony no. 40, Moonlight Sonata*, or, more recently, *Ave Maria*, whose first line—in the Literature department they had learned enough Latin for him to be able to transcribe it accurately: "*Ave Maria gratia plena*"—he carried on his lips in lieu of the promised kiss he would give the girl. But without any explanation, more than a week had passed and still she had not replied. It was the same as when she was in Ch—ău: then, she might not come out at all, despite his waiting for a whole hour in front of Hall of Residence No. 7. Although punctual in every other respect, her sense of time completely disappeared when she was with him. At most, they were together in the same space, a space devoid of events. There was no time, only distances: those to be covered (between objects) or interposed (between people). And now she was distant also in the literal sense.

When he no longer found any place for himself among books, the only thing for him to do was walk, increasingly long distances, but never at a stroll (he had no truck with the English!). The way he walked, using his whole body, made you think of Giacometti's *Man Walking*, with which he felt like дßа canoгa napa.[63] Once the mechanism was set in motion, nothing could stop it, as if he was about to regain in miles and at a good exchange rate all the time he had wasted vainly waiting for her. Movement meant not only life, but also flight from life and all its problems, a flight that no longer brooked any delay, since the four letters and the telegram sent two days previously had failed to resolve the situation, merely complicating it further. What could have befallen a country girl spending the summer holidays at her parent's house for her not to answer? And what should he do next, if Maria gave no sign of life? To force her hand in such a delicate situation as correspondence—"*laissent parfois sortir de confuses paroles*"—seemed to him boorish, but not to send him any tidings, after his telegram had thrown the Central Post Office into an uproar, not to mention, he suspected, the post office in her village, might also be called tactless, whatever the attenuating circumstances. In fact there weren't any attenuating circumstances. And then his imagination went wild, as he tried to fill all the blank spaces her absence had left on the map, inscribing them: *Ibi sunt leones.* (Her zodiac was Leo.) That she might have gone away somewhere without informing him was out of the question: the *versts* her family had travelled during their voyage to Siberia in 1949, and later back again, were enough to last them a few more lifetimes; with such an inheritance, you don't feel much like travelling. That she might be helping her parents in the fields—hers was a family of village teachers, with a small vegetable patch big enough to yield them a few potatoes and onions. That she might have got married—the thought didn't bear thinking about! That her folks might not let her write to him—absurd, given that he was a good, if not brilliant, (future) match. That she might not care about him—all too likely, but

---

[63] A pair of boots, i.e. two of a kind.

why then had she gone out with him in Ch—ău? That one thing and another—trying to examine all the things he would not have wanted to know had he discovered them, he didn't even notice that he had walked halfway across the city. He was already in Valley of Roses Park when the library caught up with him in the guise of *Romeo and Juliet*. What if she were dead? To ask such a question is like pulling the pin from a hand grenade—nothing can be the same again! Either you clench it in your fist until you become one with it, ready at any moment to explode with impatience but nonetheless putting off the answer, or you hurl it as far away from you as you can and wait for the shockwave to topple you: *Mortua est!* For a good few minutes he was unable to believe how simple the explanation for it all was—the girl's silence, his disquiet—but what a release to burst into devastating tears, which washed away all the filth (nocturnal emissions, plus "the paw" once or twice daily) of the swinish body (*corpus* is an anagram of *porcus*); and what spiritual solace to grieve her *in absentia*, thereby preserving her living memory eternally. Like in the fairytale it was deathless youth, but by default. No decrepitude. No sex life. He wept uncontrollably, rocked by spasms, as if he were pouring from his eyes all that he had had to swallow in the meantime, time that cannot be turned back. What came back to him was the all the time wasted, those indigestible evenings when, whatever he proposed they should do—read a book together, go to the theatre—the girl would invariably say, "No!" with the same vehemence as if she had been fending off temptation. Even if she had been pregnant (none other than she, the Virgin Mary, whom he had no few times cursed in his mind: "Let the Germans f—k her!"), she could not have been more nauseated by his proposals. In his turn, he had the feeling of always being out of synch with her, even now when—mourning for her with the devotion of enamored youth—he felt closer to her than ever before. Having perished, she descended from the heaven to which he had elevated her during her telluric existence and at the same time she sloughed off her earthly image, to be eternalized as a miracle-working icon.

And the miracle was not long in manifesting itself, just a

stone's throw away, in the flesh and blood of a young woman, who was turning her back on a male companion in order to put on a bikini top. He had never seen breasts in real life, and these were very close—not at all in a hurry, the girl was chatting over her shoulder to her male companion—and the contemplation of them filled him with mystical ecstasy, albeit an ecstasy that had nothing do to with the Madonnas and Childs he had discovered in art books, turning the pages with one hand only. Life returned triumphant, as if the worms of the tomb had all been transformed into silkworms, which now wove a bridal veil, albeit for a different bride. Her beauteousness hit him in the plexus and he was not even aware of his hand groping for his fly, as if unbuttoning the collar of a shirt so as not to suffocate. The palm of his hand clenched something like the knobbly throat of a gander hissing at the forest-glade sylph who was now arranging her breasts in the cups of the bikini. His fingers glided up and down, the eagle he was hand feeding gulped ravenously in its ascent to a higher realm and all of a sudden, just as the male companion was fastening the bikini at the back, he erupted, thereby sprinkling his votive offering of seed on the grave freshly dug in the upper air. For an instant his eyes met those of the woman, but instead of raising an outcry, she merely adjusted her bikini slip, baring the woodland shrubbery of her pubis. *Blitzlicht!* He saw black, turned on his heel and legged it through the trees. Having abjured the *Memento mori*, his ears were popping, as if on take-off, as if Martin Luther in person were shouting to his face: *Pecca fortiter!* There was no doubt about it: today was his lucky day.

If you cross Ch—ău on foot, in a straight line, from one end of the Boulevard of Peace to the gates of the city—the real slog doesn't begin until you come to the six picturesque miles of hill and dale, dale and hill between urbs and airport. Not so for him: having voided his lachrymal and seminal glands, the walk was a pleasure. The main thing was not to overdo it. On the way back he would take the express bus, a luxury the twenty kopecks he had been saving for a cup of coffee would allow him, so as not to transform a delight into a delict by a single faux pas. Intuitively, he sensed that there was a connection between freedom of movement and freedom of thought, and airports seemed to symbolize both, being the departure point for countless journeys "*по просторам нашей необъятной родины*"[64] and the terminus (if the airport in question was in Bonn or Vienna, of course) for freethinkers, the so-called dissidents expelled from the USSR. If his parents had known that he was heading outside the city limits on foot, they would have broken his legs. And had his father known what was going on in his head, no punishment dire enough could yet have been invented. And so it was that his urge to measure the road from earth to heaven, with his feet if it was not possible with his whole body, turned into a pilgrimage. And by a transfer of images, the airport became a heavenly Jerusalem/Mecca/Lhasa, and the airplanes as many flying churches/mosques/temples, in which the holy liturgy of ascension was officiated. He could even see himself up on the roof of the Temple (the battlements of a castle built by the strains of his lyre would also have served just as well, or the shingled roof of a church, after he would have entombed the woman he loved within its walls), tempting himself: "Cast yourself down, for it is written . . ." But here ended the reading. The bit about going arse over tit wouldn't work and that was that. Not even slogging along on foot could bring him any closer to an understanding of what, in the absence of faith, was impossible to understand: whether he levitated (like in Buddhism) or ascended to the heavens (like in Christianity), it would still be a case of the body standing in for the soul. Whereas he had just lowered into the grave, albeit an imaginary one, the lifeless body of his beloved, which meant that from here on, however far he went, he would still have one foot in the grave, her grave. There was no question of his amputating that foot. Better he dragged the grave along behind him as long as he lived. But for the moment, this didn't hinder him from advancing at a brisk pace, as if his ankles had sprouted wings like the ones on the cockades of Aeroflot pilots' caps (the only pilots you would ever see in the Soviet Union). Life smiled upon him once more, an

---

[64] Across the unbounded expanses of our Homeland.

airhostess kind of smile. And so he put on a spurt, jerking his limbs, striking wild-animal postures, his body taking up first one then another pose, in a relay race. He felt like neighing for joy and breaking into a healthy gallop. And all the while, the heat of that July afternoon was like a horse's bit of molten gold in his mouth. When he finally arrived at the airport, he felt as if he had just landed, whereas he had gone there with the original aim of taking off.

With the telegram spread out on the table, the girl read the message for the hundredth time: *Avia Maria granitsa plena*. By now she knew it by heart. She had never flown on an airplane. She had never been abroad. She had never spread her legs in front of any man—on her inner thigh a birthmark shaped like a tank told the story of a young mathematics teacher holding her hand over her belly, as if to shield her unborn baby, as a column of Soviet tanks rumbled through the village in the summer of '64—and everything she knew about relationships between men and women could be summed up by an expression she had heard countless times on the lips of the Russian girls at university, who were more experienced than the Moldavian girls: *Лишь бы не залететь.*[65] More than an hour had passed and the blank sheet of paper was still as immaculate as the girl who ought to have long since blackened it with ink (immaculate not-withstanding wet dreams and monthly emissions): it was inconceivable that she should denounce him, but nor could she get into the bad books of the militia on his account. The daughter of former deportees to Siberia could not allow the prize-winning schoolgirl of not so long ago to do her patriotic duty, and the Literature student kept tugging the sleeve of the country girl. Nothing she had learned at home, at school or, for the last two years, at university could help her in the present situation: as if the very presumption of innocence was about to exculpate an a priori trespass. And then she suddenly realized how little she knew that boy: apart from his being "a writer"—a fact that everybody knew—there was not much else she could say. To tell

---

[65] Just don't get pregnant.

the truth, she was interested in neither him nor his poems. But it was inconceivable that some other girl should take her place in his life and his writing. In addition to the *Autobiography* she had written out countless times—on joining the Komsomol, on finishing secondary school, on submitting her application to university, and so on and so on—what else could she say about herself? She had never had to continue writing on the verso of the page. She had lived the first twenty years of her life openly in this way, but now the four words of a telegraph might be enough for her to have to turn the page, this time forever. And before having something to hide in the future, she could see herself kept under close surveillance, perhaps even persecuted politically. The decision had been taken, however, and now she had to decide whether she should wait the long torturous hours for the village militiaman to return to her house, as she had been told to, or to go and seek him out at the police station, to tell him to his face: "I have nothing to declare."

On his return to town, he was forced to drop in on Nadyusha, where he had left his notes. The librarian from the Foreign Literature Room hurried up to him to inform him that his mother had come looking for him and that it was a matter that could not brook any delay. On his table he found a note—in the unmistakable handwriting of a teacher of the mother tongue and literature: his mother's—summoning him to come home imme-diately. How much time had elapsed since she wrote it? Now that he had found *Malte Laurids Brigge* again he did not feel like parting with him. How could he possibly abandon him? To keep himself from feeling lonely on the way back, he took with him a sentence, which he copied on the palm of his hand, as if to flesh out what the lines of fate stubbornly concealed from him: "His features were as orderly as the furniture in a guest room which somebody has just left." With his certificate of good behavior in his hand—the reader's pass that attested that he had not left the library all day—and the *Ave Maria* on his lips, he was heading for the exit when a young man, whose eyes he had at other times felt looking at him, signaled him to follow him to the toilets on the second floor: "Would you like to come in?" He followed him trustingly—ever since he was at school, the boys had always gone to the toilets when they wanted to have a smoke and talk among themselves. Instead of offering him a cigarette—he was even thinking of how he would politely refuse—the young man looked him up and down, glancing out of the corner of his eye at the closed door, and then pointed at the cubicle next to the window. Still not realizing what was happening, but feeling a dreadful premonition in his plexus, he suddenly experienced the sensation that time itself had drained from the room, like a painting from which the date and the signature had been erased. Near closing time, the library seemed empty, and the presence of the man filled the whole picture frame: "Today—now or never!" He still refused to understand *what exactly* would happen today, but the lack of a verb did not hint at anything good, as if the action to be concealed by the toilet cubicle door, besides being shameful, would have compromised his family honor. What his intellect stubbornly rejected as being inconceivable, his body intuited from the start: he suddenly went pale, the blood drained from his cheeks, and a violent spasm turned his stomach—an ingot of bile, the gold standard of fear. In that instant the man vanished and the bell sounded for closing time. Meanwhile, from the shock, his perspiration had erased the quotation from his palm. Which is to say, after a day of running back and forth, he had been left empty-handed.

The way home was via Pushkin Square. You had merely to cross Gogol Street, walk diagonally as far as the fountain, and thence down the bust-lined Classic Writers' Lane. The young man felt slobbery, prey to every sticky gaze, like an insect caught in a spider's web. He hadn't even managed to wash properly in the library WC. He reeked of excrement, without having shat himself, unless it was the air of Ch—ău itself that stank of shit, ever since the sewage works had been working at only half-capacity. He couldn't go home soiled like that. His parents would smell it a mile off. And so he decided to wash himself again at the public toilets on the left as you enter the square. He was beginning to cheer up as he descended the stairs, two steps at a time— not long now and he would be rid of all the filth—when in the basement gloom he came across the man from the library, who was accompanied by some young companions, and who did not even appear to be surprised. "*Сам пришёл!*"[66] he heard the man declare, more for the information of the others, words which, as far as he was concerned, might be translated as "out of the frying pan and into the fire," given that it was widely known, albeit he himself had completely forgotten, that Pushkin Square was the meeting place for the homosexuals of Ch—ău, notwithstanding the fact that "*Гомосексуализм в нашей стране изжит хоть и окончательно, но не целиком. Вернее, целиком, но не полностью. А вернее даже так: целиком и полностью, но не окончательно*".[67] He fainted on the spot—blind luck in such a situation. And so, having risked jail for pederasty, the man found himself holding an unconscious boy—now it was his turn to feel that time had stopped: he could see himself doing life imprisonment, in a cell with a dozen blokes who would put him through the grinder. "*Только не здесь, только не сейчас!*"[68] the man stammered, catching him as he fell, and helped by the boys, who flanked him forming a kind of bodyguard, he heaved him up the steps. As soon as he was dragged outside, the young man came to himself, but if he delayed opening his eyes, it was in order to watch them furtively through his eyelashes as they gesticulated above him, vying for the *droit du seigneur*, one spreading his palm, another clenching his fist, a third spreading his index and middle fingers in a V for victory sign, ready to thrust them down his throat. It was the same as in childhood, when the boys used to play rock, paper, scissors, and not one of the hand gestures was invincible. Stone beat scissors, scissors beat paper, and paper beat stone, and so on, in a circle; the first was also the last, as each would discover sooner or later, experiencing it on his own hide or dishing it out to another. (God Himself, in His three hypostases, seemed like a projection of the childhood

---

[66] You came by yourself!

[67] "Although homosexuality has been liquidated in our country once and for all, it has not been wholly liquidated. Rather, wholly, but not fully. Or rather still, wholly and fully, but not finally.' Venedikt Erofeev, *Moskova-Petushki*.

[68] Only not now, only not here!

game: God the Father was the fist in the Old Testament; the Holy Ghost brought the letter of the Annunciation; the Son of Man cut through the *before* and *after*.) When the youth finally deigned to open his eyes, the exchange of glances was two to one in his favor. He declined the outstretched hand of the man from the library, who was now affability personified, but allowed himself to be conducted to the edge of the square—"*А то ходят тут всякие!*"[69]—transfigured by anguish and trying with all his might to look as if he were on top of the situation. It was not until he was on the other side of Lenin Boulevard that he could breathe easily: the worst was behind him, but who knows what surprise was in store for him when he got back home.

From the threshold his mother informed him that a girl from his university had telephoned him and that she would call back later. This was what she had gone to the library to tell him, but he had been unable to find him. With unfailing intuition, the woman must have had an inkling of the telephone call's import, not to the girl from the country, but to her son, and she secretly prayed that her first-born had not impregnated the lass, whereas it was he who almost got raped. She couldn't see herself as a grandmother or a mother-in-law at the age of forty-one. "I'll not ask you where you have been, but rather why you weren't where you said you would be when I came looking for you." Spoken too loudly to be addressed only to him, her words were in fact a warning for him to take care what he said, because they were not at home alone. Or else, given that she could just as well have whispered, her wording betrayed the strong hand of the paterfamilias. It was at that moment the telephone rang. Maria's voice seemed to come from the world beyond, not because of the distance, but because of the interference on the line. She barely had time to ask after his health when he blurted: "I've been to the airport! If only you knew what an idea came into my head . . ." It was precisely what she did not want to hear, and at the same time it confirmed her darkest suspicions, which she had categorically dismissed when confronted with the man in uniform that

---

[69] There are all kinds of people around here.

morning. Afraid lest he say too much, or that he had already given himself away, she did not let him finish, hanging up the telephone halfway through his sentence, to the despair of the competent organs, who were recording the conversation. There was no doubt about it: the boy was a hopeless case, he had his head in the clouds, and now he had turned her life upside down, unless it was she who had turned his upside down[70]—there was no question of her boarding an airplane with him. She was not even going to let him see her tank! And so she set about writing, dictating to herself *à haute voix*: "I the undersigned, [surname, forename], domiciled in . . ., I hereby request to be transferred to the extramural section . . ." and, before turning the page, *sotto voce*: 'From now on, you're a dead man to me.'

---

[70] Consequently, in order to read Cap. 3-bis, you should turn the book arse over tit, the way the author had to adopt the first person singular in order to get inside the character's skin.

who wished into their unearthly ring dance; the engines, too, roared, the airplane picked up speed, the glans of the airplane ("a Boeing, in other words!") was about to jab into the sky, lifting the skirts of the horizon, having attained an erection—"*With-out his knowing / the coupling of male and female / his organ was aroused*"—when a voice (from beyond!) announced the Milarepa Airline Company's flight from Xining to Lhasa, and I watched through the porthole as one by one the foreigners, i.e. *nous les autres*—the real ballast that had prevented us from taking off the first time—, were ejected, at which I felt myself take wing and I would have flown to the end of the night, even to the end of my days, had the parachute not opened and had not a voice (a different one, but also from beyond) brought me back down to earth, not so much the land promised to me, as much as the I promised to it: "Repeat after me:

je te suis, croyance,
toi qui suis la mort".

to the skies; wherefore one of the stewardesses rolled forward an altar on gilded wheels, like a drinks caddy, while the others went up and down the aisles handing out sandalwood incense sticks. Behind them, two older stewardesses twisted the passengers' heads around to face the Buddha, the way you would rotate a prayer wheel, and then they all threw themselves to the floor for their ritual gymnastics. The passengers did not sit idle, but rhythmically waved bunches of lit incense sticks, and the smoke soon turned the inside of the airplane if not into a temple, then at least into a zeppelin. I knew that some pilgrims arrive at places of apostolic worship having prostrated themselves the whole way; from the zeal with which our stewardesses threw themselves to the floor, again and again, it was plain that they wanted to attain flight altitude on foot, and not just for their own sake. There was no longer any need for lit incense sticks, since from the head of each bodhisattva a streak of smoke rose to the heavens; the hundreds of fat men were inflated balloons about to lift the passenger cabin to the firmament from the inside. Not that I had a fear of heights (whereas in early childhood, they called me Gagarin, to the chagrin of my grandmother, who had sobbed in grief when the first cosmonaut died in an airplane accident, as if he were a member of the family, at the age of thirteen, I became Mowgli, because I used to climb the crane that was constructing a twenty-two-story tower block; a few years later, there I was, at the top of the tower from which you could paraglide, on the hill of Komsomolist Lake in Ch—āu), but in the instant when, looking out of the porthole, I saw exactly the same magnificent vista that had presented itself to me a week previously on the upper terrace of the temple in Xining, with the city lying at the foot of the sacred hill, I felt a knot in my stomach. "I'm sitting here like I'm over there," I thought, imitating the peasant woman from in front of the Central Post Office in Ch—āu, more and more aware that, through some unknown miracle, I had boarded a flight, bélas! other than Xining-Beijing. In that moment, the airplane started to move, lumbering toward the take-off strip; the stewardesses, now stark naked, had intensified their tantric yoga, riding each other foaming at the mouth and dragging all those

safety belt, to ease the airplane's take off; but all the fat men seemed to sink deeper into their seats, like weights to drag the iron bird to earth. The plane raced and it raced down the runway, which never ended, reluctant to tear itself away, as if the runway had turned to flypaper. Instead of taking flight, we suddenly heard a screeching of brakes, the reek of burning rubber in our nostrils, and the plane (a Boeing? an Airbus?) swerved at the end of the runway, but without leaving it. "With so many fat men on board," I said to myself, almost overjoyed at the turn the journey had now taken, "it's no wonder we couldn't take off." From the way it limply returned to gate A8, you'd have thought it had suddenly felt sick (of us!), which can happen to anybody—as the poet says: "Lord preserve us from premature ejaculation and tardy riposte!"—, especially when the imagination veers out of control, potency pants behind as it tries to catch up: "*Wholly devoid of desire, / you can contemplate her inner penetralia; / wholly filled with desire, / you can contemplate her outward appearances.*"

Wherefore, the loop split into the crinkly strands of a gigantic pubis, which the devil kept trying to smooth; the shaven-headed stewardesses vanished, the fat men leapt from their seats, almost weightless, even the pilots, thitherto invisible, appeared to be perplexed. Somebody then came up with the idea of seating us in a different order, so that the initials of our names would join together to form a message that by its own power would lift us into the sky, or so I supposed, whereas in fact, fat man still ended up next to fat man, from one end of the airplane to the other. Viewed from above, the full seats now formed an abacus whose beads were made of fat, which an invisible hand kept moving from one side to the other, unable to work out the sum. "*You've made a mistake,*" it was as if I could hear the voice of Ioan Flora, not long before he died, "*you're scratching my balls not yours* . . ." But what was happening to us was not a Serbian joke, nor did we resemble the beavers that eat their own testicles when in mortal peril. It so happened that each passenger was seated in his own place, taking his own flight—as many flights as there were passengers—, and the task of the crew was to melt down those separate wills into a single breath capable of praising us

I had had my photograph taken in the square on my first day in Xining. Instead of showing us how to put on our oxygen masks in the event of cabin depressurization, they went up and down the aisles making prostrations, performing a kind of holy gymnastics, and I counted to a hundred before the exercise came to an end. All the passengers, apart from me, had lit sandalwood incense sticks and were taking part body and soul in the edifying ritual of departure—soon, the smoke enveloped everyone, and it was only then that the airplane began to move. In the meantime, the stewardesses were spinning prayer "pinwheels" with even movements of their palms, the way I had seen everybody do in the temple at Ta'er, the engines roared, the airplane raced along the runway, on the ceiling buttons with two hands joined in prayer lit up, supposedly telling you to fasten your seatbelt, and before long we would leave the ground. My theory, a fantastical one to be sure, was that in order to take off, the airplane had to overcome not only the earth's force of gravity in general (g), but also a specific territory, and that the force was equal to g multiplied by the surface area of the country in question. In other words, it was one thing to take flight from Ch—áu International Airport, conquering the resistance of RM's 33,700 km², and something completely different to do so in China, with its area of 9,596,000 km². No matter how fantastical, my theory seemed to explain the frequency of aviation disasters in Russia (17,075,000 km²)—except that what also had to be taken into account was the large number of important people who perished in such disasters (General Lebed, far more entitled to be president that Lieutenant Colonel Putin; General Troshkin, hero of the Chechen war, which had been waged by the Kremlin grave-digger). As an irony of fate, that colossus with feet of clay that spread its legs across two conjoined continents, as if to urinate in the Volga, was called "Небесная Россия" (Celestial Russia), with a bicephalous eagle for its emblem. More modest in its claims, China called itself the Sub-heavenly Empire, populating its territory compactly and gazing ever more insistently over the fence at boundless Siberia, which in the midst of a demographic crisis. I almost felt like standing on tiptoes, despite my

Book of the Dead—"our father who in heaven art a hawser as I on earth am thy the cow tethered by the rope mu"—, pulled me aloft, ever higher (who was it who said: "Хорошо что коровы не летают"?73), thereby drawing me into the world, into various publishers & languages, and from time to time, into flesh and bones. And now here I was invited to China. After I was transposed into Mandarin and transported by airplane into the Sub-heavenly, my return home closed a loop; but in the end, I was to place this Xining-Beijing flight in parenthesis—by comparison it was barely a curl. And exactly like in the fable of the woman and the devil that smooths her curly pubic hair, the longer it took for the plane to take off, the more the passengers squirmed in their seats. From my seat by the porthole, I watched as the plane filled with fat men one by one, who as they advanced in single file up and down the two aisles felt more and more in their element. Absorbed in the sight, and with my broken wristwatch in my pocket, I had lost track of what was happening, and the living chain of fat men was never-ending, as if they were going around and around in a circle, advancing up the aisle on the right and retreating down the aisle on the left, a circle that delayed take-off. Fearful lest my presupposition come true, I didn't even dare turn my head—and even if I had, what else could I have seen but the enormous ear of the fat man next to me, from which could be heard, in an undertone, the unmistakable music of that prayer without beginning or end that had drawn Radu and me into the temple in Xining. It was then that I set about counting them, and I soon had to add a second zero after the 1, and then after the 2, 3, 4 . . . "It's impossible," I said to myself," as incredulous as the Transylvanian at the zoo, "no A-380 could fit so many people!"

As I counted, the files of fat men dispersed, each taking his seat. The stewardesses were just as spectacular: their heads shaven, they wore swastikas over their chests (not to be confused with the inverted fascist swastika), and their dark cherry red uniforms looked more like the robes of the monks with whom

come to an end, as a result of a telephone conversation that the
telegram's recipient cut short, fearful lest we were being listened
in on (could it have been otherwise, when the former head of the
KGB was now General Secretary of the CPSU?), but it had not
put an end to my burning desire to go away, to travel as far as
the eye could see. And now books had become paper airplanes,
the Book of Books had become the international airport, and
yours truly had become a long-distance pilot, whereas they had
called me "Gagarin" as a child. I had just discovered that in a
world well and truly grounded, the flight of fantasy, as soon as it
deviated from the Party line, was to the authorities tantamount
to a hijacking, and when on September 1, 1983, a Soviet fighter
shot down a South-Korean jet with two hundred and sixty-nine
passengers on board, on the grounds that it had violated USSR
air space, it left no room for illusions. My intuition told me
that you become what you read, but practice showed that—
exactly the same as in the joke about the sewing machine spare
parts which, whenever they were assembled, still came together
to form a Kalashnikov—the qualitative leap, if it occurred at
all, was sooner due to banned authors & titles, to read which
(furtively, wrapped in a *Pravda* or *Izvestiya*) gave you the sensation of hurling yourself headfirst from the top of the tower. This
state of pure weightlessness, all the more desirable given that the
gravitational field of the system could not be overcome, had a
name: *levitation above the abyss*, like Nietzsche's reaction ("If you
gaze too long into the abyss, after a while, the abyss will gaze
back at you") to the Temptation of Christ ("If thou art the Son
of God, cast thyself down"), only to end up at the phrase that
gave me sweet chills: "For it is written . . ." Reversing the order
of the words, Being itself ("it is") was conditioned ("for") by its
having been "written." And after I mourned my love, that girl
"frightened of airplanes", one summer afternoon, believing her
dead, and after one December night in Moscow, when I almost
flung myself from the fourth floor, I had decided that life was
worth living not in order to read about how Goethe lived it, but
in order to write my own life. In the end, what saved me was
my poem "VACA~", whose first line, inspired by *The Tibetan*

its nimbus above our heads. It made me feel the same as I had in the upper courtyard of the temple in Xining a few days ago, when, alongside Radu and Anna, I had contemplated the gilded statue of a gigantic Buddha, its belly displaying its swastika, to the strains of ceaseless chanted prayer. Not that I had been transported (in parenthesis let it be said that whenever anybody spoke to me of being transported aloft, I would immediately recite the Virgil Mazilescu poem: "the transportation of an old cupboard from dining room to balcony / that has agitated me lately", which would immediately bring that person back down to earth), rather I was experiencing a kind of exaltation prepa-ratory to inspiration; but since I'm not in the habit of writing in railroad stations, I gave up the idea. The apparition—impos-sible to tell whence he had sprung up—of the second fat man instantly projected me back to the lateral courtyard of the same Buddhist monastery, in front of the stupa of a monk whose spectacles made him look like a diver or cosmonaut. Only in the temple of Neamţ Monastery, whither I had descended one frosty evening, January 15, 1991, had I ever experienced such a sensation of peace—I could have remained there forever!

In the airplane by now, having passed through the seem-ingly endless bellows of a corrugated corridor, I was startled by the swastikas on the backs of the seats, the same as were to be seen on the walls of the Buddhist temple. I would have liked to point them out to my fellow poets, but either they had not yet boarded or they were sitting too far away from me. "I'm sitting here like I was over there" were the words that came to my mind, spoken once by a woman from the country, sitting down in the middle of the street to catch her breath, and whom the newspa-per vendor in front of Ch—ău's Central Post Office had asked to move aside. And as for me, where was I? I was in my allot-ted place, not going by the seat number on my boarding pass, but by the implacable logic of events which after a given point become fateful: after the post office clerk made me transcribe the "Ave Maria gratia plena" telegram into Cyrillic in the summer of eighty-three, and the telegraphist reproduced it as "Авиа Мария граница плена," my walks all the way to Ch—ău Airport had bring me any luck; I found myself humiliated by her once again on the return leg, when, with eyebrows meaningfully raised, she delivered her rejoinder: "*Rien à foutre!*" In a country of billions! . . .) Arms and legs spread wide . . . Da Vinci's universal man must have been born in an airport, while passing through the metal detector!

We were all waiting to board, at gate A8, and beneath my very eyes time was turning into lines, written ad hoc, from Serbian Dragan Stanić's travel diary, but also into a retrospective of the videoclips & images stored in the captive memory of the cameras that Radu Andriescu from Jassy and Szabo T. Anna, a native of Cluj resident in Budapest, were showing each other. I asked Jalal El Hakmaoui to let me have a quick look at his *Le ciel en fuite. Anthologie de la nouvelle poésie chinoise* (Circé, 2004), long enough for me to copy out a poem by Bei Dao, whose enchantment had been haunting me for two days—"*je te suis, croyance / toi qui suis la mort*"—, even though I knew it by heart. All around, I could see little groups splitting up, having formed during our stay in Qinghai province. It was as if on the Xining-Beijing flight, each of us were taking his own airplane (Beijing-Frankfurt, Beijing-Paris, Beijing-Vienna) and only the prospect of another Festival (Struga, Rotterdam, Nicaragua) kept us together, bound us to each other by a complicated system of recommendations, some of which were reciprocal. It was not apparent when exactly the first of the fat men made his appearance among us (in the absence of the other four, with whom I might have compared him, I had no idea what was his previous ordinal number) or, more to the point, how he had passed through the metal portal, which he would have been able to straddle; what is certain is that not one poet, not even the octogenarian José Corredor-Matheos, whose childlike curiosity made the world more vivid to him, interrupted what he or she was doing, or, in some cases, his or her dozing, to cast him a glance. Introverted creatures as they were, the grandeur of the human spectacle in the flesh and blood had nothing to do with them. Nonetheless, something in the air had changed, as if an enormous fan, as big as a helicopter's rotor blades, had suddenly begun to whirl

formed in the atmosphere of that morning, but nobody seemed to be attending the spectacle that was unfolding behind us. Nature had put all her yeast in a single lump of dough; but from what oven can such a plump, golden-brown loaf have emerged? Made in China? Or—as poet Dan Sociu said—"as big as China"? Standing next to me, Estonian Iaan Kaplinski raised his eyes from his English-Chinese phrasebook, and the horizon became one with his eyelids, with which—as he himself confessed—he had leather-bound the *Tibetan Book of the Dead* countless times. "Only when the disciple comes to renege the very existence of the Buddha," he told me unexpectedly, "can he be said to have learned the lesson." "Yes, but not even Marpa treated his beloved apprentice all that nicely . . ." I started to reply, but the poet had taken refuge in his phrasebook, remarking to me over his shoulder: "Do not take the Lord's name in vain!" when we were in fact just about to fly over the Gobi Desert. It was then that Jalal El Hakmaoui joined us, and our duel of words thereby became a childish game of "rock—paper—scissors", in which the Buddha reveals his empty palm (the void), God the Father clutches two religions (Judaic and Christian) in his fist, and Allah, like a Tristan Tzara *avant la lettre*, scissors from the Old and New Testaments the pages that suit him. Each on his own wave, we headed to the hand luggage inspection area; as implacable as a guillotine, the metal portal was about to expose what we were about—but without it having buzzed, I was taken aside by a uniformed local beauty to be patted down, although I would have been more than happy to pat her down. (With foresight, I had transferred my box of prophylactics—three-pack, MASCULAN brand—from my bag to the back pocket of my jeans, after an incident at Vienna International Airport on the outward leg, when a middle-aged customs official had rifled through my hand luggage in search of the square metal object—the foil wrapper!—that had struck her as suspicious on her computer screen; when she finally found it, she cast me a wondering look—I didn't look like a sex tourist!—and the words instantly came to my mouth: "*Mais je ne parts pas en Cine pour faire des bébés—elle en a déjà trop!*" Her "*Bon succes, Monsieur!*" didn't

to embody the very essence of the "fat man", what's more, in its folk version, "Fat and handsome", so beloved by my grand-mother, since it was identical with the person of her son. But more astonishing still was the lack of any reaction on the part of the hundreds of passengers who were shepherding their flocks of luggage toward the holds of the airplanes, as if on an aerial transhumance, with stopovers that would—for some—exchange not only time zones but also the meadows of northern skies for the pastures of the southern hemisphere. I looked around for the flying Dutchman, Germain Droogenbroodt, who within a week would be on his way to the Struga Festival, via Shanghai, where he would launch *The Frontier Tide. Contemporary Chinese Poetry* (Point Editions, 2009); his blue globetrotter's eyes showed the two hemispheres, the first, Eurasia & Africa, the second, the Americas, and the glint, as big as a welding flame, that was flickering now in the left, now in the right, already divided the sky into parallels and meridians. Behind me, Hennayaka Mudiyanselage from Sri Lanka was smiling—from the beginning of the Festival he had communicated only by smiles, a sign that with the departure of the colonists, the English language had also fled the island; Afghan poet Sayyed M. Farani kept glancing at his mobile telephone, already acting in his capacity as minister and close associate of President Hamid Karzai; Lebanese Ziad Mahmoud Ali Kaj, who throughout his entire stay in China had not spoken to anybody, not even to Palestinian Rose Shomali Musleh or Moroccan Jalal El Hamkaoui, Arabic speakers both, was probably wondering why people took no notice of him, despite his more than 120kg critical mass; the others were of every variety.

"Mr. ---n!" (how far do you need to go for your name to suit you? . . . a foreign voice pronounced it syllable by sylla-ble, wrongly stressing the second), called out the operator, in front of whom I had stepped without my even realizing it, as she handed me back my passport and boarding card, when the deflagration of another light, ten times more powerful than the last, twisted my whole body toward the entrance: "Another in the queue!" A huge crater, the size of an ancient amphitheater,

furtively at first, then unabashedly, although this did not seem to bother him in the slightest. I was picturing to myself how the airplane would fly tilted to one side, that is, if the man's huge gut were able to fit inside, when a powerful light coming from behind him set him off in golden relief, like the yolk of an egg raised to the sun—not ten steps away from him, another fat man, a fat man squared, by comparison with the first, joined the queue. "At least he doesn't have luggage," I thought to myself, "the same as hulk no. 1 . . ." Nonetheless, it was strange that nobody seemed to pay the men any mind, not even Kiwao Nomura,[71] whom I was about to ask whether that was what sumo wrestlers from his country looked like. My (just over) 60kg shuffled a few more steps forward, mostly on my heels, and to the file of fat men was added a new jewel, a fat man cubed in comparison with the second—he too with his hands in his pockets. "At this rate," it occurred to me, "the aeronautical industry will only be able to cope with the situation if it starts mass-producing the A-380." But a general indifference could be read on the faces of those around, most of them poets from all over the world, who were on their way back from the *Second Qinghai Lake International Poetry Festival*. No doubt about it, the queue (*de dragon chi-nois*)—my entire childhood rests under the sign of "в порядке живой очереди" (standing in line)[72]—must have unwittingly lost its head.

At the people's feet, like pets weighing circa 20kg a piece, plus 5 euros per additional kilo, the luggage dragged itself forward across the floor of the waiting room, which was now traversed by the wave of the fourth explosion of light, a sign that another heavyweight had been added to the chain of fat men. I instinc-tively turned my head, and the sight that presented itself, rather than terrifying me, filled me with admiration: the man seemed

---

71 All the names of the characters are real and can be found in the anthology *Transcending Reality and Matter: Poetry Collection of the Second Qinghai Lake International Poetry Festival*.

72 In French, the word *queue* means literally "tail." In Russian the term for queue is *živaja očered'*, literally a "living line/file/sequence", and here the author places the emphasis on the adjective *living* (under communism, life itself meant endlessly standing in line) — *Translator's note*

Cap. 3-bis
Milarepa Air Lines

The tone: "*I wish only to take journeys in time to which I would
not have the respite to say:* I want to go back!"

Roland Barthes, *Journal de deuil*

I WAS QUEUING at the check-in gate for the Xining-Beijing
flight, at the end of a week that concluded unexpectedly—outside the airport, for the second time recently, the strap of my
wristwatch came undone, a black Omax I liked to call *Cernă
hodinka*, and thus the time I'd spent in Tibet literally shattered
on the asphalt—, when all of a sudden, a hulk of a man joined
the queue, the way you would add a zero after a unit. I'd never
seen such a handsome man—and for better or worse, I was
well-travelled, the sort who studies not only monuments & landscapes, but also human types, it being my (mis)chance to live
above a young centenarian named Gratia Plena Three-in-One.
Paradoxically, the big man didn't darken my view, nor did the
poem by Cezar Ivănescu spring to my tongue: "¡ there are some
fat people / you only need to poke them with your finger / and
they burst (fat people who fatten the eye)", as it usually did on
the occasion of such an apparition; on the contrary, the man
seemed to consist of a luminous material, which he poured in
abundance over the onlookers, anointing their hearts. I shuffled
forward slowly, twisting around to see him in all his splendor,

Cap. 4
Portrait of the Peerless Artist as a Crowd

The tone: *"Those who loved each other when they were alive, who with their dying words asked to be buried next to each other, might not be as insane as one might think. Perhaps their remains will blend together and unite . . . Who knows? Perhaps their remains will not have lost all sensation, all memory of their original condition; perhaps in them still smolders the warm breath of life . . ."*

Denis Diderot, *Letters*

It was their last anniversary to be celebrated *in corpore*, the twentieth since they finished school. Understandable given the distance between Sighetul Marmației & Borșa and Ch—ău, by no means negligible in wintertime, there were only few absentees, and Florin and Miron I. exerted a greater presence at the table than if they had actually been there (the girls who had married and moved away didn't count!). A woman classmate sighed dreamily: "Увидеть Париж и умереть!"[74] only to be contradicted by ---n over the top of that worthy assembly: "Why 'умереть' necessarily?! . . . I've seen it a number of times, as plain as I see you and you see me!" But the bad deed had been done, the idea of death had been set in motion within a small circle of people the same age. A number/name could not yet be read

---

[74] To see Paris and die

on the ivory ball, not even its color was known (white? black?), and the coup de grâce, struck by the pool cue, had whizzed past the ears of the partiers. The festive table was starting to look like a pool table, with six pockets around the edges, empty as yet, but who would be the first to be potted? and *le suivant? les suivants?* That such a thing never crossed their minds was obvious as morning approached. Ever delaying the hour of parting, they had agreed to meet again, all of them together, for a weekend somewhere in the country, in order to celebrate the birthdays of those of them born in June; in the end, they decided on the twenty-second, "всем смертям назло."[75]

And death was to draw the winning lottery ticket for one of them: it was sufficient for ---n to submit an application to the Centre National du Livre for a grant to stay in Paris to translate Roland Barthes' *Journal de deuil*. True, nine years after the commemorative meal, which came after no fewer than three other commemorative meals from August 2001 to December 2005 (plus another one in a different town, in the absence of the former classmates, as was later discovered). The cumulative effect of these serial deaths, every two years, might have broken up the class had it not been defused by none other than their former tutor at another anniversary, the twenty-fifth, when she asked them to keep a minute's silence for Miron I., Dorian, Aurel and Valentina, during which she kept her eyes on the clock—she opened and closed her eyelids the way other people mouth the words when they read!—, timing exactly sixty seconds, no more, no less; but after a while, they all found themselves thinking about the empty passing of time rather than their deceased classmates . . . On the contrary, to see Paris, even for only a month, meant another life or—since it all went according to Roland Barthes—even a *Vita Nova*. At which point the question arises: how much of him had the departed classmates taken with them to the other world, and how much of them would remain with him, wherever he might go, before he in turn made the journey? Rhetoric aside, there are three famous graves (plus one about

---

[75] In spite of death

which he knows nothing) which he has to pack in his luggage whenever he makes the trip from Ch—ău to Paris, via Budapest or Bucharest. As President V. V. Putin said: "Котлеты отдельно, мухи отдельно,[76] which means that somebody sees the city of light (again!), while somebody else glimpses death. Both the one and the other through dark glasses: borrowed ones, worn only as long as ---n is translating the *Journal de deuil*; their own black-earth goggles, in the case of all the others.

Now, try to extract a single life-story, that of somebody in particular, without disturbing all the other life-stories with which you come into contact, like in the game of dexterity, where you empty a box of toothpicks onto the table and start picking them up one by one, until the first wrong move. (N.B. during the game, you're allowed to use another toothpick as a lever.) But if the attainment of perfection means not dislodging anybody, the opposite performance of scattering is preferable: a single movement, and a pile of logs (in the eyes of the player, he himself an insatiable reader of memoirs by survivors of the Gulag, catastrophes are measured in cubic meters of timber) rolls downhill, taking with it the lives of all those who lent a shoulder to erecting the pyramid, prisoners and guards, victims and executioners, *requiescat in pace*/ may they have no rest! The pyramid (alias Lenin's Mausoleum); the logs (subsequently replaced with red granite); the heap of toothpicks (if not the Caudine Forks that the heroes of the first five-year plans underwent); the lever-toothpick ("I've got something stuck in my teeth" "Pick it with ---n!"); the film spooling *à rebours* has neither beginning nor end—a good job we have long-defunct Soviet technology and the human factor, always blind drunk, yelling: "Fore! Because things were better before . . ." Freeze frame: Moscow, 1987. Just like in the Russian joke about the epitome of insolence—"Сидеть в глубоком тылу, ебать жену фронтовика и искать себя в списках награжденных за храбрость!"[77]—,

---

[76] Cutlets aside, flies aside

[77] To stay behind the front line, to sleep with the wife of a man on the frontline, and to look for your name on the lists of those decorated for bravery in battle.

on the morning when everybody from one sixth of the earth's land mass is hurrying to the Leninist *subbotnik*[78] dedicated to the seventieth anniversary of the Great October Socialist Revolution, to wake up in your bed in the student hall of residence, with a first-first communist—not one who's just pretending, like the others: "*first* you ask to marry me, then the *first time!*"—, who you find out only by accident is a Party member, when, in response to your deliberately macho dirty joke: "The member and the membrane!" she curtly shows you the red card, alias the membership card with the head of Ilyich on it. "Remember your day of rest . . ." the young man says, trying to stay her, so that they can have *une grasse matinée* together; not that she would have been against it, quite the opposite, but: "The Party calls!"—and with those words, off she went. The day too leapt to its feet, still sleepy, in a hurry to pick up its pace, switching from its usual weekend gait to a striding forth to do *subbotnik*. But the sun rose differently after a night of entwined legs. In the meantime, he had got out of bed to go to the toilet, where—not unexpectedly—he had bumped into Vanya Novitski, a.k.a. *sca-ca-rabeus sacer*, not because he stuttered, but because he spent his life on the bog: a member of the "вечный студент"[79] category, he waited until his victims shut themselves in the cubicle, and then he would recite to them the poems he had written that day. The more cynical would ask to read them with their own eyes, whereupon Ivan would pass them the A4 sheet under the door; his heart must have been sorely wounded whenever he heard the rustle of crumpled paper between buttocks, but he would come back to life as soon as somebody remarked: "Очень своевременные стихи!"[80] (It's no less true that lately, a new and

---

[78] Collective voluntary work, thus named because usually performed on a Saturday (*sub-bota*) — *Translator's note*

[79] Eternal student

[80] "Very opportune poetry!" A paraphrase of V. I. Lenin's remark ("A very opportune book!) about Maxim Gorky's *Mother*—a kind of bible of socialist realism *avant la lettre*. Later, Lenin's words were placed in the mouth of the wolf from the joke: A rabbit is hopping through the woods with a book under his arm. From the bushes, where he is having a shit, the wolf says: "What have you got under your arm?" The rabbit: "A book!" The wolf: "Quick, give it here—a very opportune book!"

redoubtable predator had encroached on Vanya Novitski's hunting ground, none other than Valeriu Matei, whose whistling on the bog—always to the same tune from *Lăutarii*[81]—could have moved even Gheorghe Zamfir[82] to tears; whereas *sca-ca-rabeus sacer* moved you to pity, the nightingale of the bogs moved your bowels.) On his return to his room, the unmade bed looked as if it were tutting at him: look at this ad libitum Sabbath on a *subbotnik* day. But before he could make the bed, there was a knock on the door. The surprise, pleasant at first sight, soon gave way to puzzlement draped in the politeness dictated by the circumstance: in the doorway, behind the beautiful Persian girl from the fifth year, Translators class, peeked the soldierly face of Vasili Zyoma[83] from the second year, Poets (Lev Oshanin's seminar). From the look of them, you'd have thought they'd knocked on his door to inform him he'd won the lottery, whereas in fact they were just about to sell him the ticket. On the threshold, they roped him into their social welfare plan—after lunch, they intended to visit the domicile of a war veteran, who was said to have been Beria's lover. A detail not lacking in importance, in the context in which *Novy Mir, Neva, Zvezda* and other "fat journals" were at the time competing to churn out documentary prose by Shalamov, Nadezhda Mandelstam, Lev Razgon et al.; the Gulag was topical once more, this time from the victims' perspective. Since he had nothing better to do, he immediately accepted, happy to put on a show of being busy. Inera's *clin d'œil*—"Это не совсем то, что ты ожидаешь увидеть . . ."[84]—, far from making him wary, merely whetted his curiosity. "Я бы сказала — совсем не то!"[85] As if he for one spent his days visiting the mistresses of Lavrenti Pavlovich. And before they settled on a time for the visit, it flashed through his mind: "In other words,

---

[81] *The Fiddlers* (1972), famous Moldovan film of the Soviet period, about a nineteenth-century band of Gypsy fiddlers — *Translator's note*

[82] Gheorghe Zamfir, famous Romanian pan pipes virtuoso — *Translator's note*

[83] Zioma, from the Russian *zemlyak*, "(fellow) countryman, brother."

[84] It's not quite what you were hoping to see

[85] I'd say—not at all

it doesn't matter what time you get up in the morning, but who you're in bed with, if you want to get ahead!" but at the same time he knew that no matter how early you rose, and whomever you were with between the sheets, if you weren't called, you wouldn't get anywhere.

"Ahead" was right next door—you merely had to go out the front door of the student hall of residence, an edifice in the shape of a Russian П, built in the fifties, and, after crossing an inner courtyard the size of a handball court, in a state of abject neglect—stunted trees, dilapidated wooden benches, dislocated metal swings—it was the first entrance on the right. Climbing a stair so narrow that to get it around the corner you would have had to pass a coffin through the door of the apartment at the end of the landing—strangely, this wing of the building didn't have a lift—, they wondered whether they'd end up in the back of beyond. As if it weren't enough that the babushka lived up in the attic, they also had to traverse a labyrinthine corridor, which was all angles and seemed to be part of the building's load-bearing structure itself, before they arrived at the door of room No. 49. Inera gave a coded knock: it was like the opening measures of the *Ode to Joy*, and then made a sign for the two young men accompanying her to wait. Five minutes passed without anything happening, except that all three physically sensed how, behind the locked door, the whole house had been set in motion, even though no human breath betrayed its presence. "What the hell is taking her so long," wondered the boys, at which their guide explained that she was just opening up the way for them. "More like she's preparing her retreat . . ." said ---n on the off-chance and the beautiful Persian instantly rewarded him with one of those looks of hers that clenched his balls from the inside: "Вижу, ты всё уже понял . . ."[86] All of a sudden, the door opened, without the click of the latch making itself heard, and in the doorway appeared an elderly woman, over whom time had washed in every direction—furrowed brow, withered cheeks . . .—, enough to mark its territory before consigning

---

[86] I see you've already understood everything

her to oblivion. After the introductions had been made, the old woman stretched out one hand to each boy, not to shake theirs or, God forbid! for them to kiss hers, but to feel their faces (Vasili's covered in molehill-like purulent pustules, ---n's all smiles); she was completely blind. "Neither of them is yours," she said to Inera over the tops of their heads, "this one's still a virgin, the other already has a woman," after which she signaled them to come inside. The door closed by itself behind them, as silently as it had opened, and the narrow hall led them to the only room available, a day room, bedroom and—to judge by the chamber pot peeking from under the bed—toilet all rolled into one. "I don't have electric light," she chided Vasili, who was groping for the switch, ". . . or candles either, except the one for when I close my eyes for the last time." A yellowed newspaper, hung in the window who knows how long ago, caused the light, dim enough as it was, to settle in semitransparent layers on the objects in the room, like the lard which Grandmother used to spread on his bread as a child. All around, before their eyes, there opened that variety of dusk which, instead of gradually becoming clearer, grows more and more opaque, finally filling your eye sockets with walnut jam/plum preserve, making your eyelids feel sticky without your being sleepy. The veteran thanked them for the foodstuffs, attempted to pay for them, but encountering resistance on the part of the young folk, instantly resigned herself and then vanished. A moment later, she reappeared from nowhere, with a bottle of the hard stuff, and now here they are clinking glasses as big as thimbles, "за знакомство"[87]. Now that the rules of both guest and host had been obeyed, they could talk as among old acquaintances. First things first, she asked them about what the papers were saying, paying no great attention to the flatulent official discourse of *Pravda, Izvestiya* and *Trud*, but showing great interest in the latest revelations published in *Moskovskie Novosti*. Quite simply, she couldn't believe such things were being said openly, in signed articles, without anybody paying a price. As they talked, one of them happened to mention

---

[87] For getting to know you

the name of V. M. Molotov, recently deceased (November 8, 1986), at which the old woman let slip: "Я хорошо знала его жену — по лагерю!"[88]

But she stubbornly refused to say anything more than that, by the only possible means she could steer the conversation in the direction she wished without giving the impression of avoiding the subject: she recounted in great detail how she had come to meet Polina Zhemchuzhina. Half an hour later, she was still on the frontline, always hauling a wounded man off the battlefield, and that was how she came by both a medal and a husband. The medal wasn't quite the Order of Lenin, but the husband, the future husband, proved to be a SMERSH officer! How he had managed to get shot, when he was the one who went behind all the rest, holding a pistol, ready to shoot any soldier who took one step back, remains a mystery; but even peppered with shrapnel, he hadn't lost his gift of speech: "Мы с тобой как две рифмы — кровь и любовь."[89] Their marriage was founded on that rhyme. Sealed on the very first night, during which he more than she had bled copiously. (At this point in the narrative, Incra blushed to the very whites of her eyes, and then blanched—at the student hall of residence, the boys laid bets as to her virginity, as doubtful to some as it was indubitable to others; it was a wonder that they didn't drag her off to a gynecologist to have her checked, despite her being twenty-five.) After their return from the front, each looked for a job—he in the ranks of the NKVD, she among the auxiliary medical staff of an emergency hospital, and peace and harmony overflowed in their house. Not only had they escaped with their lives, but also, they had avoided the juggernaut of repression, immediately after Germany's surrender, when a large part of the soldiers and officers of the Red Army who had embraced the Allies on the Elbe in May '45 had been declared "enemies of the people" and hauled off to Siberia along with the Soviet prisoners of war, for whom the end of hostilities meant swapping a Nazi extermination camp for the Stalinist

---

[88] I knew his wife well—in the camp

[89] We two are like two words that rhyme: blood (*krov'*) and love (*ljubov'*)

Gulag. In the few hours they used to spend together (both of them toiled from dawn till dusk!), they didn't have much to say to each other; luckily words weren't required when doing that business in the dark, he wearing his long johns, she her night-dress, barely hitched up. Like on the shooting range (bang! bang!), careful not to come to the boil (or as she put it: "not to let the milk boil over"), for which reason they did it strictly by the cal-endar, and even then, practicing coitus interruptus. She never asked him anything, he never told her more than was necessary: a real model family. After a period of relative calm, there was a change of direction and a new wave of arrests. "Дело врачей."[90] Not even then did her husband tell her anything, but she knew for sure that something was happening: not because he came home later than usual and more tired, but from the way they made love. Whereas before it had been a mere formality, like tearing a leaf out of the calendar, on a date established in advance, now the act was stormy, an onslaught, like a bayonet charge. They were back at the front, the invisible front. Not that he would have unloaded on her, rather, you might say, he was taking his work home with him—not the work proper, but the skill, the savoir faire of which the *Torturer's Handbook* speaks; but since the SMERSH officer was now an NKVD interrogator, torturing victims to their face had replaced shooting them from behind. Whether he came home after midnight or whether he arrived on time—the old woman did not bother to explain to them what "on time" was supposed to mean—, all physical contact, now increasingly spontaneous, smacked of an interrogation, not that he asked questions, but because he quite simply voided her inside. She might go to bed with the "bad interrogator" and get up in the morning with the "good torturer"; whereas after the first, she could at least sleep till morning, the second spoiled the whole day for her, so that by evening she would almost be praying for the "bad one" to come. After a few weeks of such mute "cross-inter-rogations," nocturnal and matutinal, a frothing-mouthed dawn gallop suddenly loosened her husband's tongue, and the only

---

[90] The doctors' trial

words he flung in her face were: "Враг народа!"[91] (which rhymed with the "врачи-отравители"[92] on everybody's lips in those days). She shut herself away in silence (what was the word of a mere nurse worth against that of an NKVD officer?), which only enraged him the more: "Молчание — знак согласия".[93] Now, he was not content merely to rape her regularly, with the sanction of family law: he also had to trample her underfoot, at first verbally, then literally. He beat her without leaving any mark, in the most sensitive places, with the precision of a marksman. He hit the target! And once again she got used to enduring stoically the regular beatings of the "bad torturer," but it was enough for her to sense the "good one" from afar and straightaway her flesh would start trembling on her bones. What did he do to her? Or rather, what didn't he do to delight her (nothing was left of the woman who was a veteran of war . . .), only then, in the last moment, when they were on the point of explosion (a million-volt discharge in the eiderdown!), he would suddenly slash her with a razor blade. Short circuit. Once . . . every time . . . In vain did she try stripping him naked, whereas before, when they did it, he had been in his long johns, she in her negligée; in vain did she feel every inch of the sheet: by some kind of miracle, he would manage to introduce the cutting edge (since the object was not to be found) into the bed, and with it the pain! Within a short time, she was covered in runes, which she had to hide from the "bad NKVD man," in whose presence she never went naked. "I think he hid the razor blade in the pillow, between the pillows, but I never caught him . . ." concluded the old woman, but it was only now, as she gave them to understand, that the real nightmare began. All of a sudden, the "bad NKVD man" stopped beating her, but now he would tell her in lurid detail about everything he had done during the day in the Lubyanka basements; no sooner would he finish his confession than the "good torturer" would start wheedling her, begging her

---

[91] Enemy of the people

[92] Poisoner doctors

[93] Silence is a sign of conspiracy

amid increasingly voluptuous sighs not to tell anybody, for her
own sake, for the sake of them both, and to be on the safe side,
he threatened to cut out her tongue. It was no empty threat: he
kept half a razor blade secreted behind his teeth, which he tried
to thrust into her mouth with his tongue during a passionate
kiss. But she realized what he was up to, and so what might have
seemed an endless kiss à la Paolo and Francesca was in reality
nothing but a life and death battle of tongues, each trying to
wield the same blade. Seldom did it not end up in bloodshed!
Within a short time, she had become the storeroom of his burdened conscience, and he was the first to threaten to break into
it. Whereas up until lately, as the wife of an NKVD officer, she
had thought herself safe from the arrests in the middle of the
night, after the arrest of Polina Zhemchuzhina (since Stalin was
a widow, Zhemchuzhina, the wife of Molotov, Foreign Minister
at the time, took on the rôle of the country's first lady), she knew
for certain that nobody and nothing could rescue her from the
infernal machinery, except, perhaps, the work of her hands. If
you live with a Minotaur in a labyrinth, she must has said to
herself, you should at least not get caught; on the contrary, make
the labyrinth your oşşşwn and whenever the Minotaur hits on
you, try to surprise him! No sooner said than done. Using the
few items of furniture she had in the apartment, every day she
knocked together a kind of crossword puzzle, always different,
which made moving through the apartment a real obstacle
course. At the same time, she scavenged all kinds of objects from
the streets of Moscow, from chairs with their bottoms knocked
out to discarded shelves, which she would assemble at home
according to a well-articulated defensive logic (beaver's den? ant
hill?). It was amazing how capacious their poky apartment
proved to be; and how she hard she toiled, hauling to the top
floor—for some obscure reason, their building didn't have a
lift—old trunks, cupboards, shelves, stools, boxes, bed back-
boards etc. etc. The real challenge was incorporating them into
a world already overladen with objects, and that was when she
had the bright idea of connecting them within a closed circuit,
which she would be able to control remotely, without leaving

the house. Only she knew how she managed to get hold of the pulleys and cables or how much it cost to assemble the materials, in accordance with ever more complicated diagrams; and every time—death expresses itself in the present indicative—, white makes the first move and wins in six, in twelve, in twenty-four moves . . . She didn't hold out any hope for herself in the long term, but for the time being, she could make the game drag on for yet another move. On the other front, her husband was no longer content to recount to her his feats of arms—the "черный воронок,"[94] arrests in the middle of the night, summary executions in the Lyubyanka basements—, but like an AKM-47 he stripped down the entire mechanism of repression that privileged preventative punishment for potential crimes. You might say he was warning her, but then he would give way to the "good torturer," who—armed to the teeth, as we have seen—demanded bloodshed: "Умри ты сегодня и я умру завтра!"[95] was spoken in the mind, the way you might make the sign of the cross with the tip of your tongue on the roof of your mouth, and openly: "I'm going to cut your throat!" He didn't get the chance: on the night when they came to arrest her, he let the "three in civilian clothes" enter (the labyrinth—but they couldn't have known that!) while the armed men searched the apartment—now a well-honed system of traps, operating independently as a kind of rudimentary home perpetuum mobile—, she managed to crawl out of the toilet window, climb down the fire escape, and even had the presence of mind to call the police from the nearest phone box to report that persons unknown had just broken into the apartment of an NKVD officer. And then she vanished . . . "What about the gulag?" "What about Polina Zhemchuzhina?" cried two voices at once, the boys' (Inera was more dead than alive); no matter how hard they tried to hide it, their disappointment was obvious. "The Kustanai region, the summer of that year. What can I say—a beautiful woman!" And after a pause

---

[94] Black van in which the NKVD drove away the people they arrested at their homes

[95] You die today and I'll die tomorrow! — a slogan expressing the entire philosophy of the Gulag

that seemed to them endless: "When I finally understood that it would take me a hundred lives to build a labyrinth fit for Moscow, let alone one fit for the endless expanses of Russia, I quite simply let myself get caught." As they were leaving, when the old woman apologized for not conducting them to the door—in her lap, her hands seemed to be unwinding from an invisible ball not the thread of Ariadne but the lifelines of all those who had crossed her threshold—, all three must have felt their legs give way beneath them. He couldn't vouch for the other two, but ---n for one never returned to that room. But nor did he wholly escape the war veteran's labyrinth, since even two decades later he still returned there in his mind.

It was from the same Muscovite period that the debate about evicting Lenin from his mausoleum dated, the idea being that only after his earthly remains were buried would his diabolical work come to an end. Others, supposedly more initiated, claimed that if Vladimir Ilyich had been the root of all evil, the umbilical cord of the Great October Socialist Revolution remained Kaganovich (b. 1893), the only man from the "first circle" of V. I. Lenin's close associates whom Stalin hadn't touched, and therefore as long as he was alive, дело Ленина живёт и побеждает.[96] The concoctions of fervid minds, you might say; was it therefore a mere coincidence that less than a month after the death of Lazar Moiseevici (July 25, 1991), the ГКЧП[97] putsch took place, on August 19, 1991, defused in less than three days, but which was to deal the death blow to the USSR? . . . It was also the period—the ninth wave, as it were, after Gorbachev started glasnost—when the political joke entered its final throes, and in those anniversary days, besides numerous "bearded" anecdotes, a caricature was also doing the rounds, in the manner of Mayakovsky and his famous Агитки,[98] which depicted Ilyich doing *subbotnik*, except that instead of the traditional girder (inflatable, according to the jokes), he and his comrades in arms

---

[96] Lenin's cause lives and is triumphant

[97] State Committee for Emergency Situations

[98] Agitprop placards, usually satirical

were carrying on their shoulders his great big *membrum*. As for
---n, on the morning of that day in the dark April of eighty-
seven, rather than hauling his member to a Leninist *subbotnik*,
he stuck it in a thoroughbred Communist—and a good thing
too! But instead of thinking about his *first-first*, he couldn't get
the old woman and her labyrinth out of his head. A hairpin in
the brain, or rather a metal shard!

An open coffin, that of Miron I., from which wafted—
despite the formaldehyde—the unmistakable scent of putrefac-
tion; another coffin, in which the swollen body of Dorian almost
spills over the sides; and a third, showing Aurel setting off on the
journey without return, the cadaveric blotches on his forehead
and throat preceding him—all three as many bookmarks in his
Parisian text of *va-et-vient*. March, 2006. To leave a communist
country, even if fifteen years have passed since the fall of the
USSR, to set eyes on the red flag, with the hammer and sickle, in
the middle of Paris—now there was a good start to the trip! The
Hexagon was in the grip of a strike the likes of which hadn't been
seen since May sixty-eight. A throng of more than 100,000 demonstrators had invaded the city center, and overnight *la vie en rose*
had become *la vie en rouge. Allez les Bleux!* (And to think that in
1848, during the February 25 uprising, it took the intervention
of Lamartine, Foreign Minister in the provisional government,
to save the tricolor at the last moment: "The red flag is (…) a
pavilion of terror (…) which has only ever done a circuit of the
Field of Mars, whereas the tricolor has travelled all around the
world, bearing the name, the glory and the freedom of the motherland . . ." From the Place d'Italie, the column of demonstrators
went down the Avenue des Gobelins as far as the Boulevard Saint
Michel and then poured over the river to the Rive Droite via
the Île de la Cité, where the torrent swept up clumps of tourists
filming the student performance, yet another attraction of the
City of Light that ought to be included in the specialist guides
désormais. Close to the Jardin du Luxembourg, the first clashes
took place: rocks, empty bottles, plastic chairs and even Molotov
cocktails were lobbed at the riot police; in response, the police
water cannons dampened the inflamed communards. To look

at them, the most diehard of the stone-throwers haven't opened a book in their lives (otherwise, they wouldn't have thrown stones at *Mona lisait!*), but that doesn't stop them from being in the front ranks of the striking students. *Entre chien et loup*, the strike of the above-average IQ's takes a dramatic turn, thereby proving—for the umpteenth time—that *ideas drink blood*: broken shop windows, burnt-out cars, the first of the wounded, one in a coma. He loves France too much to wish these incurable *sans-culottes* success, even though they'd deserve a Socialist Revolution—if 1789, 1848, and 1871 didn't knock any sense into their heads. Mingling with the crowd, he got to talking with a young woman who was rather mechanically waving the flag of the USSR ("parce que c'est le bastion de la liberté"), drawn not to her beauty so much as to the feeling of déjà vu (or déjà lu, to be precise: "Looking at Pulcheria, who seemed to be around eighteen years old, I sometimes could have believed that she was the perfect creation not of nature but of craftsmanship. (. . .) Every movement she made might have been the mechanical movement of an automaton. 'Might she be an automaton?' And I began to study her walk: there was something strange in that walk, something impossible to describe. I began to study her gaze: wonderful, calm eyes that moved simultaneously with her head. Her face and her hands were so graceful that they might have been lined with fine leather. But Pulcheria spoke . . . As did Albert's golden-browed android. I spied on her conversations: she would listen to her chevalier, answer him with a smile, and merely say: 'Qu'est ce que vous dites!' and sometimes 'Qu'est ce que vous badinez?' Her voice was gentle, her pronunciation had something unusual, unclear. 'Might she be a second Galatea?' I wondered . . . 'Pulcheria is not a living creature,' I thought, 'but does her father, who might be a genius of mechanical inventiveness or who might have bought himself a mechanical daughter, insist on marrying her off?" A. F. Weltman, apud Ioan Halippa, *Kishinev in the Time of Pushkin. 1820-1823*). "Et le Gulag?" he asked her abruptly. "Tout cela est faux! En avez-vous connu un seul detenu politique?" "Oui, une detenue—il y a presque vingt ans . . ." The demonstrator's name was Inesse and obviously she had never heard of Inessa Armand, the flamboyant mistress of V. I. Lenin, the one who came up with the *theory of the glass of water*. Walking beside her—in fact, mostly standing still—, he told the girl about Ilyich's comrade's proposal to set up sex cabins on all the major Muscovite boulevards, for a start, and then all over the country, cabins rather like the public toilets of 2000's Paris, but to serve all those who suddenly felt a different kind of pressing need. Even if, at first, she didn't believe it, the young communard proved to be worthy of her name: "J'ai soif!" and without giving him an opportunity to reply: "Chez toi ou chez moi?" If two decades ago, on the day of the Leninist *subbotnik*, when he had woken up in bed with a *first-first* Communist, he had ended up meeting the woman who had been in the camps with Polina Zhemchuzhina, where would this one-night stand lead, an affair with a petite-bourgeoise pretending to be a rev-olutionary and who was ready to abscond from the *manif* with the first foreigner who crossed her path? He preferred never to discover the answer than to answer his new acquaintance (acquainted as he was with the dictum: "Knowledge means knowing that which, once you know it, you realize you would rather not have known.") "Chez moi il y a ma femme et ma fille de 18 ans," his voice passed for the voice of reason, even though it was sheer madness to tell her such a thing in so bare-faced a way, "et chez toi—je suppose—c'est plutôt chez tes parents!" while saying in his mind: "That's why the artist is beyond com-pare, because he doesn't pair with just anybody!" "C'est où, chez toi?" asked Inesse, undeterred. "En *Mal de Vie*!" came the reply. On his way back to the hotel Manet in Place d'Italie, on foot as always, by the Pantheon he got the feeling that during those days in Paris something important had passed him by: not the *manif*, not the communard, but who? what? In the meantime, evening after evening a young woman in love left the Pantheon building after work, on her way home to the XVI-ème before the strike degenerated into street fighting; when ---n was to meet her, in December 2007, in Ch—ău, after returning from Paris for the umpteenth time, he was to recognize Marianne in that girl, without any shadow of a doubt!

They say that in his final months, political prisoner Osip Mandelstam refused to touch the prison camp food, being nauseated by it. He survived by reciting to the non-political prisoners, the delinquents—in return for a slice of white bread—reams and reams of poems, the favorites being Yesenin's poems from *Москва кабацкая*, although he was a poet he couldn't stand; likewise, in *Непридуманное*, Lev Razgon recounts how he escaped the Gulag alive thanks to his talent for composing complaints—*lăcrămații* in the Moldavian rural dialect[99]—, that were juridically unbeatable, even for Soviet jurisprudence, with the result that numerous prisoners had their sentences shortened; ---n would now be unable to say when he metamorphosed from a *grămătic* with a certain amount of literary skill into a *lăcrămătic*,[100] since the process itself stretched over long years, from the composition of love letters larded with sentimental poems that were then passed off as his own by a boy in his class at university (he was never to discover whether the boy got to sleep with the girl he was in love with) to making clean copies of the autobiographies of people with little or even no book-learning, for whom he thereby acted as a confessor, exactly the same as in Danilo Kiš's *Encyclopaedia of the Dead*, all of which culminated in his translation of Barthes's *Journal of Mourning*. Less than two months after going on a picnic with his erstwhile schoolmates, on June 22, 2001, at which ---n was conspicuous by his absence, Miron I. died. It's against nature to bury a schoolmate before your grandfather, but that was what happened one August morning—the former, aged just thirty-seven. Rodica N. didn't get a chance to say: "The countdown has begun . . ." when Justin Panța—not that he had been at school with them, but quite simply he was the same age—also passed away, while the

---

[99] From the French *réclamation*, but possibly influenced by the Romanian *lacrimă*, "teardrop" — *Translator's note*

[100] *Grămătic*: scribe in a boyar's chancellery (from the Greek *grammatikos*); *lăcrămatic*: composer of *lăcrămații* (see previous note) — *Translator's note*

whole Romanian literary world kept vigil at the bedside of Gellu Naum[101] as he lay dying in hospital. It was as if a dispensation had been given to those born in 1964; but who had opened the sack? could it have been the former classmate who in her sweetest dream had imagined herself in Paris (why not Venice? it would have been better suited)? and what could be done to sew it back up (the mouth of the sack, not the classmate)? The answer— abiding by the principle of one fire drives out another—was not long in coming, when first Gellu Naum, aged eighty-six, and then ---n's grandfather, aged almost ninety, crossed the Styx to re-establish the natural course of affairs. In the newspapers, he learned that Gellu Naum had been in a coma for more than seven weeks; his grandfather, on the other hand, had not been able to sit still during his final days, as if trying to elude "baba Anica" by breaking into a run. When he finally took to his bed, he lost his speech along with his physical mobility. When ---n leant over him, all he managed to say was: "The lips"—meaning he wished him to kiss him farewell—, before collapsing into unconsciousness. *Bref, il a vécu très mal sa mort.* (What reserves of tenderness remained to him, after losing his father as a child, after receiving a head wound in the war and falling prisoner, after burying both his mother and his first-born son in forty-six, to depart with "The Lips" on his lips!) At the funeral, he walked not alongside Grandmother, but at her head: as the procession left the village, he went before and she three paces behind (at last, under the same law: "only then, in the time to come, will I be able to be with you and you alone, and the molecules of your decomposed lover will start to move, to awake, to seek the traces of your molecules scattered throughout nature!"); they weren't able to find a black tie for him, even though one had been specially put aside, and so he was placed in his coffin with- out a "Ибиоматъ"[102] around his neck, as he used to call that sartorial accessory when he was alive, one that was required of every "nachalnik" (boss) he had during his almost fifty years of

---

[101] Gellu Naum (1915-2001), Romanian Surrealist poet — *Translator's note*

[102] "---- your mother"

working for the state—, his brother turned up with a new wife, four months pregnant. Life went on. Since then, ---n's sentences have been of two kinds—the way you might sew a dead man inside a sackcloth and the way you might rupture a placenta to extract the fetus from therein.

And if Paris—another kind of Paradise, from which two letters have fallen: A[nno] D[omini]—was procured at the expense of lives dear to him, it crossed his mind, during another sojourn in France, after his talking parrot died in his hand in January 2002, and the second of his old schoolmates was killed in a car accident in the summer of 2003—*son meilleur ennemi* at school—, at whose funeral he wept inconsolably?! He all but developed an obsession when, in March 2003 and then February 2005 Mariana Marin and Ioan Flora were added to the *Departures* list; it was they who had stayed with ---n until after midnight in the beer garden behind Bucharest's Museum of Romanian Literature in September 1996, and it was Flora who had then accompanied him to Boulevard Unirii (where he was to catch the 783 bus to Otopeni Airport), walking him all the way down Calea Victoriei in the early hours of the morning. It was they who were the last to wish him bon voyage before he left for Paris. Such things are never forgotten—as they sat *at a table long and rich* (in bottles), Traian T. suddenly sat up straight and contemplated Mady as if seeing her for the first time, and then he asked her to marry him (luckily, he was in the middle of a divorce with his nth wife), at which Ioan retorted, for the benefit of the rest of the table: "Go on, then, marry each other for love—but who's going to f—k the two of you?!" By the end of the year, they had joined the third of his schoolmates, after which there came a full stop. As many dead as dots on the i; words—longer, shorter—are only the lines that join them in a single, ever-changing circuit (serially or in parallel? that is the question), reminiscent now of a constellation (the funerary Big Dipper versus a little wain with an infant therein?), now a garland of fairy lights on the Christmas Tree (by the old calendar or the new?), now—but, oh, this one requires a lot of imagination—a map of the Paris Métro ("My thoughts have always been in Paris," Ioan Flora once told him, "so much so that when the coroner weighs my brain, he won't help but observe that the two hemispheres reproduce, down to the smallest detail, the city on the Rive Droite and Rive Gauche, expanded throughout the cerebrum—the Île de la Cité, with all its historic buildings & monuments in miniature, and the Eiffel Tower thrusting out through my brow bone!"). Before all else, getting on track means a descent into the underworld, where all those who have made their quietus regain their identity: *Hic jacet* [surname, first name; date of birth—year of death] . . . The hard part (of the loam) henceforward begins: to shape a well-proportioned sentence after the given punctuation marks, one perfectly symmetrical with the lifeline on the palm of the hand, except mirrored. Like He who said: "Live your life grammatically!" *Grammaire*, in French. It sounds almost the same as *grande-mère*, whose *lăcrămatic* he never ceased to be: "You are the *grande-mère* and on your tombstone will be erected the Syntaxine Chapel!"

Three meals to commemorate the dead every day, not counting the nine- and forty-day commemorative services: this was what his diet ought to have been when he was writing. Boiled-wheat *kollyba* replaces the Proustian madeleine. For the souls of the departed Miron I., Dorian, Aurel, and—for five-o'-clock tea—the late Valentina. As if the souls of the dead were pecking from his palm. *Kollyba* was Grandmother's specialty; tea, at any hour, was his. Cups of black tea throughout the day gave him white nights. Neither counting sheep, nor undressing in his mind the women he had possessed or desired helped him fall asleep. And it was then that he would enter the labyrinth in the old woman's head (since to judge soberly, it would have been impossible for her to build it right under the nose of her husband from the Organs without his realizing it!) or rather the labyrinth of the young woman from the winter of forty-nine. Usually, he fell asleep before finding out whether the "glorious organs" managed to lay hands on the enemy of the people or whether they fell into her trap. But one night, the usual scenario took a completely different turn: suddenly, he recalled in vivid detail, as if he himself had been present, how his grandmother had got lost at night, in

the summer of forty-six, carrying a great big sack of corn on her
back. Her eldest son had recently died, still almost a young lad,
having fallen off a horse, and in the same year—that of the famine—she had also buried her mother-in-law and built her house,
and now she had to find—in the earth—the wheat to make the
commemorative *kollyba* for her dead son. It was rumored that
in the harder-hit villages, they had started garnishing the dead
with ring loaves made of clay—as if the deceased would not eat
his fill of earth in the next world! . . . Luckily, her husband, a
war veteran, worked as a watchman at the Cereals Collection
Station at U—ești station, around six miles from the village of
that name; it wasn't a question of him stealing—he wouldn't
have touched what wasn't his even if the fence had had a single
lath—, but rather a question of borrowing a pot of flour from a
bread oven. He made an agreement with the shift manager, and
after midnight Grandmother appeared in the place they'd agreed
on: a clump of bushes by the railway track. She shouldered the
sack and off she went—but she had to be wary of both police
patrols and any villagers who might be wandering around at that
hour of night. She took a roundabout route, along the edge of
the forest, over the hills that the locals called *munturi*, which
were something between hills and mountains, sweating with
fear—not because she was creeping through the thickets with a
sack on her back so much as because she was worried about her
other son, aged just seven, whom she had left home alone. The
night was on her side, since not a star could be seen in the sky.
But since she knew all the roads within a thirty-mile radius, the
darkness heartened rather than terrified her. Once she had put
enough distance between herself and the station, she paused to
catch her breath and then continued at a slower pace. She must
have been walking for about an hour when she sensed that she
was on unfamiliar ground. According to her inner clock, she
ought to have reached the edge of the village by then, but there
was no sign of human habitation anywhere. She quickened her
steps, so far as the heavy sack allowed. For quite some time she
had been shifting the weight from one shoulder to another. She
was fit to drop, but she didn't give up. It was as if her dead son's

grave were carrying the sack across the stubble field. But the farther she advanced into the night, the farther receded her hope of ever arriving. Time had not stood still, and soon it would be dawn. It was then—as Grandmother recounted a quarter of a century later—that she suddenly stopped and prostrated herself: "Holy Mother of God . . ." and in that instant it was as if the mist lifted from her eyes. She was far away from U—eşti, which she had left behind her somewhere in the distance. How terrified she must have been to have passed right by the village in her mad flight without even realizing it! The fear stayed with her for the rest of her days (far more days than she could carry, so much so that toward the end she prayed: "Take me to Thee, O Lord!"). The village ate the *kollyba* for her firstborn, at Radonitsa, year after year, and her blind flight in the middle of the night, with a sack on her back, barefoot over the stubble field, brought into the world her youngest son, who at one point was to weigh more than a hundred kilos. As happens more often than not, we search elsewhere for what is right under our noses: in the nineties, ---n had struggled to write an article, on a tip from Vasile Vasilache, about a nutcracker *à la moldave* whose baby almost died when her breast milk dried up, but finding a walnut in the attic she ground it up and fed it to the infant, bringing him back to life and raising him to be a fine young tree (now a towering walnut!); and then another second-hand story, about a young forester, a proud, handsome man, who, when he felt starvation gnawing away inside him, fled the village before it could show its hideous face and died shielded from the gaze of his fellow villagers, who thitherto had feasted their eyes on him, thereby teaching them an immortal lesson about beauty, which, too, demands that it be saved; when in fact it would have been enough for ---n to make a fair copy of his grandmother's fugue, which saved his family from perishing and the family name from shame.

From 0 to 9 are digits, from 10 to 99 numbers, and with 100 begin the anniversaries; the digits bring you into the world, the numbers sit well in a biography, on the anniversaries are built a myth. Although the year 2009 promised to be a triumph of life, death joined the race as early as January, with the appearance of

Roland Barthes' unpublished *Journal de deuil*, a work that came
to ---n in the proofs stage. You don't necessarily have to see your
name among the dedicatees of a book to know that the text in
question is (pre)destined to you and that, if not all humanity,
then at least your own humanity ought to be poured into a book
like that. It was as if his grandmother—officially illiterate (the
only thing she knew how to read was the family memorial, unless
she had learned it by heart)—had sent him the book from the
other world in the year that would have been her hundredth.
And so, instead of writing *The Testament of a Translator from the
French*, which he had promised to a publication in Romania, he
set about transposing—without even having signed the contract
with the Parisian publisher—the (Barthian) swansong into his
own language: "November 15, [1977]. There comes a moment
when death is an *event*, an ad-venture, and in this way, it acti-
vates you, interests you, dreams you, sets you in motion, stuns
you. And then, one day, it is no longer an event, but rather a
duration, tightly packed, devoid of importance, untold, dreary,
unavoidable: the true mourning, insusceptible to any narrative
dialectic." A day from the journey (which meant a number of
notes, seldom just one, written on fiches that the author had
made *manu propria* from standard sheets of paper, cutting them
in four) each day—the way you might practice a musical phrase/
note with a pebble in your mouth:

> "24 March 1978
> Sadness, like a stone . . .
> (from the throat
> into my depths)"

You might say Barthes' journal was a Japanese garden that ---n
intended to turn into an Eastern Orthodox graveyard. The lap-
idary text was at its most solid where disintegration and decay
began: "May 31, 1978. That whereby Mother's presence is in all
I have written: by the fact that everywhere in those writings there
exists an idea of the Sovereign Good." And not long after that:
"January 18, 1979. Since Mother's death, no desire to 'construct'

anything except in writing. Why? Literature = the only region of Nobility (as was Mother)." The further he advanced, not only in his transposition, but also in his assimilation of Barthes' journal—by now the rights contract had arrived from La Seuil—, the more he got the feeling that he was in a realm of shades, like the king in the Indian story who tried to remove a corpse from the burial field and was caught up in an endless back and forth as long as his reason answered "present!" to the challenges of the spirit that had taken control of the corpse: "If you know the answer and do not say it, your head will shatter in hundreds of pieces," but breaking off as soon as it asked him, at the end of an impossible riddle: "What was each for the other and what was it not?" Likewise, translation meant to shoulder the other's tragedy—forever and ever, amen. "*O! ciel, Madame rêve . . . Madame rêve . . .*" The buzzing of the telephone—too early in the morning for somebody who went to bed after midnight, and then torturing himself for another two or three hours before he managed to fall asleep—tore him from his reverie: Radio France Internationale. *Vous êtes ---n? Mais qu'est-ce que se passe chez vous, en Mal de Vie?*" The night before, he had received the following e-mail: "The young declare April 6 a Day of National Mourning in the Republic of Moldova. If you didn't vote for the Moldovan Communist Party, light a candle and join the demonstration!!!" Around 15,000 people of all ages had answered the call, and thus the Twitter Revolution arrived in Ch—ău: on a Monday. Tuesday, with its proverbial three unlucky hours, was about to begin.

It had happened to him once before: to go to bed in one country, the largest in the world, the *Motherland* at the time, and to wake up—or to be more precise, to be woken up by an early-morning phone call—in another, a tiny sliver of a country amputated from the rest (not Bukovina, not even Budjak; and lately, even Transdniester was about to break away), on the morning of August 19, 1991; but on the contrary, on April 7, 2009, the police-state regime of the General of the Dead-Army, quick to shed intellectual blood, seemed impossible to budge, despite his death foretold. After it had been said again and again *haut et fort* that something was rotten in our Denmark, it was as if the men whose feet stank still couldn't believe it. The size of the demonstrations came as a surprise to both the self-proclaimed winners of the April 5 election and the leaders of the opposition parties: ever since Iuda[103] Roşca's PPCD had decamped lock, stock and barrel to the side of the regime, there had been no major demonstrations in Ch—ău. A mass of simmering people chanting their legitimate rage: "I refuse, I resist—I'm an anti-communist!" "Another election!" "Down with the mafia!" etc. etc. in National Assembly Square, where, eighteen years before, the six-feet-six Ion Ungureanu had read the *Proclamation of Independence*; meanwhile, the riot police, in black uniforms, equipped with shields and truncheons, were trying to hem the demonstrators within the perimeter of the Triumphal Arch, Government House, Parliament and President's Office, unless, that is, they were there to lure the crowd to the latter two edifices, symbols of state Power, precisely because they had been posted in front of them. An invisible hand turned the section of Boulevard Stephen the Great between Pushkin Street and National Assembly Street into a declivity, so that the human lava, about to be extinguished in National Assembly Square, was able to flow in the appropriate direction, with the hotheads at the fore, as was only natural. As the atmosphere grew more and more inflamed, a number of masked youths made their appearance among the protesters, chanting in unmistakably Russian accents: "Unification!" And it was also they who were among the first, at a signal, to break the police cordon in front of the President's Office. In fact, the police were there more for decorative purposes than anything else, standing around like village girls by the fence watching the swains go by and ready to retreat beneath the parental roof at the first stern summons. Hard to say who was so sinless as to throw the first stone or how sanctimonious were the others who lobbed rocks at the tinted glass of the building through which the General of the Dead-Army had gazed on his people over the last eight years as if through sunglasses. Power dazzles! Under the pressure of the people still

---

[103] Whenever ---n writes Iura Roşca , the computer corrects it to Iuda [Judas] Roşca.

pouring from the direction of Government House, a first wave
of young people broke on the steps of the steel and glass colossus, popularly known as the Corncob. After a while, the crush in
front of the High Double Door was so great that you could have
walked on the heads of the besiegers like they were cobblestones.
In raw if not freshly laid heads, the yolk exploded, and their
mouths extruded long tricolor ribbons: "Long Live Moldova,
Transylvania and Wallachia!" From the smell of brimstone,
it was suddenly plain that the rotten eggs of the professional
demo-breakers had gone into action. Equipped with rucksacks
in which rocks took the place of books, they seemed specially
prepared to surf the crest of the crowd, which was still foaming
but already calling for calm: "That's enough!" The main thing
was to "catch the wave"—and there they were riding the wave!
Sensing that it was going to end in bloodshed, most people were
watching from the margins, more and more worried by the turn
the peaceful demonstration was taking. It was as if the Day of
National Mourning decreed the night before was now claiming
its obol of human lives (after they had shouted: "Communism
is what the dead choose!"); those who had struck a blow for
another election had ended up smashing the windows of the
Regime, behind which cowered frightened young people just like
them, except that they wore uniforms. Their uniform had once
been their protection, but now, given their association with the
Dead Army, it made them moving targets, all the easier to hit
given they were just a handy stone's throw away. By chance, other
policemen were busy demolishing a wall behind the President's
Office and throwing the rocks at the demonstrators, unless they
were actually supplying them with missiles. In the meantime,
the larger part of the platoon of carabinieri had barricaded themselves inside the building, as if in a bunker, leaving behind a
living shield, which was quickly smashed. Before the thugs even
had a chance to share out the spoils of battle—shields, helmets,
rubber truncheons—, somebody signaled them from an upper
story to enter the building, even if they were greeted with water
cannons from within. But the cannons soon fell into the hands
of the besiegers, who were further inflamed rather than cooled

off by the increasingly flaccid jets of water, all beneath the gaze of spectators who marked their separateness by taking a step back. Rolling the dice, like in the time of Charlemagne, the General sacrificed his bishop and got ready to deploy his castle, alias Parliament (he kept his queen until April 9, long enough to give his speech as Premier and *я-сама-мать*: "The police will use all necessary means (…) including firearms," which made him go down in history as Zina Carabina), to win the match. Half an hour later, the presidential security detail was giving guided tours of the lobby of the Presidential Palace ("One group of people entered as another left"), and, with the permission of the chief of police, two young men raised the flag of the European Union from the top of the Corncob, while others hung from the front of the building a map of Greater Romania, partly covering the emblem of state. The entity the General of the Dead Army deemed to be the beneficiary of the coup was emblazoned in large letters: "ROMANIA MY HOMELAND." The desperate attempts on the part of the leaders of the opposition to make the demonstrators return to National Assembly Square, where loud-speakers had in the meantime been set up, only half succeeded—on the one hand, centripetal force was driving the besiegers more strongly toward the Parliament building; on the other hand, the need to find out news other than that which was too blatantly served up on a plate made the others go back the way they had come. The city center was a head with two vortices. The left hemisphere versus the right.

Reminiscent in form (& content, from 2001 to 2009) of the membership booklet that had replaced the five-pointed star on the Moldovan Communist Party emblem, Parliament had been a lucky horseshoe for the General of the Dead-Army: in a presidential republic he would never have been elected president! It was now the final card to be played in a game in which—and here the experience of Judas Roşca giving up a place inside the tent in "Freedom City" for the chair of vice-chairman of Parliament was not to be overlooked—the one who lost won. Whatever the case, it was his turn to make a move, the final move, putting a puppet at the head of the country and ensconcing himself in the chair of speaker of parliament, but to do so the *bâtiment*[104] had to be burned down—fire purifies! As quick as you could shout: "Пожааааар!" (fiiiiire) the first Molotov cocktails broke the ground floor windows, and at 16:34 hours the same two young men raised the flag of the European Union above the Parliament building, again with permission from the police—in the person of General Vladimir Țurcan: "They [the demonstrators] need to see it: You made the declaration, you climbed to the top, you hoisted . . ." They saw it, but differently than was intended: "From up on top, from the window of the Parliament, as the rocks were flying, it could be seen that there was an organized, operational plan" (Marian Lupu). To mark the difference now that there was a different strategic objective, the masked men who had stormed the Presidential Palace were now wearing gas masks, which were all the more necessary given that nobody was in a hurry to extinguish the fire. And while the country went up in flames, ---n was whirling like a Dervish between Parliament and National Assembly Square, amid the finely crafted dolls and golden-browed androids of the "New Generation," produced by a genius of mechanical skill, seeking in the crowd his friend from the Alliance Française, whose offices were situated nearby. It was none other than the enamored young woman from the Pantheon, which he had passed every day for the length of a week in March 2006; as if she were being punished for missing the *manif* back home, the young people's revolution had caught up with her in a foreign country, in the very center of Ch—ău. When he finally glimpsed Marianne's head silhouetted against the backdrop of a Romanian tricolor, he couldn't believe his eyes—his Frenchwoman was *à poil*! In the last year and a half, whenever he had tried to undress her with his eyes, she had never given any sign of wanting to play along, but now she was parading in broad daylight down Boulevard Stephen the Great, in her birthday suit, as if she had just stepped out of Botticelli's *The*

---

[104] The word hit upon by Marian Lupu, the then Communist speaker of the legislative, on the very evening of the day when Parliament was burned down, while he was giving foreign diplomats and journalists an impromptu guided tour of the building gutted by furious demonstrators.

Birth of Venus. Written by. 12-point font, Times New Roman: "following her, I observed only her passing—her gait, as if holding an overripe pomegranate (in French: *grenade*) between the thighs." Not that she was playing *Liberté guidant le peuple*—she too was carried along on the wave, like everybody else, she even seemed unaware of the state she was in. Stark naked, she was wandering aimlessly among men and women demonstrating in the street and now milling around, trampling each other—a crowd pumped in and out like an accordion against the broad chest of National Assembly Square. In the instant when their eyes met, it was confirmed—literally: "each person's gaze confirms each of us" (Gellu Naum, *Journey with Stelică*)—from head to toe, and he then read in the Parisian's eyes her amazement at his coming upon her naked, shamelessly displaying, despite his status as a public figure, his weakness for the fair sex in general and hers in particular. As they walked side by side, during which time ---n kept peeking at her from the corner of his eye or turning his head left as if obeying some (inner) marching order: "Eyes left!" both he and she knew that no matter how far they might go, they would never arrive together, and it was this that liberated them from the constraints of a relationship, even a casual one. Their walk among the people had barely begun when ---n saw another naked person, and then another, and another, and another . . . It was as if everybody that entered his field of vision disrobed at the entrance, without taking a cloak-room ticket; the same as sheep and cattle are flayed before being hung up on hooks.[105] A sea of naked people washing up against

---

[105] Not at all accidental, the "bestial" comparison—see also *Emerging from winter* at www. europalibera.org: "After the Teheran Conference, where Europe had been divided up into major areas of influence, we knew that our fate was sealed. The main problem was, as Anton Golopenția put it, how to hibernate, how to save our national identity during this new Dark Age, which might last for many generations" (Mircea Eliade, Memorii, Humanitas, 1991).

(. . .) For many years, doves come to my kitchen window, not to bring me the Annunciation, but lured by the crumbs I leave. I know that it is not hygienic, that the bird chosen to symbolize peace carries germs, that elsewhere you risk a hefty fine if the police catch you feeding the pigeons in front of Notre-Dame de Paris, etc. etc. Notwithstanding, after every meal, I play little Hansel, the only difference being that for better or worse, I'm not lost. I like to believe that after pecking up the crumbs at least once, any bird might find my window, even when another (and I'm not necessarily thinking of "Je est Autre") will be looking at the sky.

the black rocks of the riot police in battle dress. The demonstrators were as unaware of their primordial nakedness as the riot police were fortified (by their breastplates emblazoned with the insignia of statehood) in their confidence that they were defending the constitutional order. Sans culottes versus loyalist troops. Ten thousand groins on show, curly, shaggy, shaved, male and female, full of the joys of spring, and as many (x 2) testicles and tits, jiggling at every step, parading back and forth, between the Parliament in flames and Government House, like beads on an abacus, impotent witnesses to the impotence of both the one (the Regime) and the other (the Opposition), when, as darkness fell, the General of the Dead-Army ordered over the police radio, even before recording his speech for the nine o'clock news, the commencement of the operation to clear "the occult, extremist forces that want to compromise our country" from National Assembly Square (formerly Victory Square, and subsequently, after Ch—ău municipality street-cleaning vehicles washed the blood and filth off the asphalt, just like on June 24 ,1945, at the Victory Parade in Red Square, with the sole difference that in forty-five the street-cleaning vehicles came behind a column of German P.O.W.'s, fed rotten cabbage the night before, and washed the feces and intestinal hemorrhaging from the ground where they had trodden: a humiliation piled on that of defeat). Not since the funerals of Ion and Doina Aldea-Teodorovici[106] had there gathered so huge a crowd—you just had to close your eyes to imagine you were back in the midst of the endless funeral procession of 1992, when it was as if the whole nation conducted the late Ion & Doina on their final journey. Back then, the uniforms formed a black border around the crowd crammed into the funerary corridor along the section of Boulevard St. Stephen the Great between National Assembly Street and Pushkin Street, and the same as in the old days, all the names of those present had been set in Cyrillic type, 7.62mm caliber, I'm sorry, I meant font, and printed. "Tra-ta-ta-ta! Tra-ta-ta-ta! Tra-ta-ta-ta!

---

[106] Husband and wife singing duo, who after the collapse of the Soviet Union campaigned for Moldova's reunification with Romania. They were killed in a car crash in 1992 and were given a state funeral, which drew massive crowds — *Translator's note*

Tra-ta-ta-ta! Tra-ta-ta-ta! Tra-ta-ta-ta! Tra-ta-ta-ta! Tra-ta-ta-ta!
Tra-ta-ta-ta! Tra-ta-ta-ta! Tra-ta-ta-ta! Tra-ta-ta-ta! Tra-ta-ta-ta!
Tra-ta-ta-ta! Tra-ta-ta-ta! Tra-ta-ta-ta! Tra-ta-ta-ta! Tra-ta-ta-ta!
Tra-ta-ta-ta! Tra-ta-ta-ta! Tra-ta-ta-ta! Tra-ta-ta-ta! Tra-ta-ta-ta!
Tra-ta-ta-ta! Tra-ta-ta-ta! Tra-ta-ta-ta! Tra-ta-ta-ta! Tra-ta-ta-ta!
Tra-ta-ta-ta! Tra-ta-ta-ta! Tra-ta-ta-ta! Tra-ta-ta-ta! Tra-ta-ta-ta!
Tra-ta-ta-ta! Tra-ta-ta-ta! Tra-ta-ta-ta! Tra-ta-ta-ta! Tra-ta-ta-ta!
Tra-ta-ta-ta! Tra-ta-ta-ta! Tra-ta-ta-ta! Tra-ta-ta-ta! Tra-ta-ta-ta!
Tra-ta-ta-ta! Tra-ta-ta-ta! Tra-ta-ta-ta! Tra-ta-ta-ta! Tra-ta-ta-ta!
Tra-ta-ta-ta! Tra-ta-ta-ta! Tra-ta-ta-ta! Tra-ta-ta-ta! Tra-ta-ta-ta!
Tra-ta-ta-ta! Tra-ta-ta-ta! Tra-ta-ta-ta! Tra-ta-ta-ta! Tra-ta-ta-ta!
Tra-ta-ta-ta! Tra-ta-ta-ta! Tra-ta-ta-ta! Tra-ta-ta-ta! Tra-ta-ta-ta!"
Nobody was missed out: "We'll die and then we'll see!"

Cap. 5
"Jus vitae necisque"

The tone: *"When they are sorely upset at an inanimate object or living creature, regardless of kindgom or species, Romanians allot or to be more precise assign that thing or creature back to its natural origin. I don't know whether the reader realizes the philosophical profundity contained in the expression . . ."*

Paul Zarifopol, *Register of Delicate Ideas*

::: THE DICE, CAST hard, disarticulate, each exposing a single dotted face, with punctuation scattered—*grains de beauté*—over the skin, taut to bursting point, of an ouroboric sentence, 21 dots in total, like in the card game. To write means to cast the die after cajoling it every which way—not necessarily *nompers*, *plommez* or *longnez*[107]—, with the sure hand of a freckle-tamer, twisting it around and around to examine every facet of the idea of hazard (or every face of the Judea of Khazar), in order to match words and events, sounds and letters, intonation and punctuation. Double six. It's the same with making love: two rolling epidermises, offering each other the braille of its erogenous spots—his numbered, hers dotted everywhere —, so that they can pair with each with an unpaired number; seldom do they roll a double.

---

[107] *Nompers*—dice with one face repeated twice; *plommez*—dice with one face heavier than the others after being leaded; *longnez*—dice with a magnetized face.

They have no choice, they have to go the Neighboring-and-Friendly-Country in order to love each other freely. "It's as if I were running away from home," snorts the girl, and what's more"—the grave note, like a metal strand, lends authenticity to the words—"with a foreigner." The almost deserted station platform, tacky against their soles because of the globs of chewing gum spat out left and right; the morning coolness seeping down the back of their collars; finally, the few passengers—they can be counted on the fingers of one hand—taking their seats in a broken-backed minibus; the journey would have been a pleasure, were it not for all the bags with a month's worth of food, the bales of goods, and all the sundry items awaited on the other side of the frontier. "Could you take some cartons of cigarettes over for me?" a middle-aged woman asks them, looking at them closely, but then gives up. "What do you care, eh? Lovebirds. . ." Three policemen in black uniforms are walking an unmuzzled Alsatian; "One of them knows how to read, the other to write, and the third feels honored to be in such select company," somebody laughs. "What about the dog?" "It's a bitch . . ." "Molda, к ноге!" barks one of the policemen, and the state quadruped hastens to obey. Finally, the inspector gives the signal for departure; but nobody moves. Haven't you heard of the Moldavian automobile's four gears: slow, slower, standstill and stop? Fortunately, it's a Mercedes on the Ch—ău-Jassy route; unfortunately, it's driven by a Bessarabian driver. Punctuality isn't the natives' strong point; in the best case, they'll set off *at around* eight. Here's the newspaper vendor; only after he does the rounds of all the vehicles will they be able to leave. Once he gives his "imprimatur," as it were. A last check on the passengers ("Have they all got passports?") and, we're off! Voices muffled by the rustle of the Friday papers, which are thereby good for something; indeed, what could have happened in the world overnight? The platform is left behind, landscapes rush through the windows on both sides, which means they've left Ch—ău: "Bon voyage!" can be read in the rearview mirror. While the man ruminates, chewing the cud of the morning silence, the girl chews a candy-pink stick of *Dirol Indian cinnamon* gum, her air of being absent bordering on alienation. "Blow a bubble big enough to fill your head on the inside," says the man, breaking the silence, "I'll hammer it on a pink anvil until I correct the shape of your skull which was deformed at birth (unless it's a congenital mal-formation). Would you like that with or without a brainwash?" She turns him a cinnamon-scented smile, then blows a bubble, like a cartoon speech bubble framing the reply: "Love is . . .!" It doesn't occur to her to offer him a stick of gum to fragrance their communication *de bouche à l'oreille*; he has been taught never to ask for anything, only to be thankful for what he gets. The silence is ballooning, ready to explode, when all of a sudden: "Another policeman's been born," somebody observed. On the back seat sit huddled together two young men who seem to dis-guise their sexual identity beneath an appearance of indifference to what anybody else thinks of them. They are so ugly that their ugliness is cancelled out whenever they look each other lovingly in the eye. In front of them, a young woman whose beauty con-trasts strikingly with the means of transport; she methodically schools her son: "You're a big boy now. Do you know how many boys would like to be in your place?" "My place is here beside you," says the son curtly, wavering between pressing up against his mother and turning his back on her. The progeny is as ordi-nary as the mother is thoroughbred; "like casting lead letters in a platinum mold," thinks the man, perfecting the comparison. The girl next to him is restless; suddenly she presses her ear to his: "What's that you're listening to?" It sounds like a seashell, like nothing; difficult to say who's phoning. "I brought the CD player," she goes on. "Would you like to listen to some Jacques Brel?" Temple to temple, they share the same set of headphones, each with a small receptor in their ear, like bodyguards. When they hear him gulping, as if choking for air—the song *Le plat pays* was recorded when Jacques Brel was already ill with throat cancer—, after the line: "Avec des chemins de pluie pour unique bon soir," they hold each other's hand in complicity. The acoustic syncope is as loud as a bel canto tremolo. The other passengers stoically endure the cacophonous siege of *Russkoe Radio*, turned up full volume, in accordance with the unwritten rule of all

Ch—ău minibus drivers. Nobody objects, probably fearful lest
the driver put on a cassette of *manele* instead, which in any case
they won't escape after they've crossed the frontier. Music for
ears that can swallow anything except silence. Ladled out, like
in a soup kitchen. And this only to follow the recipe of ideal
governance: "The emperor empties his subjects' hearts and fills
their bellies." Till the demonstrative belch, in the Asian tradition
of doing the meal honor. Some of the passengers have started
to open their packed lunches; the acoustic effect soon combines
with an olfactory effect to match: not food from home, not fruit,
but cheese/cabbage/potato pasties purchased (three for one leu!)
on the bus station concourse. Cuisine fit for public transport! In
the headphones, the voice of Jacques Brel attacks *Quand on n'a
que l'amour*—"Au jour du grand voyage" sounds different from
the inside; on the outside, the others have to put up with the
same blah-blah-blah every day, a round trip, first thing in the
morning/as dusk is falling, which, for better or worse, is how
they make their living. Therefore all the more discordant is the
presence of the young mother on the seat in front. From the way
she looks, she's one of those escorts who garb their naked bodies
with the white/black of a luxury limousine, dream they are the
queen of the ball for one evening, and end up in some motel on
the highway, testing the mattress with a pea under it. The way
the driver kept looking at her and weighing her up said nothing good to the man, who had been around enough to detect a
"problem" passenger because of whom all the others were more
than certain to suffer. At around "Pour tracer un chemin / A
chaque carrefour" he realized what was causing his feeling of
unease: with studied gestures, the woman was putting on a show
of being a loving mother; any moment, you expected to hear a
voice offscreen: "You feel good in Lenor." The World as [lack of]
Will and [Advertising Hoarding].

Only the evening before he had been torn away from his desk
by repeated knocks on the door; "knocks" is saying too much,
they were fingertip taps at best. In the doorway, a kid begging
food. That was a first: usually, they're sent to scrounge money.
Through the crack of the door, he handed him a *Green Hills*

shopping bag with a few crusts of bread, two tomatoes, and a pie (apple? cherry?) he hadn't had a chance to eat. But the little beggar on the other side of the threshold was in no hurry to share the man's dinner. "A toy," and in his eyes could be seen how proud he was to have dared to say it. "Don't you have a toy for me?" It was a plea for his right to a childhood, alongside little girls and boys raised within a proper family. The man rummaged in his daughter's bag of toys, in which were stuffed a dozen dolls, a few teddy bears, countless plastic animals, and all sorts of other things. When he returned to the threshold with a toy car, the boy still hadn't looked in the bag of food. He received the toy with a kind of impatience that betrayed mistrust, he tested it in front of the door to see whether it went, and then he decided to confess to the stranger: "When I grow up, I'm going to wash cars." Maybe he's fey, thought the man, using his grandmother's words, who, had she been present, would have spat to ward off the evil eye: "Ptju! bahure de kopkil!" But the enchantment was peeled away as soon as the lad said: "A pistol. I wanted a toy pistol . . ." Without a word, the man closed the door in his face. "When I grow up, I'm going to be a bank robber," he continued, speaking in two voices, without realizing it: "But when you were seven, didn't you buy yourself a popgun for your birthday, which you used to shoot at flies all summer?" The incident of the evening before came back to him more and more insistently as the mother made her presence increasingly felt in the minibus, despite his resistance. He was quite simply overwhelmed by her attention, the young woman going out of her way to thank him. "Who would want to be a mother!" sighs the middle-aged woman. On the back seat, the two uglies smack their tongues, as if one had been dipped in a barrel of honey, the other in a barrel of shit, and now they were licking each other. "Very ugly and consummately beautiful people oughtn't to have children," opined the man, "so as not to perpetuate the exception, good or bad." "I take it you're a racist . . ." laughs the girl. "I know people of only two races: the superior—those shaved on top (the armpit)—and the infe-rior—those shaved down below (guess where?); which race are you?" She retreats back into the auricle, the last redoubt holding out against the outside world, urging him to follow her: "*Ne me quitte pas*." From time to time, the minibus stops, picking up passengers from the side of the road or bags full of who knows what. In the station at Călărași, the driver announces a five-minute toilet break. URINBURG, it says in crooked letters on the bog, a structure consisting of a dividing wall and two doors. A gentleman enters one door, and a lady emerges from the other; appearances aside, they are nothing but a man and a woman who drop their trousers/hitch their skirts and let rip. No privacy whatever. (A line from a different play, about a wannabe who laid out all his pieces of paper in the beer garden of the Writers' Union Holiday Home, spreading them over four tables, to mark his presence, and then loudly complaining to the manager: "No privacy whatever!" A sentence that ensured his posterity.) "Let's cross species of plants and animals with the names of towns," says the man, becoming animated, amused by the inscription on the bog. "Hamsterdam." "Londonkey." "Viennuniper." "Praguorilla." "Berlynx." "Zebrazzaville." When proper names come into play, the competition abruptly takes a completely different turn: "Abelgrade." "Cainnsbruck." Twinned towns. "All aboard!" orders the driver. "Everybody seated?" On the platform, three policemen are walking an Alsatian with a muzzle hanging over its chest; they're a perfect match: the humans with unbuttoned shirts, the dog with unbuttoned maw. "I get it," someone says, slapping his brow. "The Alsatian's part of the uniform." "In Moscow, in eighty-eight, eighty-nine, it was thought tasteful to name your mutt Lavrenti Pavlovich," the man whispers in the girl's ear. "The intelligentsia in particular were unburdening their former fear and complicity, even if they knew it was Beria who was responsible for the first wave of released prisoners, albeit the common criminals, in the spring of fifty-three." In time, history's telephone went on the blink, tragedies replayed as farce, as if you were to translate—in the best tradition of harmonious Soviet bilingualism—"three years' imprisonment as "три года расстрела" (three years' shooting). The words whiff of brakes. By the time the driver shifts gear from "standstill" to "slow," some more policemen turn up, dogs and all: Molda and Lavrenti Pavlovich, Lavrenti Pavlovich and Molda.

". . . what if your dad has told them to be on the lookout for you at the border?" laughs the man. "Don't joke about it," the girl says curtly, definitively, surprised at how often what he says comes true shortly thereafter. "Or are you sick of life?" "Of death," he murmurs, changing the tone: "They don't have anything to do with each other except that they're both part of the show: Sometimes a stunning girl walks down the street, the kind that every idler undresses with his eyes and whose very passing sets off all the car alarms in the parking lot. Well, do you know how they console themselves? By saying there must be somebody somewhere who's sick to death of her!" "When I listen to you," somebody butts in, "I understand every word, or almost every word, but I'll be damned if I know what you're talking about. О чем это вы?" Taken by surprise, the two of them fall silent, but the same voice straightaway encourages them to keep talking, genuinely interested in forcing the match to go into extra time: "But please go on . . ." How could he miss such an opportunity? "In the spring of eighty-six," says the man, plucking up courage, now speaking for the sake of prying ears, "I received a summons from the KGB. I didn't sleep a wink the whole night, and the next day, without saying anything to my family, I reported to the Planetarium.[108] Two shocks, one after the other: the officer on duty who opened to the door to me was our teacher of Scientific Communism, by far the most democratic member of the social sciences department; as I was waiting in the antechamber, from the adjacent room could be clearly heard the voice of somebody informing on a colleague, a long-distance driver, concluding, in the spirit of the period: 'I can't understand anything of what he says, but I understand what he's getting at!' Was that you by any chance?" he asks, abruptly turning in the direction whence the voice had come. Two ears as big as a boxer's jawbones bracketed the expression of surprise on the face of the man who had just been

---

[108] In the allusive language of Chişinău's inhabitants, the Planetarium was KGB headquarters, whose building was indeed located next to the planetarium.

dealt a knock-out blow. All wrinkles, he looks like a boot-scraping grate ("Mais vieillir, o! vieillir . . ." Jacques Brel gurgles in the headphones) on which time has wiped its feet whenever it happened past; "a peasant face," one can read between the lines. "Those were the days . . ." says the jug-lugged man, unimpressed, making them both feel the same icy chill up their spine. "But what about the people?" The others say nothing: Why would they work their jaws for nothing? For minutes on end, the man watches the unbroken line that divides the road in two, and then, suddenly: "Just after the war, there were French women who, using an eyeliner pencil, used to draw a line up the back of their bare legs, from the heel to inside the hem of their skirt, in place of a stocking. At least a woman never contradicts herself. À jamais!" he concludes, talking to himself. What interests him, in fact, is the line drawn by her pause: has anybody ever crossed it? The milestones they pass show an ever-shorter distance to the border and therefore to a potential answer.

At the entrance to the Moldovan border post, an enormous hoarding depicts a border guard with an Alsatian on a leash; from one end of the country to the other, statehood is linked together in a chain, like a dogs' wedding; one going at it, with the others chasing behind. "We've harrived," says the same unknown voice, recognizable by its aspirated h. But nobody moves. The woman gives her final instructions to the child and, aware that they're watching her, feels obliged to explain: "It's the first time I've been abroad with him . . ." From what she says, the boy will be spending a week at a children's camp in Ciric, which is not exactly to his liking. But she has to work and doesn't have any time to look after him. Public opinion is on her side or at least shows some sympathy. After the routine passport check comes an additional humiliation: after being stamped, they are surrendered to the driver and then passed from hand to hand, open at the photograph page—the names are called out, some of them mispronounced, all part of the spectacle that goes hand in hand with public transport. "No privacy at all!" All the while, the child is staring like an aimed rifle at the border guard on the billboard. Or, given his tender age, like a silenced pistol. His mother casts him sidelong looks, ready to be the first to explode. The day unfurled its orange parachute, brighter and brighter against the clear sky, the same sky as above the Romanian customs post. "The purpose of your journey?" asked the customs officer at the foreign frontier, mechanically, and as the woman recited the story about the summer camp, the lad suddenly wrenched his sweaty hand out of hers and bluntly declared: "The lady isn't my mother!" Before she recovered from her shock—"The lady isn't my mother!! The lady isn't my mother!!!" the child kept yelling desperately—, the woman clouted him across the back of the head. "You little bugger!" she shouted in his face, discharging all the hatred pent up over the course of the journey. "How much longer are you going to drive me out of my wits?!" The speed at which this miniature family drama unfolds is inversely proportional to the delayed reaction of the officer, who is obviously overtaken by events. "Everybody stay where you are!" he orders, finally taking the initiative, looking left and right for reinforcements. "Shut it!" says the woman, scarlet-faced, turning to the other minibus passengers, in anticipation of their remarks. "He doesn't know what he's saying . . ." But simultaneously somebody manages to call out: "Fathers are like shit flies, but there can only be one mother!" In an instant it all comes to the surface, everything she'd tried to conceal for almost three hours, dissimulating it among the regular passengers of the Ch—ău-Jassy route. She's a society lady from head to toe (male society, that is!), who's travelled thousands and thousands of miles, back and forth (across the bed); "F—k!" and "F—k!" are the only intelligible words as the lady talks broken English on her cellphone with some accomplice waiting on the other side, and seem to refer to the child, given the frequency with which she repeats: "Boy! Boy!!" "You're the cow!" yells the middle-aged woman, losing it, wounded in her amour-propre. And before the men in uniform make their entrance, the same aspirated voice lowers the curtain: "If honly I had a wee hole, even in my brow!" The Madonna and child are disembarked and led away, under escort, into the customs building. "Doesn't anybody here know her?" asks the officer, getting straight to the point. "In what way?" Biblically?"

says a wise ass, but the joke falls flat with the man in uniform. Another dozen policemen—not the ones with the Alsatians, this time, who have been left behind on the other side of the frontier—crowd inside the sweaty minibus. "Right, as if none of you were in the same vehicle as her . . ." He waves his hand in disgust. *Кто свидетель? Нет свидетель!*[109] "Each person come forward with your passport open at the photograph. The purpose of your Journey?" One by one they pass through the pen; "Not cattle, but sheep," sighs the middle-aged woman, peeved. Waiting to get their passports back, the passengers talk randomly, about organ traffickers, about girls who've gone to the West to prostitute themselves, often with their parents' knowledge, about the billion or so Euros that Western Europe pays into Moldova's budget annually, about the more than six hundred thousand people working without papers, etc. etc. The bourse of news items doesn't close even after they're handed back their passports and are invited to get back inside the minibus. The empty seats next to the driver show that two front teeth are missing. "What'll we do, boss? Wait for them?" "F—k her, by the time she greases all the right palms, I'll have made another two round trips . . ." Happy to get away from the scene of the crime as quickly as possible—there are as many scenarios as there are heads to imagine them: illegal adoption, a pedophile ring, trafficking minors for their organs—, the passengers return to their wonted occupations: looking out of the window and listening in on other people's conversations. "Since you've got nothing better to do till we get to Jassy," says the man rummaging in his bag for *The Daily Arsewipe*, "read this." INDEPENDENT BUFFET, says the signboard of a tavern, first on the left after leaving customs.

The change of scene left just the two of them in the guesthouse placed at their disposal for the weekend. "I've no idea what I did to deserve your happening to me," he begins distantly, "or whether through me you're going to be atoning for who knows what hidden sins . . ." In half-profile, she shows her six-dot, unblemished cheek, to the detriment of the five-dot one, pocked

---

[109] (Broken Russian) Who witness? No witness!

in childhood. "Nobody twisted my arm," she says categorically, "I came here with you of my own free will." Her words show off their enamel, like a row of teeth bared in a stewardess smile before closing with a perfect bite. "In any case, the punishment is included in the consummation of the act, like VAT in the sales price," he concludes, in a conciliatory way, "even if it isn't listed in the bill." "Or written in sympathetic ink." She is as direct in her speech as he is elliptical—the difference between an arrow and a boomerang. In other words, in the economy of the phrase, she represents the asterisk, he the footnote. "Like in the joke about the conscientious executioner who took extra work home with him," he says knowingly, "except that I torture words . . . maybe even myself. But that's it, I'm an imbecile!"[110] The way she laughed, with her whole mouth, in ascending shelves, was like the tumbling water of a mountain stream—it sets in motion the fourteen gearwheels of his sawmill eloquence. "You are a cascade! A puncdum!" He kisses her on the mouth, in one leap, as if throughout his speech his aim had been to hurl himself from the lip of the chasm into the unvarying torrent, shattering himself into thousands of champagne bubbles (". . . the prelude to an adventure," resounds the advertising slogan in his brain), at her feet. Falling, he traverses the distance between upstanding man, paterfamilias, and immaculate being, whose desire he feels gushing with the impetuosity of a geyser from the eternal ice. And as he follows his instinct, leaping the shelves like a shoal of salmon swimming against the current, toward the river's source, to spawn and die, her body emerges from the river's flow, her blouse slips to the floor, the buttons of her jeans snap open, her catapult-shaped panties are yanked to below the knees ("Don't scream, my knees," the blood throbs in his ears), without being fully removed, the way you might hobble a grazing foal. From one breast to the other, his mouth flows down her bosom, borne along by the undulation of forms in full spate, as if after snowmelt. All around, as far as the eye can see, the glinting primordial

---

[110] ". . . holding a can opener, wondering why the earth doesn't open up," Henry Miller, *Sexus*.

waters ebb and flow to the horizon and back, as if an unseen
little girl were skipping a rope, and only when a clump of reeds
("reeds, screeds," once set in motion the verbal combinatory
mechanism continues to whirr) brings to an end the endless
expanse does the shout erupt from his throat: "Land!" Kneeling
before this miracle of nature, he plunges into the delta, tongue
out, sending flocks of migratory birds clattering into the air—
they are unseen, but their wingbeats ripple the skin of the girl's
pelvic region—, before he finally reaches a pool of freshwater,
from which he laps like a dog. Her head tossed back, arching her
back in order to meet him at her lower meridian, she spreads her
legs, focused on the eruption of the miniature volcano in her
groin. Making a pirouette, they collapse on the bed. Their lips
have said everything they wished, now it is time for their sexes
to act. After a few failed attempts ("—n, ooo!!! it hurts!" she
keeps saying whenever he tries a fresh penetration), he pulls her
on top of him; she lets herself be penetrated by the pink salmon
that has now leapt the final shelf of the stream and is jerking on
the shingly bank; the pneumatic motion of his piston is transformed into the circular motion of her hips, a young amazon,
halfway through the twenty-fourth orbit of life; the potter's wheel
spins, the lump of clay grows compact, takes shape, acquires life;
the carousel is overrun by a swarm of cruel children, crueler and
crueler, given that only one of them stands a theoretical chance of
reaching the finishing line of the obstacle race. The arduous, slip-
pery climb, like pushing a sledge up an icy slide, clasping it on
either side, suddenly ends in dizzying freefall, *à la montagnes
russes*. "Is that what you call making love"—her first words afterward— ". . . at a great height?" "A bloody tale, sex," comes the
reply, "a good job it's not repeated. The *First Time*, I mean."
"When I was still a virgin," laughs the girl, among her tears, "I
once placed a mirror between my legs. I didn't know what I
hoped to see. The reflection of an eye framed between its lashes,
sleeping deeply in its nest of flesh, turned me inside out. It's not
looking at me, I told myself, but not a moment passed than I
felt it dreaming inside my body, I trembled at the thought that
one day it would awake, unexpectedly, but I was also dying of

curiosity to see it at work finally. In that instant *nothing* was revealed to me, except that *everything* depended on that *nothing*—hung in the balance, as long as I/it remained untouched. You can imagine how hard my heart thudded in my chest when you gave me *The Story of the Eye* to read; I remember it even now: '. . . I then found myself face to face with what, I expect, I had always been waiting for, the way the guillotine waits for the head it is to slice.'" "When I was a child, whenever I got something in my eye, my grandmother would remove the grit with the tip of her tongue," he says apropos of nothing. "You've never told anybody this before, have you?" Sitting up in bed, he watches as she unclasps herself from his embrace—left alone, the warmth left by her flesh curls up on his chest—and wrapped in a blue towel, she signals him to follow her. He lingers long enough for the little siren to deal with a matter of intimate hygiene and then joins her body of supreme joy under the shower. "I baptize thee, servant of God . . ." intones the man, swishing the rain like a priest flicking holy water with a bunch of dried basil. "What seems genuinely amazing to me is that none other than the Church that promises eternal life has done everything to make the faithful laugh at the reproductive organs. I wonder whether in vitro fertilization is the Devil's obverse of immaculate conception." "What about in Romanian folklore, where the virgin gets pregnant after swallowing a teardrop . . ." He laughs at a memory. "Don't be selfish," she says, annoyed, "tell me what you're thinking." "A friend of a friend—she works as a *traduttore* for a Moldovan-Italian company and is preserving her virginity in the hope of marrying an Italian, the cult of the Madonna being famous in Italy; apart from that, she's an unsurpassed flautist: as she says: 'The number of cocks I've sucked, if you planted them on my back, I'd look like a hedgehog! —, was all in a panic at the thought of getting pregnant whenever she happened to swallow a drop of sperm." "Do you know the definition of a superior blowjob?" she asks, not to be outdone. "To ejaculate powder on her cheeks." With a not at all rhetorical sleight of hand, he pushes the conversation down a slope where the tongue requires no words; begun under the sign of water, their dialogue ends in bed, in a consummate conjunction, through a libation to Eros, the god who is "fluid in appearance." Her flow is as majestic as his torrent is vertiginous; like superimposing the graph of frequency over that of end result. "It's not *God knows what hidden sins* that atone for a dream," she picks up where they left off. "Literally. The first time I dreamed you, we did it . . ." "*Pozna!*" (prank, jape, joke) he laughs, but realizing he's blathering, he tries to save face. "Whence *pozna*? The etymology is uncertain. I myself believe it comes from *poznanie*, knowledge." "*Cognosco, nascor*—same thing!" They are thinking of the same thing, which—all too often the things s/he has mouthed have come to pass, sometimes even in excess—, they do not say by name, but even unsummoned it makes its presence felt through the mace-blows of the heart. "What is it?" She presses her ear to his chest as if to hear the answer there rather than on his lips. "Nothing." They have yet to achieve the degree of intimacy that might shelter them from the emptiness which—without the chatter afterward, lovers resemble two sleeping bags at most—fills the crevasse of the silence; but the more the man stubbornly prolongs the suspense, the more insurmountable seems the yawning chasm, from whichever side you might look at it. Amused to realize that it was easier for him to pull down her panties than to coax out her secrets ("How about that! Putting a mirror between your legs . . ."), he chooses his words the way he might tie the cables of a suspension bridge, but even so, he still needs an outstretched hand, hers, in order to step past the embarrassment of a confession. He ought to start by going back to her origins—in the USSR, people were classed according to: those with healthy origins and everybody else; not a word about *L'Origine du monde!*—, in other words, *ab ovo* (or *ab coleo,* his), touching upon the humiliations of a puberty undermined by interdictions and unsatisfied curiosities, whose only illustrative matter, when it came to sex, was the obscene doodles on the doors of public toilets, both for boys and for girls, indiscriminately, at which the younger generation gawped—what else could you look at (the newspapers printed only photographs of Stakhanovites, the television wore the black-and-white vestments of a nun on top of the fiery body of a female commissar in charge of propaganda, and the only kisses on the mouth authorized in public were those given by the Secretary General of the CPSU, Leonid Ilyich Brezhnev, the leaders of the socialist countries, and the members of the Central Committee)?! All the tricks with a mirror gripped beneath the toes of his sandaled foot in order to position it discreetly below the skirts of the girls in his class; his first wet dreams, spontaneous erections during Russian classes (unconnected with his menopausal teacher); the competitions between boys in the upper classes to see who could beat it the fastest, and the jokes afterwards ("wankers get hairy palms!"), which he happened to witness in the school W.C.; the blind luck of a lad from his village who, after the middle school graduation party, ended up in the bed of a young widow, dragged on top of a body that was all desire, inside which, after entering again and again, he finally felt he was going to pee himself and said so, to which the wise woman advised him to pee without pulling out; the pink/turquoise underwear, like a girl's, which made him ashamed whenever he had to get undressed in the overcrowded changing room before P.E.; and not least, Dorian's exclamation, in the seventh year at school, on seeing the black knickers of the girl next to whom, the real meaning of which he was to understand only years later, after he got used to his wife wearing dark panties on delicate days: "---n и Родика поменялись трусами!"[111] He hadn't even had pubic hair when it happened, what? he wouldn't be able to tell. Anybody. They were playing up the walnut tree: he, his little brother and their cousin, who was already a young lady. She reeked of iodine, "Gvozdika,"[112] and something else, indefinite, but no less insinuating. He detected the source of that mysterious perfume; it was her natural scent, which the cologne was unable to smother. A mixture of brine and thyme. A lightning intuition whacked him across the back of the head: "Might the smell come from her . . ." He didn't have time to finish the thought. His whole being was focused on a single desire: to see

---

[111] ---n and Rodica have swapped underwear!

[112] Brand of cologne

it. In the middle of the game, he jumped down from the tree
like a gymnast changing apparatus. "See who can hang the longest without falling!" he challenged, and there they were, his little
brother and his cousin, each hanging from a branch. "One, two,
three . . ." A bare-legged parachute, he grabbed her in jest, as if
to pull her to the ground. At the opposite extremity he could
feel her strong peasant fingers, toughened at the udder from an
early age, as they clenched the branch, and in a single tug he
pulled down her knickers. The act was so unexpected, as if
launched from a catapult, that both of them froze in fear: the
stalactites of the girl's legs slowly swayed in midair; the boy
instinctively raised his hand to his eyes, as if a hysterical bat were
about to burst from under the awning and crash into his face. A
black creature—not a puppy, not a kitten, but somehow similar
to both—bristled at him, beating a retreat. It was bleeding! He
glimpsed the gash, but it was from the putrescent stench that
emanated therefrom that he knew it was severely wounded and
might not even survive. It resembled nothing he had seen in his
life, and the sight was all the more horrifying given that pilosity,
pubic *y compris*, was to him solely an attribute of masculinity; a
bearded lady would have shocked him less. He tried to make the
connection between his cousin, whom he had seen squatting so
many times in the past, before his parents took him away with
them to the city, and that terrifying beast that must have
devoured her from the inside and now, insatiable, was emerging
from her crotch, its grinning maw baring its bleeding gums at
the world. He all but wet himself, after foolishly sticking his own
head in the wolf's mouth—the shame of it! "A c—t," the word
was a key turning in the crown of his head, and only now did
he comprehend the ancestral objurgation: "'*te-n naşterea
mă-tii!*"[113] It was not a figure of speech in the slightest, but rather
an address as concrete as could be. "Did his mother have one the
same as that?" The leap from the girl now screaming her head
off to the woman who had brought him into the world made his
legs go limp; it was impossible for him to have emerged from

---

[113] Get back up your ma's birth-hole!

that, but at the same time, he would have given his life to be able to thrust his head inside that yawning maw of perdition. And then everything went black and he fell down in a faint. "Is something wrong?" the girl kept asking, "Tell me!" "It's nothing," said the man, twisting around to the bedside table, looking for his wristwatch, a black Omax that he called *Černa hodinka*, in memory of that Friday, May 13th, in the *Lobby Bookshop*, where he had been waiting for her and had dropped it in the exact moment when he was making a sarcastic remark about that ill-omened date, causing the glass casing to crack. "Time for a bedtime story. I've just come up with one . . ." And after a lengthy pause: "In her waking hours, the Sleeping Beauty was of an ugliness that only her jeweled earrings could eclipse. Their diamantine dazzle would catch your eye, especially on the evening of the Ball in the Hall of Mirrors, when, by the light of the chandeliers, the starry sky was reflected above the courtiers—the constellations of the northern hemisphere from the right ear, those of the southern hemisphere from the left ear. The whole kingdom depended on this knife-edge play of symmetries. And it was self-evident that there was not a man in all the kingdom who did not dream of the jeweled earrings. The only one who did not have eyes to see them was a young insomniac, the pupils of whose eyes proved deep enough to hide them in at night. As soon as lights out was called, the Sleeping Beauty took off her earrings and, the way you would slip a crystal pendant inside a black silk pouch, she let them be swallowed by the orifices of his irises, before recovering them the next dawn when, feigning to kiss his eyes, she imbibed them with her gaze. What did she care that the young man could not sleep because of ocular lesions, so long as the jewels were safe and the kingdom was closely guarded? In her sleep, she took with her the images of the day to keep her company, and it was then that all the beauty of the world came together in her visage, but a mere flutter of her eyelid was enough to put it to flight. And so it went, night after night, year after year. 'How about I pull off a heist?' thought the young man after a while and closed his eyes forever. 'Why don't I exchange the jeweled earrings for all the beauty of the world?' she happened to say, and never awoke again . . . Aren't you asleep yet?" "Here's the female version, à la Milorad Pavić," she replied, maliciously. "At night, Prince Charming, conceals the family jewels inside Snow White . . ." Intuitively, he realizes he has upset her somehow; could it be because of the last-moment substitution of a story made up as he went along for a tale from three decades ago?" "The very conjunction of man and woman . . ." he clings to a sentence from the *Symposium*, but it fails to unfurl. With one twist, like unwinding a roll of Japanese silk closely copying the gesture of the *Woman with Makemono* by Hosodo Eishi—her postures are as many color reproductions of the "Beautiful Women Playing Cards" series of master Kitagawa Utamaro—, the girl allows herself to be denuded (". . . and you ain't seen nothing yet!"); the Blinding Brilliance appears now in the form of *Maja Nude*, now as *The Great Odalisque*; Munch's *Madonna* meets Uecker's; the luminescence of the flesh, as breezy as it is in Renoir or Degas as it is saturated in Modigliani's *Nudes*, flickers, gutters in her body, drained after a night of love, at the end of which the nymph became a silk moth, *Cio-Cio-san*.

On the way back, they take the same minibus from in front of the Billa supermarket. "The last time I saw Mihai Ursachi, from behind, was as he was crossing the street over here," and the man points at the zebra traversed by the tram line. "He was like a walking ghost; I'll never forgive myself for not running after him . . ." An angel working late among mortals rushed into the breach opened up by his absent gaze before being absorbed back into the June air. Beside him, the young woman sat down gingerly, as if seating herself on the blade of a sword whose hilt was in the trousers of the man next to her. "We're off!" announced the driver after counting the passengers in the half-empty minibus. At the edge of Jassy, he picked up a few more; another two or three would surely board at the border, which meant he had a good chance of making the day's journey with a full bus. "Want some?" she offers him a stick of *Dirol Indian Cinnamon*. "Cinnamon gum . . . cerebral?" he ruminates. "I was in the sixth year at school, the seventh at most, when I discovered its existence. I can't remember what lesson it was, but what I do know

is that I was sitting next to Rodica M., the daughter of the
Minister of Education in the Mircea Druc government, and the
boy in front turned around to her and said, 'I know what you're
chewing there.' She was by far the prettiest girl in the class, and
was perfectly aware of her precocious femininity, which has only
improved with time. 'What am I chewing?' she asked, feigning
interest. 'I'll whisper it to'—and here he said my name—'in his
ear.' He told me a long word, which I didn't hesitate to repeat *à
haute voix*, the better to memorize it: 'A prophylactic!' The girl
burst out laughing and turned completely red. Just then, the
teacher hauled me to the blackboard by my ear, to expose me to
the opprobrium of the rest of the class. For better or worse, I
knew dirty words, even if I avoided saying them; you could see
them scrawled on every fence, but 'prophylactic' wasn't one of
them. The performance took a completely different turn when
everybody realized (the teacher being the last!) that I had no idea
what the word meant. It's one thing to laugh at the impertinence
of a classmate and quite another to laugh at him when his naivety
is exposed in so amusing a manner. In short, they stoned me to
death! Do you know how I felt? Exactly like in the Sermon on
the Mount [of Venus, as it were]: "Blessed are they which are
persecuted for righteousness' sake, for theirs is the kingdom of
heaven" (Matthew, 5: 10). Afterward, in the break, the boys lined
up to enlighten me as to what one was and what it was used for
. . ." She laughs heartily, still undecided as to whether she ought
to reward this little story with another of her own to match. She
will do so at the first opportunity, in bed—the locus of all *con-
fidences*—, but for now she contents herself with glancing at the
*Néant*derthal from the corner of her eye (". . . because you are
not everything through what you are, because you are not what
you would like to be, because you are not more than nothing,"
Miguel de Unamuno). He feels her breath on his cheek — now
that they have spilled innocent blood, hers, he will have to lend
her Ivan Bunin's *Легкое дыхание*[114]—, before the so eloquent
phrase: ". . . to the last breath." In less than half an hour they

---

[114] *Light Breath*, a masterpiece of Russian short prose.

arrive at the border. They are greeted by an officer reeking of the barracks, who emits (nasal) words in fully buttoned-up uniforms: "Weapons? Drugs?" Not so much the questions, which are routine, but the way he puts them, with an excess of zeal (as if pointing his finger or, worse, making the thumbs-down sign: "*Macte!*"), is the first sign that border checks have been tightened. The driver discovers that the reason for the hostility could not be more banal: the woman with the child two days earlier. The commandant of the border post had witnessed a spectacle that would have outdone even a Dumitru Crudu novel: while the woman wrung her hands, protesting her maternity, the boy kept yelling: "The lady's not my mother!" In the end, it took the authorities on both banks of the Prut a good few hours to convince themselves that the lad was shamelessly lying just to punish his mother, who was about to build a new life for herself with another man (the one who had called her on her cellphone). But since the boy was adamant she was not his mother, she resorted to a strategy as simple as it was effective: "Give us both a DNA test right here and now!" knowing her son fainted even at the sight of a hypodermic needle. "Blood is thicker than water . . ." concludes the driver, philosophically. "It's as if we're doomed never to escape the whole business with that boy," complains the girl. What doesn't even cross her mind is that without anybody knowing it, she herself is crossing the border with a boy, a forty-eight-hour-old fetus, conceived in the Neighboring-and-Friendly-Country and smuggled into the Motherland on crossing the Prut. "You think that was the end of it?" he asks her, on the Moldovan side, after a sustained pause. "Some stories need time to unfold. Let me tell you one our accountant Roman Roman told me one trip. Well, it was in eighty-eight, in a modest two-room apartment in Ch—ău, a funeral repast was held for Ion Gheorghe Roman, born in 1949 and died of shame because he was reluctant to wake the neighbors in the middle of the night so that they could call him an ambulance. Heart attack. At the head of the table sat his old father and the priest, of around the same age. They got to talking and discovered that both of them had been deported to Siberia; after another round of drinks, the name of the place was mentioned: Serpnyovo, Tyumen region; they talked some more and all of a sudden, the priest remembered that in forty-nine he had baptized a first-born Moldovan child, in the first year of *ссылка* (exile), whose mother brought him to his *землянка* (hut) wrapped in birch bark. 'That was my son, father!' the old man exclaimed, bursting into tears, overwhelmed. 'The lad for whom you've just held a wake . . .' 'Mountain meets mountain, then man meets man!' Can you imagine what a loop in time fate made in order to fulfil what was written . . . That's what I call a *берестяная грамонта!*" (birch-bark letter) What he passed over in silence, lest he expose himself to ridicule, the way life itself had made mock of a man, was that after his death, fate had proved inimical to I.G.R., since on the ribbon of one of the wreaths laid on the newly dug grave could be read, in gold letters (over-assiduous, the engraver had transcribed both the text and the customer's instructions): "MAY HE REST IN PEACE ON BOTH SIDES." "If he was deported, it means he was a *гулак*,"[115] somebody remarks. He doesn't answer, even if he knows, from the same workmate, that it had been a case of rivalry in love: the spurned lover had become secretary of the village soviet and taken care to put the name of his luckier rival on the list of "enemies of the people." They make the rest of the journey in silence, listening to Jacques Brel ("J'arrive / J'arrive / C'est même pas toi qui es en avance / C'est déjà moi qui suis en retard"), ear to ear and tightly holding each other's hands, so as not to lose themselves among strangers. The landscape delights the retina— "A beautiful country, wasted on the locals"—, until in the larger bus stations and towns, the first ambulatory insignia of the state appear: three armed policemen and an Alsatian with lolling tongue. In Călăraşi, the driver pulls up in front of the bogs, as if the translation of URINBURG were CARPARK, and makes a point of directing his passengers: "*Мальчики налево, девочки направо*" (Gents to the left, ladies to the right). The concourse looks the same as two days ago; it's as if they hadn't even left the station. The main road is like a strip

---

[115] Portmanteau of *kulak* and *gulag*

of flypaper. The final thirty miles are the hardest to bear; everything has been said, there is nothing more to see. CH—ĂU. In letters as tall as a state official. He, a man of letters. She, a blank page. Before they part—the man heading home, the young woman to the lodgings she shares with two other girls, one a Russian, the other a Gagauz—, they walk a few paces together; coming toward them is a gentleman in his seventies, with the bearing of a Soviet officer, retired with full honors before the arrival of perestroika, a firm step, an implacable mien, like the faces on posters from the Great Patriotic war, pushing a chrome wheelchair in which in his son sits rigidly, almost as grey and soldierly as his father, holding an Alsatian on a leash. "Holding" should have a minus sign in front: one end of the leash is merely wrapped around the disabled man's right wrist and in all likelihood, he would not be able to grasp it in his hand. They process at a walking pace, from time to time the old man gives the Alsatian a clipped order: "Рядом!" ("heel!" in Russian, obviously—the language in which all the mutts of the former USSR were trained), calm, in charge of the situation, like a superior officer to a lower rank. The disabled son then becomes animated, repeats the father's order, shaking the leash (a transmission cable for the paternal will) and barking like a corporal, hysterical at his impotence. The Alsatian walks alongside—let it be noted in passing that the leash, never taut, trails over the asphalt—, his whole attitude revealing that the real leash is acoustic, the old man's voice, even if he strategically turns his head toward the wrist around which the leash is wrapped. "*Honor thy father and thy mother that thy days may be long . . .*" can be read in the dog's eyes, in italics. "I was in the tenth year at school, at the most," blurts the man in the girl's ear. "Every evening our parents took me and my brother for a walk, even though a peripatetic parade *en famille* was the last thing we wanted. We would hop along two or three paces in front, attentive to the slightest change in our father's tone of voice. He was a lieutenant in the reserve, and both we children and his parents called him: *The Army!* I no longer know what started it, but I was unable to pronounce a sentence from start to finish. 'Repeat what you said,' father would order, 'without stuttering!' Instead of flowing like water, my voice burbled an excuse, which made him lose his temper. 'Stand to attention! You have ten sentences. No more, no fewer. You will repeat them one after the other without stumbling. If you make a mistake, you will start all over again!' Back then, I used to read voraciously, and I hardly lacked a broad vocabulary. On my first go, I managed to reach the fourth sentence, when, attempting a subtle transition from the subordinate to the final clause, I botched the number of the verb. I was even less success-ful on the next attempts. I kept stumbling at every step; I was afraid even to open my mouth. My father yelled full in my face: 'Just you wait, I'll put the horse's bit in your mouth!' Again and again, until we were almost home. I knew the ten command-ments by heart, and would have been able to recite them as a last resort—but I congratulate myself even today that I didn't! ('Don't tell on me to your Dad!' Grandma would implore me whenever we recited the *Lord's Prayer*, the *Creed or the Decalogue* together)—, if I hadn't sensed the entire absurdity of the impro-vised rhetorical exercise. Let him fill my mouth with pebbles to correct my diction. Or with soil! He didn't care that he himself, the Father-Word, was behind the speech impediment. *Say it right or I'll kill you!*—there was no middle way . . . It was many years ago, but whenever I write a text, I get the feeling that I'm repeat-ing that evening walk, over and over again. If it's true that our tongue is what expresses us, then man, Impotence is thy name . . . I don't know why I'm telling you all this." "Yes you do. You're afraid of the emptiness that yawns open after . . . That wasn't it . . ." "No. Do you really want to know?" And without waiting for her to say yes: "That same Rodica M., whom I sat next to in class, the troublingly precocious girl, had made me swear, in the fourth year, that I wouldn't tell on her to anybody after she con-fessed to me, carefully choosing her words, that since she was an only child, her parents couldn't bear to lose her, whereas she would have been strong enough to get over the death of either of them. 'What about you?' she asked, taking me by surprise, the way somebody might plonk a hot potato in your palm. 'What kind are you? The kind who just has to close his eyes and he imagines his mammy and daddy grieving over him, or is it you who imagines your mother dying?' 'My mother? More like my father!' At which I then burst into tears. I was still *маменькин сыночек*;[116] she was already *la fille à papa*—but in less than half a year, her parents were to give her a little brother: Doru. It was thirty years ago, and I still can't forgive myself for that answer of mine. And now I've made you an accomplice in that-which-cannot-be-said . . ." "I would kill for you," she fires off the words at him. "And you'd be the first!"

There was a series of coincidences. They burst out laughing when, just a few days after they had talked about the insects trapped in conifer resin that enhance the value of amber, and he compared her to such a creature, captive *à jamais* in the light of an endless August afternoon, a droplet of pine resin fell on her head; "The story is too wonderful to keep to myself. Besides, it couldn't be timelier. A peasant lays his hands on a fairy—I'm merely repeating a French *fabliau*—, who, in exchange for her freedom, offers to grant him three wishes. In exactly that moment, the man's shapely young wife walks past. 'I want her to be covered from head to toe in *cons*,' exclaims the man. No sooner said than done. But he straightaway realizes that there is no way he'll be able to cope with such an abundance of *cons*. He thinks no more than a moment before asking for a forest of *pins* all over his body. Nothing could be simpler. But things become complicated as soon as the young peasant couple abandon themselves to the joys of spring, impatient to take advantage of the fairy's gifts—you can imagine the scene: she looks like a human cheese-grater, and he attempts to fit his magnificent pine forest, bristling all over his body, into her thousand holes, without success. He ponders how to overcome the difficulty, and what do you think occurs to him? 'Make us like we were before!'" Another time, lifting her up onto a rectangular stone that was like a miniature plinth, he pressed his ear to her no longer entirely virginal womb ("Once doesn't count!" as they say), on an impulse that surprised him more than

---

[116] Mammy's boy

it did her and which both pretended not to notice. It had been decided that between them there was no room for a third—"We won't have children; I'll have you, and you me"—, ostensibly on the grounds of Rhesus incompatibility, unless blood-group incompatibility (his A(II)Rh, hers A(II)Rh+) is a valve to release reproductive logic. And as if the gesture in itself were not telling enough, he gave her Ruxandra Cesereanu's *Uterus* to read on the very morning of the day when, having missed her period, she did the test. Positive! She would have cried to herself with her nose in the book, without breathing a word to anybody, if he hadn't phoned her shortly before midnight. He. "It's too long to wait till Monday; let's see each other tomorrow." Saturday. Three p.m. She was dressed all in black, with an ESPRIT t-shirt, a tight miniskirt, leather sandals, with panties riding up between her buttocks like the night of June 22nd-23rd vanishing between the two days on either side, she emanated such ingenuousness that he could barely refrain from teasing her—"Say the word over and over again really fast: *nerwie*"; she, on the other hand, is in a quandary as to whether or not to tell him . . . "Black suits you," says he, irrepressible. "Are you in mourning for your maidenhood?" "---n, I'm pregnant!" She bursts out laughing so as not to burst into tears: "Fathers swarm as thick as shit flies . . ." She would have placed a full stop there, doubled, squared: :: *For E—a, my lucky die, may she never stop rolling*, went the dedication he wrote in the book, directing her to p. 48, and which he gave her one May evening, after they went to see *The Seventh Seal* at the OWH-studio and watched the wandering knight play an endless game of chess with Death ("What eludes Bergman, probably due to ignorance—otherwise I doubt he would have omitted such a significant detail—, is that in the Middle Ages they cast dice to decide whether to move such and such a piece, which made the game—one of chance, how could it be otherwise?—particularly inimical in the eyes of the Church. 6 : 6."), reckless of the outcome. Who could have imagined that in less than three months they would be going hand in hand to the gynecologist's to terminate the pregnancy. And as the girl lingered interminably in the doctor's surgery, he was unable to tear his eyes from a little girl playing hopscotch all alone in the yard of Hospital No. 1, at the Gates of the City, casting a pebble into one of the squares—the sixth—and leaping the decalogue all in one breath. He could not sate his eyes looking at her when, having emerged from the door of the clinic to inform him that in the event of an emergency, somebody would have to decide whether she would be kept alive or not—"*Jus vitae necisque*," said the irrepressible Latinist in him—, the young woman asked his consent—"A mere formality . . ."—to give his name.

* *The only child of a large family*
"1. 'What do you mean he didn't have an elder brother? What about the hanged man? . . .' said the tremulous voice of the f—kographer-in-chief—a member of the old guard, trained in the spirit of 'Мы пойдем другим путем'[117]—, like a wire along which the subaltern's denunciation has just travelled: 'The prime-f—kographer doubts the non-existence of the elder brother.'
2. For some time, the life of Sin-Guru had become the true model and statute for every family in the Republic, a constitution and brief course in national history, so much so that every f—kographic detail was first debated in the supreme forum—Co-Fathers of the Nation—and only then passed to Sin-Guru for his signature and communicated to the nation
3. at certain fixed intervals of time, like weather bulletins, sea-level reports, the rate of exchange between the national currency and the principal foreign currencies, possession of which is punishable "по всей строгости закона,"[118] the party line, etc.
4. by which subjects set the course of their lives, births and deaths, engagements and weddings, meetings and partings, in accordance with the updated f—kography of Sin-Guru,
5. each citizen keeping at home a copy thereof, always the latest revised and corrected edition, which is as indispensable as an identity card, as necessary

---

[117] "We will take a different path!" Words attributed to the young Volodya Ulyanov after his brother Aleksandr was hanged for a failed plot to kill the tsar.

[118] "With the full severity of the law." The words whereby the maximum punishment was demanded in Stalinist trials, a phrase subsequently adopted by Soviet propaganda.

6. as in the old days—before Sin-Guru came to power, following a coup de grâce—when every celibate kept multiple calendars of his lovers' menstrual cycles, with red lipstick marking the days that were 'out of the question . . .'

7. Ah, tu, Motherland, whose calendar has so many red leaves . . ."—

thus begins the novel by the late Albanegrin writer Ippolit I. Kamare, *The Only Child of a Large Family*, Fata Morgana, Ch—ău, no date. The quotation, long enough to give an idea of the author's idiosyncratic style, is but a segment of an interminable DNA chain, "broken" into 666 poetic lines parodying—both textually and in their layout—the message of the Annunciation, as demanded by the narrative logic. Thumbing his nose at the Gospel according to Matthew ("The book of the generation of Jesus Christ (...) Abraham begat Isaac; and Isaac begat Jacob" etc.), the "back-to-front *ebangelia*"[119] according to Ippolit I. Kamare proclaims: "The book of the Generation of Need (...) Cain slew Abel, Romulus slew Remus" etc. etc." for twelve pages, long enough to reduce the population of the novel to an insignificant minority. And what regime needs a minority?! In next to no time, the Co-Fathers of the Nation draw up a "model f—kography" of Sin-Guru, in which his life is arranged in such a way that every episode refers to the everyday reality: "Born into a large family, after becoming a fatherless orphan, Sin-Guru is given the noble mission of standing in as his younger brothers' and sisters' father . . ."

Thus, once the ideal is proclaimed—the large family—, a subtle semantic shift is employed: the "fatherless orphan" replaces the "father," and not just for his "younger brothers and sisters," of course . . . Contraceptives are banned; sterility is treated not as a medical condition but as shameful sabotage; abortion, homicide; sexual minorities, "enemies of the people." At the same time, extramarital affairs are viewed positively, as long as they "bear fruit," and illegitimate offspring have the same rights as their legitimate siblings. There is an anthology piece, dozens of pages long, in which Ippolit I. Kamare describes a night like any other in the city Ch—ău, after lights out and the playing of the national anthem *Procreate*

---

[119] From the Russian *ebat'* (to f—k)—*Translator's note*

on the radio: the author piles together in a disorderly heap a host of ordinary substantives, among which swarm the verbs, without employing a single adjective or adverb, and after a certain point, you get the suffocating physical sensation that the text is being written with human bodies in the midst of copulation and the prose takes on the substance of an ancient bas-relief.

After a few pages, the figures in the "bas-relief" begin to vanish one by one, which means that the state's demographic policy has undergone a change, and this is because cereal production falls short of the number of "mouths to feed." The new direction is heralded by the second revised and condensed edition of the "model-f—kography": "Born into a large family, after becoming a fatherless orphan, Sin-Guru is given the noble mission of standing in as his younger brother's and sister's father . . ." In everyday life, this sentence translates as food rationing books only for the first three children born into a family, the rest—if they insist on coming into the world—are left to starve or crawl back inside the womb. Before issuing the third drastically revised and reduced edition, the Co-Fathers of the Nation debate for weeks on end the delicate question of choosing between a boy and a girl, with the "maternal line" finally winning out, as can be seen from the following: "Born into a large family, after becoming a fatherless orphan, Sin-Guru is given the noble mission of standing in as his younger sister's father . . ." Thus, sisters can remain in the bosom of the family, while their brothers are taken away to orphanages converted into barracks, with survivors becoming army children. But the "paternal line" takes its revenge with the publication of the fourth, snipped and castrated edition (aim: "One family, one child!"), which leaves no room for speculation: "Born in (year), the only child of a large family assumes the noble task of paterfamilias early on . . ." The letter of family law was invariably applied, and the "excision of infants" from the lists of the new born entailed their erasure from the ration books (in the case of twins, priority was granted to the first-born, regardless of sex). In parallel, a black market of adopted children burgeoned under the noses of the authorities. An end was at last put to this through the cutting of the Gordian knot: to the strains of the (morning) national anthem *'te-n mă-ta! (get back up your mother's*), the male population was put to the sword, or rather the scalpel, as part of a national voluntary sterilization campaign (a late echo of St. Bartholomew's night), which meant that the "line of the immaculate conception" was to triumph.

Reading Ippolit I. Kamare's book is doubly instructive: first of all, because all these things are not happening to you, the only child of a large family; and secondly, because nobody has got it into his head to make *Unageing Youth and Deathless Life* a model to be followed by the citizens of the Republic of Moldova.

Signature

Cap. 6
F.M.D.

F(ATALLY BEAUTIFUL AS the cause of a lost war, since only after taking up the conversation where it had left off the last time ("I don't know whether there is any connection between the way you live and the way you are to die; but what's for sure is that the death you'll die says something about the life you've led!"), when she stretched out her hand to him across the table, making herself noticed, this after she had barely made herself heard throughout the recording of the TV broadcast, although out of all that rabble of an audience she alone had read his *Gestures* ("That's how I introduce myself!"), a hand that was pure gesture, only then did they reach the terminus station. "You only have to imagine me six feet under, with my bones all lined up like matchsticks in the grave's box of darkness for the thought of death to keep me alive. Through reading, *quamanec* or esoteric & ascetic practices, you can conquer F(ear of) D(eath), but not the horror of the corpse. It stinks! Alyosha Karamazov naturally reconciles himself with the death of Zosima, but the Christian in him—imagine a perfect religion, in which the holiness of the deceased is known by the nose, by the smell emanated by the candidate for beatification; every saint has his own perfume; there are as many scents as there are "blessed"; and here and there a whiff of . . . God, forgive me, I'm talking dirty! . . . a female martyr—cannot forgive the elder for having putrefied. That's why he rushes out of Zosima's cell! Straight into the secular world. I'm mad about Baudelaire's

The Corpse, but it's still F(yodor) M(ikhailovich) D(ostoevsky) that I believe in. And I also believe in the sceptic of the Paris mansard: *Let me live and die in the third person.* I want nothing else. Nothing." The man seeks the girl's eyes as he speaks as if reciting from a book—"One of Papini's daughters, Viola, also remembers this: in 1917, Ungaretti, returning from the front at Bulciano, lay for hours and hours on the grass, looking up at a few wisps of clouds trailing slowly across the sky. She asked him what he saw, and Ungaretti answered: *Nulla*"—; he noticed her contact lenses, minuscule pellucid jellyfish sucking the sight from her pupils. "I want to be cremated," comes the girl's reply to a question that has not been asked. She lights another cigarette— Lucky Strike/AN AMERICAN ORIGINAL—, he counts the stubs ("Four") in the ashtray. "Me too," says the man delight-edly, sliding himself under the duvet of the same desire, "and to have my ashes scattered on the wind." The waitress changes the ashtray, both of them wait in silence for her to go away—it's a privilege of the *bien nés* to talk in the presence of servants with-out noticing them—, and then he continues: "There's a high bridge in Voronezh, *The Alcoholics' Death*. Legend has it that one night, two friends were crossing the bridge, dead drunk. One of them wanted to relieve himself from a height. He did so, straight onto the electricity wire that passed below the bridge. A rainbow of death arced between man and electrical charge; in a fraction of a second, all that was left of him was a small heap of ash, just enough to fill this ashtray. Which means that he leapt his own corpse straight into death." His words have the effect of a well-shaken thermometer—they're to calm others; even if it no longer betrays *Dostoevsky fever*, his speech reveals an indescribable disgust, of the "so much fuss over empty words!" kind. The man sinks into silence ("Don't *gruzi*,"[120] says the girl, testing her voice like a wallpaper stripper), inventorying the human ashes, from Auschwitz to *E la nave va*. It's his way of broaching heavy sub-jects, entering by the door behind the anecdotal, then climbing

---

[120] From the Russian *грузить*, here: don't burden your mind with things of trifling impor-tance; don't get annoyed; don't take it seriously.

the (dialectic) spiral stair of parentheses up to the mansard, to break out through the roof. "I've told everybody about it, not just my family, that thing about scattering my ashes. So that I'll be prepared, so that they'll be prepared! But it's absolutely beyond me to draw up a *Will and Testament of a Translator from the French* (when in fact I was destined from birth to be a *translator from the Russian*). I the undersigned _____, resident at No. __, _____ Street, make it my dying wish that . . . Now of all times, when the city council has decided that all writers should be buried in the Central Cemetery, the cemetery where I literally grew up in my apprentice years. From which I grew . . ." "Why? Why?" It's her favorite question or simply her question; asked twice, it thrums like a tuning fork that sets the right tone for the conversation. "I'll try to explain it to you later, in writing." "Later when?" "In writing: during my lifetime." He has no way of knowing that he'll keep his promise, which he makes now only to escape the girl's tenacity; he will keep it by translating, years later, Roland Barthes' *Journal de deuil* (how easy it is to speak another's words, transposing them into your language at best, appropriating them as you go along: "I don't want to talk about it, lest I don't write literature—or without being sure that it might become literature—, even if literature is born from such truths"), and because, in order to get his hand in, he'll have to dip his quill—in a manner of speaking (he uses a mouse)—in the black inkwell of his grandmother's grave, may she rest in peace. But for the time being he settles for reciting to her, all in one breath, in a language that smacks of *roquefort*—let it be noted that the "mold" of his French is no common or garden fungus, but verdigrized bronze, attesting its age & nobility—, Gu Cheng's (1957-1993) poem, *Une generation*: "La nuit noire m'a donné des yeux noires / moi je m'en sers pour chercher la lumière," *pour la bonne bouche* as it were. Her eyes insist, and the only thing he can do is to resort to a childhood trick. He recites slowly, separating the syllables:

"La po-pa la poar-tă
Es-te o mî-ţă moar-tă
Ci-ne-a rî-de şi-a gră-i

Drept în gu-ră i-a țîș-ni"

[At the priest's gate / There's a dead moggy / Whoever laughs
and tells / It'll leap straight in his mouth]

> *(C'est un homme. C'est une femme.*
> *Qu'est-ce que c'est?*
> *C'est un stylo.*
> *J'ecris*
> *tu ecris*
> *il ecrit / elle lit.*

The late met the early on the third day, first thing in the morning, at the hour when, *n* years ago, an envoy arrived to take
him, as if fresh from the egg, to war. He had just been dreaming
of being buried with military honors (even though he was the
consummate civilian!) when the National Anthem resounded,
probably from the radio that he forgot to turn off before going
to bed. He twisted around in the sheets so violently that he managed to glimpse his dream body stretched out in the coffin, the
hands laid over the chest, holding a candle stump. *He had putrefied!* "Me too . . ." All of a sudden, he discovered what it was like;
therefore he could no longer keep putting it off. "I the undersigned, +++"—he used to die of pleasure in the evening, hearing
her over the phone: "Hello, ---n, how are you?"—"resident at
No. __, ____ Street . . ." He has to get rid of the body (to swallow the "dead cat," as it were), at all costs, in order that he might
think of death unhampered. He climbed into the shower and as
he was turning the faucet, he felt gush from above, along with
the tepid water, long, slender woman's fingers. They flowed cease-
lessly—he could feel the varnished fingernails running down his
back to the base of his spine—, tracing every part of his body,
inside and out. They flowed into him. He lopped them off with a
single abrupt twist of the stainless-steel faucet, and a pitter-patter
of fingerprints came after him as he went from the bathroom
to his typewriter. "Do you know that *you will die?* Yes, man is
mortal, I am a man: therefore . . . No, that's not it: I know you

know that. What I'm asking is: have you ever been *certain* of it, absolutely believed it, believed it not with your mind, but with your *body*, sensed how ultimately the fingers that hold this very page will be yellow, icy . . ." Zamyatin's words, which he copied in his diary on January 29, 1994, opened wide to him—sometimes, he would begin his mornings by reading random pages of his diary, in search of his lost 'I'—, shagreen leather shrinking as fast as the eye could see up to "the fingers that hold this very page," "this very page," "page." He had to write, while there was still time. Or rather to buy time, as if life belonged to him only in writing. "I the undersigned, +++, resident at No. __, _____ Street, don't want anything." But oughtn't the verb not to be in the negative? What then? "I the undersigned, +++, resident at No. __, _____ Street, want nothing." Not bad, for the author of *The Trilogy of Nothing*—from Aurel Pantea's review of the book (*Vatra*, No. 4, 1998), he recalled the following idea: ". . . a possible approximation of +++'s *nothing* would be the world of consciousness as an unbridled spectacle of forms"—, except that "I want" and "nothing," at least for one baptized into the Orthodox Church, were somewhat at loggerheads. He couldn't write that. He crumpled the page and tossed it in the wastepaper basket, like a three-headed Indian monkey, "I see nothing" / "I hear nothing" / "I say nothing," after eating its brain. It was only then that he realized that what had woken him that morning was not the National Anthem—he might very well have heard it in his dream too, as he lay stretched on the catafalque in eternal slumber, receiving the military honors due to those who die *pro Patria*—, but the taste of death on his tongue. It was as if he had smoked all night long or—an expression he had heard her use—as if he had kissed an ashtray. He had not smoked a cigarette since the *Civil War*, when, following Flaubert's prescription, he had puffed through a whole pack of Marlboro—albeit Soviet ones (produced in Kishinev!), with the inevitable Russian health warning: "МИНЗДРАВ СССР ПРЕДУПРЕЖДАЕТ — КУРЕНИЕ ОПАСНО ДЛЯ ВАШЕВО ЗДОРОВЬЯ!"[121]—writing a few

---

[121] THE HEALTH MINISTRY OF THE USSR WARNS – SMOKING DAMAGES

pages of text. It had all started with Eugen Cioclea's words "Such-and-such, since he's alive . . ." (except he wasn't, but he was to learn this later), taken out of context by Nicolae Popa, for the sake of their consummate beauty, and appropriated by ---n to serve as a character, only to end up, almost instantly, at the story with "why it's unlucky for a smoker to take the third light." (". . . because by the time the third smoker takes a light, the sniper in the trench opposite will have had time to take aim," explained Cioclea, a diehard smoker.) All three promised to write a text about "giving up smoking"; in the end, he was the only one who kept his word, even if the text took a completely different turn. Now, from his viewpoint ("Who knows what the date is today?"), he managed to re-read "in the mirror" the prose piece dated "October 18-19, '89. Moscow," with the feeling he was dictating his last wish, without forgetting that in ninety-two . . .

(When two armies of equal strength
measure up in battle,
the one that fights in despair will prevail.

"Practice beats grammar," he liked to repeat in situations unforeseen by the rules. That he was down to his last three cigarettes and had as many prisoners to execute gave him no peace. "You can say that again: 'gave him no peace!' During wartime." After carrying out the capital punishment, So-and-so, since he was alive, was in the habit of taking a breather, right there on the spot, smoking in the sepulchral silence and watching the tobacco smoke mingle with that of the gunshots. In his soul he was a poet, even if his body wore a uniform ("Right . . . but the uniform, patched as it was, represented the Motherland.") "F—k this Civil War, if the victor can't grant the final wish of a defeated man. A good job nobody cuts Pachkulya's cigarette rations!" By decree of the President, who was also Supreme Commander of the forces and guarantor of territorial integrity, they were henceforward to be regarded as victors: 1) because it was they, as the official communiqué specifically stated, who were fighting for a just cause and 2) in order to raise the morale of the national army, presently at rock bottom, something nobody admitted, even in his own mind, out of the fear of talking in their sleep straight into the ears of the informants. The fact that the Supreme-Commander-Guarantor-of-Territorial-Integrity had undermined him, giving the order to retreat—after they had succeeded in taking the bridge across the Dn—r, "splattering every inch of the ancestral soil with blood" (ah! the matchless charm of the cliché)—counted for little in the general economy of the war. Or even not at all, for the handful of men from his unit killed for the Motherland. There was more and more talk of an agreement between the two riverbanks, at the level of the "top commanders," to the effect that neither side should carry out military operations on its own territory in order not to degrade precious military hardware and in order to expend fuel on the labors of spring instead. In this way, they are supposed to have calculated the average number of deaths in action per diem, in both the one camp and the other, with each side to cover the number (of the dead) using its own human resources, as it were, in the spirit, in fact no, in the letter of the Daoist postulate (*Wage war unnaturally*), and obviously under the strict supervision of international organizations and multinational peacekeeping forces (in the person of the Russian Fourteenth Army). Monitoring commenced immediately after the Anthem, when the newsreader from the radio solemnly read out the lists of losses incurred overnight, and at first there were no few cases in which two or three of the names listed were still in use by their rightful owners, who had no idea that they had "fallen heroically in the line of duty." But they found out by evening, in front of the firing squad, when, having been declared Heroes of the Republic (post mortem), their sentences were read out. The nation required martyrs; they were, so to speak, the bricks and mortar of the nation. In some cases, when they were not to be found on the base (even "cannon fodder" has ears, and not necessarily like a donkey's! which not only obey its superiors but also its instincts), the "living dead" were declared fugitives from justice on both sides of the river. After which it was every man for himself. Till they came up with a solution—the lists of losses were read out over a special frequency, 100.1 f.m., the Scheherezade Frequency, at the same hour as National Radio broadcast "Melody Medley" and, on the secessionist bank, at the same time as "Песня с приветом" (Songs with a Dedication). But all this might equally have been nothing but rumors, machinations of the enemies of state, although it is no less true that where there's smoke there's fire . . .

. . . that he had to execute three and all three had a "final wish," the same wish, and he only had three cigarettes, setting aside the last—like the last bullet—for himself . . .

Out of the blue, he started playing by himself ("Like a fool . . .") a game of "aristocratic football." Unsurpassed in their elite unit, except by talking parrot Mil Arepa, from which he learned the trick of twisting the box so that it would always fall upside down, his comrades added to his codename—all of them had secret codenames—the noble particle *de*, and the former Literature student (three years of foreign languages) now answered to the name *Proust de Rage*. He put the box on the edge of the table, with one end slightly protruding, then with a calculated movement flicked it up into the air, to the height of a "hand raised to vote yes." The box made a *salto mortale*—at least one, although two or more would have been appropriate—, then fell back onto the wooden board. Either "zero," or "five," "ten," "fifteen." Usually, they played up to a hundred, for bullets. After a botched strike, the box hit the ceiling—if the concrete lid of the cellar can be called a ceiling—and an entire barracks of matchsticks scattered over the concrete floor. He made to pick them up but stopped short. White, fragile, slender, the heads like patellae, the matchsticks looked like the dislocated bones of a headless skeleton, let's say that of *Marie Antoinette* (*marionette*, as Mil Arepa pronounced it. "Не был сердце . . . Здесь был пуп . . . Здесь был член . . ." "Не был, а бывал! Это женский скелет."[122] He Hamletised *à la russe*. "Byl ili byval? . . . To be or

---

[122] "Here was the heart . . . Here the bellybutton . . . Here the membrum . . ." "Not was, but has been. It's a woman's skeleton."

to be *intra?*" In the end, he had to pick them up off the floor; they were army supplies—a box a week. Once the final match had been struck, six small holes were made in the empty box: in all four corners, plus two in the middle of each long edge, and after a scrap of khaki cloth was laid on the bottom, the snooker table was ready. Using burnt matchsticks sharpened at one end as cues, the players had to "pocket" a dozen tiny balls made from pinheads, an exercise recommended for snipers in particular. Unlike "aristocratic football," this glass bead game required greater powers of concentration and was rightly regarded as the prerogative of the elite forces; the grunts played "rock—paper—scissors." "The execution? The execution . . . a sort of half-duel . . . pure death, without no riposte . . . one-hundred-percent death! *Classic instant death.*" Since the very first days of the War, the hours prior to an execution had made him uneasy, when, knowing the exact number of men sentenced to death, he would try to picture each in turn, to remember him . . . the way he would draw the cigarette from his cigarette tin, the way he would smoke it, with which hand, down to the filter or just halfway, with pleasure or just for the sake of it. It was his way of feeling solidarity with those about to die ("We're all sentenced to death, but for some there's a delay in the execution . . ."), he always offered them a cigarette from his own tin, as if they were equal in rank to him. The men sentenced to death (in all his time as a lieutenant, there was never just one at a time!) and he himself, the commander of the firing squad, were to prove that regardless of the time and place, there was never smoke before you yelled, "Fire!" After the execution, while the soldiers lugged the lifeless bodies across the minefield (they had a special map, but sometimes they put a foot wrong), he would pick up the cigarette butts and put them in an empty matchbox, inside whose tray he would write the date and time of the execution, the names of the men sentenced to death, and a short Latin maxim by way of an epitaph (the dead speak Latin, don't they?), then stow it in his knapsack. After the Civil War degenerated into an endless series of executions, on both sides, he managed to create an ambulatory cemetery of such "mass graves," the ideal cemetery,

The Final Wish Dovecote, as he named his treasure hoard in secret. With a little imagination, it could be turned into a train (as many matchboxes as there were eternal sleeper cars!), the *Train of Death*, as it were, enough to diversify *le train-train de la vie*. Others pilfered personal items from the shot men, as amulets to ward off the bullet; it did them no good. When caught, they were taken "в чистом поле, лицом к стене и пулю в лоб."[123]

He slept with his rucksack for a pillow, like Ivan Turbincă in the service of General Creangă.[124] Death purred at his ear, told him bedtime stories, sent him prophetic dreams. Like the time when, waiting for dawn to break, he had a *rêve eveillé*. He saw himself pull his cigarette tin out of his pocket and open it, but inside he discovered three men sentenced to death, two alive and one dead. He took the dead man out of the cigarette tin and smoked him, passing him around in a circle to the other two. They agreed by looks that whoever was smoking the cigarette when the ash fell from the tip would be next. A dead man is hard to smoke, he's clammy, probably he's wet himself in fear or broken into a cold sweat. The other two were scrawny. What would they taste like? The stub was passed from hand to hand, soon somebody's fingers would get burned, but it refused to shed its cap of ash. The ash grew like a molehill, like a termite mound, it grew and it grew, as big as an Albanian bunker, as Lenin's mausoleum, as an Egyptian pyramid and in the moment when the D(ead) pharaoh came back around the circle to the commandant's fingers, a bang on the door wrenched him from sleep. In the doorway appeared the freshly shaven orderly—the young, healthy blood was visible as it danced in his cheeks, as if doing its morning exercises; it was obvious he had splashed himself with "Тройной"—, but with bleary eyes, and reported that the prisoners were ready. "I'll be right there." He went out the door like a bullet from a gun. He didn't even have time to think: "Hmm, like a bullet. . ." as he trod on the orderly's heels. Outside, the white day chucked

---

[123] Into an open field, up against the wall and—bang!—a bullet in the forehead.

[124] Ivan Turbincă is a Russian soldier in a fairy tale by Ion Creangă (1837-1889), whose exploits include a descent to Hell and an ascent to Heaven — *Translator's note*

a bucket of sunlight in his face. He saw black and then . . .
"What's with this . . . F(ata) M(organa)?!" The orderly hurriedly
explained: "She's a sniper! It says so in black and white in the
accompanying documents. And . . . ," he didn't know whether it
was worth telling him, although he himself was greatly pleased
to hear such a thing, "the lads all said that she f(—ked) d(og-
gystyle)!" The commandant didn't hear him; he was standing
rigidly, his head resting on his shoulders like a pyramid in the
desert (a pyramid from one of those dollar bills that circulated
clandestinely, even among the military), gazing at all four cardinal points of the world simultaneously. Somehow or other, he
found himself asking him: "Blood pudding"—that was his nickname for his orderly, who held the rank of sergeant, although not
necessarily because his always freshly shaven cheeks were rud-
dy—"what do you make of the looming war?" He let his reply
pass through one ear and out the other; in any case, he talked
to himself, like in a silent film whose subtitles—"So far as I can
remember, grandmother wove at the loom. The worn clothes,
that is, ones that weren't worn any more, were torn into strips for
weft and tamped down on the warp to make rugs and mats; the
loom transformed the cheap material and sometimes preserved
the warmth of the human body in the living tissue, laid on the
floor or hung on the wall. She wove constantly, for her own
household needs, but also for relatives, close and distant, using
the old clothes of whoever came to her with a commission. It was
as if she gave new life to the rags. As many clippy mats as family
chronicles. Illiterate though she was, Grandma wrote her own War
and Peace on the loom! Her mats and wall hangings were missives
that only the older generation knows how to read. The generation
that still knows how to say: 'The front ran through here in the war'
and 'My husband fell at the front.' You seat yourself at the loom
in the morning and evening, as if on a milking stool, you milk the
family cow, which is kept next to the house and which keeps the
house . . . In short, the loom is the most civil tool possible, whereas
civil war weaves destruction . . ."—don't really coincide with the
action on screen. "Where are they?" he finally asked. The prisoners, huddling together, made him feel cold. They looked at

him coldly, absently rather than indifferently, from *beyond good and evil* (like Him who said it), as demanded by the rules of the game. He signaled them to break ranks; two of them stepped sidewise, the one in the middle — *F(emale)? M(ale)?* — stood still. Without reading out the sentence, which was always the same—"Расстрелять и не допустить бумажной волокиты!" (V.I. Lenin, Полное собрание сочинений, vol. …, p. …)[125]—, he took the tin out of his tunic pocket and handed a cigarette to the first. The woman took one too, with her left hand ("Is she really so good in bed? . . . Maybe she's even a mother!") He'd never shot a member of the fair sex. The hand of the last one waved impatiently when the commandant snapped the tin shut. "Temp?" he asked the man sentenced to death, although it was unclear whether he did so with disguised interest or poorly simulated interest. The commandant took umbrage, for the Country as much as himself: "Temp, you f—ker? Marlboro!" It was only then that he recognized him. Or rather he let himself be recognized: "Nothing personal, as you might say . . ."

The two smoked, the third took a short step back. The commandant cast him a quizzical glance. "I need to . . . go." "Go on then!" He didn't have anywhere to go. There wasn't a fence or a tree he could stand up against or behind; they'd all been burned for firewood. (In parenthesis let it be said that in order to stand them against a wall in accordance with regulations, they were forced to stretch a traditional wall-hanging between two hoes poked in the ground—such was the extent of the psychological support he could grant to the condemned, without disobeying the orders of his superiors, which would have automatically put him in front of a firing squad.) He slipped away from the other two like a shadow—as the sun was shining low to the ground, he could have made a run for it—, but he froze to the spot. He had got a hard-on, now of all times. "I can't . . ." He went back in front of the wall, holding his hands in front of him, like a goalie about to defend a penalty kick, while the lieutenant watched

---

[125] "Let them be shot without any great bureaucratic fuss!" (Telegram in which V.I. Lenin asked the commissar in charge of grain collection to put an end to the uprisings of starving peasants in Povolzhie by liquidating entire families that had been taken hostage.)

abscntly, having just recited in his head: "La popa la poartă . . ." He didn't know where to get another priest. The one in the rhyme would do. "Fire!" A short burst felled all three in one go. The cigarettes were still smoking between their stiff fingers, like snuffed candles, when the commandant stooped to pick up the butts and close their eyes. He cupped his palm of his left hand over the face of the first, ran the fingers of his right over the face of the second, the woman; then he looked at his hands as if studying two death masks. The third was lying face down, oblivious. "That's what you call luck! To meet death with a hard-on, like a man, and then to have the soil take the cast of your death mask . . ." He cast them a last glance, over his shoulder, as if to forget them.

At the writing table, the commandant inscribed the names of the two, of him and her (had there really been a third?) in calligraphic letters on the tray of the matchbox that contained the cigarette butts, then the Latin maxim—EX NIHILO NIHIL—, one word for each. Since he started drawing up lists of quotations, he had collected, if not a book, then at least a *Tibetan Booklet of the Dead*; say what you like, but he for one knew, and not from hearsay: "The fact is that in the trench, I swotted up on the whole of Nietzsche Goethe and Ko[...]"—*arse longa, victual brevis*. Stooped over the sheet of paper all through the afternoon, a poor Narcissus contemplating my reflection in the mirror of the page, I must "constantly invent words capable of dispelling the corpse reek lest it waft in my or my reader's face" as I think about how to get him off scot free in the next ten to fifteen lines, while the commandant calmly smokes his final cigarette. I feel him getting away from me, and there he goes: he shot through the door of the shelter like a bullet, went to check the guards on duty. It was as if he were driven by an evil spirit: he was seen here, there, on this side, on the other, all at once. Each seeks his own death all by himself; blessed is he who finds somebody to record it. As for Such-and-such, as he's alive, none other than A.S. Pushkin himself was to confess, *avant la lettre*, with the clairvoyance proper to genius: "С героем одной уже я не встречался. Сказывают, что Сильвио, во время возмущения Александра Ипсиланти, предводительствовал отрядом етеристов и был убит в стражении под Скулянами,"[126] as for the undersigned . . .)

. . . none other than Grigore Vieru in person, the author of the poem *The Shirts*, who originated, did he not? the Moldovan lyric poetry of the 1960s; you will remember: "There was a war. / Its echo / Still lives on . . ."—tersely wrote the following P.P.S. in the Easter issue of *Literatura şi Arta* weekly, published on April 23, 1992: "Whoever reads carefully and, in particular, whoever knows how to read a person's psychology will easily observe in the article 'Good for the East' the great despair that envelops the soul of this not-so-young young man. But as somebody once said, Despair means not knowing the reasons why you fight or even if you really need to fight. Stop it, my man. There is room under the sun for all. And there is room enough under the Cossack bullets. Get down into the trenches for once . . ." He had a light touch, that maestro whom the Romanian Academy had proposed for the Nobel Peace Prize no less! Now, n years after the incident in question, the man feels the same chills down his spine as on that morning in June ninety-two—although at twenty to five your head's still in the middle of the night, like the bag they put over your head in front of a firing squad—, when somebody rang and then knocked insistently on his door. "Thus does fate . . ." It was an envoy sent to take him, without too much talk ("Talk is cheap!"—apposite given Russian premier Pavlov's monetary reforms), to the war. His wife, long since awake (as if she had been expecting it!), opened the door, but not before hiding her husband's shoes. In that very instant, she realized what was going on—the name on the conscription papers, signed by the General Executor of War, was +++, which was a pen name. "He's not here. But the envoy was unwilling— he wasn't allowed—to leave *with nothing*. "Put it in writing that he's not here. Собственноручно!" (*Manu propria*) A mute scene: between the envoy on the threshold craning his neck to

---

[126] "I never met the hero of this story again. It is said that during the Eteria, Silvio led a band of rebels and died in a battle near Sculeni."

look for signs of the man's presence and the woman walking the length of the hall to her husband's office to write—at the same table at which he now sets down these words—"he is not at home," and between her and him, in the bedroom hiding under the quilt, the man being looked for, ready to claim to be his wife's lover should the intruder burst in on him. No sooner had she closed the front door behind the envoy than the National Anthem resounded—she had forgotten to turn the radio off the night before—, *Romanian, awake . . .* The anthem was like a healthy erection after an appendectomy. "My God!" he said, slapping his forehead, "The anthem that raised me from the dead this morning (if of course it was the anthem that raised me!) wasn't *Our Language*, but the other one, from ninety-two, *Romanian, awake . . .* The early hour, the National Anthem, my wife, long since awake—the links in the chain rapidly came together—, what's missing is the Envoy." In fact no, he'd announced his presence *differently*. In his mouth: that unbearable taste on his tongue! To rid himself of it by speaking it! In a word, to "declare in writing that he's not here." He reread *Civil War*, from eighty-nine; the text didn't need further editing, except for perhaps a few updated commentaries. "Why should it be any surprise that one and the same word—*război* (war, loom)—expresses life and death, when the very notion of language also means—as it does in the mediaeval chroniclers—nation, and our nation, as is well known, sits with its arse in two boats / *with its boat in two arses*?!" His brother returned from the front line for long enough to change his clothes, and with a little luck, to get some action between the sheets: ". . . and that makes me wonder: whose *război* am I reporting on? the loom? defense of national territorial integrity?" Like a two-tone typewriter ribbon—with the heading: "black for the dead / the living in red"—, the frontline leapt from one bank of the Dniester to the other; the Dniester itself seemed to have laid its bed along the River Bîc, dividing the population of Ch—ău into "patriots" and "Mankurts". (But before he ever laid hands on a typewriter, first his father's, on the sly, and later his own—the very same Moskva—when he left home to go to university—"To Moscow! To Moscow!"—, as a small child he served an apprenticeship at his grandmother's loom, watching her in fascination, sometimes taking a seat beside her; his entire poetics was a response to the command of long ago: "Tamp it down well!") Like a shuttle, Charon's bark wove back and forth between the banks. "The Motherland!" ---n took up the refrain. "Every foreigner has possessed her, first to the Prut, then to the Dniester, and still she act *po tselka*!¹²⁷ *Teritorial'naya tselostnost*! Which is to say, territorial integrity, translated *ad libitum*! And that ever since it was put up for grabs, in 1812, taking it now in one hole, from the front, now in the other, from behind. And in ninety-two it hobbled eastward, into a position where it could be buggered more readily by the Muscovite." In other words, the historical frontier along the Dniester abruptly broke, after both the one side and the other repeatedly tried to move the zipper now to the Prut, now to the Don, and it got stuck somewhere between Dubăsari and Tiraspol, which, if you look at a map of the republic hanging from a wall, corresponds to the trouser flies, as if the young state had just caught its manhood in the metal teeth of the infernal mechanism. On the railways, the women of Galina Andreyevna's *Interfront* were on strike against the Romanian language and Roman alphabet, diverting the trains eastward. It was as if the switch to the Roman alphabet meant that life itself changed the gauge of its tracks, when in fact the larger Russian gauge was, it's said, the result of a misunderstanding anyway (asked whether they ought to increase the distance between tracks slightly, given the state of the roads in Soviet Russia, Stalin is supposed to have replied: "На хуй больше?!"¹²⁸ which was taken literally, with a palm's width being added to the European standard gauge). In the meantime, amid the increasingly impassioned patriotic calls, the cries of grief were making themselves heard irritatingly often. Against this optimistic backdrop, it was decided to mobilize the reservists, even though a national army had yet to be created, and so it was that ---n too almost entered

---

¹²⁷ The vestal virgin

¹²⁸ The Russian obscenity here is equivalent to "Wider my arse!" but can be literally construed "Wider by a cock!" – *Translator's note*

the fray, feet first, thanks to maestro Grigore Vieru: "There's
plenty of room under the Cossack bullets. Get down in the
trenches for once." Who knows, perhaps a dead son of his native
land is worth more than the living father of a four-year-old
daughter. The upshot is that he had just thrown away the chance
of a lifetime to die for the homeland, and in order to live in view
of other people for or rather with the homeland—"Почувствуйте
разницу!"(Understand the difference)—he would have to produce a doctor's note, wouldn't he? But instead he contented himself with having as little contact with other people as possible.
"They used to call the wall carpet a *război* (war/weave), the one
that adorned the main room like an iconostasis, at the center of
which the Holy Family had placed the wedding photograph, and
around the edges, photographs of the sons in the army," he said,
but his brother had already walked out the door, leaving him to
draw the conclusion all by himself: "And that's how it's been ever
since the world began, the men go to war (*război*), and the women
remain behind at the loom (*război*). In other words, *Iliad* and
Odyssey." He carried on reading, which was heavy going: ". . . with
two men at once!" It was no secret to anybody that war potentiated the sexual appetite, both male and female, even to the
point of paroxysm; whence mass rape as a weapon, but also
mobile brothels, serving as gyms where the combatants could
unwind. The incident is supposed to have taken place in Ch—ău
in May-June ninety-two—less than thirty miles from the front
line, the capital of RM was on a war footing with Tiraspol, and
Bender/Tighina, even though they were on the right bank, had
gone over to the other side—; passing from mouth to mouth, it
reached his ears in the form of the following nasty tale. "Listen
up—it's well past midnight when a man in a white coat comes
out the door of the emergency hospital and heads to the nearest
waiting taxi. 'Are you free?' 'Yes, I am,' says the driver, overjoyed,
'I've been twiddling my thumbs here for half an hour . . .' But
the doctor's in no hurry to get in the cab. He looks the young
man behind the wheel up and down before deciding: 'Just
between us men—I'm on duty in the gastrointestinal section;

there's a patient there, a Russian woman, *бой баба*! who wants to do it with two men at once, and she's willing to pay for it. Since you're just sitting here waiting . . .' In a word, he persuaded him. So, he leads him to the gastrointestinal section, through an endless labyrinth of corridors. Once they get there, he takes him into the showers and locks the door from the inside. Apparently, the young taxi driver didn't realize what was happening until the doctor demanded he suck him off . . ." A few lines later: ". . . f—king Temp! . . . Marlboro!" The truth is that the information came to him by way of the photojournalist from Ch—ău's M. Kogălniceanu Museum of Literature, Nicolae Răileanu, a classmate of a commanding officer in the national army, who, during the war in Transnistria, was in charge of distributing humanitarian aid on the front—, according to the most conservative estimates, every soldier in the ranks is supposed to have smoked a carton of Marlboro and eaten five kilos of dark chocolate daily. The next sentence stopped him in his tracks, like an insurmountable barrier: "It was only then that he recognized him. Or rather allowed himself to be recognized . . ." The story told by his brother, a war correspondent for *The National Soviet* at the time, about how he arrived on the front and seemed to recognize among the prisoners who were digging a square pit some two hundred yards behind the frontline (a tank trap? a mass grave? God knows!) a lad with whom he had studied Russian at university, originally from Tiraspol. He stopped to look at him more closely than would have been appropriate in the case of a prisoner. Sensing he was being looked at, the man cast him an interrogative glance and then fixed his eyes on him. His smoldering eyes scorched him, but, his brother continued, he had to endure his gaze, in order to give him courage. "I didn't see him again, and I don't even know whether it was him or another; probably they shot them all. But his eyes still haunt me . . ." As for the Pushkin quotation at the end of *Civil War*, which serves as a *deus ex machina*, well, there wasn't a single person in the whole of the Great USSR who didn't cite it when in a bind: "Who will clean (wash, cook, write, learn) for you, Pushkin?!" Quite simply, he was sorry to kill his character, but nor could he leave him in peace, and so . . . "Ай да Пушкин! Ай да сукин сын!"[129]

The smoke (cigarette smoke? gun smoke?) that gagged his mouth frayed until it unraveled. He sat motionless at the writing table, caught in the vise of an infernal machine, as if waiting for the harrow to carve upon him the commandment he had broken. "*Thou shalt not kill.*" He felt he would suffocate if he didn't . . . and then . . . beneath the bell jar of morning . . . The blunt, cold-edged cry, like a coffin with a corpse inside and six invisible bearers bumped blindly against the walls of the house, the bedroom door, the windows overlooking the yard, the walls of the labyrinthine hall between office and kitchen, booming beneath the skull's cupola, but without finding an egress. He stood all alone in the middle of the house—a close-fitting Khrushchev-era "rubashka", tight in the sleeves and collar, easier to pull on than off—, in the crystal of the now consummated cry. Nobody saw him. Nobody heard him. Only the Virgin Mary saw and heard him . . .)

Her legs crossed—crooked as if she were holding a slender cigarette between index and middle finger, so slender as to be invisible—, she hangs transparent veils of smoke from the skirts of the outdoor restaurant sunshade (smokescreens of what theatre of war?) from which she looks like a besieged city. She bears a name predestined for war: Elena. "Not even incinerated!" she says, taking up the conversation where it left off. "Ideal is to be snuffed out all at once, completely, like in the countryside, when they turn off the electricity for the night." The waitress changes the ashtray for the third time and makes her presence felt, remarking over her shoulder, at the girl: "I've been watching you. You're a real smoker . . ." For an instant, the remarks short-circuits their conversation; they require a "cultural prosthesis"— and the man extracts it from his memory with ease: "Between the man who has the sentiment of death and him who hasn't yawns the abyss between two non-communicating worlds"—in

---

[129] That's the way, Pushkin! That's the way, son of a bitch!

order for it to re-enter its groove. "Do you think she"—and here he points his head at the waitress—"has it? How can you die when you're wearing a new uniform? Particularly a white one, even if it's stained . . . A well-starched apron protects you from Baba Anica—by the way, is that what you call death where you're from?—better than a suit of armor!" But with long practice at eavesdropping around the tables, the waitress picks up the thread as she walks away and feels obliged to interpose: "In our village it was a man and a woman; whenever they went to a wedding or engagement, he danced with all the young wives, as bumptious as can be, unlike his baba, who sat stony faced and silent at the side with the bairns and the old folks. All until one day when she got sick of the other women's snide remarks: 'Keep that cockerel of yours in your own yard, because he keeps jumping the fence into other folks'!' So she starched his underpants—the passion-killer kind—ironed a crease in them, and off they went to a wedding. And here he is trying to dance, with his galvanized sheet-metal *dessous*! after two or three dances, he was skinned raw, as if he'd been riding a hedgehog. Look at him tugging his wife by the sleeve for them to go home, even before the bride's dance, whereas other times they were the last to leave . . ." As she speaks, *Dessous chics* plays on Radio d'Or, with Jane Birkin in top form, having taken from another woman's mouth—and what a woman: Brigitte Bardot!—not only her man but her song ("Je t'aime . . . moi non plus"), but here the coincidences come to an end. With feigned insouciance, she asks: "What would you like to have been in a past life?" He knows she knows the answer—"Nothing"—and waits for her next question: "Why?" She pretends to have got something in her eye and as she cleans her reflection in her pocket mirror, she asks, in passing: "Would you be able to shed blood?" He laughs to himself: "As long as it's a virgin's . . ." "You've got a dirty mind," she says with almost childish disgust. "I'm talking about whether you'd be able to kill somebody?" He tries to catch her eye, and then peers through his contact lenses into her eyes, which have "a seven-month baby bump." From where he's looking, she seems *a highly delicate body, almost a non-body and almost already a soul, or almost a non-soul and almost already a body,* i.e. an open and at the same time closed parenthesis, which either encloses or excludes him, he hasn't yet found out which. She is the horizon of his desire, unattainable, toward which his *tempus irreparabile fugit,*[130] as much *tempus* as he has left, as they sit smoking on the terrace of the Seasons Restaurant in Ch—ău. "I had a cat when I was a child, while I was still living in the country. It used to eat chickens. It was vicious! Until one day my cousins Silvica and Snejana came around, on the off-chance, but with a sack from home (they lived on the other side of the fence), offering to get rid of it for us. You can imagine how hard it was for us to put the cat in the sack . . . They told my parents they were going to their grandparents' in the next village and that they would be doing us a favor, they'd take it with them, but no sooner had they walked out the gate than they turned in the direction of the gulley. I followed them at a distance; I was convinced they were going to drown the cat. When they reached the edge, the eldest, Silvica, tied the neck of the sack really tightly and . . . at the last moment she seemed to change her mind, and then all of a sudden, I saw Snejana running home, which was just over the road from the gulley. Before long, she came back carrying two spades. At which Silvica dumped the sack on the ground. What can I tell you? I couldn't take my eyes off them: two fatherless little orphans, one in her third year at school, the other still in nursery school, using their spades to hit the tied sack with all their might. And all the while, the sack emitted ear-splitting mewls. You should have seen it writhing in the dust of the road (and believe me, I wouldn't quote Eliot's "fear in a handful of dust," but rather I'd mention Fyodor Mikhailovich Dostoevsky, sentenced to be shot along with other members of the Petrashevski group, who, on the morning of December 22, 1849, with sacks pulled over their heads, like oversize nightcaps, experienced 'десять ужасных, безмерно-страшных минут ожидания смерти'[131]), as the sack became soaked with filth-caked

---

[130] Irreparable time flies. Virgil, Georgics, 3.284 — *Translator's note*

[131] Twelve dreadful, endlessly terrifying minutes waiting for death

blood—living tissue, no less. And you know what? As I watched them, I would have given anything in the world for them to let me hit it with a spade just once . . ." "The cat was going to have kittens, wasn't it?" "How do you know?" he exclaims in shock. "Five little kittens . . ." she says, as if she hasn't heard him. All around, young people are drinking beer, smoking, talking, as if communicating among tables. But the reality is that a sense of absence has descended on the Seasons outdoor restaurant, an absence that gapes in each person like a fishing hole in the ice, and one after the other each goes to the hole, without the others noticing, and a dozen empty chairs are left behind. Soon the only ones left are the Fay and the Minotaur, in an infinite labyrinth of words and silences. "I know who you are! I recognized you when, getting up to go to the toilet, you stumbled—you, a professional dancer of ten years' experience!—, because your right leg was numb. Just after I'd told you about my friend Aurel Dumitraşcu, the poet from Neamţ, who, before laying his hands across his chest, asked to be taken to the toilet so that he could die clean." He refreshes himself with a sip of mineral water; the water tastes like a numb leg. "Now that you know . . . In ninety-two I searched for you at the front, in Coşniţa; officially, I'd come to the front to perform in a folk-dance show. In your *Civil War*, you yourself told me to come and meet you at the Dn—r . . . You were supposed to be there; they even sent for you. You didn't come! I danced, I sang at the top of my voice: 'F(air) M(aria) D(ear . . .),' I had my picture taken with the soldiers—one of them hung a Kalashnikov around my neck!—; looking at them now, I try to guess which of them came back from the war, which were left behind, in your place, where you ought to have been!" "That bit about 'in your place' doesn't hold, because I'd just become blood brothers with Ioan Flora, at a poetry festival in Romania and since we couldn't swap shirts, as is customary—have you seen the size of him?—, I put his passport in my pocket, he put mine in his; it was only later that we realized: in the middle of the Balkan/Transnistria war, we'd exchanged the (still valid) passports of two non-existent states, the USSR and the SFR of Yugoslavia. Now try to guess who's in whose place . . ." ". . . and when you went your separate ways after the festival, which was Flora and which was fauna?" "It was obvious which was which, otherwise he wouldn't have titled his final collection of poems *The Dinner on the Grass*." "And you wouldn't have titled yours *Eloquent Arms*." "Every bird dies by its own song . . ." "Since you mentioned *Death to the Alcoholics* earlier," says he, singing a different tune, "let me tell you one last story, so that we don't end up with me owing you one. One spring, two mates went up the hill to tend the vines. The road was so muddy they could barely keep their footing. After a while, one of them held onto an electricity pylon to keep his balance and started shaking the mud off his boots, kicking like a restive horse. The other, a short distance away, thought he was being electrocuted and, running up to him, whacked his arms with the handle of his shovel with all his might. The doctor who put his arms in plaster an hour later had to grit his teeth to stop himself laughing, and all the while the man who had hit him with his shovel swore by all the saints that he was just trying to help him . . ." "Is that what you came here to tell me?" "The rest—as you very well know—is silence . . ." "What about what remains?" "Ask the dust!" Born in the year of the seventy-seven earthquake, which he for one had missed, sleeping like a log, it's as if the girl consists of seismic waves, whose magnitude—mild to medium—and continuous frequency varies according to her inner *Scream*; blessed be the man able to trigger a shockwave in her. Indifferent to those around her, she talks calmly, staring into space, her little snub nose turned to the wind, as if she were reading the half-past-five news on Radio d'Or: "You have no love in your life . . ." He grins at a memory: "A girl I was at university with, she used to borrow money from everybody, without ever paying it back. And when you said: *I've got no money!* she'd immediately ask: *Got any life in you?* In the end, we all chipped in to give her a monthly bursary, but she continued to scrounge, until one fine day, the head of her group told her straight out, in front of everybody: 'Those hands of yours are always taking, never giving. I'd like to see them folded across your chest, *Venera Milosskaya*!' (Venus de Milo) It was like she'd whacked her over the hand with a metal ruler. But she didn't lose her cool. 'Is that so? Well, I'm going to throw clods on your coffin with both these hands of mine!' came her reply. Take that!" The girl reaches for a cigarette—"The last!"—; their gazes intersect on the packet of Lucky Strike. "Make a wish," she says. "I'd like to leave *Civil War* in your keeping. I wrote it n years ago, so that I'd be ready. For you." "How about another wish? For yourself . . ." He remains silent. She remains silent. They remain silent. "Let me have the last puff." The ash falls away. The moments fall away. The quotation marks fall away. What was your favorite game as a child? Blind man's buff! It was like an initiation, *avant la lettre*, into the F(ear) of D(eath), and at the same time, model lesson about time. Silence. Then after a pause as long as life. Can I ask you something too? And then, without waiting for her to say yes. When are you going to come? Without further a)Do

Cap. 7
Decamiron and the Bodiless Beauty

The tone:
"(…) Because
Behind the first row of curtains were
Other curtains, and behind
The second row was a third,
Behind the third, a fourth, and through
None could be glimpsed the light of day and
The face of the beloved waiting in the doorway,
But only
Red-and-black and again
Red-and-black and again
Red-and-black."

Alan Brownjohn

HE DIDN'T SLEEP a wink until daybreak, as if he had ingested the white flesh of a nocturnal game animal. The counting of sheep, which in the past came to an end before reaching the zodiac of Aries, the first in the carousel of twelve, continued with the slaughter of the paschal lamb, he lingered lengthily, long enough for him to examine the sacrifice from every side, the representation thereof as it "stood a Lamb as it had been slain, having seven horns and seven eyes," from the Revelation of St. John, before finally sliding down the secular slope of the cloned Dolly to reach the grim television images of the foot and mouth disease then devastating Britain, the black sheep of the EU, and threatening to cross la Manche, tugging at the Continent's sleeve—all against the background of the childhood refrain: "White field / Black sheep . . ."—, with no end in sight. Not even undressing women he knew, item by item, brought him the slumber of which he dreamed; no matter how many skeins he unwound, the spindle of night was endless. He retraced uroboric lists of lovers, beginning with Bianca, thus rechristened by turning her surname and forename inside out, after he had mourned "his Maria" in the Valley of Roses park. "Even if I look—and don't forget I also am—black," her vaulted voice, the way you might mount the neck of a violin on the resonance box of a viola or perhaps a cello, sounded in his ears just as clearly as twenty years ago, when they first met, amid the arches of auditorium no. 1, formerly a chapel, where they were attending a lecture on The History of the Party, "I regard myself as—and pass for—a white woman, albeit one with a *grain de beauté* in a certain place, which only my lover can see, and which is as big as myself." The textual graft—the pencil lead replacing the spine's marrow—worked in her unwitting flesh with the tenacity of the subconscious within a consciousness if not puritanical, then at least spotless; to read her fully you had to begin by writing her. He was having the waking dream of writing a *White Book of What Would Have Been Had It Been Otherwise Than What It Was*, whose covers were his eyelids heavy with sleep—on the point of giving birth to monsters!—when an angel—"Jeder Engel ist schrecklich . . ."[132]—got tangled in his eyelids. The angel seemed surprised, as if it were the man who had landed in his, the angel's, eyes and not the other way around, and as if someone were now to remove him with the tip of his tongue. "Who are you?" one of them asked. "Wrong number," apologized the other. They didn't have anything more than that to say. They looked at each other, weighing each other up, like two boxers, one bantamweight, the other flyweight, before climbing into the ring. "I could break his bones

---

[132] Every angel is terrible. From Rilke's *Duino Elegies* — *Translator's note*

just by interlacing my eyelashes," the thought flashed through his mind and in the same instant he heard a sound like that of a matchstick snapping and a pizzicato voice (the angel's?) coming from nowhere: "Don't blink!"

By dawn, he had plucked the angel bare. after which he laid the stark-naked body—the photosensitive epidermis turned indigo in the blink of an eye and was as airy as a paper kite instantly carbonized in flight by the sun's polaroid flash—between two sheets of white A4 paper, which he inserted into his typewriter. He stuffed the bunch of feathers inside a pillow—a square pillowcase the size of a mediaeval Bible, the posthumous work of his officially illiterate grandmother ("… who had learned only to sign her name"), bequeathed with her dying breath to the grandson who was her very likeness and, what's more, bore her name: "Find yourself a woman you want to grow old with on the same pillow . . ."—, never soft enough for sleep to creep up on him before he had to resort to counting sheep. Lest he wake the rest of the house, he carefully placed, the way you would carefully place a hen on its eggs when it lays for the first time, his dear Erika—he had paid for her twice, once when he bought her and the second time when the craftsman had replaced her Cyrillic with Roman letters, for the same price as she originally cost—on the pillow's downy nest. The two being more than mere personal items, the very cause and effect of his sleepless nights thereby came together, nights that were otherwise perfectly reversible in the consecutiveness with which they denied themselves to him, and each of which had, ever since the morning of August 31, an angelic component, which was now of great worth, given that ---n had just thrown himself—body and soul—into translating Robert Muchembled's *Une histoire du diable (XII-XX siècle)*. His fingers ran over the keys, each connected to a number of letters—always the same ones—upon which ultimately depended the fate of the character, as it were; the author himself is nothing but a marionette dangling in midair from the invisible threads of taut gestures, fit to burst, amid involuntary movements and repressed urges. A man at the Faustian age at which, still hale, the flesh hurls itself, as if in a wrestling bout, without flooring it, but without hitting it,

it looks as if it wanted to hide, juggling the bones of its own
skeleton beneath the skin tent of the inner circus—he said: "Like
a surgeon working the night shift who leaves his rubber gloves
inside the patient's belly, God left His hands in the first man after
he closed his flesh back up"—the missing rib. Into that imaginary
bone with the ivory luster, one and the same figurine had been
boring for many years, without form and bare at first, then ever
slenderer, until finally it was transformed into a dagger with a
hilt in the form of woman's torso and a blade in the form of legs
tightly conjoined to form a mermaid's tail. "Style is the prerogative of insomniacs and rheumatics," he continued, in his mind;
"the sentence writhes on the page, can't lie still, the joints grind,
muscle contractions make themselves felt as cramps of the
tongue, not a single word works, to the inner ear the skeleton is
at best a bunch of sounds, *Vir-o-con-go-eo-lig*, scattered from the
(writing) hand to the mouth (that will articulate it). No position
is comfortable enough not to be changed at the first demand
made by numb limbs; no syntax is so rigorous as to hold in check
the writhings of the tongue. And in both the one case and the
other, *the bones speak*." He inherited his rheumatism from his
grandmother; to judge by his name, his dark hair, his blue eyes
and a certain way he has of expressing himself—as if blowing on
the words, the way you would pick up in your bare hand a potato
baked in the embers—, he is the worthiest descendant. "You know
a man by what hurts him. Gourmandizers and tongue-smackers
suffer the most often from internal diseases, heart and digestive
system; pleasure attacks the soft tissues, thins the blood, perfo-
rates the intestines. A shitty existence: your whole life you carry
death in your belly, you feed it, crawl on your hands and knees to
keep it happy, but in the end, you fatten the worms. On the other
hand, lumbar pains, slipped disks, osteosclerosis, rheumatism befit
simple folk, the temperate or downright ascetic, the workhorses,
the oxen of labor, call them what you will, who are always ready
to put their shoulder to the wheel, in the name of an order of
things wherefrom they cannot abscond. For each of them, the
skeleton is nothing but a cowbell around the neck of eloquence."
He rests his head at the old woman's rheumatic feet—and, as if

this were not enough, she broke both her legs in her final year (had she completed it, it would have been her eighty-fifth), in her son's apartment building, where, two decades earlier, he had asked her to move from her house in the country, probably more emphatically than would have warranted: "Mama, I kiss [*pup*] your feet [*picioarele*]! Don't speak ill of Anastasia—she's family!" to which she, bitterly quick to take offence, didn't even realize what she was saying when she retorted: "Break [*rupi*] my legs [*picioarele*], mammy's darling, but why?" How often she rocked him on those legs when he was a bairn! And if she dozed off, he would wake her up demanding to be rocked. Everybody in the world would have laid him on their knees, swaddled like a cocoon, and rocked him back and forth, night and day, anything to stop him bawling. But now, *requiem aeternam*. In the light of day, he sits up, rising from the pillow of his insomnia; in vain might you command: "Take up thy bed and walk!" For the last seven years, August 31 has stretched its legs beneath the quilt of grass where his grandmother sleeps her eternal sleep. "What is it like for her, there?" No sooner did the words come to him than his mind began scrabbling in the soil like a pig. "Would I still recognize her?" He closed his eyes, as if clasping the whole world to him, lest he be left on the outside, lest it slip from his grasp. The graveyard had turned into a children's playground, all the graves were open, each standing in for a canoe, a toy car, a slide, and all kinds of wooden playthings. There was not a soul to be seen, as if the earth had swallowed everybody up. Standing upright on a freshly dug mound of earth there was a wooden board, wider at one end than the other, a coffin lid, as he immediately realized. He was sitting on one side of the lid, his grandmother on the other, as on a seesaw. At first, he was unable to lift her from the ground—"She can hardly have taken root," he thought—; and now he is trying with all his might to counterbalance, if not by his own weight, then by an effort of will, the bundle of bones at the far end. "A heavy loss," kept twisting in his mind, seemingly without any connection, when all of a sudden, the wood gave a long creak and the old woman leapt up. Once the balance had been thrown out of kilter, things hurtled at a hellish rate. As he

and his grandmother rocked on the seesaw, every time he managed
to lift her from the ground, she looked younger by one photograph
in the family album, here she is the last time, in her "portrait" (her
word) for her identity card, a few years before she died, here she
is in the country, working in the garden, during each of the yearly
vacations he and his brother spent in U—eşti, finally, here she
is in that period photograph with serrated edges, from 1968,
when his father, an officer in the maritime aviation, arrived on
a week's leave, on which occasion the village photographer "took
her face"—here, the reverse-order series of grandmothers in the
family album breaks off, with the imagination having to fill in
the rest—, the woman in her prime, taking care of the house, her
husband, her two children, her mother-in-law (in just one year—
and what a year: 1946!—she buried her mother-in-law, one of
her sons, the eldest, "as well-behaved as a maiden," she would
never forget to add; the year she built her house), as a mother,
again as a mother, as a young wife, as a bride, as a fiancée ("Will
you follow me?" the freckled youth with the flame-red hair asked
her, after Sunday mass), as a maiden, as a little girl, and finally,
as a babe in the cradle through which at almost yearly intervals
passed another ten brothers and sisters. At the other end of the
plank, ---n was growing (easily said: "when he was one year old,
he looked five; and when he was five, he looked fifteen . . ."), he
was in search of the [personal] myth, which changed as he grew
older: Wunderkind, Romeo and Juliet, Don Juan, Faust . . . All
of a sudden, the graveyard filled with people, living and dead,
families went from one grave to another, with the insouciance
of gymnasts moving to the next piece of apparatus, on which
they are about to perform: the beam, the floor mat, the parallel
bars . . . Like He who said: "I have seen the terror of naked circles, squares and trapezoids . . ."

He awoke with a dull ache at the back of his neck, with the
feeling that he had rested his head on a pillow filled with soil rather
than the eiderdown and angel feathers he had placed under the
typewriter to serve as a muffler. "Probably she's turning in her
grave, poor woman," thought ---n, unable to loose himself from
the spell, "ever since I started translating that infernal text. The

things a man will do for money! But I haven't sold my soul . . ."
Empty words—he set no store by pecuniary gain, what interested him was the book in itself, whether he could transmute
it into flesh of his own flesh, depending on the extent to which
and, above all, whether or not he had the *daimon* in him. Apart
from anything else, Bianca Negru must have been a witch, one
of those witches who didn't even need to fly to black sabbaths
on a broomstick. Her congenitally milky skin, as if bathed in
the Milky Way, was impregnated with the night of the sabbath,
with its full moon and a starry sky. "Cuckoo!" trumpeted the pillow. "Cuckoo! Cuckoo!" From the typewriter rose Grandmother,
down to the waist, and turning in half-profile toward the type-
written page, she cast a glance at the text. "Delete it! Delete it all!"
the old woman gently admonished. "How do you expect the girls
to love you when you ramble on about an old biddy?" The apparition vanished as quickly as it had arisen, and he would not even
have believed in any apparition if he had not read, immediately
after the line with "the beam, the floor mat, the parallel bars":

"When your grandmother was a girl . . ."

(He was struck by the suggestiveness of the phrase, a felicitous phrase, no doubt about it, albeit commonplace; suddenly
he realized that the very perception of time, or rather the passing
of time, was expressed in bodily terms, in the feminine, ranging
from "when your grandmother was a girl" to "widowed times."
All that remained to do was for him to embrace it, the long-gone
epoch, as if you were to flip the body of an old maid on top of the
wastepaper heaped on the writing table and—"Fair Marie dear, are
you a maid?"—copulate with her madly, like in those American
films where the female hitchhiker hangs from the tattooed arms
of the young man, face to face, and he presses the accelerator, the
car tears away, the passenger's ass jiggles up and down with every
bump, and he races on and on, chasing the "love of his life,"
looking at the highway through a maid's body (old or young,
what does it matter now?), which has been polished to the trans-
parency of a stained glass window of the Virgin. And on and on,
the mad dash for ideals comes full circle back to whatever you
were able to get your hands on, the horizon is framed in the arc

of the windscreen, takes the form of the girl's shoulders, she rises from the pile of manuscripts scattered over the table, she adjusts the shoulder straps of her dress, as if placing in parentheses what has just happened, she replies: "Some say yes, others say no . . ." Time, like a maidenhead . . .)

". . . Grandpa was a young swain at the time," ---n picked up the thread, at the end of which the groom, none other than Ion Potoroacă (from Poltorac, i.e. "a man and a half"), put on his parade uniform, with gold braid and a sword at his hip—it was the bride's wish that he marry in uniform—, gave his final instructions to the orderly, bid farewell to old man Calestru and madam Ileana, with whom he lodged in C—ii de Sus, laughing uneasily when they voiced their alarm at his setting out through the forest at night to make the journey of a few miles to the girl's parents in Vadul Raşcov, where the wedding was to take place, and off he went. "He was fixing to die," madam Ileana was later to say, when at gloaming the next day emissaries arrived from Vadul Roşcov to ask after the groom and, on discovering that he had set out the previous evening, sent word to halt the wedding until he was found, alive or dead. (Those present say that the bride replied: "Let the wedding continue—I'm as good as married," and the ceremonies did indeed proceed, from the blessing of the ring loaves to the disrobing of the bride, and at the break of the next day, at the hour when the newlyweds' sheet would have been taken out into the yard, instead of swelling the ranks of the wives, the woman was already knocking on the door of Japca Convent.) In the meantime, soldiers from the military base in C—ii de Sus combed the woods, but apart from a few tunic buttons—his? somebody else's?—they found nothing. The search continued the next day, and on the third day they found him, stark naked, on an ant hill. He was unrecognizable. They found no wounds or trace of violent death—as if he had ended his life by an effort of will!—, but the industrious insects had disfigured him to the extreme, as if they had carried his features away with them under the ground. The day after that, old man Calestru and madam Ileana, along with the priest, a guard of honor, accompanied the sealed coffin from their house to the family plot in the village

graveyard. Since the good Lord had not blessed them with children, and since Potoroacă had been an orphan, Death was to
grant what Life had taken away from both the one and the other.
After the funeral repast, the elderly couple, now the more aged
for having added another name to the list of departed souls to
be prayed for, were crossing themselves, about to go to bed, when
suddenly they heard footfalls in their lodger's room, along with
snatches of military orders, which did not cease until daybreak.
And so it went, night after night. "God smite him, he comes
back," said madam Ileana tearing her hair out, "whether or not
you lock the door or not, he still comes back." And it was true, on
the stroke of midnight, they would hear the gate creak, the dog
whine piteously as it got out of his way, the latch of the front door
leap from its keeper, the door fly open to bang against the wall—
dressed in the tunic of an officer of the Romanian Army, buttoned to the neck, wearing a sword at his hip, Potoroacă would
salute his hosts, who cowered in fear, and then enter his bachelor
room, where the orders would continue, occasionally pigmented
with "Holy Mary's slippers!" (where he got that oath is another
story, which he took with him to the grave), until the third crow
of the cock. After forty days, they held a commemorative service,
they gave alms (speaking of which, the girl's name was Pomană
[Alms], Dochiţa Pomană), the priest sprinkled holy water around
the house, but he continued to come, and every time he lingered
a little longer (the nights were leavening—it was past the autumn
equinox). All until one fine day, old man Calestru was unable to
take it any more—as soon as the latch leapt, he planted himself
in the doorway and no sooner did he say: "Mr. Potoroacă, when
you were among the living, we treated you well, now that you are
no longer, why don't you let us live in peace? Go back whence you
came!" than the reply rang out: "Old man Calestre, if you couldn't
stop me when I was alive, why do you think you can stand in the
way of a dead man?" Realizing that there was no escaping the
importunate lodger, old man Calestre didn't sleep a wink the
whole night and at daybreak he said to his wife: "We'll tear the
house down in the summer. We'll build another down the hill."
And that's just what they did. It was then that Grandfather made

his entrance, a young swain (this last detail will be of greater or lesser importance to the story as a whole), greeting the old couple—he had arrived from the next village in order to postpone having to toil unpaid as a serf for the local landowner—and wishing the men all the best as he joined them at work. The whole day he never once laid down his pitchfork, tossing clay mixed with straw up into the opening of the hayloft, where the women spread it over the floor with wooden paddles. After a while, his legs carried him by themselves to the mound of clay and back, his torso twisted by itself toward the hayloft, following the trajectory of his swinging arms; it was as if he were broken in two, as if he loaded his pitchfork with his own innards and heaved them up and over. "Ho, laddie, take a breather!" said one of the men. "Mind you don't give yourself a hernia, because then your wedding will end up a wake" (this an allusion to the unfortunate woman who woke up married to the Romanian lieutenant and went to bed a virginal bride of Christ). At sunset the indentured peasants took their meal, which was laid out on long towels from one end of the yard to the other. Then each man went to his home, while the young swain stayed overnight at his aunt's, who, although she pulled faces on account of the late hour, didn't have much choice in the matter. She laid some blankets outside for him on the porch, and within seconds the young man was fast asleep. Potoroacă arrived at midnight, as was his wont, but as he was about to go inside, he tripped over the old woman's nephew, who was tossing and turning as if in the toils of a bad dream. Groggy, he jumped up and before he knew what was happening, he found himself wrestling—as it says in the good book: "and there wrestled a man with him until the breaking of the day" (Genesis, 32: 24)—with an invisible force, which tried to fling him to the ground in a blind fury. The next day, finding her exhausted nephew on the threshold, the aunt quickly tried to break the spell, lamenting over him for the ordeal he had suffered, and giving him a stiff drink to revive him, she told him the whole story of Potoroacă's wedding. "But don't tell anybody," she said hastily, "otherwise it will go badly for us." Fear caught up with him on his way back home, exactly like in his aunt's incantation: *and he took him and he threw him to the ground / he left him fearful and in a sweat*, meaning, somewhere at the unconscious level, the upper threshold of fear. He abruptly turned around and headed to the Holy Trinity church, designed by architect Alexey Shchusev in his youth. There he saw Grandmother, Gheorghe Olaru's daughter, praying in front of the icons. All of a sudden, he felt at peace—he was saved. At the end of the hours-long service, he waited for her at the church door, determined to gamble everything on a single card: "Will you follow me?" No subsequent ordeal—and, as God is witness, he suffered everything that a man could possibly suffer: in forty-one he was taken prisoner by the Germans (managing to escape before being sent to the concentration camps in Germany); in forty-four he was conscripted by the Russians, he received a head injury on his way to the front (when two troop trains collided), he lay in a hospital bed near Moscow for a few months (the family was notified that "Ваш сын пал смертью храбрых в боях за . . ."[133]), instead of being demobilized (the military commission had declared him an invalid), he was sent to the front, he crossed the Oder, after fierce fighting in which men fell like flies, and his unit reached the edge of Berlin; in forty-six, he buried his elderly mother and his fourteen-year-old son, etc. etc.—marked him so greatly, so much so that he relived it again and again, he told his children, then his grandchildren how he had wrestled the Devil and won. What the grandfather could not have known, but what the grandson would discover—over the course of time, the honey poured into the boy's ears turned to wax, a quantity large enough to fashion a life-sized effigy of the aforementioned Potroacă—was that "Ion Potorac was obsessed with magic. He possessed a number of arcane books, such as *White Magic* and *Black Magic*, horoscopes and calendars. Many strange things happened after his death. Witnesses said that somebody or something would often throw stones at their windows; the stone would fly inside the house, but the window would remain intact. Objects were seen to move by themselves, although

---

[133] Your son died a hero's death in the battle for . . .

physically incapable of doing so. Sometimes clocks would stop, and inside them a pebble would always be found. When they threw the two books on the fire, it took hours for them to burn. Everything passed of itself, the same as it had arisen. In the end, the house was demolished" (Ecaterina Eriju, *From the Life of Ion Potorac*). Another source, namely Elena Neaga, the daughter of the head of C—ii de Sus police, mentions in passing our character's suspected "unnatural bent." And so, "when Grandmother was a girl," Grandfather, the young swain, was an unwitting participant in a love-cum-horror story involving a supposed homosexual obsessed with magic (black? white? ultimately, what's the difference?) Ecaterina Eriju claims that Potoroacă's final words to his orderly were as follows: "You ought to know that here is both a heaven and a hell. Make sure you have a good time, because even if you don't, you'll still end up in hell"), whose ghost haunted the environs of both C—ii de Sus and C—ii de Jos for a long time, and a poor young woman who put on a nun's habit over her bridal dress, an ideal pair in their refusal/inability—true, for diametrically opposed reasons—to follow the laws of nature. In the autumn of the same year he married Gheorghe Olaru's daughter. Once padded out, the story of how *Grandfather wrestled the Devil*, passed down from father to son like a congenital malformation, was to expand to the dimensions of a founding legend, not because of the hero's mythic origins (on the night in question, nobody told him: "Thy name shall be called no more Jacob, but Israel, for as a prince hast thou power with God and with men, and hast prevailed."), so much as because it established a number of taboos: whereas "the children of Israel eat not of the sinew which shrank, which is upon the hollow of the thigh, unto this day, because he touched the hollow of Jacob's thigh in the sinew that shrank" (Genesis, 32: 32), his descendants—to include Grandfather among the characters, he must invent a fitting name for him: Băjenaru, let's say—on the male side are not homosexuals, do not practice magic, and have no monastic vocation. What's left: the officer? the girl?

It was as if he found himself holding a key without anybody bothering to show him the lock that had to be opened. An invisible railroad man—pointsman Păun?—changed the points, and here he is walking the streets of Moscow in 1989 A.D., past slogans inscribed in man-high letters on red cloth, mile after mile of bloody bandages, he cannot make out the names of the boulevards, no, wait, he is walking down НАРОД И ПАРТИЯ ЕДИНЫ! he turns the corner onto СЛАВА КПСС! he intersects with УЧЕНИЕ ЛЕНИНА БЕССМЕРТНО, ПОТОМУ ЧТО ОНО ВЕРНО! he wanders down ПРОЛЕТАРИИ ВСЕХ СТРАН, СОЕДИННЯЙТЕСЬ! ПАРТИЯ — УМ, ЧЕСТЬ И СОВЕСТЬ НАШЕЙ ЭПОХИ! НАША ЦЕЛЬ КОММУНИЗМ! around in a circle, ПРЕВРАТИМ СОВЕТСКУЮ ФЕДЕРАЦИЮ В ДРУЖНОЕ, ПРОЦВЕТАЮЩЕЕ МНОГОНАЦИОНАЛЬНОЕ ГОСУДАРСТВО! ПЕРЕСТРОЙКА — ПРОДОЛЖЕНИЕ ВЕЛИКОГО ДЕЛА ЛЕНИНА, ДЕЛА ОКТЯБРЯ! [134] caught up in the schema of a circulatory system gnawed by cancer and agonizing, in the final stages, over a sixth of the world's dry land, and that's if we don't take into account the metastases of the disintegrating Eastern Bloc. The comparison comes of itself: as long as the Motherland depicts itself as such (*РОДИНА-МАТЬ ЗОВЁТ!* where *РОДИНА* comes from *родить*—to give birth), then Moscow and Leningrad must be the ovaries (the first acutely inflamed, the second on the point of atrophy), with the ("boundless") native land living according to *ses règles*. Little does he care! Irina S—va walks by his side, in step; they've just been to see *Маленькая Вера* (Little Vera)—at the "Гавана" (Havana) cinema the audience was motley, ranging from spotty teenagers to war veterans, all of them there to see (and not to believe their eyes!) Soviet youth actually having it off, her on top, him underneath, and this in a country where, as a Soviet woman put it in a TV transmission broadcast from Moscow to New York, "секса нет!" (sex doesn't exist)—and now they're returning to the student hall

---

[134] People and Party are One! Glory to the CPSS! Lenin's doctrine is immortal because it is true! Workers of all countries, unite! The Party is the mind, honor and conscience of our age! Our goal is communism! We will turn the Soviet Federation into another prosperous multinational state! Perestroika is the continuation of the great work of Lenin, the work of October!

of residence, he to his own affairs, she to her husband. The walk does them good; "it's like turning the clock back every evening at the same hour," says she, with reference to their daily deambulations at light's out. "It winds up the mechanism," he says, agreeing with her. They always choose a different route, or rather than choosing one, they cast a clod of earth before them and follow it in whichever direction it happens to roll—they've roamed the whole of Moscow on foot like this. "You know, the name of my character translates as . . ." "Понятно, *беженец*," she interrupts, and after a pause: "От себя не убежишь . . ."[135] "It's quite a widespread name . . ." The June sun is slowly setting, at the same speed as the shadows that sprout from beneath the soles of their feet like monstrous toenails. They advance toward the dwindling light among houses that spread bat wings as if about to take flight as soon as darkness falls. They both feel it on the backs of their necks, but again and again a colonnade, a passageway, an underpass opens before their eyes, at the end of which . . . "Вы ведь не кочевники, правда?!"[136] says Irina, an exclamation more than a question. "No, just a nation of deportees, every now and again . . ." he answers, in his mind. Chatting together, they are unaware that they are the only peripatetics in the entire district, a grey zone, hemmed with barbed wire—the sign, ВХОД ПОСТОРОННИМ СТРОГО ВОСПРЕЩЁН![137] has been left far behind; not that anybody pays it the slightest attention . . .—, which looks just like an inner courtyard, with countless alcoves and secret passageways. They walk briskly, without realizing they have quickened their pace, cross another courtyard, likewise hemmed in—ЗАПРЕТНАЯ ЗОНА[138]—which looms in front of them, swallows them, disgorges them into a third—СТОЙ! УБЬЁТ![139]—, then a fourth, a fifth, with no end to them in sight. All around, there is not a soul to be seen, it is

---

[135] Naturally, *fugitive* . . . But you can't run from yourself!

[136] But you're not nomads, right?

[137] Unauthorized persons strictly forbidden!

[138] Restricted area

[139] Stop or we'll shoot!

as if they are in a de Chirico painting, *Mystery and Melancholy of a Street* (from which the little girl with the hoop has vanished), framed by redbrick walls. The Alsatian muzzle of darkness gapes; it won't be long before it rushes to tear them to pieces. "Куда подевались люди?"[140] said Irina, dispelling the mystery, whereupon the courtyard (how many had there been?) suddenly fills with soldiers. They are stripped to their waists, their torsos, oiled with sunlight, emanate warmth and self-confidence—you don't have to be Leni Riefenstahl to see the blond beast in the body of a Hans, or in this case an Alyosha, flexing his back. Caught up in their everyday exercises, the soldiers pay them no mind. It is as if they and their equipment are behind a glass wall, in an open-air wax museum, at closing time. There is no officer to be seen—how can you recognize an officer in a crowd of soldiers? nothing could be simpler: while the grunts toil, he stands to one side puffing on a cigarette—; but to leave them unsupervised is equivalent to putting a pan of milk, or rather a bucket of sperm, on the stove and forgetting about it. They proceed along the dark side of the passageway, casting sidelong glances from under the cap peak of shadow at the inner courtyard where dusk slices away the edges of the amber light. "So much beauty, so much cruelty," says ---n to himself. "Ты служил?" (Did you serve?) she asks at the same time as his thought. "Who, me?!!" Their evening walk risks taking a nasty turn now that other soldiers suddenly appear to start their night's guard duty. All of a sudden, an Alsatian barks, one of the soldiers looks up, stares into space. The two of them instinctively crouch down. They look ridiculous (but who could possibly see them in the semidarkness: both longhaired, wearing jeans and baggy shirts which they haven't tucked into their trousers?) in that indecorous position. Initiating him into Slavic ontology, Irina informs him that when a Russian wants to classify somebody as beneath all contempt, he says: "Рядом с ним я срать не сяду!"[141] They laugh softly, but also nervously. "Run for it!" he shouts in her ear, and like a single body they

---

[140] Where have the people vanished to?

[141] I wouldn't squat to have a shit next to him

spring up and away from the dog that has sighted them. Behind them they hear whistles, which means they have been seen. The only thing they don't know is whether the soldiers are whistling to intimidate them before closing in on them or whether to signal they are getting away. An icy rod slides up his spinal cord, against the grain, comparable with the wire brush used for reaming the bore of a rifle. The woman is sopping wet, as if after a night of lovemaking. Instead of casting their shadows on the asphalt, they clutch them to their chests and run feverishly, like mercury shooting up a thermometer. They don't look over their shoulders—that whiplash glance might make the soldiers look closer than they really are—, it's enough that they sense them at their backs as they run. They run across other courtyards, each giving onto the next like chins cascading down a fat man's chest in garlands of lard, gathering at the gut before spilling over his belt. Finally, they espy a gap in the wall. They pass through it and find themselves on a patch of waste ground near the Savyolov Station, which means they're a stone's throw from the student hall of residence. They walk the rest of the way in silence, in the dark (whereas according to V. I. Lenin, communism meant socialism plus electrification, according to M. S. Gorbachev, socialism with a human face entails communism minus electrification—Q.E.D.). The area where they live is where Chikatilo was last seen, or rather, where the psycho's last victim was found, just a few days ago—little do they care! The photofit of the serial killer, posted on every telegraph pole at head height, falls in with them every thirty feet. In the dim light of the entrance, they look at each other and agree tacitly not to tell anybody anything, but from the way Irina's husband reacts—"На вас лица нет!"[142]— they realize the incident has marked them. In two voices, gesticulating with four hands, they told the tale, and the young woman's husband, otherwise garrulous, was left speechless. "Вас же могли изнасиловать! Обоих! Всем взводом![143] he telegraphs.

---

[142] You're faceless, i.e. pale

[143] They could have raped you! Both of you! The whole platoon!

"Покажи па нем как?"[144] says Irina, pointing her head at ---n. He pretends to bump into his wife's young companion while pushing a wheelbarrow, a gesture that wipes the tension from their faces. "Time for a game of préférance," he says abruptly changing the subject. "Who's brought the cards?"

The shockwave caught up with him more than four years later, one night in late October, at the end of a journey during which he changed no less than four trains, three historical provinces, two railway gauges, one hundred Moldovan lei, and summer for winter time. Accompanied by Vio—"double the expenditure, half the pleasure," as he teases her whenever they travel together—, he had to kill time in Dej Station, four interminable hours, starting at midnight, before the local train to Carei arrived. Few people, sad faces. The matte yellow of teeth bared in sleep, nicotine-stained fingernails, hands resting in laps with deathly resignation, backs hunched in the fetal position, the air of Brueghel the Elder's *Peasants* that hangs over the waiting room, everything makes you believe that time has stood still, even if the hands of the clock on the platform tell you otherwise. Two middle-aged railroad men turned the corner and almost tread on a furry lump, which gives a short whimper. "Nice dog, that," said the first. "Yes!" grinned the other, admiringly. In that exclamation, there was a great unconfessed sadness, a nostalgia for the wider world, which neither the one nor the other would ever see, and at the same time, a reconciliation with fate, with themselves, with the thereness of that place where even the appearance of a stray dog was an event worthy of note. Finally, the train pulled up to the platform. Abruptly roused from their numbness, the people rushed to the carriages. The two of them wasted no time running to the train, entering the first free compartment, and occupying the window seats. They were joined by a pair of young Russians, from around Orhei, who had come to the other end of the country on business. "How do you like it in Romania?" asked Vio, striking up a conversation. "Очень," answered the girl. "Не то что у нас — здесь люди культурные, говорят

---

săru' mîna, doamnă!"[145] They didn't have much more to say than that. The darkness and cold in the carriages turned the train into a high-caliber machine-pistol with four silencers screwed together all in a row; inside the compartments, the few passengers sat pressed up against the backrests as if to make room for the bullet when it finally flew. They were taken by surprise when the soldiers boarded the train, carrying all their equipment. The soldiers were on their way back from maneuvers; you didn't have to have attended military academy to know that: it was obvious from how their sweat smelled—instead of the sweat of an ordinary day's work, what hit your nostrils was a reek of gunpowder, and a metallic taste somehow appeared in your mouth, making you clench your jaws. Ignoring the civilians, in the doorway of the compartment, an officer barked new instructions. The only words that could be made out were "*futu-vă-n cur!*" and "*pizda mamei voastre . . .*" Meanwhile, a minuscule torch followed them as they obeyed the officer's orders. All you could see were his teeth, like a row of infantry spades digging a mass grave, after which he barked a final curse at them, spraying saliva, and a moment later the action moved to the door of the next compartment. In the darkness of the compartment, the soldiers seemed more numerous than they really were, all the more so since they couldn't sit still. A curt whistle announced the train's departure. The locomotive jerked forward, as if it had kicked itself up the arse. The soldiers slumped in exhaustion, more absent even than their Kalashnikovs and grenade launchers, which filled the corridor. Nobody moved. The only sound was the monotonous "π-r-squared" rhythm of the wheels, to the tune of "The train from Transylvania / Is coming full of soldiers . . ." Through the window, the darkness is a marathon runner fleeing from the firing squad. From inside the carriage, a man with a woman asleep on his shoulder ("the star on my epaulette," as he calls her in his mind) watches him, careful lest they miss Jibou station, where they have the connecting train to Satu Mare in a quarter of an hour.

---

[145] Very much. It's not like in our country—here the people are civilized, they say, *I kiss your hand, madam!*

There's no light anywhere, the athletes of breaking day are panting far behind, and there's no end to the race in sight. From time to time an isolated station flares like a match, instantaneously filling the compartment with a matte phosphorescence, long enough to capture the spermaceti faces of those present: the Russian couple huddled up against each other; the soldiers with their heads lolling on their chests, clenching their guns between their legs; Vio . . . "A soldier is merely a man without a safety catch," says ---n to himself, trying to gather his thoughts, "Chekhov's pistol . . . you never know when it will go off!" "By "Chekhov's pistol" he has in mind the soldiers in the Moscow courtyard, whom he thought he had escaped four years earlier, somewhere near the Savyolov Station, only to discover *hic et nunc* that in fact the pursuit had not stopped for an instant—on the contrary, the pursuers had multiplied, ready to roger them, without making any discrimination based on politics, nationality or sex. Closed circle. Sphincter. "*Dignus est intrare in nostro docto corpore . . .*" He almost leapt out of his seat whenever the train stopped, but each time, his flesh muffled the action of the inner spring and so nobody noticed. There was no doubt about it—time gripped him by the balls, all three of them (counting his pocket watch along with the two he had from birth), and now, as they say: "*Fuți, nu fuți, da' vremea pulii trece!*" Night undid its flies, exposing the *dessous* of the day to come. Jibou.

    Plus de peur que de mal, as was later to be proven, except that it wasn't clear which was worse, the fear of the danger proper. "Если изнасилование неизбежно, расслабьтесь и получите удовольствие."[146] Woken from his reverie, he tore the page from the mouth of the typewriter—it was the passage he had translated the night before, from *A History of the Devil*, before he sat on the seesaw with Grandmother: "A lieutenant of the guard in Lyon, La Jaquiere therefore opted for night duty, given that he was a great enthusiast for amorous visits. One evening, between eleven and midnight, he told his comrades, in a passion, that if he met the Devil that very moment, he would not release him

---

[146] If rape is inevitable, relax and savor the pleasure.

from his grasp until he granted him a wish." No sooner had he spoken that he espied a shapely woman of peerless beauty, walking alone with her maid. An amorous encounter ensued, with flowery words on both sides, and with the beautiful lady complaining of her odious husband. Accompanied by two comrades, La Jaquiere walked the lady home, where he persuaded her to yield to him, so effectively that "they abandoned themselves to pleasure" twice. The satisfied officer succeeded in persuading his lover to grant the same favors to his two friends. The three then gazed upon her, singing her praises, her ivory forehead, her flaming eyes, her blond hair, her snowy neck, the roses, lilies and carnations of her cheeks. Finally, she stood up and asked them whether they knew whom they were dealing with. "Having said that, she hitched up her dress and *dessous* and revealed to them the most loathsome, the ugliest, the most stinking and the most diseased corpse in the world." There was a noise like thunder; the three men fell down senseless; the house vanished leaving a ruin strewn with dung and filth. At the break of day, the groans of two of them— their comrade having died of fright—alerted the neighbors, who pulled them out of there, "covered in filth from head to foot as they were." They summoned a priest to shrive them. La Jaquiere died the next day, and the final survivor followed him three or four days later, after telling the tale as it is set down here." Not a word more. As if Robert Muchembled's text were a sponge that had absorbed that sentence that appeared out of the blue at the bottom of the page—"When Grandmother was a girl . . ."—, and all that followed it—the tale of Potoroacă, the irenic chase (when he had fled with Irina, the Russian woman, in 1989) through the courtyards of Moscow, the night journey in a train packed to the gills with soldiers . . . —, only to be raised on the tip of his pen nib to the author's burnt mouth. (When the author and translator of *A History of the Devil* finally met, the former gave the latter a signed copy of the original book: "*Pour ---n, qui s'y connaît très bien*".) To write means to live the life of the characters by proxy, a life which after a while becomes yours more than theirs. To translate a love story of a century ago, between a homosexual lieutenant obsessed with black magic and a bride (of

Christ, after failing to become her husband's), via a *billet doux* to the woman who, in reaction to your first (and last) declaration of love, found nothing better to say than: "Go to the devil!" which was a reply to match the beautiful woman hitching up her skirts and *dessous* at the end of François de Rosset's novel. To watch the ineffable "eternal feminine" curbing between its thighs the warm substance of an alien woman's body. To draw nearer to the woman *de ses rêves* with ejaculation into a chance womb the same as boys do in childhood when they compete to see how many globs of spit will cover the distance between fence and road. At the end of this series of infinitives: Bianca Negru. "Even if I look—and don't forget that I am—black, I regard myself—and pass for—a genuine white woman, with a *grain de beauté* in a certain place, which only my lover can see, and which is as large as me." That sentence of hers followed him everywhere; it was all of her that remained to him after he believed her lost—in the same way, probably, they burned Potoroacă's two books, *White Magic* and *Black Magic*, "at least the books themselves had long since ceased to exist"—, not enough to take her place, but sufficient (why does it remind you of the story of the loving son who, once a week, mixes the ashes in the two hourglass-shaped urns of his parents, who died in a terrible car crash, "because on Saturday night, Mom and Dad used to make love"?) in order to twst her from one side to the other.

The day took an unexpected turn. It doesn't bode well when you wake up with an iron Erika in your lap. "*On se connaît?*" Nor does the ringing telephone bode well, far too early in the morning for someone who hasn't slept a wink all night. "Are you coming to the graveyard?" ("Which one?" he would have liked to reply, given that the only graveyard for him and his family was the one in the country, whereas "Saint Lazarus" was not even a cemetery, but a huge underground parking lot of graves.) The doorbell put an end to everything. In the doorway, two girls of indeterminate age, wearing headscarves like from when his mother was young, want "поговорить о Боге" (to talk about God). He lets them come inside, shoots the bolt behind them,

ushers them to the bookcase. The amazement can be read on
their faces—never in their lives have they seen so many books
gathered in a single place in somebody's house. "All right, you
want to make a Jehovah's witness of me. Let it rip!" One of the
girls was kneading a brightly colored brochure in her lap: *The
Watchtower*, which was now of no use. "How about I call my
brother," he asked, reaching for the telephone, "and ask him to
come over for some group sex?" They were prudes. Whence his
imperious need to do them verbal violence: "Let this here old
man tell you a story. Sister to brother in bed: 'You screw better
than Dad.' 'I know. Mom told me.' Off with your knickers!" To
the stupefaction of the terrified girls, the floor did not open to
swallow up the sinner. Suddenly, he felt sorry for them. "Let me
show you something." He placed a catalogue of color reproductions of Brueghel the Younger, a.k.a. Brueghel of the Hell. As the
girls looked at the pictures, he read to them from *A History of
the Devil*, not at all disinterestedly, as we shall see. "Imprinted by
the devil's claw in a certain place on the body, preferably the left,
since this is his favorite side, often hidden in the 'shameful places,'
i.e. the eye of the witch, Satan's seal . . ." The girls' ears were ringing by now, they barely dared to breathe—the one holding *The
Watchtower* had a large, fourteen-carat mole next to her left eye.
"Now, get out of here!" At which one of them jumped, thinking
the man had called her by name. "And may the devil take you if
you keep knocking on people's doors!" Alone once more, he bursts
out laughing. A rapist, him?! A buttcracker . . . "The last thing I
need!" Back in the living room, he sets about folding away the
sheet. The whites pass through his hands like blank checks to
Hypnos or Thanatos (who can tell them apart?); he holds on to
the pillow for an unnaturally long time, as if somebody had tossed
it into his arms (who? whose?), "Forgive me." What if the angel
was a message, with each feather a letter, arranged in a definite
order, and he had stuffed the pillow with them? In a trance, he
stuffs it inside a black box, which the vacuum cleaner came in,
and on which he writes:

"Bianca Negru
*** Street, Building ***, Apartment ***
Ch—ău."

At the post office. "Please open the box." The clerk can't
believe her eyes. "What's this?" "*Opera Somnia.*" "What?" He
pays. Surprisingly cheap for such a large parcel. 13:00. In the
lobby of the Hospital of the Republic. Stop! Wrong entrance.
The entrance to the morgue is around the back. He has to hurry.
Any moment now they will be taking away Miron I., the first of
his classmates to depart for a better world, aged just thirty-seven,
after a life in which he made his name famous. With a voice as
ingenuous as a child's, an attractive, heavily pregnant Gypsy is asking every passing white coat: "Where can I find the twat doctor?"
The coffin of his classmate, closed to conceal not his death, but
his decay, which, even if invisible, the corpse transpires through
every pore, despite his having been bathed in formaldehyde. At
the graveyard. By the grave. A cubic emptiness—*alea jacta est.*
"The countdown has begun," says Rodica N. Without his for-
mulating it explicitly, ---n is thinking the same thing, recalling
that in their seventh or eighth year at school, Miron I. asked
to borrow his wristwatch during a test, supposedly so that he
would finish on time, and then returned it to him, but not
before turning it back a few hours and days. The reflex action of
a Peter Pan terrified by the passing of time? The funeral repast.
A throng of people with whom he was at school and university.
Condrea recounts how in Siberia he drank "медведь-приходит-
и-уходит".[147] The booze loosens tongues; after another two
or three rounds of drinks, the dirty stories are unloosed too.
Condrea, again: he recounts how he and a younger cousin went
off to cut down forests over the Urals, so that during their stay
in Siberia they could earn enough money to pay for weddings:
Condrea was to be a godfather, and his cousin a groom. They
both went at it with the native women, all of whom were gagging

---

[147] "The-bear-comes-and-goes." A cocktail rather like a Bloody Mary, varying depending
on the proportion of vodka to tomato juice as follows: 1:4, 1:3, 1:2, 1:1 etc.

for Moldavians. But after a while, his "tap started dripping," and the groom-to-be's todger swelled up like a bottle of "Советское Шампанское" (Soviet Champagne), and so they had to go back. Before his hapless cousin boarded the plane, he had to bandage his tool and hang it from his neck like an arm in plaster. "If you saw him from a distance, it was as if he were giving the pioneer salute with his todger!" laughs Condrea. "*Une histoire de cul*," concludes ---n, "which Miron I. would have liked too. Let's raise a glass in his memory." "Bottoms up."

There followed days and nights that were uniform, not because of the proximity of the autumn equinox so much as because of the number of pages translated daily: ten. A hopscotch in which could be felt now the hopping child, now the pebble. "*Albo lapillo notare diem / Nigro notanda lapillo.*" One Sunday, Bianca phoned him: "Come over, right now." He went straight away. You don't wait around after a lapse of ten years. She lived in a ten-story block out in the sticks. The lift wasn't working, naturally. After he bounded up the stairs, three at a time, he looked awful, like a chick just out of the egg. She, on the other hand, had not changed in the slightest. "Even if I look—and don't forget that I am—black, I regard myself—and pass for—a genuine white woman, with a *grain de beauté* in a certain place, which only my lover can see, and which is as large as me." The consummate chastity belt, locked from the inside. "You didn't need to send me the pillow—I've got my own trousseau!" "Have you got a groom?" The very question seemed to puzzle her: "A groom? What would I do with one of those?" She was sitting on the couch, leaning back on a pillow (his!), in the posture of a geisha garbed in Blinding-Brilliance. He didn't even realize when he jumped on her. "What's got into you all of a sudden?" she said, trying to temper him. "It didn't get into me *all of a sudden*—it got into me *all that time ago!*" He'd been stuck on her, and for a long time too, the way the earthquake of seventy-seven, which he'd missed by having been fast asleep, had literally stuck to the soles of his feet, after a pot of chicken soup—his other grand-mother, his mother's mother, had paid him a visit the day before, bringing him country food: a dozen eggs, vegetables, and a hen as fat as a goose—spilled all over the floor from the shockwave, and the homemade noodles spread their hieroglyphic script over the floorboards. He hurled her to the floor and as she fell she managed to pull him on top of her: all the better. He managed to unfasten her bra, slipping his hands up under her blouse. With a single jerk he ripped off her top to reveal two breasts with muzzles upraised as if scenting the air. "No! No!! No!!!" scolded Bianca, struggling in his grasp with all her might, "I beg you . . ." Her entire body was a perfect white—never had he beheld such a bust. In stark contrast, on the outer side of her left arm, above the elbow, there was an enormous mole, proportionally as large as the reunified Germany on the map of Central Europe. "Too visible," thought ---n, "to be the one promised to her lover." He felt his member throbbing to the rhythm of his heartbeats, the way a Formula 1 driver feels the gearstick when changing from third to fourth. Now he should brake?! . . . When he got to her trousers, they wrestled until finally she yielded. "Let me take it from here," she said, quelling him with a gesture and picking herself off the floor. "Don't look." Lying on the bed, she let herself be looked at freely (". . . расслабьтесь и получите удовольствие"), half-absent, half-aware of her womanly charms: "Haven't you seen *une fille à poil* before?" The throat; the breasts, "duplicates of the buttocks adapted to the frontal coital position"; the bellybutton, like a well in the immensity of a desert of shifting dunes; the pubic triangle, the calligraphy of whose raven-feather black hair is suggestive of a master's brush-strokes in *encre de Chine*, positioned in the middle of a blank page . . . But, good God! the "raven-feather black hair" is not merely figurative, in other words, it's not hair . . . they're feathers . . . the mount of Venus is covered in feathers, those of a raven or jackdaw, they are black with a bluish sheen—"*Nevermore*"—, the view dampens his appetite more quickly than the Codex of Constantine Mavrocordatos, anno 1750: "He who is caught with a stiffened member in close proximity to the generative parts of a woman shall have that loathsome organ amputated that it might never serve him thereafter."

It is not true that it is easier for the one who leaves . . . She is

the one left behind him—now translated into the words of the
man who interrogated Chrétienne, daughter of Jean Parmentier,
born in Estrée, Lorraine, aged twenty-three, during her trial in
1624: "She says that she met him but once (...) and that the
devil did her great harm, as she felt dreadful cold and immense
pain, as if he had thrust thorns between her legs, so that she lay
ill in bed . . ." (*Drole d'histoire*, somehow symmetrical—thanks
to its effect of compensation?/sublimation?—with the tale later
told by Louise, a young Frenchwoman who looked like she had
stepped from Botticelli's *The Birth of Venus*, albeit in skin-tight
blue jeans and a low-cut T-shirt, with whom he used to go out
now and then for coffee *à la turque*. As aware of the fascination
engendered by her mere appearance in public as she is disin-
clined to judge by appearances; how endearing to hear her pro-
claim, no doubt in full knowledge of the facts: "*Alors, les filles
sont des salopes et les mecs des cons; dès que tu as compris ça, tu as
tout compris!*"[148] She had had an affair with a musician, "*aussi
barbu et chevelu que toi.*"[149] Usually, they met in his small studio in Marais, where she would stay until late. On the evening
when she dumped him—"*assez tôt pour prendre le temps de flâner
dans le Marais avant d'attraper le dernier bus*"—they hadn't made
love, but "*une fois dans le bus, il suffisait de me lover sur moi même
pour prolonger la nuit et retrouver son parfum, celui de l'amour
physique, celui des rendez-vous tardifs, des heures a se préparer, des
dessous choisis, des huiles parfumées qui se fondent dans la peau.
mon odeur elle-même semblait s'être effacée devant la sienne, comme
pour laisser la place à un parfum qui nous ressemble, qui ressemble à
nos baiser, à nos sexes, qui enveloppe les draps, les vêtements, qui me
suit encore bien après l'avoir quitté. . .*"[150] And in both the one case
and the other, what the girl desired/feared and did not happen is

---

[148] So, girls are trollops and guys are bastards; once you understand that, you understand
everything.

[149] As beardy and long-haired as you

[150] Once, on the bus, I only had to coil up around myself in order to prolong the night
and rediscover its scent, that of physical love, of late encounters, of hours getting ready,
of select underwear, of scented oils that melt into the skin. My very odor seemed to have
effaced itself, as if to make way for a scent that resembled us, that resembled us kissing, our
sexes, that enveloped the sheets, our clothes, that still follows me long after possessing it

experienced *at the highest fiction* as if it had occurred like the poet says: "I don't have proof, but I remember" . . .).

Barely had he emerged from the staircase than the noise of a breaking window was heard high up, as if somebody had jumped from an upper floor. But nobody, nothing fell to earth, not even shards. The air fractured, however, like a blue bird hitting a windscreen. "Bianca!" Twenty flights of stairs at a run. The door to her apartment crashes open, hits the wall (she hadn't locked it when he left). In the one-room apartment, no sign of life; nothing but rumpled women's clothing on the floor and a ripped pillow case. He looked everywhere at once, without being able to focus on anything. Finally, he looked out of the window. Only the pane of glass separates him from the clear sky. The steam on the pane. On closer examination, the steam proves to be the outline of an angel, viewed from behind, life size, its wings folded behind its shoulders, casting a final glance—"Bianca's eyes!"—at the world it leaves behind *à jamais*. As if calling him. "Come, right now!"

Editor's note: Reading years later the typescript of *The Decamiron*, I was astonished to find that the second copy of the text was *Four-handed Writing*. But at the same time, holding the carbon copy up to the light, I was able to pick out very clearly the poem *A book knew not* . . .

Cenotaph

"A book knew not what only the signa-
    ture had learned to do"

"through the power of abstraction, walking
    among graves and crosses, to elevate the
    cemetery to the schema
of a sentence with subordinate clauses of
    time place mode cause etc., smiled the
    professor
of syntax, solely that he might pour the
    old wise language into the schema thereby
obtained. but you my pupil how do you
    establish relations of co-ordination
    and subordination?"

ever since I was a student I've known by
    heart the central cemetery all its sub-
ordinate clauses: the temporal clause by
    the gate (the plot for Russian soldiers
    fallen in the first
world war) the causal clause crammed along
    one edge (the very many young children
who died in the '46-'47 famine) and con-
    cessive clauses (graves with the star
    of Moses

unfurled on the arms of Christ's cross).
    I used to go to the
cemetery with the comforting feeling that
    I was making an unannounced visit to
joseph grand (more than just a character
    to me). and the same regret
at not finding him at home even if every
    time he left me his message on display—
    the sentence in its final

(as it were) edit. I think I've read it
  in hundreds of ways: the little dog of
  the earth
trotting along paths now in bloom now
  having shed their leaves always came to
  greet me
one day I was attending the funeral of a
  confrere when I heard sounds (like the
  voice)
of emil cioran in *exercises in admira-*
  tion): "I deleted

the adjectives." "dig more deeply into the
  word," grinned the professor of mor-
phology who doubled as a gravedigger, with
  a set of shovels additional to
requirements solely that the meaning buried in the word might remain
impenetrable to rain and rabble as long
  as possible. but you

my apprentice today when you raise the
  word to your ear and shake it like
a matchbox how many meanings can you pick
  out in its sepulchral silence?
from up on the edge of the grave when I
  gazed down on it for the last time
I saw beauty poured into new/soft female
  molds and I saw them sink into the earth
  that

(*the green ivy leaf* slipped between the
  pages of the old family bible to dry
  and which
avenging itself enters the holy writ penetrates the letter of the law reading
at random *genesis and apocalypse exodus*

and proverbs ecclesiastes and acts
until it comes to *song of songs* until it
  makes its bed in verse 5:3
            "I have put off my coat . . .")

they might advertise the open-topped grave
  perfect for honeymoon travel
I saw the void disinhabited by it the same
  as the void supposedly dislocated
in the pluperfect by an infinitive I saw
  myself years later given the burial rite
  by
bustuariae in the syntaxine chapel and I
  know my place in the sentence/in the
  schema
                    after all hadn't I seen

how on the 31st of the VIIIth A.D. MCMXCIV
  ma gra(nde-)mère emilia from whose dying
  mouth
a saint popped out who doubled as a docent
  teacher of phonetics. he said nothing,
  read
poetry. he placed a stick of chalk in
  grandma's fingers and her hand like a
  little girl's at
her first writing lesson led her from left
  to right

over my name signing herself: n

Cap. 8
Four-handed writing

The tone: *". . . he will know the diapason and dysdiapason of each voice in its rising above rising and in its falling below falling; he will see in what way are voiced the heavenly sayings and those that require rising and how are voiced the earthly sayings and those that require falling . . ."*

Anton Pann

THE VILLAGE CEMETERY silently falling back like a seesaw from which somebody has just jumped, the emptiness in the stomach spreading throughout the lone body that has reached the dead point of the curve before reabsorbing it, shout and all, in the gyre yawning somewhere beneath the clavicle, the Boeing 747 taking off in the endless night with a few hundred souls on board, including, not least, the author *without whom not one of the things that have been made would have been made* listening to *Stairway to Heaven* through his headphones as performed by a Viennese orchestra, all this linked together along the melodic line of the sentence that *eternally stretches*—the dreamed body of the Bodiless Beauty rocks absently in the silken hammock of the syntax—toward a prose that demands to be read not only with the retina but also with the diaphragm. *À haute voix.* ". . . it's like an angel just popped out of your mouth," the photographer told him all that time ago. He had been hired to take a photograph of the entire family to mark his father's coming home on leave from the naval air force. "Fend him from the evil eye . . ." he added heartily, but too late. It sickened him appallingly, that image of the angel popping out of his mouth covered in blood and spittle, like a kitten or a puppy being born, or at best a chick—although he would have preferred an angel from the womb rather than the egg—, upon which image was later to be superposed a curse he heard on a city street: a woman cursing her pregnant underage daughter: "I hope you give birth through your gob!" His face blanched, he ran inside the house, to the mirror—an old mirror from the time of Tsar Nicholas, framed in darkened wood and bearing on its lower side three identical German stamps: Rohgewich 35g GUMPENDORFER Rogewich 35g, a mirror with a daguerreotype sheen, passed down, in the absence of any photograph of his great-grandmother, on his mother's side from generation to generation and which years later would be inherited by his daughter, since his mother had borne only boys—, to look at himself. He studied himself carefully, probably for the first time ever, he even stuck out his tongue, like at the doctor's, took a deep breath, exhaled. A slight mist covered his reflected image, but then swiftly dissolved. There wasn't any trace of an angel on his face! From the mamas' mirror—both his mama and his grandma were "Mama"—an unfamiliar little boy stared at him, dressed up like a doll to have his picture taken, from whom he took his leave casting a final complicit glance over his shoulder. The photographer was calling for him. The photograph with finely serrated edges, as was the fashion in the sixties, shows a boy in no way different from any other; the only thing that makes me think that the angelic being was I, the author, is the presence within the frame of the black chick with droppings clinging to its tail that had shadowed him everywhere that summer until one day it vanished without trace, as if the earth had swallowed it up. It, which is to say, he—that's how you go up and down on the seesaw of personal pronouns until you forget yourself—, the 'I' of the day of his first appearance in a photograph was to take only the first step on that journey against the clock to the end of the world before withdrawing—"I do not dare to move forward by a *kun*[151] / rather I prefer to withdraw by a *ki*[152] "—in the terrifying face of the Unknown.

The angel will have been two thirds presumptive mood and just one third indicative mood, but even then, mostly in the imperfect or future tense; in the present, where the vacant gazes of four solitary men intersect, forming a viewpoint favorable to contemplation, it appears as if out of the blue, showing itself only to the latter—it involuntarily betrays its origin, *angelus*, situating itself at the end of the sentence like the Latin verb—, who, obviously, does not believe his eyes. It is not given to anybody to see it at rest, and for the angel in its pure state, an apocryphal grammar, attributed to Jakob[son], puts forward the infinitive of the verb, *manifestare*. Another "critique of language," *Tractatus logico-philosophicus*, whose author is too well known for us to mention him in a text already overpopulated with absences, captures it, without explicitly naming it (although sentence 6.54—"My propositions are elucidatory in this way: he who understands me finally recognizes them as senseless, when he has climbed out through them, on them, over them. (He must so to speak throw away the ladder, after he has climbed up on it.) He must surmount these propositions; then he sees the world rightly"—seems to signal its blatant absence), in proposition 6.522—"There are things that cannot be put into worlds. This makes itself *manifest* . . ."—, only to elude the final proposition, 7: "Whereof one cannot speak, thereof one must be silent." The rest of the texts pass over him in silence—with the exception of the celestial sayings that deal with none but him—, the same as a career soldier, after climbing the ranks from private to general, is put in the reserve. His absence hangs in the air, like a raincoat in the cloakroom of the N. K. Krupskaya Library, Ch—ău 1984 (or '85 or '86—it was still *1984!*), a raincoat of which only the fob remains. The plastic fob from the library cloakroom, inscribed with an unlucky 13, and now serving as a keyring can be found in the right jeans pocket of the passenger next to the

---

[151] Chinese unit of measurement equivalent to 3.3cm

[152] Chinese unit of measurement equivalent to 33.3cm

porthole marked "Emergency exit", the author in person, far too absorbed in the strains of the Viennese orchestra—*Stairway to Heaven* lowers him into the phonothèque of that very same national library, named after Lenin's wife, where for the first time in his life he wore stereo headphones, imagining, to the music of Wagner, that he was piloting a supersonic Airbus with all the writers he had read on board—to realize that he has been lured into a trap laid by his own hand, in writing, when he recorded in his travel diary the sentence that he had thought of while still on the ground: "The angel had eyes set wide apart, like two airports separated by eight time zones, so that if you took off from point A at 12:00, let's say, and flew for eight hours, you would land at point B at the same time, 12:00, on the same day, thereby saving eight hours with which to pay your return journey." It didn't fit the present trip, whose angel made himself manifest in profile and askance, like a deviated meridian, Paris—Antananarivo, but on the other hand, it fit like a glove, albeit worn inside out, if not on the wrong hand, with the journey of more than a decade ago, Ch—ău—Moscow—Petropavlovsk-Kamchatski. An inverted symmetry, the symmetry of the figures on playing cards, united these two journeys within a single unwritten book, a book in the infinitive.

To change from a Boeing 747 to an IL 82 in midair, albeit imaginarily and only in order to recapture the atmosphere of that precipitous winter of his fall, is like jumping from a thorough-bred woman-in-heat to a feminist who is puritanical and frigid to boot. He was in the air for a good few hours—he'd taken another plane in Moscow, from Domodedovo, after not being able to land in Vnukovo because of a snowstorm—; he had been flying over the polar circle when a huge black iris pressed up against the porthole that looked out on the white immensity of the icecap, peering at him as if through a pince-nez. He immediately recognized that look from the airport in Ch—ău: *he* casting a glance over his shoulder and thereby causing her to appear out of the crowd; *she* rushing to his breast as if fired from a catapult, hitting him with the glacial air of a woman abandoned and thrusting into his hands, without providing any explanation, a cellophane package with something soft inside, like some furry life-form. Before vanishing as quickly as she had appeared, she yanked off her fur hat with a theatrical gesture. Her head was shaved—the year was 1986, in the whole of the Soviet Union only convicts and conscripts walked around like that, and even then not willingly. Given how lacking in initiative she had proven to be, at least when it came to him, since they met each other, her gesture left him speechless: could this be the same woman who, after finishing her tenth year at school, had travelled from Odessa to Ch—ău on the overnight sleeper train, to hand in her university application, with a thermometer still in her armpit—because nobody at home had asked her to extract it after her mother insisted on taking her temperature, caught up in the fever of getting her ready for the journey as they were—, without breaking it. "Not only will she not spread her legs, but she won't even lift her arms from her sides," was his first, not at all decent thought on hearing the story. "You won't break her on the first or even second try!" But what he asked her was something completely different: "And what was your temperature when you arrived?" "36.6°C." Now, on his departure, the girl had put a bag of quicksilver in his hand. "Here I am!" The iris filled the porthole; as the airplane banked suddenly, through its crystalline lens, sensitive to the stripe-like play of light and shadow, the night passed in the blink of an eye. It was only after he pulled down the plastic blind that he looked around to see whether anybody was watching him and slipped his hand inside the cellophane package; her raven-feather black hair, with its bluish iridescence, still warm, reacted to the familiar touch, let itself be stroked, curling around his fingers and glinting in all the hues of the aurora borealis, then suddenly, as if somebody had turned off the electricity, it was extinguished. He would have preferred the instant death that lay hidden for Cleopatra in a basket of vipers. The darkness seeped under his fingernails into his writing hand, envenoming his life and handwriting; even in his most nondescript gestures an infinite disgust was to be read, a repulsion and an exhaustion that only irrevocable loss can lend you. The stewardess served lunch. Cold, obviously. He masticated in disgust—every food item tasted of paper written on and then crumpled up; it was probably in exactly the same mood that Flaubert swallowed rat poison, before making poor Emma Bovary do the same, but at least he came out of it with a line that has gone down in every anthology of world literature. He didn't require arsenic; on his tongue, the body of the night before, a body with a bitter name, was dying, convulsed with chills, burning with a fever, writhing in the toils of labor before giving birth to "a hedgehog" (her words), because she was unable to have children or imagined she wouldn't be able to: a little more imagination and he will feel her cadaverous poison seeping into his bodily tissues. And he imagined her dead, *already dead*, whenever their relationship came to an impasse; as long as he had not penetrated the mystery of her corporeality, the game sooner had a cathartic function—absolved, she was all the more desirable—, but since once cannot die at peace before falling into sin—and she fell! they fell!—, the vision of her martyrdom struck him with the concreteness of its details: the soles of a girl who'd grown up on a grazing field, with strong toes, as if harnessed to walking, the elongated ankles of a model (Modigliani comes to the lips, not just because of the phonetic similarity . . .), thighs generously arched to support the Grail of the well-buffed posterior, you'd call it flawless were it not for the precipitous fissure of the sex which in turn casts you, *de profundis*, a glance of seething magma welling from the abyssal gulf and about to burst its banks, the pubic triangle, the calligraphy of the crinkly hair suggestive of a haiku placed in the middle of a blank page, the belly button like a well in the vastness of a desert of shifting dunes, the breasts, "duplicates of the buttocks adapted to a frontal coital position," the throat and—new paragraph . . . Spanish mystic Colomba da Rieti, the object of his erotic fantasies—he recognized himself in one of the members of the gang of rapists who, attacking the maiden on Friday, August 22, 1488, ". . . began by tearing her clothes off, pausing only for a moment when they heard a jingle that might have been coins in her pocket, but which proved to be the sound made her crucifix knocking against its flagellum . . ." (long pause to catch his breath) and: "They continued to rip off her clothing, baring her until they came to the iron belt, three fingers wide, with which she mortified her bare hips, the cilicium and the two nail-studded iron chains tied around her neck and over her breasts"—he beat a retreat from this real as well as naked body, of *tertium genus* (the Christian mystics placed virgins between humans and angels), giving himself to her in the very moment when he was about to turn his back on her. The world of abstract ideas, swallowed whole from books and placed end to end with the painstakingness of a lover of systems, abruptly crumbled like an iconostasis struck full force by the unbelief of the congregants, it was enough for her merely to ask him, no! to command him—he was cack-handed around women—, in a peremptory voice: "Undress me!"

"Don't be afraid, it's me who's afraid for you!" a voice said in his left ear, coming from the porthole, barely perceptible, more like a breath of air—they were flying above the Frozen Ocean of the North, when the IL hit a magnetic storm, like it says in the poem, "Lightning bolts passed through our hair / Thunderbolts crashed behind our necks," which, *mutatis mutandis*, could only be an anonymous e-mail to him: "The girls were crying for help / But the boys weren't any braver / I the youngest started yelling at them / Stop all your sniveling / It's easy for you to die / You've fucked everybody already // But how can I die now"[153]—, he had only to believe that the owner of the voice would show himself. The passenger, as was obvious from a mile away, was one of those people who dream of flying, the sound of the alarm clock or the buzzing of his phone in the morning interrupts him when he is already in space, at one with it, in free fall or gliding over an earth now concave, now convex, on which he can no longer gain a footing. In their day-to-day lives, such people have a springing step, as if they're in a hurry, and even when they're forced to stand still, their bodies carry on striding in their minds, as if they were inside a wheel, acting as its motive force. If you let them, each and every one of them would be capable of lugging their own lifeless bodies to the grave; anyway, doesn't the final journey still begin underfoot? Ultimately, they're no longer people, but

---

[153] From Vasko Popa's poem *The Upper School of Love*, which evokes Emil Cioran.

functions; once substantives, now they're adjectives, passing—on
the street, in vehicles—passengers. With infinite regret, a mixture
of compassion and cruelty, the angel weighed him with his eyes—
he glanced at the others, in numerical order, corpses in a Moscow
hangar, a total head count of 280; a mere statistic—; the man was
two thirds respiration and only a third of him good to die—you
wouldn't have had anything to bury. It was this final third that
he had in his care, but good God! how many fears and abyssal
urges had accumulated in that bunch of bones in the space of
just twenty-two years. But the angel and the passenger did not
have any fears in common, which made communication between
them almost impossible. No matter how hard it would have been
for him to admit it, the angel had a terrible, even pathological,
fear of heights. Whether that fear was atavistic, an ancient fear
of falling, or whether it was a recent genetic mutation—given
the air pollution nowadays, anything is possible—, is anybody's
guess. He felt his legs give way under him merely at the thought
that "God made the firmament and divided the waters which
were under the firmament from the waters which were above the
firmament." To him, the favorite of the grammarians in the first
centuries A.D., who felt dizzy even when moving from one line
to another within the plane of a sheet of paper, had fallen the
"lofty mission" of looking down from above, when constitution-
ally he was unable even to look up from down below. But he was
fascinated by the line of the horizon, whose taut rope he skipped
in his imagination whenever his celestial nature felt a primordial nostalgia. Folk remedies, hypnotism, physiotherapy, fasting,
nothing helped him. At the moment of take-off, he felt an emptiness in his stomach, which at first was no larger than the hole at
the narrow end of a funnel. The emptiness swelled as the plane
gained height (he said "gained height" the way you might say
"gained solidity"). At 28,000 feet altitude, a mass grave opened
up beneath his clavicle, into which he implacably plunged with
every three hundred feet in height that the airplane gained. His
fear took over the whole airplane, it seeped into the fuel tanks,
took control of the navigation instruments, pumped kerosene
into the engines, spewed exhaust fumes, shared out paper bags

to people feeling sick, et cetera. Even the food tasted like tainted carrion. He was no longer himself: his arms, held wing-like, had turned numb, the soles of his feet had frozen, shod in the undercarriage, the fact that the passengers were wandering up and down inside the plane like they couldn't give a shit turned his stomach, the aloof expressions on the faces of the pilots in the cockpit rang in his ears, the air corridor along which he was stretching from one end to the other seemed to him a wormhole, from which there was no escape. He consoled himself with the thought that even Aurel Vlaicu[154] was afraid of being high up in the sky; his contemporaries remember how "after he bid his friends farewell (and he did so a number of times one afternoon, since he made a number of flights), he would shake hands with those who were comradely watching his flights, bid them farewell, and then take out a hip flask and gulp down two or three slugs of raki." An angel was flying in an airplane, in a cruel frost that seeped even into the cabin. He had lost a passenger on the ground, in the waiting room of Domodedovo Airport. Heart attack. In flight, a woman gave birth. Nature abhors a vacuum. The birth had been preceded by a change in the air—how right Augustine was: "*Inter urinam et faeces nascimur*"[155]—, as if the angel had shat himself in fear. Then a fine mist of alcohol—the time is 1986, Gorbachev had banned alcoholic beverages in a nation that had never woken from its drunken stupor; but even so . . . —enveloped the young woman in labor, creating a small olfactory oasis. Lest his head start to turn—the angel doesn't have an autopilot; it's well known that it's his fear that keeps the plane aloft—, he peeked over the shoulder of his passenger, who was reading, detached from the surrounding hubbub: "It's better to stand than to walk, to sit than to stand, to lie down than to sit, to sleep than to lie down, to die than to sleep, not to be born than to die." A transparent air of pure alcohol, now fringed with heavy tassels of blood, descended over the expectant people; the woman roared and gave birth. Further bottles were unstoppered, vodka

---

[154] Aurel Vlaicu (1882-1913), Romanian aviation pioneer — *Translator's note*

[155] We are born between shit and piss

and even champagne, to celebrate the event (we owe every event to the daughters of Eve, do we not?)—saturated with alcohol, the air tasted of "Кровавая Мэри"(Bloody Mary); via the stewardess, the captain sent his "Pilot" wristwatch as a gift to the newly born babe, but then, not being able to wait to land, he appeared in person (a dead ringer for Vasile Botnaru, the Radio Free Europe Kishinev journalist, whose bird/crotch symbol is still waiting for its own airline—why not the Avia Maria State Airline, with the prima donna of the National Opera as its sex symbol? . . .);

all the while the passengers were calling out girls' names, finally voting for Angelina; in all the commotion, God/the devil knows whether anybody could hear the choked voice of the volunteer midwife: "I can't stop her bl[eeding . . .]?"

"Bloody Mary" puts him back on board a Boeing 747, Paris—Antananarivo, but only to lure him into a descent into time, inversely proportional to the height from which he contemplates the Sahara Desert, maybe this time at least he will manage to achieve, in his yo-yoing between heaven and earth, that primordial state of repose, standstill, the place where still . . .

He was to be found at Nadyusha, alias "N. K. Krupskaya", the only public space in the Ch—ău of those years where you could fill out a form in Romanian—in the "Foreign Literature" room, true—, without running the risk of being branded a nationalist to your face. He felt like he was in the bosom of God (granted, he would have preferred the bosom of an antique goddess, an Aphrodite or a Venus, the same thing . . .); he even had his own table, a table's distance from the Freak—as he mentally labelled the misshapen lump suffering from the bulimia of reading, who never unglued his eyes from his book, or rather his book from his jam-jar spectacles—, which was the first in the corner to the right of the room. In the morning, he arrived at the same time as the librarians—sometimes, he would even be waiting for them at the entrance to open the doors—; closing time always took him by surprise. Immersed in his reading, he deliberately turned his back on the world outside; only when he felt his backbone was like a horseshoe did he know that, whatever they might say, he had a feeling for the spine. Reading (as his Grandmother used to say: "Why so much reading and reading?") was the ideal form of escape from a world that changed its slogans at the speed at which general secretaries of the CPSU died—three in less than four years; the loose-tongued used to joke that they were going to get themselves season tickets to Red Square, so they could listen to Chopin and Verdi in the open air to their hearts' content during the grandiose funerals—; invariably there would remain nothing but the closing words of the official announcements: "The Soviet people has closed ranks even more tightly around the Communist Party and Central Committee . . .," but it was still the Soviet people who suffocated. Perestroika had barely managed to open the window a crack, and even that was small and barred. It's no wonder that he lived vicariously; it was enough for him to come across a sentence of the following sort: "I then surmised what I was to sense much later: you have no right to open a book unless you undertake to read them all," for him to adopt it immediately, transcribing it in his own way: you have no right to write a book unless you have read them all—because you have to be able still to write books after you have read "them all." Which nonetheless didn't stop him from publishing a slim volume of poetry in the "Debut" series—"Le Rebut," as he called it, with reference to himself—, a copy of which had lately entered the library. *Vien dietro a me, e lascia dir le genti*,[156] as it were.

It was the winter of eighty-five/eighty-six, and what a winter! He would come to the "N. K. Krupskaya" through the snowdrifts—knackered boots, a corduroy suit with worn knees and elbows, a bright red sweater clinging to his shivering body, haggard with insomnia, so thin you could almost see through him—, to "read up" and become a real "library mouse". He said it with bitter irony, for whoever was able to read between the

---

[156] Follow me and let the people talk (Dante, *Purgatorio*, V, 13)

lines, since the library was as full of holes (missing authors and titles, and tomes so lacking in substance they might as well have been holes) as a Swiss cheese. Here he was in his element of not being anywhere but also everywhere at once. He was working on writing a "metaphysical" poem (never was he to write it!) meant to express his "explorations"—he had discovered the dimension of faith, realizing straightaway how unprepared he was for such a discovery; like He Who said: "When he believes he does not believe he believes, and when he does not believe he does not believe he does not believe"—; lest he lose track of it, he wrote it down in a diary, in the form of:

Model-lecture on belief

Once, the angel Gabriel—to Catholics, the messenger of God; to Muslims, the "peacock of heaven" and guardian of the divine revelations—appeared to the Pope (or the Caliph; the Rabbi isn't part of the equation, because his relationship with Yahve is direct, from God to chosen people, with no middlemen) to impart to him the important news: on the night of December 21-22, God would send him a prophetic dream. He gave him detailed instructions on what to do in the meantime, and then faded away. The Pope (or Caliph) did exactly what the angel said, but on the night of the winter solstice, as fate would have it, he couldn't sleep a wink. He did not fall asleep till morning. Meanwhile, elsewhere, the worst sinner woke up with the feeling that he had dreamed something forbidden, something unspeakably . . . "In my dream, I was . . ." he starts to tell his wife (or concubine), but she turns over in bed, uninterested. Meanwhile, the Pope (or Caliph) jumps out of bed in alarm—somebody else has dreamed his dream! First of all, he decides not to reveal his loss to anybody, but saying his morning prayer (*namaz*), for the first time ever he senses that he is not heard up there, on high. He then sends spies to all four corners of the world, to apprehend the miscreant who, more than certainly, will not have been able to hold his tongue. But since the poor culprit is terrified and illiterate besides, he is unable to read in the book what was revealed to him in the dream, and so, the spies come back with nothing. Depressed, the Pope (or Caliph) raises his eyes to heaven.

His (im)patience having run out, God looks down to Earth in search of the lost dream, examining the right-believers as they unsuspectingly pray to Him, morning and evening (five times a day), or whenever they thank God for the things that they have done themselves. He also examines those who blaspheme Him or take His name in vain. Not one trace of the dream. He then sends down to earth legions of angels and, hot on their heels, His secret police, the devils. And so it is that at every believer's bedside, an angel and a devil meet. But so what?

Instructed by God, the Pope (Caliph) tells his spies how to look a man straight in the eye, piercing him with their gaze, in order to detect the fugitive dream. Anyone suspicious is arrested: the sleepless with bags under their eyes as big as double sheets hung out to dry and those glutted with sleep. They are questioned under torture and in the confessional for the desired information. Under the red-hot iron or the leather lash, they are prepared to say anything, you only have to hint at what you expect of them. Since it is out of the question to be hauled before the Pope (or Caliph) to recount what you dreamed last night! Out of the blue, a kind of contest of false statements begins; equally sick of the howls of the apostates and the ecstasy of the apocalyptic martyrs, the Pope (or Caliph) tries to change the rules of the game, channeling their confessions in the desired direction. From the thousands and thousands of storytellers he therefore selects the best twelve, without any of them having an inkling as to the existence of the other eleven, whom he sends out into the wide world, giving his blessing to their apostleship. He wagers on the fact that the real dreamer will quickly be exposed when he keeps his priceless hidden treasure to himself, but our man understands nothing of the two-bit annunciations of all these peripatetic preachers, accompanied by wretched scribes who set down procès-verbaux of every plenary meeting. When the paths of two or more such "apostles" happen to cross, they fall to quarrelling, smear each other with the first insults that come to their mouths, their followers clash, cudgel each other. Shameless! The people gather around, like at the fair, but only a few wretches follow them. The ancestral religion is under threat from every side, blood and ink gush (it's not apparent which is the affluent of which). But then

God Himself intervenes, *ex machina*, to restore a little order. He officially appoints four bookmen to summarize the host of apocryphal "gospels", reducing them to a common denominator. They set to work, each in his cell, isolated from the world and from God, and finally four completely autonomous books see the light of day, in which the similarities merely highlight the differences between the irreconcilable texts. Disgusted at so much quarrelling, God gives His blessing to all four.

"What are you reading?" the woman mockingly asks our man, who has taken more and more to staring into space. Her words induce great disquiet in him, but also great pleasure. In secret, he has started learning to read—the dream, as he remembers all too well, was revealed to him *in writing*—, using one of the four authorized gospels, obviously. At first, he reads letter by letter without understanding anything, until one day the letters adhere together in a familiar-looking way to become syllables, the syllables cohere into words, the words into phrases, the phrases into sentences. The alien text reveals itself to him in all its splendor. "It can't be true!" the man cries out in his heart. "*It so happened that . . .*" He immediately sets about making a clean copy of the dream, but his eyes, accustomed to the canonical text of one of the four gospels, cannot distinguish the revealed text from that composed by another's hand. The sentences therefore interlayer, the dreamed with the undreamed, from their conjunction are born small hybrid monsters he is unable to get rid of. In the end, he recognizes neither the gospel nor the dream. As a last resort, he decides to give up writing, which is not at all easy for somebody addicted to the pleasure of the text. Only after he forgets the alphabet and puts all the books on the fire (or rather the one book—the book of books) does the dream reappear, this time as if through a mist.

Unredeemed, the Pope (or Caliph) wasted away in his palace, poisoned by the loss of what, although predestined to him and him alone, never belonged to him. He tried everything in his power (and as the Lord Above sees, his power was boundless within his bounds): he hypnotized his flock or stopped them sleeping, depending on the times, but never did he dream with his own eyes. At the bedside of the Pope (or Caliph), four bookmen read to him in turn passages from the four canonical gospels, each from his own version. "I believe not!" said the Pope (or Caliph) with his dying breath.

On his deathbed, our hero calls a confessor to shrive him. One of the Pope's (or Caliph's) spies, long since ordained a priest, with the four gospels tucked under his arm, comes and hears the dying man without believing a word: how many such wretches has he mutilated with his own hands, enlightened men, men with book learning, poets, philosophers! But since the man does not beg absolution for his sins, the confessor gives him it anyway—why wouldn't he?—adding, just for the sake of it: "Thou shalt not steal!" and then hurries off to the next deathbed. In this part of the world, the plague is raging—a divine scourge. But our hero does not die of the plague, rather he dies of God's absence. Before he closes his eyes, the dream reveals itself to him one last time: its face distorted, haggard, looking more like a nightmare than a divine revelation, when he chides the man, not for what he has done so much as for what he has left undone, it is as if all the devils are quarrelling in his gob. With a last effort, the dying man strangles it, puts it out of its misery, and then goes to the Last Judgement with his soul at peace. He walks and he walks, until he reaches the crossroads between Heaven and Hell, which are separated by a wall the height of a man, known as the Weeping Wall. Not a peep. His face to the wall, God is fast asleep.

The farther the poem progressed, the more the ineffable part, standing aloof before the pre-eminence of the word, became an increasingly powerful entity unto itself. The verses merely high-lighted the blank spaces between the lines, the rhymes and pros-ody emphasized the absolute perfection of the silence, the whole existed only as a (formal) part of nothing. He ended up com-posing an unwritten poem with the intensity of those Buddhist monks who, at the end of the initiation process, are given the final and most difficult test: to meditate on the non-existence of the Buddha. In writing, the poem slipped between the lines the same as daylight seeping through the blades of drawn blinds— the main thing was to make room for *nothing*. The dialectic of plenum and vacuum opened up before him—"In the full lies concealed profit, / in the empty lies concealed use"—, he merely had to believe in the power of his hands. When he intuited that which was later to be revealed to him, at the end of a cycle of twelve years from the publication of the first book, namely: in the relationship with transcendence, the written page will always function as the screen of a confessional—you confess without being sure that somebody is listening to you on the other side; you forgive while absent, without knowing the person you have just shriven, until one day unseen hands, hands of silence, abruptly pull down the blinds. "My face is nothing but a grater that has completely grated away the face of God." But the blank page provoked in him a dreadful disquiet, the disquiet of a man raised under the open sky, who suddenly finds himself beneath a ceiling not supported by any wall.

Her appearance in the doorway of the reading room—as he sat at his table, he sensed the door open, but in a different way, as if for the first time; he ought not to have looked over his shoulder, a gesture that ever since Orpheus has brought nothing but irremediable loss—, no, it could not be her! she had refused to follow him whenever he had called her to him, but it was her! her appearance in the doorway of the reading room presaged nothing good. From the doorway, she cast him a glance, the way one might toss a homemade bomb at one's victim's legs, heedless of the surrounding crowd, in the name of an idea, and then she turned on her heel. He followed her. In the corridor, she gazed at him for a long moment—she had huge eyes, with heavy lids, like those of the Virgin Mary in Byzantine icons; when she suddenly opened her eyes wide in amazement, it was as if two twins were born simultaneously—, then she told him in a colorless voice, a voice *sine ira et studio*, you might say, since only a dead language can convey the utter indifference of that voice: "I hate you to death." It was a sunny day in late Febu-March; in the light of the library corridor, they seemed two prehistoric insects trapped in a huge block of amber, which she was slicing away from within, with her short, saw-like steps, as she went down the stairs. As he watched her in fascination—her passage from one landing to another, an enjambment in Eminescu's *Sonnets*—spring arrived. The falling of icicles . . . the melting of snow . . . the awakening of Mother Nature . . . He felt a hot flush. Nobody budged an inch when he went back inside the reading room—a door creaks differently when you open it every day—; barely had he taken two or three steps within than a huge chunk of ceiling came crashing down right on top of his desk. In that instant, every head—apart from the Freak's—jerked around, from his desk to him, who was no longer seated at it. He was laughing. A loud gurgling laugh, as if he had just heard a good joke. Since her departure—"Thou, eternally lost, eternally adored"—no more than a minute had elapsed. He cast a final glance at the "earthly remains" of the poem, now buried under a heap of plaster, along with his library books. Approximately two feet above the table, the angel Gabriel showed himself to him, sorrowful, frightened, his face contorted, but the young man was in too much of a hurry actually to see him. He had dashed out of the door, to catch up with her, even though he had no way of bringing her back. "Angelic protection," he heard behind him, without knowing to whom the voice referred. He shot past the cloakroom—he had no time to lose—; outside, he espied her not three hundred feet from the building he had just left. Standing stock-still, like Lot's wife, a pillar of salt, she was looking up at the windows of the third floor of the Foreign Literature Room, where . . . "What was that that fell?" she asked him. "The angel," he muttered, and then, to himself, "mine." By that evening, they were both to fall, each through the other. (In parenthesis let it be said that a man describes a past conquest only for the sake of a new conquest; as it were, he uses the body of the first woman as a *billet-doux* on all his subsequent loves, while remaining loyal to the first love. Like Him who said: "*J'ai jamais trompé ma femme et j'ai jamais trompé ma metresse.*"[157] It is enough to receive the text from his own hand and if you don't give it back to him before reading it, you have as good as entered the four-handed text.) Forgotten the anger of the previous day, when he had been hours late—he'd never been

---

[157] I have never cheated on my wife and I have never cheated on my mistress.

late before—, he had made a fool of himself in the only way a lover can: he hadn't been able to do anything to her. And this after the girl had placed up for grabs the priceless treasure of her virginity, before ever being brought to the altar and before he even asked for her hand in marriage. She suspected he had been with another woman, she even knew her name, that of a string instrument. (It was at a time when the line: "You can't take the man from another woman's mouth"[158] had not yet been written, a time even before he had become a man and she his woman.) It never even entered her head what he had been through (what corridors & offices) that day. But since the young man had just signed a piece of paper that required him not to divulge the content of the discussion, he avoided telling her that he had come straight from the Planetarium, alias the KGB, where, having been summoned by citation, he had spent the whole day, the longest in his life, questioned about everything under the sun, put in the crossfire, and no sooner had he recovered from the initial shock and intimidation—it wasn't the continuous crossfire questioning so much as the silent presence, in one corner of the room, of a grey-haired smoker ("Could it have been Pachkulya?"), who, unruffled, read a book without even casting them a glance, that kept him in checkmate throughout the discovery of "everything under the sun"—, than they told him that he would do well not to compromise his future with all kinds of nonsense typed up in four copies (the very word samizdat was banned), him of all people, who published in the press of the republic and the union, and that if he had not been his father's son, their discussion would have been very different. Fear gripped him by the balls and did not unclench its fingers the whole day; he hadn't signed anything but he still looked as if he had just sworn an oath of poverty, chastity and obedience. What he had no way of knowing was that they had they had demanded that the girl keep seeing him,—at which point the optimist in civilian clothes had given her a wink, as if to say he wasn't going to teach her how to go about it—otherwise she could kiss goodbye any thought

---

[158] Floarea Țuțuianu, *Leul Marcu* (The Lion Mark), Editura Aritmos, Bucharest, 2000

of getting a job in Ch—ău. And so it was that when they got into bed together, each had plenty to conceal from the other, even if both bent over backwards to appear natural. He had thought the two of them weren't a couple, but the next day, she burst into the library, the ceiling almost fell on his head, they went outside together, and so on and so forth, until they were to wash away with blood the shame of the botched first time. The night before his departure for Petropavlovsk-Kamchatski, he wrote in his diary: "I looked death in the eye: soaked by the melting snows of the last few days, the ceiling of the Foreign Literature Room—an enormous chunk of plaster in the corner of the room—crashed down on top of my table. I was a few feet away from the spot, and she had just flung in my face: 'I hate you to death,' for an instant I even pictured myself crushed under the mound of rubble, my brains smashed to a pulp . . . It was not to be. But if the falling ceiling had caught me at my post, I would have died like a bookman, on duty. Although it would hardly have been original: in January 1556, Homaym, the son of Babur and father of Akbar, died when he slipped and fell down the stairs of his Library in Delhi.

"(. . .)

"I saw her p[*iste d'atterrissage*] . . .!"[159]

He was flying inside fear that had materialized into aerodynamically shaped hard aluminum seating hundreds of passengers on an Air Madagascar flight with a name (Boeing 747) and number. On the screen in front, a tiny airplane overflew the globe— presently, the southern hemisphere—, thereby indicating the Boeing's position in space, air speed and altitude. It was like in the Ungaretti poem, "nel volo dall'altezza / di dodici chilometri vedere / puoi il tempo che s'imbianca e che diventa / una dolce mattina,"[160] from which he was about to parachute himself, for the third and last time—before that journey into the lower world

---

[159] *Piste d'atterrissage*—landing strip (French), but with a pun on the Romanian (and Russian) *pizda* (= *cunnus*) — *Translator's note*

[160] In flight at an altitude / of twelve kilometres you can / see time whitening and becoming / a sweet morning

came to an end—*una dolce mattina* of the beginning *n* years ago, when, asked for the umpteenth time what he wanted to be when he grew up, he didn't answer "a cosmonaut." The slight disappointment on the faces of those present—his father, an officer in the navy air force, was home on leave; it was his ears that his firstborn's "cosmonaut" ought to have regaled—was as nothing—easy to say nothing, but the lad was like an indoor plant, sensitive to the slightest change of air in the house—compared with the news of the death of Yuri Gagarin, announced that morning on the radio. The cosmonaut's crash pulled down with it a whole world of dreams—one of which recurred with unusual frequency: he would be gliding above the village, not very high up, but nor just above the blades of grass, he would recognize the houses and gardens, the graveyard coming downhill like a huge toboggan, at first he would not feel his own weight, but then, as he learned to control his amazement, he would pilot his little body with the skill of a Gagarin (who else!), until his grandmother woke him up to eat; he would not even get a chance to land . . .—, but also the grown-ups' world. They were left open-mouthed by his question, repeated twice so he himself could understand it the better: "But how can the earth fall?" Instead of answering, his father picked him up by the armpits and threw him in the air; the flight was as short as a fall. The arrival of the photographer in his grandparents' yard changed the course of that day. All of a sudden, everybody was in motion, some sprang up in doorways, others popped up in windows, things vanished as if swallowed up by the earth or at least didn't find their way into the hands of those searching for them. Left by himself with the photographer in front of the house, he wanted to repeat the question to him, but the prospect of being tossed up in the air once more, particularly after he had dreamed of flying the whole night, was not in the least bit tempting. He waited for the moment, ready to meet the challenge, which was not long in coming: "Do you know any poems by heart?" There was not a peasant in the whole of Moldova that did not ask the same question; he would hear it years later, addressed to his daughter by his peers, who had lived in the city for ten or fifteen years, and who were sick of

everything but literature. Why then did he give a start, as if
the mere amiability of the itinerant photographer touched his
unconfessed desire to "express something which, were it not for
him, would never have been spoken"? He paused briefly, long
enough for his heart to rise to his throat, and then, all in one
breath: "On land and in the air—sky, only sky." He didn't know
the rest; it hadn't come to him. The photographer looked at him
in satisfaction, thoughtfully even, choosing between "Bravo" and
"That-a-boy", but found himself uttering, without un-dissimu-
lated admiration: "Well I never! It's like an angel popped out of
your mouth." The lad turned white, ran away, and hid.

He had not slept for more than forty-eight hours, but even
so, he asked for a coffee—he was like a shirt soaked with instant
coffee—, the last. Beneath the slanting wing of the Boeing, as
large as the graveyard of his native village, Africa rose darkly into
the sky; in all his life he had never seen a firmament so dark. It
flew endlessly, transforming hours into miles in accordance with
the flight map. In front of the Boeing, space parted like the legs
of an interminable African woman who, swaying absently in the
celestial hammock, goaded you the more she rejected you and
rejected you the more you desired to possess her, naked, at her
ultimate root, that impenetrable *locus pessimus atque profundus* of
every origin. What eluded the physical gesture—he could feel the
Boeing between his legs (even on the ground he had remarked
the glans of the cockpit), as if he were afflicted with priapism,
unless his cultural memory had appropriated Kenzaburo Oe's
A Personal Experience, given how many hours of flying he must
have accumulated in his life: "Himiko had collapsed into orgasm
countless times, in the beginning at short intervals and then after
lengthier and lengthier pauses. Every time, Bird remembered the
sensation of launching a model airplane at evening, on the playing field of his primary school. Himiko rotated around the axis
of his body in ever wider circles, trembling and groaning against
the sky of her orgasm like a model airplane struggling under
the weight of an overly large engine. He then descended to the
landing strip once more, where Bird was waiting, and a period of
mute and stubborn repetition recommenced (. . .) Himiko was

still flying, gliding toward earth and then soaring back up, as if
in a dance, like a kite caught in an updraught"—was precisely
the absoluteness of the absence, which defines her whose genital
apparatus is defined by amateur anatomists as a "hollow penis".
He had learned the lesson by heart: as a rule, the man expresses
himself through the verb *to have*, the woman through the verb *to
be*; but since there exists no man in the pure state, and the same
goes for woman, more often than not they are auxiliary verbs to
each other (He *will have had*. She *will be*). More rarely to themselves: the man, in order to reinforce his sense of ownership (He
had); the woman, in order to affirm her surplus of being (She
is going to be). At the intersection of the male and the female,
in the divine proportion of one to three, the angel is born, *it
would have been about to be*. "A creature bewitched," thought the
author, with his eyes on the screen, where Africa showed itself
to him like an elephant facing the calf of Madagascar alongside
it, "I bear him aloft and he drags me down to earth. Diabolical!
. . ." Near him, he felt one of those absences more eloquent than
the most insistent presence; its nearness was betrayed by fingers
clenching the armrest of the chair alongside him, eyes staring
into space, beads of cold sweat . . . From head to toe, the angel
was an endless fear of heights, its plumb line, a divine marionette
hanging from the fingers of a drunk puppeteer in a fairground
performance about the creation of the world, the standard measure of the fall from *illo tempore* when "out of the ground the
Lord God formed every beast of the field and every fowl of the
air, and brought them unto Adam to see what he would call
them, and whatsoever Adam called every living creature, that
was the name thereof" (Genesis, 2, 19), and only he, the good-
for-nothing, knew not how to utter them before the Lord.

The sky retracted like the undercarriage beneath the wings
of the Boeing: the countdown began, 9—8—7 km . . ., the
passengers quickly fastened their safety belts without having to
be asked twice, the stewardesses burned the final fuel reserves
of their smiles, 6—5—4 . . . ; not long to go, at 3 he felt as if
somebody were covering his eyes—he peered through the transparent, slightly cupped palms the way you would look through

the seamstress's spectacles of your great-grandmother—, a voice out of nowhere asked him: "What do you see?" "Nothing." The hands glued themselves to his retinas like contact lenses: "And now?" "Darkness . . . pitch darkness." Painlessly, the way only light can penetrate, the hands slid into his eyes, up to the elbows, stretching into two rainbows, one white, the other black: "Not even now?" "I see . . . I see the fetus floating in the amniotic liquid like a cosmonaut in his capsule . . . It looks like me, the way I looked in a photograph a few weeks after I was born . . . It's breathing, smiling . . . All of a sudden, it's world fissures . . . He turns arse over tit, flips toward the widening breath . . . The hole sucks him into it with superhuman strength . . . The fetus is afraid, closes its eyes . . . The tunnel! . . . swift hands drag it outside, unknot the umbilical cord from around its neck, slap its body once, twice . . . a silent film . . . as if somebody has turned the sound off . . . and not waiting for him to announce his arrival in the world, the resigned voice of the midwife, as if in a hurry to wash her hands: *May he die sinless on this earth, may he be an angel in the kingdom of heaven.*" On his face he feels the face of the angel, contorted by animal fear, you would think it a freshly cast death mask were it not that it kept blinking, with the transparent hands joined together in prayer over his own hands, which he keeps raising to his eyes: "Who are you?" "I am you." "And I?" "You are you." "Then who was it who died at birth?" "It is unknown . . . sometimes I think they swapped us, immediately afterward, in the register of births." "And after that?" After that . . . it can be told only in blank verse:

can you have been that child? can yours have been the miracle?
you sit naked in the middle of the house. nobody pays you any
    mind. you are—still
an only child—like a milk tooth tied with string to a handle,
    with your eyes on the front
door, when suddenly somebody opens the door and—blit-
    zlicht—stands on the threshold.
a woman, against the light—the sun gilds her outline—, through
    whom

you foresee yourself, she bursts into tears for
no doctor was able to . . . "what am I supposed to do with two?!"
never have you suffered a worse fright. from that dreadful fright
    flows
self-consciousness, whacking you across the back of the head:
    the other is I!"

The passenger next to him steals a glance at him from the corner of his eye, then turns to him in half-profile and says, with the
same intonation with which Corin Braga must have whispered
in the ear of Sanda Cordoș: "Brace yourself, we're about to die,"
in September 1993, when their airplane wasn't able to land at
Roissy-Charles de Gaulle: "*Mais vous parlez tout seul, Monsieur!
On ne connaît aucun cas quand l'avion n'est pas revenu sur terre!*"[161]

The Boeing 747 landed at the end of the night, with a few
hundred souls on board, not least among them the author *without whom not one of those things created would have been created*,
up to his elbows, like a village midwife, in a text intended to be
read not with the retina so much as with the diaphragm—all in
one breath, the hollowness in the stomach spreading through
the body whose arc has reached dead center before being reab-
sorbed, cry and all, into the yawning vortex somewhere beneath
the clavicle.

---

[161] Speak for yourself, sir! There are no known cases of an airplane not having come back
to earth!

Cap. 9
Chaliapin's Darling

The tone: *"Il m'a fait lire du Proust, du Tolstoï et du Dostoïevski, déclara la malheureuse, avec un regard à vous fendre le cœur. Maintenant, qu'est-ce que je vais devenir?"*[162]

Romain Gary, *La Promesse de l'aube*

NONE OF THE children lurking behind the corner, at the other end of a sleeve-like archway, neither Felix, nor Joshua nor Miriam, could have imagined that by tossing a purse tied to a thread under the feet of the passers-by they were, in a (profane) way, repeating the gesture of observant Jews who hang multicolored threads from their girdles—a sign of religious observance; but even without displaying Jewishness (the threads; the money bag, albeit reduced to the size of a purse stuffed with loose change), it was obvious from a mile off that the courtyard at No. 61, Strada Armenească, right next to the central market—"ВО ДВОРЕ ТУАЛЕТА НЕТ!"[163] was inscribed by the entrance in large letters, for the benefit of those without; but not in the tenancy papers of those who dwelled within, in which it was clearly stated: "Удобства во дворе"[164]—was tenanted by

---

[162] "He made me read Proust, Tolstoy Dostoyevsky," declared the unfortunate girl, with a look to break your heard, "what is to become of me now?"

[163] NO TOILET IN THE COURTYARD!

[164] CONVENIENCE IN THE COURTYARD.

the seed of Israel. Even the fact of their being moved from a hostel for married couples at the edge of town to the historical center of the capital, where they occupied two small rooms, at the end of a corridor that also served as the communal kitchen, was thanks to a family of Jews that had chosen the path of exile, finally managing to emigrate to Israel. "Новенький хочешь играть с нами?"[165] asked the lurking children. He did not even have time to introduce himself, in the way his father had taught him: "Меня зовут…" (My name is). Without giving him time to reply, they said: "Гони монету!" (Give over a coin) The fact that the kid didn't immediately run away to complain to his parents made them like him; in any case, they had no intention of robbing him—they themselves had all chipped in to fill the purse, to make it more believable: at the end of the game, each would get his money back. "У тебя что, языка нет?"[166] But since he spoke Russian only in his head—without wishing to, as if a tape recorded all the sounds he heard over the course of the day—, and his eagerness to become part of their gang urged him to do it, he couldn't let them go without an answer: "Нельзя!" (Not allowed) It was the only word from the adults' speech that he had consciously retained, given its unusual frequency, whose sonority, that of a skillfully wielded ninja sword, captured your attention: "Нельзя!" Who knows how many generations had had to mouth it repeatedly before they forged it into a lethal weapon; the language itself seemed to have found its consummate expression in the slashed calling card—the film *Zorro* had just come out, and in the whole of the USSR there was not a single kid who, openly or in secret, had not attempted that sword stroke— of the foreign word: "Нельзя!" An explosion of laughter, like biting an overripe pomegranate without peeling it, splattering everybody with juice of *Punica granatum* and spittle, revealed a dozen front teeth, all of them bone, a sign that the milk period of childhood had come to an end. And they went back to playing their game—yanking passers-by with their piece of string—,

---

[165] Want to play with us, newcomer?

[166] Don't you have a tongue?

when a well-built man, perhaps a little corpulent for his age, came to a halt by the archway. He hesitated for a moment, to make sure nobody was looking, then bent down to pick up the purse. Which jerked away, vanishing as if by magic up the sleeve of darkness. Instead of continuing on his way, the man entered the yard, putting the little conjurors to flight, all except one lad, who seemed lost—the "Новенький"—and who did not budge, allowing himself to be grabbed by the ear and dragged home, without putting up the least resistance: "You made a fool of me!" The legitimate fury demanded immediate assuagement, in front of everybody: "Вы видели как он со мной поступил?"[167] His father spoke Russian not only in public (understandable, since his audience was mainly Russian-speaking) but also, above all, when he was furious (something that his family were at a loss to understand). Whenever he did so in the presence of his eight-year-old son, the latter knew that he was being berated as if the blood thudding in his ears translated the paternal dissatisfaction into words he could understand. There was no room for doubt in this respect. He merely had to discover what he had done wrong, and as quickly as possible, in order to beg forgiveness before his father could demonstratively stop talking. If he did not hasten to declare his *mea culpa*—couching it in the exact words the pater-familias wished to hear—, he ran the risk of days of detention. His father would turn his back on him, without speaking a single word. He addressed him only if there was an urgent need to do so, and then only obliquely, giving him orders via his mother—the apogee of humility—or younger brother. "Мальчик тут ни при чем . . ."[168] somebody interjected in his defense—but ha! but it was like pouring gas on the flames at the height of the conflagration—, which might charitably be translated: "Don't lay hands on the lad, don't hurt him . . ."; but this time the sacrificial lamb that was to take the place of the son became a scapegoat. "Put your nose in the slops and the pigs will eat you!" roared the father, in response to the stranger's unsolicited interjection? as

---

[167] Did you see *what* he did to me?

[168] The lad isn't guilty of anything . . .

a warning to his son?—it wasn't clear. The denouement would have occurred far from strangers' eyes, in the seclusion of the family home, had not a timid knock been heard on the door of apartment no. 16, thwarting the lesson about to be taught. In the doorway, two little boys and a slightly older girl—could they be the same ones from archway?—mumbled a kind of apology, probably forced to do so by a parent who had happened to witness the episode, insisting that "Мы ненарочно!";[169] a smile played across the man's face, as if to say, "Who has ever heard of a well-behaved child or a beautiful old woman?" But then, contorted with fury, the same face turned to his cornered son: "Which of them played the trick on me?" In the unbearably long silence, a fly could be heard agonizing in a spider's web; why do they let themselves get caught? Without waiting to be told to leave, the children had already turned on their heels when all of a sudden, the little girl planted herself in front of the man, who was increasingly impatient to resume teaching his son a lesson: "Нельзя обижать детей!"[170] Like tossing a grenade into a room before beating a hasty retreat . . . "Спорим, он его убьёт после этого!"[171] the little girl burst out laughing, once outside. "Кто пойдёт со мной подслушивать под древью?"[172] You could expect anything from Miriam—hadn't she been the one who had taught Felix to fasten his trousers on his bellybutton, so that the lad ended up with them around his ankles on the first attempt?—but nobody would have suspected her of such courage. With her heart in her throat, she climbed the wooden stairs—the way you would count the steps of the scaffold(ing of this text, to which she too has put her shoulder, has she not?). How long she was gone is hard to say. Hard too to say what exactly happened to her when, her ear pressed to the door, she made out a metallic tapping, coming in short bursts, which made her wet herself, but somehow differently, as if she had voided

---

[169] We didn't do it on purpose

[170] Hurting children isn't allowed!

[171] I bet he'll kill him after this!

[172] Who's going to come with me to listen at the door?

her innards. Instinctively, she put her hand between her legs, the searching fingers felt raspberry jam—it was blood. Hers. She stifled a scream by biting on her fist. When she returned, she was not the same girl. To the lads waiting for her outside, she merely remarked, over her shoulder: Somebody was typing inside.

The more Russian he learned—within four weeks, he had gone from being nicknamed *Мальчик-Нельзя* and *Писуля*[173] to being called by his name—, the more welcoming the court-yard became, expanding, overspilling its bounds into countless little bays hidden away from the eyes of the world, when they played hide-and-seek or tag, only to contract abruptly once he was called to come inside. He wasn't allowed to climb out of the marsupial pouch except to go to school and sometimes, after les-sons, to run errands to the shop; but the inner pockets, large and small, lined with moss or spiderwebs, streaked with silvery snail's trails, he could explore to his heart's content. There were places that smelled of armpit, others of homespun wool, sometimes, more seldom, of a shirt collar worn for a week without being taken off, and one hiding place—you could smell it from afar—that smelled of an incontinent old man's trouser flies. But after all, it was the ill-smelling places that were also the most fre-quented—first of all, because only a few of the tenants had indoor toilets, and secondly, because the bunkers where the fam-ilies stored their winter coal were situated around the latrine. Once every three or four weeks, a public health vehicle arrived to pump out the month's filth, at which times the whole court-yard stank of shit. Как в том анекдоте (Like in the joke): "Doctor, when I eat black caviar, I expel black caviar, when I eat red caviar, I expel red caviar. What should I do?" "Have you tried eating what everybody else eats?" It was a sight to be seen: the holy family walking in line—the children in front, the parents a few paces behind—, immediately after the nine o'clock news, to do their business at the bottom of the yard before bedtime, and his solo trips outside in the wee hours of the morning to empty his brother's chamber pot. It was an injustice that cried

---

[173] *Not-allowed Boy* and *Pisser*, but also *Writer's Son* (from *pisatel'skij synulja*).

to the heavens—he for one didn't get up in the middle of the night—, established as such with the tacit complicity of the whole family: if he hadn't taken it outside, nobody would have done it. The only time he rebelled, his revolt was crushed in the egg: "Today you can't be bothered to take F.'s chamber pot, tomorrow you'll refuse to bring me a cup of water." No doubt about it—his father knew how to make his wishes known in no uncertain terms. A pity that F., the younger, didn't obey or perhaps, who knows? that he, the first born, didn't rebel against his word. (The stick had two ends and didn't necessarily punish disobedience, but rather defiance of his word.) He thought nothing of trotting to the privy in broad daylight, holding a page ripped from an exercise book or newspaper, despite the blatant indecency of it, but his legs gave way under him whenever he had to cross the courtyard holding F.'s chamber pot: it was as if the contents hidden beneath the lid—that would have been all he needed, a lidless pot to display whether the younger's business was "wet or thick"!—were carrying him by a handle to the bottom of the yard; and nobody likes to be led by somebody else's shit. How could he have known back then that the most prized position at the court of the Sun King was *porteur du pot du roi* and that the knights of the bedchamber were the best off? "I'm not going to take it outside for him much longer," he sometimes consoled himself, thinking that the following year F. would start school and therefore have to get up at the same time as him. Night was for dreams and since they shared a bed, their bodies formed a pair of binoculars through which their parents, bending over to wish them good night, could see their own future, whereas strangers, once they got to know them better, were to wonder about their past: "You wouldn't think they had the same father," said some, ". . . or the same mother," said others. "Why isn't F. like me?" he sometimes thought before he fell asleep, trembling at the thought that his mother might have given birth to F. and himself inter-changeably. "How did she know I was I and F. was F.? Why am I not another?" After a few months of "'Как тебя зовут?' 'Меня зовут . . .'", during which he decided to learn enough Russian to be able to ask the others questions, a curly-haired cherub made his appearance in their courtyard. He was probably visiting his grandparents. He bore a striking resemblance to the wee Volodya Ulyanov on the Little Octobrist badge. "Ты кто?" asked he, sidling up. Silence. "Ты мальчик?" "Нет." "Ты девочка?" "Нет." "А кто? "Я ев'ей!"[174] He had learned the lesson—and that *leninskij urok* from the first day of school was to be a lesson to him for the whole of the rest of his life—, he knew that certain words were never to be uttered, lest you put yourself to shame; he had a list of them in his head. He didn't even realize what he was doing when he blurted: "Нельзя . . ." The rest of the sentence: "сказать еврей"[175] plopped out like a lizard sloughing off its tail. The little angel abruptly burst into tears and ran away. Why the little boy reacted like that was beyond his ken, but even so, he suddenly got a hollow feeling beneath his clavicle, although after that he went back to playing and forgot all about that derogatory word. Out of the blue, he was grabbed by the arm and frogmarched to the door of their apartment—he didn't even know who the harridan was. The woman's impatience manifested itself in the form of angry knocking—there was no doorbell, to save money on electricity—, which interrupted syncopated bursts of metallic tapping from within, as if a dozen fleas wearing miniature horseshoes were running back and forth across a sheet of aluminum foil. Nothing enraged the man on the other side of the door more than being interrupted while writing. Capable of committing homicide whenever one of the boys opened his mouth during his writing hours, he nonetheless comported himself with the utmost respect toward the harridan, who wasted no time yelling: "Ваш мальчик обозвал моего внучка *жидом*!"[176] He assured her that such words were quite simply never uttered in his house, then blamed the lad's pre-school years spent in the country, and finally promised to give him such a good hiding

---

[174] "Who are you? Are you a little boy" "No." "A little girl?" "No." "What then?" "I'm Je'ish."

[175] "It's not allowed to say Jewish!"

[176] Your boy called my grandson a Yid!

that he'd forget he'd ever been born. "Вы печатаете?"[177] the woman asked, taking a different tone. Her question was not at all innocuous, if we remember that in the seventies, the heyday of samizdat, every typewriter had to be registered with the police, who took a fingerprint of its letters, as if it were a (potential) criminal. But he was fully law-abiding—"the license to carry a gun is a license to be,"[178] as it were—, unthinkable that he turn his weapon against those who had placed it in his hand. Wounded in his pride as a man of letters, he evinced offence: "Нет, я печатаюсь!"[179] Full stop. "Контрольный выстрел.[180] Rather than being impressed, the harridan shook her head disparagingly, something between, "Is that right?" and "Выучили вас на нашу голову!"[181] turned on her heel and left. And as she moves into a distance measured not in paces but in years, between them creeps a filler story whose only quality is that of having been true from beginning to end, whether it be told in the first person or whether it be written in the third. At the beginning of the fifties, just after the second wave of deportations, I was teaching Russian language and literature at an evening school in Ch—ău. He was taking evening classes, the only place where he could conveniently meet girls of his own age, as well as women past the first flush of youth, and after classes he would go out with now one, now another. I wouldn't have noticed him had he not asked me one day to recommend him for Party membership. It was a calculated move. On the one hand, he thereby touched the soft spot of the stern former underground activist, who larded her lessons about Pushkin—"Pushkin is completely ours, completely Soviet, since the Soviet state has inherited everything that is best in our people. Ultimately, Pushkin's work flows into the October Socialist Revolution like a river emptying

---

[177] Are you typing? [literally: Are you printing?]

[178] Andrei Codrescu, *Gun license.*

[179] No, I'm in print! [literally: I am printed]

[180] Checking shot, i.e. additional shot to make sure (in an execution).

[181] We taught you to our own detriment.

into the ocean . . ."[182]—with memories of her revolutionary youth, and on the other hand, he padded his file with a name ending in -stein; abiding by the same principle, he was to choose a wife whose name ended in -ova. I was fearful of a provocation—the word "cosmopolitan" had not yet drawn level with "enemy of the people," but it amounted to the same thing—, at the same time, my actions might tip the scales, in the event that (my God!) I promoted non-Russian cadres. Clean-shaven, with features as large as a *Pravda* frontispiece, he claimed to be a poet. Seeing my hesitation, he produced the ace from his sleeve: "Я печатаюсь!" (I'm in print!) And without waiting for her to recover from that, he slapped a portfolio on the table, with copies of *Moldova Socialistă* and *Советская Молдавия*.[183] It wasn't easy for me to search out his name, there in front of him. The young man's impatience to be discovered was inversely proportional to the slowness with which she turned the pages. He was nowhere to be found, but nevertheless, she had to winkle him out, by hook or by crook. As luck would have it, he slipped through her clumsy fingers, issue after issue. In a moment of weakness, with a look I begged him to take pity on me, as if he were a policeman in whose eyes—two empty handcuffs—I was nothing but the ex officio perpetrator. His blunt forefinger jabbed the newspaper as if nudging it awake. I felt a chill up my spine when, among the signees of a letter of condolence, I came across him: I. Ciocan (Hammer); with such a name—the most communist name possible—you really did deserve to marry a Serpukhova. Tens and hundreds of deceased, of every station in life, publicly mourned by I. Ciocan; there was not one box in the Deaths column that did not provide him and "a group of comrades" with lodgings for at least one night (some of the announcements were republished two or three times). The coup-de-grâce was not long in coming: after a while, he gave me a haughty look, the way you might look at some bespectacled piece

---

[182] Quoted from the *Pravda* editorial marking the centenary of the poet's death in 1937.

[183] *Socialist Moldova* and *Soviet Moldavia*, the "Moldavian" (i.e. Romanian)-language and Russian-language Party newspapers of the Moldavian Soviet Socialist Republic — *Translator's note*

of shit (the gospel according to V.I. Lenin: "Интеллигенция не мозг нации а её говно"[184]), before placing under my nose the *pièce de résistance* of the whole portfolio—the collective of the Central Print Works expressed their boundless grief at the death of comrade Stalin, whose signees also included man of iron I. Ciocan. Only somebody who had been raised in a family without book learning and who was the first to break the chain of illiteracy passed down from generation to generation of peasants like the DNA of the tribe, would be able to appreciate the importance of such a claim, pronounced in the classroom of a night school, after lessons, before a daughter of Israel, fully versed in the scriptures: "I'm in print!" The temporal breach closed back up; the time was April 20, 1973 once more.

Clamped within the girdle of two-story houses that formed a closed, almost rectangular perimeter, the courtyard clasped him like a belt—one with fitted with the holster strap of the father, a.k.a. *The Army*, given his formal interdiction that the son leave the yard without his permission—, fastened at its only hole: the archway; in order to make egress, he had to put on his school uniform—full of coercive buttonholes—, or to accompany his mother to the shops, more and more frequently, until finally he would be trusted to go for bread and milk by himself, on the days when his mother was in hospital. He had learned to hide from his parents while always remaining in view; strangers, on the other hand, found him *exterior to himself*, without having the leisure to read him all the way through—*therefore more interior than ever*. He had barely passed the age of the first corporal punishments, which were trifling compared with the canon of silence, when his father, enraged at who knows what, quite simply stopped talking to him. The father and God were one and the same and if, as it were, *the Word was with God*, it meant that his father's silence was with nobody. Banished among the dumb animals, finding himself reduced to a third-person pronoun or completely ignored, the boy was unable to pray to anybody for forgiveness, as long as God the Word had turned his face from him. And as

---

[184] The intelligentsia isn't the brain but the shit of the nation.

if his annihilation was not sufficiently manifest, the father's power demanded to be expressed, literally *ad usum Delphini*, in the highest degree: "On my word as a Communist!" When he was spoken to again, at the end of endless days, this time being addressed by his pet name, his life would resume its normal course, the chamber pot—school—homework—(errands to the shops, followed by a question mark)—play, until the next outburst of wrath, never the last, since the peace of the house directly depended on how much distance he was capable of placing between outbursts. *L'amour à la papa* did not prevent him from volunteering, in one of the first weeks of the summer vacation, to stand to attention at the end of a plank three-palms wide, laid across the fulcrum of a poplar log, when two other lads, holding each other around the shoulders took a running jump off the sandbox and landed on the other, raised end of the seesaw. Catapulted into the air, he made a *salto mortale* and crashed to earth. For an instant—an eternity to those who witnessed the scene—he lay unconscious, then they lifted him up, from the heap of planks—some of them bristling with nails—and set him on his feet. Still dizzy from the sensation of cosmic void that bulged beneath his clavicle, or, to put it in terms he might understand, when the earth flipped arse over tit, he was marched to the water pump in the middle of the yard, splashed to bring him around (even if he himself hadn't done so, the others had wet themselves from fear), coached to say at home that he had fallen from a tree (sic), and finally, dubbed "Gagarin". The washing of his face with cold water, which was like grating a beetroot, made him bite his tongue in pain. He didn't realize how much peril he had been in—the main thing was for his parents not to find out!—, as for the others, they couldn't believe he had escaped with his life. But since it was inconceivable that the lad should not conclude the whole episode without getting a healthy fright, somebody recounted, among other things, that when their building was under construction, a bad man had been entombed alive in one of the outside walls—you only had to press your ear to the plasterwork to hear him scratching with his fingernails. The lad's imagination did the rest, during his first night of insomnia, when, lying on the couch next to F., he did not close his eyes even once as he strained his ears. From what had been said, it seemed that the skeleton could slip between the stones inside the wall, in search of a crack large enough to allow it to emerge; at the very entrance to their staircase, somebody had scrawled a V split vertically right down the center, just under a bulge in the plasterwork. If women give birth through their willies (Miriam herself had told him—there could be no question of it!), why wouldn't the bad man be able to enter the world through such a crack? From his parents' bedroom came the sound of muffled groans, then grunts—neither tears nor laughter. "The bed is shaking under them, they're so scared," thought the lad, tossing in his sheet. All those people, men and women clutching each other in their beds, night after night, their eyes closed, their senses alert, only increased his fear. The women in particular, given the crack they get by giving birth. And as he pulled the quilt over his head, without poking so much as his arm outside, he suddenly remembered how, tipping over the basin of dirty laundry one day, among the pillowcases, sheets and underlinen all tumbled together, his eyes had been struck by a pair of his mother's knickers, or rather not the knickers themselves, but the bloodstains at the crotch, which defied his understanding. And then he screamed at the top of his lungs, but since his mouth was clamped shut in horror, the scream went around and around inside him, filling him like the funnel of a loudspeaker, amplified by the chest cavity from which his heart was fit to burst and achieving maximum volume beneath the dome of the skull. Death greeted him with a chatter of the teeth, his own. A presence henceforth to be familiar, with or without the skeleton beneath the wet plaster. "Gagarin!" Whichever of his playmates had said it, the name suited him as well as the plaque of white marble engraved with gold letters that sealed the urn with the ashes of the first cosmonaut inside the Kremlin wall, even though, like the hero in the fairy tale, he had had to turn head over heels to obtain it. The thought of his own earthly remains, inchoate, but seeping into his bones together with the fear of death (although in his seven pre-school years he had been raised in the religion of "fearing your parents"), harrowed him:

ashes or skeleton? the Kremlin, at the end of the journey, or, at
its beginning, the entombing wall of an ordinary house in Ch—
ău? Unable to sleep, it was not the fearful answer, which in any
case he would never know, but the question itself that gave him
no peace. If only his mother was there, at least to draw a chalk
circle around his bed, like in Gogol's *Viy*. Eight hours a day, six
days a week, his mother never let go of the chalk, as if, from a
surplus of calcium, she kept growing a sixth finger, now on one
hand, now on the other, which she could only wear down by
writing on the blackboard, if not completely, then at least to the
symbolic size of a written sign. You could feel its presence by the
air of the classroom where she labored the whole lesson at the
chalkboard, an air that her very being exuded, as if sifted through
a sieve. It was not out of the question that he had sucked powdered
milk at her breast. The whole of her was a chalk outline, not of
the kind that the police draw on the asphalt around a body
before removing it from the scene of the crime, but of a kind
somehow drawn from the inside, with a hand of bone held up
in warning—*Noli me tangere*—in order to remain impenetrable.
"Closed?" "Yes!" The ashes (of "Gagarin") and the (nameless)
skeleton were still vying for his earthly remains when, unexpectedly, the Angelouette showed herself to him in profile. She
looked like E.M.—the initials, silhouettes of the name—, if he
went by the cockerel-pecked face, except that she didn't wear
earrings and always avoided his gaze. "The good children have
long since gone to sleep," the Angelouette scolded him. "The boy
who can't sleep dreams with his eyes open." From the way she
said it to him, it sounded like a life sentence, without right to
appeal. And before he could come to his senses: "Cockerel or
hen?" Hard to say what she meant, but his mind leapt to the
"cockerels" of melted sugar, 15 kopecks a piece (almost the cost
of a loaf of bread), that made his mouth water, without him ever
tasting one: "Cockerel!" Reprovingly, the Angelouette shook her
head, spinning around and around, before lifting up her skirt:
"Hen!" He was too little to know that angels have no sex, let
alone to have seen one, in transversal section, and one so hairy,
besides. Like a scythe with droplets of dew on the lip of the blade

and the inevitable clump of grass at the base of the (missing) handle, you could have shaved just by looking at it, even though its sharpness demanded to be touched, to be tended—regularly hammered, smoothed, scraped free of rust—to be put to work. He couldn't believe his eyes, so real did the reverie seem, but then, realizing she had gone a bit too far with the lad, the Angelouette vanished, after a brief initiation into the phases of the moon, of great use to a future *homme à femmes*: "Draw an imaginary line between the two tips, as if you were writing a calligraphic *p*—*première*—for the new moon, or a *d*—*dernière*— for the last quarter." In its place in the sky, inscribed within the window frame—"New moon!" whispered the lad, as if in a dream, before falling asleep. With the first crow of the cock, dawn twinkled *de bonne heure*, with the speed of a Moskva type-writer's black-and-red ribbon.

"Gagarin!" today, "Gagarin!" tomorrow, not that he disliked how it sounded: "Ga-ga-rin!" on the contrary, he felt in his ele-ment wearing the borrowed diving suit—the urn of ashes was forgotten—, the main thing was that it not reach his parents' ears, which it very soon did. In the meantime, the event had dwindled in importance, but not the fact that it had been con-cealed. In the land of the law "за недоносительство",[185] where denunciation rivalled the per capita output of steel, self-denun-ciation was practiced on a large scale, enough to produce the shorthand records of the famous show trials against the "enemies of the people" in the thirties and forties, and, more recently, the public sessions of voluntary self-criticism in the workplace; at the same time, "явиться с повинной"[186] nonetheless entailed a certain amount of clemency toward the victim. "Where did you get the nickname?" asked his father, taking him by surprise and determined not to let him get away with a *ne znayu*. "It didn't just fall out of the sky . . ." He stopped short, surprised at what had just popped out of his mouth, you'd have thought it was an angel, if he hadn't been talking to that devil of a child.

---

[185] (Convicted) "for failure to denounce"

[186] To surrender voluntarily, to present oneself for self-denunciation.

But was he one to talk! He wouldn't have "chirruped" even if you'd flayed him alive (it's no less true that the last thing the genitor wanted in his house was a Pavlik Morozov[187]), not to mention that corporal punishment, rather than slaking his (legitimate!) wrath only burdened his parental conscience all the more. Not even with a pair of pliers would you have got anything out of him! Let alone a hammer, always ready to spill anybody's brains. A devotee of Michurin[188] and himself the product of the crossbreeding that was also known as cadre selection, he would have liked to sow in the lad's soul a miniature father into whose mouth he might blow, as if into a ring for making soap bubbles, exactly the words that he, the gardener, wanted to hear. Unbelievable how much his son's muteness could infuriate him. Meanwhile, the son was searching for some guilty act he might admit to in terms that might please the father. The lad was still examining the faces of the new moon that was his borrowed name, to match them up, when the fiend hissed between his teeth: "Недоносок!"[189] but in terror at what he had been capable of saying, he reiterated in terms more to the lad's understanding: "Puță-Patret."[190] Two clouts to the back of the head placed parentheses around the sorry tale, whose moral, in the end, was reduced to just a few words, but not those that either the one or the other would have expected: "Dad said something rude!" In the lad's exclamation there was something of the ingenuousness of the child in Hans Christian Andersen ("The king is naked!"), combined with the astonishment of Ham at the sight of his father's nakedness; after all, the old man was not in the habit of "undressing" in front of just anybody (it is said of him that when he was headmaster of a vocational school in S., one of the pupils voided himself on the desk of the teacher of the mother tongue;

---

[187] Pavlik Morozov: probably invented child "hero" of the 1930s Stalinist Terror, who denounced his own father as an enemy of the people and was then murdered by his family, subsequently becoming a secular martyred saint of Soviet propaganda — *Translator's note*

[188] Ivan Vladimirovich Michurin (1855-1935), founding father of agricultural genetic selection and plant hybridization, scientific hero of the Soviet Union — *Translator's note*

[189] Miscarriage, but also person who fails to make a denunciation.

[190] Spitting image of a weenie.

summoned to the scene to take cognizance of an act punishable
with expulsion, the polite director saw fit to enquire: "Where is
the item?" "What item?" "The stool."), and as for walking backwards with his head turned back, his first-born had his whole
life ahead of him in order to get the hang of it. There was no
punishment more fitting the son's crime when all of a sudden F.
requested he be sent outside. He had been obliged to use the
chamber pot in broad daylight. The father looked at his first-
born, as if to say, "What are you waiting for. Take it outside!"
And as if to fulfil that which was written: "Cursed be ---n! Let
him be the servant of his brother's servants!" Rather than swallow
such a humiliation, he would have made F. wear the pot on his
head, contents and all; but since he had no choice, he obeyed—
with the feeling that he had just been given somebody else's
chamber pot, and that the handle was on the inside. Inevitably,
the courtyard was full of people. Barely had he taken two steps
than he heard behind him: "говнюк!" (shitter, shithead). The fall
to earth of Gagarin, the real Gagarin, could not have been more
vertiginous! Along with the name, he also lost his capital letter,
reverting to what he had in fact never ceased to be: "малый"
(little). An anonymous Peter Pan, condemned to childhood for
life. He diminished as fast as the eye could see, a little more and
he would have been swallowed up by the ground, in front of
everybody. He couldn't have said when or how Levy sidled up
behind him —Levy was one of the older lads who had catapulted
him into the air—, in that somewhat out-of-the-way spot where,
sheltered from indiscreet view of the outhouses and heedless of
public health regulations, the more fastidious housewives
chopped the necks of poultry bought live from the Central
Market. Nor could he have said whether he shat himself in fear.
Quite simply, Levy was staring at him with eyes that were like
the holes of none too clean privies, to judge by the gum encrusted
around them. He was trembling all over, as if wracked by the
plague, biting his tongue lest he blurt something that might scare
the lad and smacking his lips in his impatience to make himself
understood: You show me yours and I'll show you mine! But
since the lad seemed to ignore his proposal, he added, in the lad's

own language: "Pula!" (Cock!) But the word meant nothing to him, or at least no more than the "*Notre* poule *dans votre cour*" that he had nonchalantly uttered to the cheers of the classmates who had made him translate into French the words: "Our hen in your yard." It was not until Levy gestured for him to unbutton his flies that his turn came to feel chills up his spine. It was understandable to want to see Miriam's, but *his*? As if Levy—no matter how big and hard he made himself out to be—didn't have a cockerel too . . . Then suddenly it was revealed to him—he'd heard about such things from the grown-ups, without believing a single word—that which he wished he could have un-seen, namely that the sons of Israel are circumcised, from an early age. That was why that little angel visiting his grandmother, who looked like the young Volodya Ulyanov on the Little Octobrist badge, hadn't been able to say whether he was a little boy or girl. And before Levy could take the next step, he put him in his place: "Ты — еврей" (You're a Jew). As ingenuous as it was insolent, the lad's coup-de-grâce came as a verbal kick in the nuts, causing umpteen generations of Rabinovitches to gasp. Now he really did have cause to exclaim "Pula!" But not before trying to grab the pot and empty it over his head. A mistake. A big mistake. The hand clenching the handle jerked and splash! right in Levy's face. (In other words, it had been number ones on F.'s part.) Silent film. *Blitzlicht*. The day showed its polaroid tongue, half poking it out, 06.10.1973, smile please, Mr. Einstein! Instead of tearing him to pieces, as would have been expected, Levy beat a retreat, with his tail between his legs, his eyes begging him not to tell his parents. It was the older lad's absolutely unexpected restraint, overturning a natural order based on who had the heaviest fists, that frightened him: what had he wanted to do to him, in fact, if he was willing to overlook such an affront? In its sheer awfulness, that which eluded his understanding surpassed every other danger thitherto, as if a cupping glass had been pressed to his skin and sucked up all the fever of a cold within its bell jar, and now he was to carry around with him that starless firmament, that perfect void, till he ended up humpbacked from toil. A lump of fear—to the grave. You had to have a "нос с горбинкой" like Levy's to sniff out danger from a mile off, even before the threat took shape in the head of the potential aggressor. They turned their backs on each other without saying another word— the way you might close a parenthesis (Levy), only to open it again years later (---n, when he was to superimpose over the childhood incident the *décalque* of Thomas Mann's novella *Death in Venice*); not the act itself so much as his awareness that he was capable of such an act caused him to go back upstairs if not on a white horse, then at least wearing gloves, even if he was still carrying the same chamber pot with the handle on the inside, now voided.

Over summer, when various families went away, the court-yard echoed hollowly. It now resembled a huge, dismantled clock, of which all that remained was the dial, whose hand had come to a stop at II. The baba and the old man. As if, drawn by a purse tossed in the passer's-by path, a skeletal hand deigned to pick up the alms, the coins for the ferryman. They had drunk a bottle of vinegar together, then agonized for hours, only calling for help shortly before they gave up the ghost, to alert the neighbors to come and remove their corpses. They didn't have anybody else, two solitudes potentiating each other according to the formula: $(a + b)^2$. Their act was all the more terrible in the eyes of the neighbors for their having taken care of everything down to the last detail: the money for the funeral, the clothes set aside for charity, even the two coffins, which he had made with his own hand, and against which were propped two wooden crosses, with their names and dates of birth/death carved on them, towering in the middle of the room like two double basses in an orchestra pit. The only thing they hadn't taken care of was the death certificates. In memory of the poor wretches, the only thing they could do, no matter how absurd a gesture it might have seemed, was place an announcement in the paper. Holding a barely legible handwritten obituary, a man and a woman knocked on the door of apartment no. 16; they were politely turned away, on the pretext that his typewriter was being repaired. Ultimately, what else could he have told them? That in that basilica, services were held only for the living and that the text of the funeral announcement was, no matter what you might say, nothing but a dead letter? But to the boys, he said, half-jokingly, half-seriously, that the typewriter fed on the fingers of the typist, and by way of proof, he waggled his bandaged index finger under their noses: "It bites!" Shut inside its box, which you would have thought was for an accordion, if it didn't wallow on its belly, the father's *Moskva* was like one of those giant tortoises that live two or three hundred years, and which only its master was allowed to hand-feed. Nobody else was allowed to touch it, under threat of, "I wouldn't like to be in his shoes!" and you only had to see the expression on his face to be deterred from testing the water with one finger. One day, F.'s birthday to be exact, the pseudo-accordion case gave birth to an oblong box, which the parents presented to the youngest son. Within, recumbent on red velvet, was a violin as big as a baby girl, which made up for the little sister that had refused to arrive, no matter how hard they wanted. Before giving him the violin, his parents had delicately asked Lyubov Josifovna—the neighbor on the other side of the wall, with whom they shared the same corridor and communal kitchen, whether she had any objections. "I once went to a concert by Georges Enesco!" was the answer of the ageless woman who passed as aristocratic and who, it was said, once wrote to comrade Stalin in person, during the first wave of deportations after the war, emphasizing the name (the patronymic, in her case) they both shared: Josif. Hard to say whether or not the backbiters were right; what is for sure is that despite her doubly unhealthy origins—aristocratic and Polish—, she had managed to avoid the Gulag. But not persecution mania. The whole building, courtyard and all, was upholstered with her ultra-sensitive tympanum, or rather, the whole of the republic's capital was her music-loving auricle, able to detect in the most ordinary human sounds the first strains of Beethoven's Fifth. F., who was incapable even of emptying his own chamber pot, was now about to start two schools at once, middle-school and seven years of music school. But his parents seem to have thought of everything in advance, providing him with an older brother to take care of him. They would set out to school in the morning, holding each other's

little hands, and the younger would wait for the elder after lessons so that they could go home together. Twice a week, he
accompanied him to music lessons. In other words, not only did
he have to carry his chamber pot, but now he had to carry his
violin as well. (The shame of being the younger brother's turd-
man was now augmented by a feeling of imposture, particularly
when some passer-by took him for what he was not—a budding
violinist.) It was somehow understandable not to dispose of your
own waste, but to entrust to another's hands the instrument on
which you expressed yourself defied all imagination. For his part,
F. carried his brother's words, intentionally or unintentionally
distorted, home with him and into the courtyard. To avoid his
brother's spite, ---n had sworn to bite his tongue whenever his
mouth ran away with him; *peine perdue*, after "But ---n said x"
naturally there followed, "But ---n did x," which was no better.
On the other hand, whatever tricks F. got up to, ---n had to cover
for him, thereby allowing himself to be trapped in a complicity
from which he saw no escape. At the first opportunity, he was
taken out of class on the grounds that something had happened
to his little brother, two classrooms down. Oops! F. had shat
himself. He wiped his little brother's arse in the school WC, with
all five blotters, one for each of the exercise books in his satchel,
without saying a word. Back home, he had hidden his little brother's dirty underpants under the pillow; there was no question of
his telling their parents—he would still have been the one who
was punished. Now, he really did need a breath of fresh air. At the
entrance to the staircase, Miriam signaled him to follow her. He
had helped her a few times before, with her Moldavian language
homework, but every time she had come and knocked on their
door. He let the young lady lead him to her room, where, on a
windowsill as narrow as a bench, there stood a row of flowerpots.
In one of them, a pencil as thick as a finger had been poked in
the soil to serve as a prop for the plant stem. He couldn't have
said what the flower was called, nor did it catch his attention at
first. Only on closer inspection did it become clear: on the serrated leaves, the consistency and color of pink blotting paper,
could plainly be read letters written in ink pencil from inside to

out, as if Mother Nature herself were trying to communicate a
secret message. He couldn't believe his eyes, nor his ears a
moment later: "They're in Hebrew. They began to appear on the
day when we were granted permission to emigrate to Israel . . ."
The novelty abruptly occupied his whole brain, making him
forget the misfortune with F. The afternoon was unusually long,
deliberately putting his patience to the test, and he was restless
throughout. It was incomprehensible that somebody should
leave her homeland—"the land of the happiest childhood," as
they always had crammed into their heads at school—, merely
because somewhere at the other end of the world there existed
the Promised Land. Let alone that they would allow them to
take their flower! There was only one way to return Miriam's gift,
tenfold at that. He would let her use Papa's typewriter. The mere
thought that he could do such a thing made his heart leap into
his throat. The two boys were already in their little bed when, as
if smelling something, Papa came into to wish them goodnight,
but found himself asking: "Which of you farted?" They both
denied it in unison, but he was not a man to leave it at that. He
made them get out of bed and stand to attention in front of him.
"Let the culprit take a step forward!" (It was to be expected: the
business—number twos—had begun to stink.) Neither budged.
"Down with your underpants!" It still stank, and badly too, but
the boys were as clean as whistles, front and back, likewise their
underlinen. He ripped off the quilt. Nothing. The following
gesture was demonstrative—one of annoyance at everybody—,
but only now did he get to the bottom of the matter. For the
first time in his life, he felt he had no appropriate question to
the answer that displayed itself to him in all its repulsiveness.
The *item* was there, laughing in his face. How could he of all
people tolerate such a thing? The boys stood stark naked, huddled up against each other like recruits in the entrance to the
showers. He was interested not in the truth—it was obvious from
a mile off who had done it—but in the confession of him who
did it; but in order to make him talk, he would have to resort to
a ploy: "You will each put them on—" and he pointed his head
at the dirty underpants "—and the one they fit will clean up the

mess." Lights out. Night, redolent of *odore di femina*, was for adults. Despite expectations, there was no sound from the parents' bedroom, neither tears, nor laughter, when all of a sudden, the voice of the wife berating the husband—like jabbing a knife in a door over and over again—shattered the silence: "Give them a thrashing! flay them alive! hit them over the head! but don't humiliate them!" This bayonet attack was greeted by frantic words on the part of the husband, who saw himself forced to beat a retreat, spraying verbal bullets both blank and live: "I'm leaving you! I'm going to throw myself under a train!" Throwing himself under a train was the keystone of the whole repertoire (he was the grandson of a railroad man, after all), usually followed by the more mundane threat: "I'm not staying in this house a moment longer!" You might call it throwing a time bomb into the fray of hand-to-hand combat, but the wife defused it with her bare hands: "Before you pack your suitcase, go and say goodbye to the boys." The shrapnel failed to detonate. Whenever anybody in the house raised his voice, the neighbors on the other side of the wall turned the music on. This time too they heard the crackling of the needle on the record, then the crystalline voice of Ivan Kozlovsky: "Ве-чееер-ний звон . . ." (Evening thrum) The angels too have to have a human voice. And his Angelouette, wherever she might be, to whom was she now showing (exposing) herself? The song came to an end, but nobody played the B side. The next day, at lunch, just after they came home from school, their parents solemnly announced that they were going to be living with their grandparents from the country, whom they had finally persuaded to move to Ch—ău.

Grandmother didn't speak Russian, at best she *pribluia*—a dialect word which, for better or worse, translates the manner in which the entente cordiale between the liberating soldier and the native populace was conducted, as in the typical post-war exchange: "Не кричи [*krichi*], баба!"[191] "I'll spraddle [*crăci*] as best I can in my own house . . ."—a few words, without shaking

---

[191] Don't scream, woman!

off the feeling that whenever anybody addressed her in the language of Lenin, he wanted to rape her; Lyubov Josifovna had forgotten even the few words of Romanian she must once have known—born in Ch—ău in the 1880s, she had no reason to leave in 1918, nor between the wars, given that she had grown up here, gone to the Gymnasium School for Girls, dazzled from a young age at aristocratic balls, married a society man, brought a daughter into the world, and so on and so forth, in short, she had lived her life among the indigenous people—, but that wasn't why the two women didn't find a common language. You would have said that, given the different worlds from which they came—Grandmother had been born during the reign of the Tsar too, not Alexander III, but Nicholas II—, from the peasantry, on the one hand, and from colonists & functionaries posted to the frontiers of the Empire, on the other, they quite simply had nothing to say to each other, if it had not been for their pregnant silences. Neither felt comfortable in the presence of the other— Grandmother because she could not rid herself of the memory of being a "skivvy to the boyars," Lybov Josifovna lest she give away what it meant to be "из бывших"[192] in a world in which the present was sacrificed for the sake of the future. Even their appearance—stewed cabbage (the former), boiled cauliflower (the later)—, rather than bringing them together (ultimately, they both belonged to the cruciferous family—each uncomplainingly bearing her cross), merely highlighted their undeniable difference. This was why the small communal kitchen that until recently had been redolent of vanilla and cinnamon cakes now reeked of borsht and lovage—the revenge of sweat of the brow over face powder. With the end of her olfactory matriarchate— ultimately, they were nothing but two elderly women, each marking her territory by the only means at her disposal: kitchen smells—, Liubov Josifovna bade farewell to the atmosphere of her parents' house, where, by an irony of fate, she was now a tenant. It was only a matter of time—the passage of time expresses human impotence—before she manifested her discontent. One day, the

---

[192] One of the former (classes)

old woman remarked on the fact that Grandmother kept going outside during the night. (Grandmother's rheumatic gait was unmistakable.) "I go outside because I need to," she said in her defense, which merely provoked the older woman: "Ночью, надо ходить на горшок".[193] To say such a thing to a woman from the country, and in front of people, too. "City folk!" Grandmother must have said to herself, "they take their shoes off at the door, but they shit in the house . . ." And then she flung in her face, even though she had no way of understanding the words in Moldavian: "Don't eat shit!" Which is to say: What do you know, my dear woman, about going "на горшок" in a room six by twelve feet square, where a baba and her old man sleep crowded together in two beds with their grandsons? or what it means to come to the city and live in a matchbox after living your whole life in your own house, built with your own two hands, in 1946, the year when you buried your first-born son, in a village you seldom left, and even then only to travel a stone's throw away? or about being a woman in her prime, with a husband and a smallholding—you know nothing! Nor could you! Chastened, Lyubov Josifovna swallowed the insult, which she didn't even seem to have understood. But that evening, at dinner, the paterfamilias spoke up: "Mama, please don't talk nastily to our neighbor." None of them enjoyed their food after that. The transition from one character to another, like changing legs in mid-stride, is achieved by a transfer of name from grandmother to grandson. He continued to take out F.'s chamber pot, but not his violin, since Grandfather voluntarily offered to accompany him to the local music school, where he chatted with the older parents or bantered with the younger mothers as they waited in the corridor for their offspring to finish instrument practice. From time to time, he went to see what new letters Miriam's flower had produced; since her family's emigration had been put off for the umpteenth time, her (blind) grandmother had come to believe—and was ready to tell anybody willing to listen—that only when the plant was covered in words, not in any random

---

[193] At night you should use the chamber pot

order, but reproducing the Torah to the letter, would their exodus be permitted. Sometimes he would be wakened in the middle of the night by his grandparents' whispers—sitting on the edge of the bed, they would marvel in unison at how they had agreed to it, to sell their wonderful homestead, and to an incomer too, and had ended up among strangers, in Ch—ău, so that maybe, just maybe that way (the father's name) would get on the list for his own *kvartira* (apartment). It was blindingly obvious that they had made a mistake, but they couldn't go against their son. He was an educated man, he knew what he was doing! At school, for a joke, somebody had taken down ---n's 3cm x 4cm photograph from the "rocket" (he was still an eminent pupil, but not for long) and pasted it in the "cart", making him tremble at the thought that his father might get it into his head to come and collect him from lessons one day, and then . . . (Somebody else, just as discreetly, put an end to his sufferings, without his teacher or parents ever finding out.) In the meantime, depression had taken hold in the communal apartment and threatened to stay for the whole winter. When the first frosts came, everybody felt crowded by the others, they all tried to stay out as much as possible (his parents at work, his grandfather walking one grandson to the music school, the other to the reciters club at the Palace of the Pioneers, and only his grandmother had nowhere to go), as if the walls of the apartment had contracted in the cold, reducing the family home to an igloo. When they ended up talking in a whisper in their six by twelve feet-square room—lest they wake their grandchildren in the night; lest they bother (insert the father's name) when he was typing, during the day, and then even in his absence—, it was as if his grandparents were somewhere else, even though they didn't show it. The only person who laughed out loud in their building was Miriam, and her mind was elsewhere, too: twice a week she came to have her Moldavian homework checked (since Grandmother had attended a Romanian school, the girl's main difficulty was transcribing the words into Cyrillic the old woman dictated). It was from Miriam that they learned news of the constantly postponed departure, and of how they were all terrified lest their baba die, since it was her pension that was going to feed the whole family in Israel. His grandmother in particular took the worries of her neighbors to heart—as it happened, the girl's father was called Jacob—, given that during the war she had sheltered a young Jewish girl in her attic, who had fled to the village after her family were deported to a camp in Transnistria, God knows whether she escaped with her life, after . . . Long forgotten, the thirty-year-old episode had caught up with her, except that this time she was the one being sheltered, and against her will. After the feast of St Basil, by the Old Style calendar, the frost left ice flowers in Miriam's window, unless the old woman's cataracts now somehow extended to the pane, and so when he came home from school, he didn't see her vervain when he looked up. And was his grandmother less clever than a plant, be it only a vervain? Didn't know how to read, did she? Not at all, she'd learned to put her signature on the slip when she collected her pension from the post office, but you don't get very far with just that. (What her grandson couldn't have known was that necessity not only teaches, but unlearns, as had happened during the war, when, not receiving an answer to her letters sent to the front—her husband had been called up in forty-four—, a wife had advised her to look for somebody to write them for her in Russian. Less than a month passed and she received not a postcard from her husband, but a *pokhoronka* (notification of decease). By mistake, as it would later transpire: the military commissariats churned them out, based on estimated losses, in contempt for human life: ". . . и как один умрём";[194] but the language of statistics has no knowledge of the singular. After which, she neither read nor wrote.) And where could she go in winter anyway? Willy-nilly, she wintered indoors. On the evening of the same day, on the radio they announced that pupils from the first four years would be kept at home during the frosts. He could therefore sleep as long as he liked. At night, he woke up needing to go to the toilet. He pulled on his warm clothes and plunged outside into the cold, even though

---

[194] ". . . and we shall all die as one," line from "Смело мы в бой пойдём" (Valiantly go we to war), a song highly popular during the Civil War.

the chamber pot was right by the stove. (Accustomed to his grandparents going outside, his parents didn't lose their temper.) The cold air took his breath away and, despite him being set on going to the privy at the bottom of the yard, he found himself peeing from the front door. Nobody could see him, in any case. In the morning, he almost died of shame: its yellow gush having arced and then fallen frozen to the ground, his piss traced a glittering rainbow that could lead to none other than him. He blushed like a girl and then paled: swaying back and forth as if she were in front of the Wailing Wall, his grandmother was scraping off the pee-pee with a kitchen knife, lest *her* grandson become a laughingstock. (A chip off the old block, not only the name, the facial features and hair color, but also the serene eyes—eyes *en fleur de tête*—, stood witness that the inheritance was genetic, that blue blood of the gaze having come from the heart did not vanish into the ground with her first born, but rattled the buckets of blueness from which drinks the sky, skipping a generation, not without the help of her daughter-in-law, whom she recognized, if the family legend is to be lent credence, by the way in which her lapis lazuli eyes struck her as soon as she crossed her threshold.) A human eraser, Granny rubbed out her grandson's mistake before the lad's father could make him correct it with the red ink that ran in his veins.

Besides taking everybody by surprise in the first days of Febu-March, the spring thaw also brought two changes: after months and months of bureaucratic running back and forth, and just when any prospect of exodus was receding, Miriam's family finally managed to obtain passports; having gone to the country without telling anybody, Grandpa was to return to Ch—ău a week later, with the deeds to a homestead in U-eşti in his pocket (not the old house, even though he had done his utmost to get it back). All of a sudden, their courtyard took on that waiting-room sort of air when time seems to stand still, like a train carriage on a siding, which only the departure signal can tear from its inertia. Life followed its course; for the umpteenth time Grandpa imitated the sounds the goods trains made as they lazily left Moldova, packed to the gills: "Хлеб-поставка-хлеб-поставка", and how they raced back from the depths of Russia, whistles blowing, as if spitting the husks of sunflower seeds between their teeth: "Спички-махорка-спички-махорка";[195] at school, they were all getting ready to be made Pioneers on the eve of Red Army day, February 23; F. didn't make much of an effort at either his schoolwork or the violin, but invented all kinds of scary little stories; two or three times a week, Miriam came upstairs to their apartment to check her Moldavian homework, but mostly stared at the walls; as for Grandmother, well, surprisingly, she was getting on with Lyubov Josifovna better and better, albeit mostly by sign language, to the delight of his parents, out all day at work. Until the first stumbling block. It was the lunch break, and as usual the boys were running around the classroom, when suddenly he found himself unwillingly caught up in a game of tag. Ruslan chased him into a corner, about to tag him, the others had just scented the quarry—he had no escape!—, when suddenly, he dodged to one side and his head crashed through the Red Corner display case with the photographs of the future Pioneers (he himself was not among them). The glass pane shattered before he even knew what was happening. Two classmates, Aurel A. and Miron I., picked him up and took him to the first-aid room, where, unbelievably, he had to wait, because a girl from F.'s class had punctured her cheek with a fountain pen nib while trying to put it in her mouth. And while two unseen hands wrapped around his neck a red silk scarf—the first in his class—, tying it under his chin in knots thicker and thicker with scarlet, he could not tear his eyes from the girl's bloody mouth; through a strange inversion of viewpoint, he could feel on his own tongue what, given the circumstances, the girl alone would have been able to describe: "The blood tastes of ink." But only in the instant when the patient turned her disfigured face toward him, with a species of mute reproach in her suddenly mature eyes, the very image of fragility, you might say, only then did the intuition that he had almost died clobber him over the back of the head; on the verge of fainting, he was quickly bandaged and sent home.

---

[195] Cereal-quotas-cereal-quotas. Matches-baccy-matches-baccy.

(Strong by nature, his grandmother took advantage of the fact that his parents were at work to cast a charm, wafting the smoke of burnt dog hair over him—like every other courtyard in old Ch—ău, theirs had no shortage of stray dogs, or yard dogs, as they were called—and sprinkling him with holy water.) Throughout his convalescence, he re-experienced the long-forgotten sensation of being an only child, even if F. didn't fade into thin air: the prospect of his death made him more alive than ever; a pity that none of his schoolmates, not even Ruslan, who anyway passed their house on his way to painting classes, came to see him. Compared with their forgetting him—highly unfair, given they were the ones who roped him into the game—, his death would have been a mere trifle. His life, not even that much. Too short to soar into the sky like a paper kite, he gave himself airs as if he were about to receive Airbus, Boeing 747 and IL 82 passenger planes from all four corners of the globe, an unavoidable checkpoint for one of Concorde's four stopovers around the world, and therefore also for the Tu 144, its Soviet twin, which craved to knock it off its top spot, even if for the time being it was gathering flies. When he was least expecting, his class tutor paid him a visit; rather than his feeling touched by her gesture, it put him on guard—a woman on the verge of retirement wouldn't pay such a visit merely to pat him on the head. In front of him, but choosing her words with care, as if talking about somebody else, the teacher told his mother something that his family probably found hard to accept: ---n was no longer the same boy he was a year ago. It wasn't grave, he still studied hard, he was still well behaved, but unfortunately, he let himself be trampled underfoot in his efforts to be liked by everybody else. "What does he lack?" asked the tutor rhetorically. "Meanness." Now that he had learned to take it, it was time that he gave some back. "How much longer is he going to turn the other cheek?" the question might have been left hanging—in any case, it didn't enter the category of questions that demand an immediate answer—if the image of the girl with the punctured cheek hadn't come back and hit him full force: "Will she be scarred?" In other circumstances, she would have made light of it—something like: "до свадьбы заживёт!"[196] but who would have wed her, disfigured like that?—but not in front of him, who had seen it all with his own eyes, and so she found herself mumbling: "The scars of good behavior . . ." After her pupils had cracked open his head, here was the comrade teacher breaking it again. From the doorway, she wished him a speedy recovery, and off she went. That same night, Angelouette showed herself to him, in profile, and only the part with the punctured cheek: "Heads or tails?" This time, there was no cause for hesitation: "Heads!" Wrong: this must have been the meaning as Angelouette jerked her head from right to left, as if somebody had slapped her. "I'm going to be tails," she said. "The tail of the griffin that will lift you from the lower world. Hold on tight and be very, very careful: whenever I turn my head, you'll have to give me something to drink or eat. Until you see the upper world. Поехали!"[197] But since he didn't have any food or drink, whenever the Griffin turned her head, he held out his empty palm. She bit it, ravenously, it would seem. It was amazing to feel her hot breath on his palm! At the same time, his hands were itching to wring the devil's neck when it reached the end of its strength. The spell wore on, and then he found himself in the upper world. "Don't complain that I ate your life," said the Griffin on parting, before giving way to Angelouette: "Sleep tight, sweet dreams—with legs spread!"(On waking, he was to glean two words from the whole episode—*Wormany*, for the lower world, and *Angelermany*, for the upper world—, which he uttered convinced that pronunciation alone is what makes the difference, although it is well known that articulation intrinsically depends on one's level of culture: "Blessed are the poor in spirit, for theirs is the kingdom of heaven.") There followed days without number, the chamber pot—school—the Palace of Pioneers; from their club for young reciters were selected six children—two Komsomol members, two Pioneers, and two Little Octobrists (he and a little girl!)—to hail in verse the proceedings

---

[196] It'll pass by the time she gets married

[197] "Let's ride!" Gagarin's words when his Vostok 1 rocket took off on April 12, 1961.

of the nth Congress of the Union of Communist Youth, held in
Moldova, which is what happened one April evening in the State
Philharmonic Concert Hall. First applause, first appearance on
the small screen, first award (a commemorative badge). After
which their club was disbanded, having completed its mission.
What with one thing and another, the departure of his grandparents, rather than lightening the atmosphere, darkened it even
further; unspoken by both parties, reproaches floated in the air,
even if they all had tears in their eyes on the day of parting.
Whereas the children's room had looked like a box enclosing two
musical instruments, one stringed, the other wind, now it suddenly half-emptied, and in the most disagreeable way, keeping
the bow (from the violin) and the slide (from the trombone).
Under the conductor's baton, in the hands of whom required.
The musical score of those days would have been incomplete
without the writing hour (for four hands), a genuine open lesson
with the paterfamilias dictating two missives—both addressed
to the grandparents in the country—one to the mother, in which
it was possible to read between the lines the anger caused by the
treachery of the old folks who had left in him the lurch just when
he needed them most, and the other to ---n, in which he
recounted, among other things, how hard it was for the mother
and father to cope with the given situation; finally, he asked the
children each to add something of their own, and while the first
strained to convey to them a mood, an idea of his, which would
have satisfied his father, who was to inspect their first drafts, F.
quite simply copied from the ABC, word for word, to the delight
of his father, who hadn't been expecting to set him as an example:
"The whole family misses you." It was to prove correct, but in
an unexpected way. Less than a week later, his mother was taken
to hospital. Nobody seemed to know what was wrong with her,
only that "it would pass." Father was the first to utter a terrible
word, which the doctors quickly and in unison denied, assuring
him that in two or three days she would be back on her feet. A
week passed and—nothing. On one of those days of dashing all
over the place, home—work—home—hospital, a Friday, in
other words, ---n left his key at home, the one he wore around

his neck on an elastic thread, next to his skin, instead of a crucifix—; his father didn't come home that afternoon, and so
Lyubov Josifovna fed him. It was also she who made sure that
the boys did their homework and that F. wasn't late for his violin
lesson. Afterward, she made him practice, proving as well-dis-
posed as she was exacting. She then let them go and play outside,
meanwhile making their supper. Father had still not arrived.
"Кабы дед с бабой были дома,"[198] Lyubov Josifovna let slip as
they ate supper. Not even after nightfall did he make his appearance, and so they watched the nine o'clock news together, then
a gala concert, then the final news bulletin . . . The crackling
screen announced the end of the schedule, but still Father had
not arrived. Even the walls seemed to have turned their backs on
them. Only when the old woman send them "на горшок и
спать"[199] did the children discover their neighbor did not have
an inside toilet, a discovery all the more astonishing given that
in more than a year of close proximity they had never seen her
visit the privy at the bottom of the courtyard, not even once. F.
entered a little room only a little larger than a closet, whence
issued a crystalline tinkling, while ---n stubbornly refused to go
inside the house, and inside a stranger's house at that. Just like
his grandmother, Lyubov Josifovna was saying to herself sourly,
when there came a knock on the door. Papa! Upset—is it much
to ask that your sons be asleep in their beds when you get
back?—, but also embarrassed on account of the late hour, he
tried to explain himself—an attempt cut short by Lyubov
Josifovna with a gesture that might equally have meant, "I don't
want to know" and, "Never mind, I was young too once . . ."
But Father was like a bottle of champagne: once shaken, you
only had to pop his cork for the froth of words to flow. His vol-
ubility, rising and falling like a rollercoaster, wound around and
around the old woman—it was clear he took pleasure in talking
to her and above all in her listening to him—, encasing her like
a pupa, it wouldn't be long before the human larva became

---

[198] Would that that grandpa and grandma were at home!

[199] To the chamber pot and bed.

invisible in its cocoon, but all of a sudden, the woman gave a start, shaken by a cry that demanded release: "[имя-отчество], какая я дура была."[200] And heedless of the children, who were present, but too small to understand, or her husband, who was too old to do anything about it—his presence has been so insignificant throughout the narrative that quite simply it has not been detected hitherto, nor will it be hereinafter—, she threw herself on the gallant man's chest. Amid sobs, she recounted how, as a pension girl, she had met Chaliapin, who was on tour in Ch—ău, and after the recital at the Hall of the Noblemen's Assembly, the singer had invited her to the ball in his honor, where they waltzed until late. When, about to retire to bed, Fyodor Ivanovich had invited her to follow him . . . "в номера" (to his hotel room), she hadn't gone after him, and now she wrung her hands for her insipid life, during which she had had good days and bad, but never a night with the Russian bass. What exactly made her reveal all this, at an hour when everybody was fast asleep, to a man of less than thirty-five, but who already had what might be called a biography and his whole life ahead of him, was impossible to say: perhaps the faint hint of another woman's perfume that her nocturnal guest wafted, perhaps his vague resemblance with the great singer. She abruptly came to her senses and before closing the door behind them, she said to him calmly, as if to emphasize that her late-night confession had not at all been a moment's weakness: "Живите красиво!" (live beautifully) That was all. (How old can she have been—eighty? ninety? [insert the father's name] must have asked himself, but it was his son, ---n, who was to discover the answer, thirty-odd years later: the ball episode had taken place on the evening of June 25, 1899; Chaliapin was twenty-six, the pension girl, the age of Natasha Rostova, at most.) Within the week, his mother was discharged from hospital, after refusing, in writing, on her own responsibility, to have an operation (later, Tetradov himself was to operate on her). Left to "die at home," she had a few days, but nobody would have wagered on her living. Not even her

---

[200] [Name and patronymic], how stupid I've been!

husband, who, horrified at the prospect of becoming a widower with two children, somehow managed to get hold of a ticket for her to take treatment at the Kislovodsk spa. The absences—first the grandparents', then the mother's—therefore knitted themselves together in larger and larger loops, laid like a macramé over their house. Miriam, too, no longer crossed their threshold, since she was due to leave before the end of the school year. Their train carriage was still on a siding in Ch—ău Station, waiting to be joined to the Moscow-Bucharest train—the only country in the communist bloc that still had good relations with Israel, Romania was the (aerial) bridgehead to the Promised Land—, when the rumors began to fly: since each family had been reserved a compartment, the backbiters claimed that they had managed to dismantle all the metal handles, replacing them with ones made of solid gold, but covered in a film of metal, with the connivance of the railway workers; the girl's father was a train dispatcher. But when you went inside their apartment, there was nothing much to see except poverty. As for Levy, he didn't come across him again until the start of the spring recruitment campaign; to avoid the draft, the young man wet the bed night after night, and his parents, aware of their son's passion for small boys, which might cost him dear once in the ranks, kept taking him to hospital in the hope of having him declared insane. As for the others, every which way . . . Deserted for the greater part of the afternoon, the courtyard was as if broken down into separate play areas, some in full view, others hidden from prying eyes, and each child went off to his favorite place or portion thereof. The world of drawers, wardrobes, suitcases & boxes under beds was waiting to be discovered—a new world, albeit without capital letters. Everything had to be explored, weighed, plugged in, and, where the case, tried for yourself (Father's razor, Mama's hair dryer). The only condition was that you put everything back without leaving a trace. Mama was the first to realize that somebody had been interfering with her things; she threatened to put everything under lock and key (whereas in fact she was scared even to lay a mousetrap lest the little one put his finger in it), but aimed only at warning them. Once she even took upon herself the blame for losing the pencil sharpener, after having taken care to extract from plant pots the six colored pencils that had been poked in them point downward. Another time, in the presence of her husband, she was rummaging through the suitcase of documents and, as if by accident, locked it. She didn't have enough keys for all the things that needed to be kept locked up. As their inventorying approached its end, the boredom returned in force, threatening to drive them outside. A fresh discovery obsessed them—they climbed the fire escape to the roof, whence, lying on their bellies, they spat into space to see whose sputum could trace the finest acrobatic figures as it fell to the ground by the entrance. Another time, they launched paper airplanes and water bombs. If the fire escape had reached to heaven, they would have long since been on the topmost step. All-powerful, their own insignificance drove them to reckless deeds, whose grandeur was directly proportional to the danger they entailed. Their lives hung from a thread, but since they had never experienced anything so exhilarating, they ventured forth daily on endless expeditions, again and again, till their heads whirled. Beneath their very eyes, the courtyard became an inland sea, bristling with the peaked sails of sheets hung out to dry, whose steep slopes made it impossible to moor. Likewise the roof was able to become the coast of the Blue Ocean, as well as the quay from which the pirates of the air were to set sail, led by God the Father, with his monkey, man, perched on his shoulder. Unsurprisingly, having once been inside the "rocket", at the end of the term ---n found himself in the "airplane," whence he risked taking a parachute jump if he didn't get his act together. It came as a surprise even to him to find that his much-lauded good behavior was in fact a species of pretending, unlike F.'s blatant impertinence. Torrential May rains and lightning bolts put an end to their celestial peregrinations, presaging their precipitous descent, if not into learning, then at least from the roof. Under the new conditions of staying inside, the very snare laid around the forbidden objects—a snare that was assumed, but no less present in the form of signs disseminated everywhere, whereby the parents believed that they p r o t e c t e d t h e i r p o s s e s s i o n s—was transformed into a fuse. The boys only had to repeat, on a smaller scale, the experience of the dizzy heights, climbing up on the chairs, in order to achieve a different viewpoint, one that opened up to them new possibilities for exploration. The two conjoined cupboards, one full of books, the other full of clothes, formed a single continent, a North and South America (the wardrobe and the bookcase respectively) that they were to rediscover in their Viking ships (supplied by Ch— ău's furniture factory). In the midst of cardboard boxes of every shape and size, their father's typewriter, padlocked and impregnable in its carapace, rose like Greenland among the icebergs. The formal interdiction on touching it, which applied to everyone, guarded its solitude like the curse laid by Yahve on the Ark of the Covenant. The contents of each box were revealed in turn, before retreating back inside just as discreetly. Sundry items of no importance. He was wracking his brains as to how he might let Miriam try out father's typewriter—a priceless gift from him that she would take with her on the day of her departure to Israel— , when F., as if reading his thoughts, perched on a stool and, far more easily than would have been expected, opened the lid. From within its lair, the *Moskva* grinned with all forty-four metal gnashers. The Cyrillic set of teeth chattered a greeting that boded ill. ---n tried to stop him—too late—F. had poked his fingers in its mouth. At first touch, a few letters engaged, but without making that clacking sound, like a cat purring, their father was able to produce; the plastic pads suddenly unsheathed their claws, the mechanism arched its back ready to pounce, and the younger brother quickly pulled down his crusader's vizor. They were still trembling in fear—as well as indignation, in ---n's case: he for one would never have dared to do what F. now did— when somebody knocked on the door. It was Miriam, all smiles. She had come to say goodbye to the brothers. And that he might be forever in her debt yet again, she gave ---n a vervain leaf on which could be read (as long as you knew Hebrew): "Do not bear false witness against your neighbor." Her unselfconscious gesture sooner betrayed presence of mind than premeditation at home, even if the reverse were true. But the wheels and pulleys of fate had been set in motion, ineluctably, and he would have to answer for others' actions. In short: one evening, inspiration having struck, the father sat down at the typewriter, after lifting it off the top of the cupboard, cradling it in his arms like a bride, and just as he was about to straddle it, he found it had been *tampered with*. His surprise was so overwhelming that for an instant he quite simply refused to believe that anybody in his right mind could have done such a thing. (Everything that was done in their house was in the name of the father, by his will or—God forbid—against it.) The three raised typebars, almost forming the sign of the cross, were the most telling proof of schism—"do not take the Lord's name in vain." He brushed aside the thought that somebody in the family had disobeyed him; it was inconceivable. Then who? He accorded them a respite—whom? his enemies, malefactors of every stripe—, long enough for him to check the key lever springs. Finally, he was forced to speak out; the way he posed the question, omitting the predicate, as if to shorten the distance between the crime and the criminal, presupposed that he knew the answer and only out of mercy did he allow the villain to admit his guilt: "One of you, which one?" (The question mark, opening up like a parachute in midair, did not mean that he expected the person to whom it was addressed to have an easy landing; unless, that is, it was in fact a vociferation mark . . .) The interrogative was still hanging in the air: beneath it, far below, as big as a poppy seed at first, and then growing to the size of a fist, the lower the canopy descended, a full interrogation was heaving into view, when F. blurted: "It was ---n!" But since each of them had been thinking of somebody else, the whole scene took on a carnivalesque aspect of mistaken identities: the father's face frozen into a mask, ---n's mask of innocence ripped off, F. donning the mask of the obedient son. Silent farce. But it was the calm before the storm: Behold, now the handsome father thunders and fulminates, the genitor agonizes, the paterfamilias pours his righteous wrath on the head of the malefactor: "God smite you!" Then he issues his final judgement, the New Order in the House of the Father: "F. is my rightful son, and ---n is nothing but his brother!"

! I kiss your hand, good Father, I kiss your hand and bow . . .[201]
Like Him who said: the father's curse is but the inversion of his
blessing—against the unjustly punished, against him accused,
and, not least, against him who uttered his name. Twelve or
thirteen years elapsed, a "чертова дюжина"[202] as it were, and,
when ---n left to go to university ("to Moscow! to Moscow!" the
gospel according to Chekhov), his father, *manu propria*, placed
the *Moskva* in his arms, and the Violin—not a quarter, not half,
but all of it, and all his—, its head on his shoulder; gifted with a
musical ear, F. was to abandon the violin, but in time he would
develop a true passion for strings; always goading them to vie
with each other for first place, the old man was to find that of
his two boys, neither would surpass the other, but rather each in
turn would become a Prodigal Son. In other words, since he had
broken his commandments, ---n was driven from the home, and
in honor of F., who returned to the bosom of the family whenever he grew weary of being nobody's child, the fatted calf was
slaughtered, again and again. By now in Moscow, in response
to "Life is worth living at least in order to know how Goethe
lived it," the way he might pay an insurance policy in the name
of the father, ---n set about writing the story of Chaliapin's darling, which he tried out, unsuccessfully, on a number of repre-
sentatives of the fair sex. But none of them was prepared to love
him by proxy, not even for one night. Therefore he changed the
record—he let himself be sought. When she stayed at his place
overnight, the first few times he did not so much as touch the
girl with the name of a violin, for fear of violating her, to which
he would have abandoned himself shamelessly had not the young
woman confessed to him in an upsurge of sincerity: "I want to
have a child with you." (No sooner said than done!) When he
was least expecting to see her again, believing her to be a sickly
hallucination at most, the Angelouette appeared to him: "Boy
or girl?" With a typically male surge of pride: "Boy!" (He had
even chosen a first name for him, after the two of them had

---

[201] Line from Cezar Ivănescu's poem "My Father Russia".

[202] A devil's dozen.

watched Miloš Forman's *Amadeus* together.) The Angelouette said nothing, but before turning her back on him—identical with Vitalie Coroban's Eve* twisting around in a final gesture of recollection, filled with desire ("Open me!)—, she looked him up and down, to remember him, farewell, farewell forever! He had sat half the night on the window ledge of his fourth-floor room in the Literature Institute hall of residence, his legs dangling, his thoughts elsewhere, when the doorwoman came to give him the big news: "You've got a baby girl!" (It was the same middle-aged woman, nicknamed the Sphinx of Gizeh, who had let the future mother of his child enter whenever she came to visit him, without asking for her identify card, which meant that Vio was able to spend the night with him.) Now, he really did have no choice, he had to live. Krasivo, if possible.

---

*

Eva. Mezzotinta, 36 x 12cm, 2000

Cap. 10
"Ibi sunt leones . . ."

The tone: *"Scappa, che arriva la patria!"*

Italian peasant woman to her son, 19th century

During daylight hours he lays his calligraphy of shadows, a fair copy, upon the application form for a SHENGEN visa downloaded from www.ambafrance.md—*faute de l'électricité*, given Moscow's energy war on Ch—ău, he finds himself forced to fill it in before darkness falls. The printed letters stand to attention, the handwritten letters, at ease, like soldiers answering the evening roll call in the barracks yard. The calling of his name— NOM *BĂJENARU* (the Slavic origin of the name must also betray danger, *bîja! [flee!]*, apposite to the character being summoned to leave)—brings with it the echo—AUTRES NOMS (*nom à la naissance; alias, <u>pseudonyme</u>; noms portés antérieurement*) *ȚĂRANU* [*Peasant*] (superfluous to say that the chosen pseudonym is the inside-out-glove of the name he received at birth; he would happily also have answered *RAC MOZGOV*— Rac [Cancer] by zodiac, Mozgov [McBrain] from Brain-ache—, had anybody ever called him that)—only to fade into PRÉNOM ---*N* (since the death of Grandmother E—, his forename has resembled a funerary vault that houses her, the same as a violin's sounding box conserves its music even after the final strains have forever left the instrument, only the final *N* (it would take more than a lifetime for him to grow as far as Her Initial) belongs to him one hundred percent, like an answer *avant la lettre* to the fourth question on the form: SEXE. Since we're on the subject, it was the grandmother who gave him his first—and most concise—lesson in sexology. He must have been the same age as the little Volodya Ulyanov on the Little Octobrist badge . . . He was yet an angel when a little girl from the village squatted in front of him and, without trying to hide it or betraying the slightest shame, piddled. Enthralled by the sight, he could not tear his eyes away from *that place*, where he espied nothing, absolutely nothing. In a panic of incomprehension, he ran home as fast as he could, shouting from the gate, for all the village to hear: "Mamaaa, Snejana's got no willy!" His grandmother was all smiles and soothed him as she saw fit, saying more to herself: ". . . I'll die happy if I live to hear you *ask to be given what she hasn't got.*" Not long before she passed away, the old woman's wish was granted—on the male side of the family, the first little girl made her entrance, and her grandson's daughter resembled her completely, from her appearance to her name (which showed that *it was given to him*, albeit not by Snejana). Whenever he fills in DATE ET LIEU DE NAISSANCE— *JUNE 22, 1964, U—EȘTI—*, the reaction of those around him can usually be summed up by the exclamation: "On *such* a day!" (it doesn't bode well to have your birthday mentioned in a conscription song: "On June the 22nd / World war broke out"), otherwise a natural reaction on the part of people who were, until not long ago, citizens of a country who had succeeded in turning an official holiday, May 9, Victory Day—with its military parade and working masses marching *of their own free will and without duress* across Red Square, as if to lend it a dash of color, under the indulgent eyes of the Methuselahs poking up from the granite trenches of Lenin's Mausoleum and waving their hands as if to prove they weren't masturbating under the viewing stand—into a lively shindig with brass bands, picnics and vodka till you puked. The imagination went wild when, on reaching section no. 6, PAYS DE NAISSANCE, the reality proved to be—the gospel according to King Carol—not an arse in two boats, but *one boat in two arses*: four generations of Băjenarus had been born in the same village, but in four different states, as follows: his grand-parents had first seen the light of day in the Russian Empire, his parents in Greater Romania, I the undersigned in the USSR, and his daughter in the Republic of Moldova (even if shortly after its proclamation, the RM was to be divided into three entities, not so much ethnic as political, each with pretensions to being subject to international law). A real family of neo-Kantians (it is known of the author of the *Critique of Pure Reason* that he never left his native city, although 142 years after his death Königsberg became Kaliningrad, obviously without moving an inch). Between ourselves, there is always something dubious about the number 6 (on the one hand, the *Sixtine Madonna*, which apparently has a six-fingered cherub, and on the other, Joseph Stalin, who had six toes—two of them conjoined—on one foot); likewise, the break-up of the USSR (N.B. it covered one sixth of the world's dry land) was triggered by article no. 6 of the Constitution, the one that stipulated that it was a one-party state under the CPSU. Further proof that regardless of tongue (including in the archaic sense of tribe, people, race), words shape, if not also create, the reality in their image and likeness. In which case, instead of *Moldavia*, why not *Mal de Vie*?

He has no words for what he has got into his head; the ones that come to his tongue lead nowhere. Like Him who said: ". . . for my words and tongue are tied." The answer given by Moses (which translates, *I drew him out*; a prophetic name), in reality, a pallid attempt to get out of things, determines God to give him a brother—I wrote "give him a brother" as if we were talking about any other woman, but of Moses' mother it is written, "And there went a man of the house of Levi, and took to wife a daughter of Levi. And the woman conceived and bare a son" (Exodus, 2, 1-2), after which we discover, "And Moses was fourscore years old, and Aaron fourscore and three years old, when they spake unto Pharoah" (Exodus, 7, 7); which means that in the meantime, the woman (?) or God (?) gave Moses an elder brother of whom, until the time was ripe, he knew nothing: Aaron, the Levite, who

"spoke well"; similarly, the author invents a character to whom he will "speak and put words in his mouth." But for what he has in mind, he would require camel-words ("...for it is easier for a camel to pass through the eye of a needle . . ."); he can only get hold of ass-words, and these are often borrowed/stolen, thereby breaking the tenth commandment: *"Thou shalt not covet thy neighbour's house; thou shalt not covet thy neighbour's wife, nor his manservant, nor his maidservant, nor his ox, nor his ass . . ."* The ass-word serves everybody; it is, as it were, the Trojan Horse whereby the Old Testament—"And Moses took his wife and his sons and set them upon an ass, and he returned to the land of Egypt" (Exodus, 4, 20)—enters the New Testament—"And Jesus, when he had found a young ass, sat thereon, as it is written, Fear not, daughter of Sion: behold thy King cometh, sitting on an ass's colt" (John, 12: 14-15; see also Matthew, 21: 1-7, Mark, 11: 1-7, Luke, 19: 33-35). In other words, words not only draw reality to them, they drag it behind them, carry it on their back, transport it from place to place, unloading it from the mouth of the speaker into the ears of the hearer. As it is written: So-and-so, since he is alive, "took his wife and children and set them upon an ass . . ."
—SITUATION DE FAMILLE marié CONJOINT (Nom) xxx prénom xxx date et lieu de naissance xxx nationalité(s) xxx ENFANTS nom xxx prénoms xxx date et lieu de naissance xxx nationalité(s) xxx NOM ET PRÉNOMS DES PARENTS xxx— and went out of his native land. No, that doesn't work. His going out can, at most, be written over the distance between *NATIONALITÉ(S) d'origine and actuelle(s)* (The story is far too significant to be passed over in silence. In the nineties, when the newly reunified Germany was granting citizenship/residence rights to the victims of the Nazi regime and their descendants to the third generation, a man from Ch—ău did his utmost to find himself a Jewish grandmother, aunt or cousin. What was more, once he had (re)discovered his Jewish origins, he had to get himself circumcised, but since the rabbi was no surgeon, his member became inflamed and thereby threatened to deprive him, through amputation, of the only physical proof of his newly recovered Jewishness, keeping him in hospital for

a good few weeks. For weeks, if not months, after that, he had to trail around offices, courts, ministries, in order to obtain a repatriation certificate. He was to take up residence in Augsburg, southern Bavaria. Methodical as they are, the German authorities even laid on transport for the newcomers: along with a number of other families, his was to fly from Ch—ău to Timişoara to Munich, where they would be met by a welcoming committee. It should be noted that thitherto neither the head of the family nor his wife had been farther than the seaside at Odessa, which required only an identity card, whereas now they needed passports and permanent visas. In the fever of preparations for their departure, our man sold everything he had, his house, his car, his "fazenda"—at knockdown prices—, and partied until the very night before. The day of the journey—the first time his two children had ever flown—, at the end of which he was he was to discover his country of adoption, passed normally, lubricated with a few beers during the flight, and another few in the transit lounge of Timişoara Airport. However, it wasn't the booze, but his education as a *Homo sovieticus*—from an early age, he'd watched war films about the Russians and Germans, he'd played Russian and German soldiers, and later he'd told (political) jokes about Russians and Germans—that spoke volumes when, after landing at Munich International Airport, he flung up his right arm to salute the members of the welcoming committee and uttered the only German expression he had ever known: "Heil Hitler!" Right there and then, he was bundled back on the plane and sent back whence he came. For a time, he could be encountered in Ch—ău's *Fulguşor [Snowflake] Café*, drinking away his sorrows—scrounging beer from whoever was willing to stand him a drink—and complaining about how every single German was a fascist . . .) In which case, it remains only for him to elevate (a verb of dramatic rather than apostolic resonance) pedestrian words—, "about six hundred thousand on foot that were men, beside children" (Exodus, 12, 37)—, joined by the 600,000 citizens of the RM (according to the official statistics, with the real figure being at least twice as many) who earn their living outside the country's borders.

Dotted line (n times): the frontier of this country is marked out by a hundred thousand maidens sleeping on their sides head to toe, who have bared their birth in their sleep. Possessing enough geography to lift its knees to its gob, adopting the fetal position, and enough history to be born prematurely, by caesarian, it is what is left of it after everybody has known it, in the lay or biblical sense, each according to how his sow-like heart dictates. Given its shifting nature, it can be located only approximately, somewhere between the rivers D—r and P—t, encompassing the metropolis Ch—ău, the bellybutton of these regions, at the intersection of the meridian named "she was a wife before she got married" with the parallel named "after she got married she became a maid". *Ubi bene*, to the locals, as long as they haven't left her, *Ibi sunt leones*, to foreign suitors, as long as they haven't invaded her, she is what you would call the *Motherland* to her face; but since the stepmother spends her nights around the continent's slums, we, her children, call her *Cleopatria*. If you ask her: "Who's my father, Mama?" she straightaway calls you her little Pharaoh, but without her telling us to our face, we sense we're *nobody's children* (in this respect, the quatrain of a little girl of just ten, Angela Ciobanu, could not convey better the contradictory sentiment of love of country: "My native land is Mother, / My homeland is Father; / Even if it weren't, please understand, / I would still love my native land"). A change worthy of note occurs as soon as you enter the adult world: suddenly, she yells in your ear not "my little Pharaoh!" but "idiot!" (it's as if, after feeling yourself the master of your childhood's Egypt, somebody were to evict you from your native delta, chattels and all, driving you forth like "flocks of sheep and herds of oxen"). Proof that you have grown up enough to "*pro patria mori*," which, and of this you may be sure, is something that hasn't eluded her. Given how many people have died for the patria, this country ought to girdle the earth thrice. Seen from as high as the crane flies, it looks like the print of a bare left foot, with the big toe splayed, as if the other four toes were not its brothers or as if day and night it were flashing the "V"[ictory] sign. Unless, that is, the big toe wasn't deliberately sundered, in accordance with the example set by

gulag prisoners sent to cut down forests who were determined to
obtain two or three weeks in the infirmary, thereby saving their
lives at the price of their own mutilation. It makes you want to
dredge up the remnants of your Latin to ask, poignantly or else
disgustedly: "Quo vadis, Respublica?" "Up the arsehole," comes
the reply when you least expect. The history of the patria is the
day-to-day life of a woman whose husband beats her over the
mouth; when the judge asked him why he didn't beat her over
the arse like everybody else, the man serenely replied: "It's her
mouth not her arse that is bad!" Which means we've arrived back
where we started. Dotted line (*n* times): the frontier of this land
passes through the *birth* of the hundred thousand women who
sleep one next to the other on their sides, with their arses poking
outward, abroad.

He ought to get it out of his head, with the indifference of a
peasant howking dirt from under his nails, but how? No matter
how he might divide it up into squares, on a scale of 1 x 131,
according to the number of inhabitants per square kilometer, his
memory isn't big enough to remember for every single person all
the things that are to be forgotten. His three-dimensional mind
balks at imagining 131 abstract people, armed with shovels and
wheelbarrows, voiding a square kilometer of space, leaving it stark
naked, like a white square in an arithmetic exercise book. Things
are further complicated, in geometric progression, once the time
factor is taken into calculation: each patch of soil becomes the
site of an archaeological dig; each corner of the natural world has
its own legend, passed down from mouth to mouth—as many
mouths, as many legends—; every brick a memento: the exodus
of the Israelites from bondage begins when, without them being
given straw to make bricks, but being asked to make the same
number of bricks as before, "So the people were scattered abroad
throughout all the land of Egypt to gather stubble instead of
straw" (Exodus, 5: 12)—it is a book of clay, with uncut pages,
whose words, once you've opened it, you spell out one by one:
"The book of the tribe of (so-and-so), son of (so-and-so), son of
(so-and-so)". But those who upset all the calculations on paper
are the country's citizens: more than 4,000,000 *curricula vitarum*

x 66 years life expectancy x 365 days per annum etc. Thus, the equation of forgetting is insensibly transformed into an exercise in remembrance; it is as if you were to cast over people, places, times the net of multiple-zero figures—the net is nothing but a conglomeration of holes stitched together with white thread—, in the hope of hauling ashore a geopolitical fiction; not even a fiction, a blas*femina* (a play on words inspired by Horace, for whom bad taste translated as a beautiful woman ending in a fish's tail; in the original: "*Desinit in piscem mulier formosa superne*"). And to which shore anyway? When the two shores spread apart like the legs of a woman about to give birth: nobody ever enters the world willingly. To push (a verb that sums up the process whereby life begins, from: "He/she pushed me into it," and the self-condemnatory version: "I was pushed into it . . ." to the commands of the midwife: "Push! push!") the reality to the point where *Nobody is the patria, not even the magnificent horseman* (depicting Suvorov on the other shore—not to the native reader) in order to turn the page. Point. No, semi-colon: P—t and D—r.

Or on the contrary, to get it into his head once and for all! There is no need for him to imagine his bonce in the form of a porcelain piggy or kitty bank, with a slot in the top of his head; suffice it that he describe his geography teacher. Her lessons invariably commenced with "you blockheads" and concluded, just as predictably, with "get it into your heads". All until one day— April 22, a red letter day—when the lads from the tenth year came to class, every last one of them, with their heads shaved, this during an out-of-control period of expansion for the beatnik movement throughout the communist bloc—their oval craniums made up a figure in the millions—, and Pîslaru, for whom the old maid had a soft spot (just two days earlier she had overlooked his answer to the question of what countries bordered the Soviet Union: "Whichever ones it likes!"), had tattooed on his bald head the northern hemisphere. The incident would have been overlooked, once again, had not the teacher's beady eye chanced to notice the absence of "our republic" in favor of the "neighboring and friendly country," which absence could be explained by the political ignorance of the tattooist: he had

copied the map from an inter-war atlas. At the teachers' meeting
convened on the afternoon of the same day, the headmaster—
he, too, a war veteran and local Party secretary—demanded the
head of the boy, but not before making him redraw the map
with its post-1949 boundaries; his tutor finally managed to prevent him being expelled, at least in theory, by stipulating that
"pupil Pîslaru will be allowed to attend lessons only after his hair
grows back" (the quotation is from the procès-verbal). Despite
this, he was not allowed to sit his final exams, on the grounds
of mental illness, but in reality, so that he wouldn't obtain his
attestation of ten years of schooling, with which he could have
attended any institution of higher education, given the head he
had on his shoulders, and in the autumn of the same year—he
had just reached his "eighteenth spring"—he was enlisted in the
ranks of the glorious Soviet Army and once again shaven bald.
Needless to say, one of his fellow countrymen, otherwise a good
lad, with an education—three years of Literature at university—,
denounced him to the sergeant; the latter's reaction was an order:
"Рядовой Пысларь, тут же отрасти волосы!"[203] As for the
geography teacher, she died prematurely, just over a year after
the "nationalist incident", she herself now almost bald; despite
this, letters addressed to her (care of the school) still continued
to arrive from the army. The sender? None other than private
Pîslaru. Each letter went into copious detail and often employed
"грубый солдацкий юмор" (coarse soldierly humor). One
example: Political education class, unit *xy*. The officer takes
from his knapsack a red brick and puts it on the table. "Soldier
Ivanov, what comes to your mind when you see this brick?" "The
construction of communism!" "Very good! What about you,
Petrov?" "The unshakeable unity of the Soviet people." "Bravo!
What about you, Sidorov?" "A c—t!" "Why a c—t?" "Because
all I think about are c—ts!" Just to let her know what life a
"лысый глобус" (bald globe) led far from home, and invariably concluding with "СЛУЖУ СОВЕТСКОМУ СОЮЗУ!"[204]

---

[203] Private Pîslari, grow your hair long immediately!

[204] I SERVE THE SOVIET UNION!

Beneath which, the signature—*Pîslă siberiană* [*Siberian felt*]. She did not have the strength of character to reply to him; but the lesson followed her for the rest of her days, which, alas, were numbered, although still more numerous than his: he fell in the line of "duty" in Afghanistan just a few months before he was due to be demobbed.

In other words, he ought to make an examination of his conscience, like bringing down on his head the ten plagues of Egypt. The first—the water turning to blood—happened by itself, in two stages, by the simple fact of being baptized a Christian: had not Christ turned the water to wine, at the wedding in Canaan of Galilee, and then the wine into blood, at the Last Supper? He had no fear of frogs. But who would have believed that in a city with running water, both hot and cold, in his own home, in the year of the Lord 2000, he would be overrun with lice? They must have latched onto him in the country, after an in-ter-mi-na-ble week's stay with relatives, with whom he had nothing in common other than the blood the parasites were now sucking. He perceived the lice as such: the alarmed punctuation mark of an unequivocal divine message: "Get the f—k out of here!" (there was no point waiting for the next seven plagues, particularly since the last—the death of the first-born—concerned him directly.) No sooner said than done, except that "here" is everywhere; whenever you arrive "there", you find yourself "here." And then the only thing you can do is depart (in the sense of: "He has departed from among us . . ."); your destination: nowhere. Under cover of darkness (like a bookplate curse that catches you up: "Let him who steals this book have doors without a handle and die without a candle"). The way you might violate the border and the patria will still not let you leave her. The way you might run away from home with the country in your arms or between your legs. By between your legs, I mean between the Tigris and the Euphrates of the paradise lost and—whenever you stick a spoke in—found. His openness in matters of copulation surpassed even that of the brothers *Who-knows-the-Male-and-keeps-the-Female*. What, you haven't heard of the famous Siamese twins, brother and sister, consummate acrobats

and peerless dancers on the tight-rope—parallel wires, like a
trolleybus's—stretched no less than forty feet high, who, in their
desperation for unity, roamed the length and breadth of the
world in search of their other halves, with their every arrival in
some unknown town or port being preceded by the invariable
announcement published in the local *Evening Gazette*: "Siamese
siblings, *he* and *she*, wish to meet Siamese siblings, she and he,
with a view to forming two heterosexual couples"? Their manager, none other than their biological father, who sold them to
a travelling circus when the siblings were just a few months old
and—as was to be discovered later, too late . . .—might still have
been separated without any risk of losing either of them, and
who himself took a job as their keeper and later their trainer,
placed high hopes in the success of that matrimonial announcement, the likes of which had never been seen before. A great
admirer of Plato, he believed that in his offspring he had found
him of whom it was said that "only his name is left of him"; like
the *androgyne*, "they had four arms and as many legs; they had
two faces, exactly the same (. . .) four ears, two procreative organs
and, in short, everything else, which you can easily reconstruct
for yourselves.' It was therefore decided to marry them off, not to
fill their solitude—an illusory solitude given that neither could
go anywhere without the other, not even to the place where even
the king enters without his bodyguard—, so much as based on a
calculation like that of twenty years before, summed up in two
words: *panem* (for him) *et circenses* (for everybody else). His idea
was to put on a production of the *Symposium*, and to be more
precise, the sublime passage in which those wonderful creatures
clasped each other in their arms so tightly when they met that in
their desire to fuse they forgot about eating and everything else.
The circus tent would serve at the canopy of the marriage bed—
each performance would be like the first time! All he lacked was
the *altera pars*; when, one fine day, an inseparable couple—as
it says in the book, "never to be parted, one from the other"—,
made their appearance in the lobby of the only decent hotel in
the little town where they had stopped to give just a few perfor-
mances, the hapless matchmaker realized what a monumental

trap destiny had laid for him, and all by his own doing. Since the announcement had not specified the position of the twins relative to each other, he was presented with a mirror image of his own children. Placed face to face, they fell in love with each other: he with him, she with her. (Just like the countries, she and her, if he and him can't be had: Moldova—Bessarabia wish to meet the Republic of Moldova—Moldovan Republic of Dniester, with a view to . . .)

Others exorcise her by drawing maps in their heads, with all the skill of a traffic policeman drawing a chalk outline— the crumbly chalk possesses something of the friability of the bridal gown—around the lifeless body of the victim. She changes her map with the frequency of blood-soaked bandages; once a month, the mother-patria crosses the inner sea—the Red Sea—, regaining her appetite for food, joie de vivre, and, of course, her proverbial virginity, that of a *beauteous queen / bride of the world* (The old tale of the *Sultan of Babylon* (who) *gives his daughter's hand in marriage to the king of Garbo and sends her to him by ship; after various adventures over the course of four years, during which she falls into the hands of nine men but is finally returned to the sultan, still a virgin, supposedly, and is then sent off once more to be the bride of the king of Garbo*, or, more recently, the tale of the virtuous virgin who had managed—how? only the fundament knows the secret the mouth conceals!—to preserve her maidenhead till her wedding night, despite having lived with a man for seven years, and once sequestered in the groom's room, she fiercely defended the bastion of her chastity till dawn, when, feigning exhaustion, she raised the white flag . . . The spotted sheet, hung out in the yard of the house, thus became the blazon of a perfect young couple who had married for love). Dated maps suit her best, from which vast swaths are detached exactly the same as in the moral of fairy tales about taking children from their mothers: "Then he (the boyar) tied the Gypsy woman to the tails of the horses, along with a sack of walnuts, and he released them to wander the world, *and wherever the walnut fell* . . ." Whether by accident or not, the edges of all the country's highways are planted with walnut trees, yet further proof that the

Gypsy woman subjected to the ordeal is a reincarnation of the
fiancée in the legend of the knight who went off to the crusades
and, in a spirit of sacrifice, gave an eye to the lady of his heart;
moved by her lover's gesture, she gave him an ear; on learning
of the girl's courage, the knight gave her an arm; not to be outdone, she gave him a leg; he, four ribs; she, one breast; he, she
. . . ; when finally they met again, all that was left of him was a
c—k, of her, a c—t: going to her, the c—k collapsed—by virtue
of the now unstoppable process of disintegration—like a cannon
whose wheels fall off in the middle of the road; about to receive
him in the conjugal bed, the c—t fell apart, leaving only the
hole in the middle. Nor are the recent administrative maps to
be discarded; the card game of territorial autonomies is a game
for two, for three, and then as part of four-party negotiations:
the winner is the one who, without anybody else grabbing his
hand, manages to turn face down as many of his adversary's cards
as possible; the cards are as many *chasses gardées d'outre mer* on
which is inscribed: "*Ibi sunt leones . . .*" But the ones that move
you to tears are the housewives' maps: each leaf of onion peel
highlights the quintessence of the Vale of Tears that is the world
of humans. Nor have I said anything about the maps of tea stains
that cover his every manuscript, including this one, by whose
"relief", be it mountainous or flat, posterity will pass judgement
on the author's sleepless nights. Setting out one fine day to write
their legends, he found he had written a

Recapitulative lesson on the Great Migration of peoples
Long before the term *geopolitics* became current, the great work of
harmonizing the national geography & history with demographic
policy commenced with the colonization of annexed territories,
whose native populations either were put to the sword or voluntarily joined the colonizers, bringing their arms and baggage with
them. The nuptial bedsheets would finish what the maps of the
strategists were unable to cover—the human stains of the "mingled
fluids" took the place of the white patches; blood was shed more
and more seldom and—with a little luck—only on the wedding
night; some sheets produced two harvests a year. It is not quintals of

wheat (barley, maize, grapes, sugar beet etc.) per hectare so much as inhabitants per square kilometer that constitute a country's wealth; there are as many countries as pockets, each nation to its own pocket or moving from one pocket to another, wholly or in part. Sewn together, they make up the geopolitical map of mankind; it is (un)known in which of them God puts/will put his hands. But in any event, since most of the pockets have holes in them, whichever pocket He has thrust them into, He has always held the chosen people in his palm. Turned inside out, besides the national currency, each reveals the small change of other peoples, which are accused, usually in times of crisis, of emptying the majority's pockets. Numerous vigilant citizens, living from one wage to the next, are prepared to chip in to convert the minorities, albeit at a rate of exchange less profitable to the majority. In wholly exceptional cases, even the Train Timetable, itself thrown into disarray—from the Auschwitz death trains to the unforgettable slogan of the nineties: "Чемодан — Вокзал — Россия!"[205] (the countless "trains of friendship" don't count)—, depends on the exchange rate. Likewise, after they have lost/taken each other's pieces/queens from the chessboard, the real players carry on the match, moving the white and black squares—there are as many potential moves as there are squares, to the power of four, in accordance with the number of cardinal points—, until they manage to push the game into extra time, and until on the board there remains not a single white square, and even fewer black ones.

But the grandiose work of settling man in his own country and the patria inside the national frontiers does not stop here, since more often than not, man does not feel at home, and the patria does not fit—man among his peers, and the patria among other countries. And so, the Supreme Prestidigitator recalls the aforementioned chessboard—one and the same for numerous games—and wonders to himself: "From two things, one: should I change the pieces? should I change the squares?" At which his twin brother, Muddler, answers without having been asked: "Why not two in one: let mankind leave his country for another, once in his life,

---

[205] Suitcase – Station – Russia!

and let the *patriae* shed their borders like snakes sloughing off their skins, once in a generation?" In the end, after arm-wrestling for an eternity, without anybody being able to claim victory, they come to an agreement, exhausted: the other will lend a hand to whichever of them gains the upper hand. Which in practical terms translates as not letting him get out of hand. As quick as you can clap your hands, they take a census of the world's population and simultaneously calculate the surfaces areas of the currently existing countries, after which it is agreed: once every generation, each nation will receive a *patria* to fit, based on the number of inhabitants per square kilometer. In fact, each nation will have to move to take possession of its *patria*—and thus begins the Great Migration of peoples. On the designated date, all the people in the world, young and old, chattels and all, set off—revolving around its axis, the planet rushes to meet them/the earth flees beneath the soles of their feet—and they keep going (Like Him who said: "And so they went; there was nobody before them and nobody behind, nobody to the right and nobody to the left"), and when, at the end of their strength, they reach their destination and settle down to live, the order comes for them to be on the move again and they are given a different address. If they don't pick up and leave, they risk not occupying their place on another map; if they stay where they are, they risk being displaced by whoever lays claim to that place as their promised land. But since the change of frontiers would lead to even greater displacement of populations, not to mention the imminent collateral losses, in human life and fixed assets, everybody obeys: nation (x) rises as a single man, in one breath, and legs it—if not willingly, then lifted up by nation (y) and hauled away so that all trace of it will be lost and not even its name will ever return. Every means is good in the struggle for peace—contraceptives versus encouraging a higher birthrate; the "only child" versus "one for the mother, one for the father, and the third for the nation"; "shall we get rid of this one . . ." versus "or shall we have another?"—, now that there's a demographic war of every nation against all the rest. In any case, on the due date, the citizens, expressed as the number of inhabitants, are placed on one pan of the scales, and countries, expressed as square kilometers, on the other—Muddler checks to see that the

Supreme Prestidigitator doesn't tip the scales—, then everything is
divided on the abacus—now it's the Supreme Prestidigitator who
takes care lest Muddler gets his sums mixed up—with each coun-
try/population being given an area as large as it can handle/rule.
It is unimportant that as a result of this division some have to be
transplanted over land and sea, others across the street—correct
judgement is based solely on figures: each birth is taken into cal-
culation/not a palm's width of land is overlooked. A woman might
sooner take her knickers off in public without anybody noticing
than for countries to abandon their borders, be they too tight, be
they too baggy. Noble titles, hereditary or bought, are forgotten,
military ranks are abolished, political parties are disbanded, sepa-
ratist/reunifying movements are outlawed—the land surveyor and
the midwife are now the politicians of this world.

And just when mankind is about to complete the grandiose
work of typesetting, in the form of the Magna Charta Libertatum,
printed in two interchangeable columns—the countries on one
side, the nations on the other: each to the right of the other; but
also: *Departures* and *Arrivals*, *Births* and *Deaths*, etc.—of mankind
nears the end, one of the two, the one who came up with *from two
things, one*, says to himself: "This world is not mine, even less so
the other one," and the other, the one who came up with *two in
one*, by way of reply, with his forked serpent's tongue: "Suck my
c♂k / f—k you, you c♀t!"

Lest it remain a dead letter, he had, on the off-chance, posted
the text to two publications situated at opposite poles, *Sovereign
Moldova* and *The Land*; the first had rejected it ex officio on
the grounds that it would have undermined the statehood of
the RM, the other on the grounds that it was a blow against
the ideals of reunification. The *ubi bene* of both is above suspicion, therefore the *ibi patria* (where the *ibi* is merely written in
the Roman alphabet, but is to be read in Russian: "иби свой
— дешевле обойдётся!"[206] in the best tradition of "harmonious bilingualism") can sleep peacefully: after two decades of

---

[206] (bad Russian) F—k yours – it'll cost you less!

uninterrupted contraband, the "Land"—*absit omen!*—has not yet reached the bottom of the sack, and "Sovereignty"—as can well be seen—isn't bursting its banks. Likewise, the P—t (via the D—be) and the D—r empty into the Black Sea, but the sea doesn't rise to flood the nether lands, nor do the rivers run dry, even if there are many who, with witnesses, undertake to drink them in a single gulp.

There isn't anybody willing to lose his head for it, not necessarily in imitation of Constantine Brîncoveanu & Sons, nor, having joined the ring dance, copying the footwork of the monkey dancing on the drum (a sign that the corpse rot has not yet reached its brain and therefore the diners can tuck into the goblet of the open skull), but rather answering John Fitzgerald Kennedy's call: "*ask not what your country can do for you—ask what you can do for your country*"; easily said, albeit difficult to translate into deeds, as long as the Patria is a business proposition for every interloper. Don't even ask what you can do *with* it; at most, you can have it off with it, losing your head, and what's more, in front of everybody. Not that it would be indecent—it doesn't have anywhere to be indecent! And when it does, it still shares the place with another two. Three girls living in a two-room rented apartment, in which you have to pass through one room to get to the other. Even if she manages to get the Russian girl to go and see a film, the Gagauz girl has just come home, complaining of a headache, and so our girl has to take her dear guest to the kitchen, which means you can forget about the bedroom. The change of scene brings not change in mood, now that desire has already wound her up with its magic key for a sex session. But since there's nothing they can do, the spring unwinds without engaging the mechanism; in the meantime, the girl makes some tea, shouting through the wall at her roommate to ask if she would like a cup, not that she bends over backwards for her, but rather so that she can hear from which corner of the flat the answer will come, which frees the hands of her dear guest—he's not made of stone, after all—to push her up against one corner. Now they are two animals in heat, sharing the confines of the same cage, two paces between gas stove and fridge, one pace between table and crockery cupboard, all enveloped in an atmosphere increasingly heated. Just as the water comes to the boil, the Gagauz girl suddenly changes her mind, now she wants some tea, so she will have to add another cup for there to be enough water for three. (He would gladly dispense with the tea and instead take the she-devil who has been simmering him for half an hour.) "Who wanted mint tea?" (not *thé de menthe* but *thé dément*, given the situation), the girl says, tempting her roommate, but the Gagauz can't be bothered with anything, not even to spoil their fun, she looms in view only then to be eclipsed in the next room, where, mug in hand, she plonks herself on the couch and turns on the telly. "Mother of God, let her find a soap opera to watch . . ." the guest prays in his mind, since his mouth is full of the girl's kiss. The girl rolls her eyes at a thought: "I hope that Russian doesn't pick her time to come home now!" The separating wall becomes what it may be supposed always to have been: a tympanum; the main thing is to know whether the two are preventatively listening in on what's happening in the next room or whether the Gagauz is discreetly spying on them. On the other side, the only sound is the loudly jabbering box, and on this side, teaspoons clinking as they stir the tea. No matter how much you might force yourself to engage in conversation, when your head (glans) has its mind on love, the words won't come together, and what comes out of the mouth is seminally scented chewing-gum bubbles, the words are as many blanks, fired in the direction of the adversary on the other side of the door that has—strategically—been left half open, while the two of them throw themselves into hand-to-hand fighting. The way the girl seats herself in his lap, lifting her skirt so that the dear guest can feel her bare buttocks—the knickers that have ridden up inside are like a cheese wire—, smacks of a declaration of war; from his chair, the man keeps the front door under observation, while his hands advance on two fronts, his right beneath her T-shirt, seeking her breasts, his left up the inner thigh. With one hand, she lifts her hair so that she can feel his hot breath down the back of her neck and, while her mouth takes its snail out for a walk, with her other hand she gropes for the zipper of his jeans, thereby opening open the third front. His hands have not been idle, and the measurements they have made on the ground show that ("we wanted to shed the clothes of our homelands"—the gospel according to *The English Patient*), having swollen greatly, her breasts have spilled from the cups of her bra, and the knickers are not as dry as heretofore. "Don't scald me!" he says *à haute voix*, as if talking about the tea, but the girl understands exactly what is needed and moves to a chair, raising one leg as she does so, in order to provide a better prospect for the final assault. (She looks like a hieroglyph which, in order to grasp it once and for all, he paints as best he knows how, in the form of a haiku:

> *three lashes floating*
> *inside the glass of water*
> *black tea. sleeplessness)*

Through the semitransparent cotton he lip reads the words: "*Viens! Viens!*" but without her calling him to her, he ravishes her with his gaze. It is the moment of truth, when the gods laugh at mortals: either they stop halfway, regretfully signing a shameful armistice, or they shamelessly have it off right under the nose of her roommate, with the risk of being caught in flagrante delicto. His head (glans), popping up outside the elastic of his underpants, votes aye; she twists around to look at the door one last time and then pulls off her knickers: "Add a spoon of honey before it cools down . . ." They are so close, their knees interlocked, that before he knows it, his fingers are inside her honeycomb, the girl's body buzzes with impatient like a hive without a queen. "Do something, anything, just do it!" croaks the girl straight into the microphone, a silent scream, with her mouth over his glans. The guest feels as if he is in a Max Frisch play, *Don Juan or Love for Geometry*, he is fearful lest he end up like the Italo Calvino protagonist from *On a carpet of leaves lit by the moon*, the chapter that the girl guessed from the very first would be his favorite in *If on a winter's night a traveler*. And then he makes the cleverest possible move in the given situation—he doesn't pull her toward him, as he sits on the chair by the window, but holding her up, he steps toward the middle of the kitchen, whence he can see the Gagauz girl reflected in the windowpane of the half-open door as she dozes in front of the television. With a sure hand, he twists his partner around, she is attentive to his movements, which are peremptory and tender at the same time, she is firmly convinced he knows what he is doing and that whatever happens, he's going to pleasure her. Letting her hang forward, holding her arms to form a suspension bridge above the void, the two are now a system of *poids-contrepoids*, whose equilibrium resides in his ability to guide the assembly work. When finally he penetrates her from behind, he feels his wand engulfed by a pot for smelting gold ("What has she got that is greased with gold?" wonder at one point the wives whose husbands' have the hots for the heroine from Gabriel García Márquez's *Incredible and Sad Story of Eréndira and Her Heartless Grandmother*); the sacs pump scorching air from both sides; the *bielle-manivelle*—'the beast with two backs'—'*and he pulled and he pulled, and he pushed and he pushed*'! A herd of horsepower galloping from one body to the other, the engines racing until they reach a hundred miles an hour in just a few seconds, the combustion of desire achieves an explosion readied by mutual agreement, love is a Formula 1 race down the wrong side of the road, a hurtling fireball eating up the asphalt. They both finish simultaneously, all in one breath, one of those (few) cases where haste (or rather speed!) doesn't make waste, but rather makes the head spin. For an instant they remain welded, she having received her day's royal jelly, he covered from head to toe in her wild honey; "I'm just going to nip off and get washed . . ." she twists around to his left ear, where she meets his lips: "You f—ker!" Viewing one side of her—in general, but not in the present case—got you nowhere; it was only when you experienced her in the flesh that she acquired mythical dimensions, with even God exclaiming *la joie de vivre*. "Few people know that the story of the Queen of Sheba begins long before she herself makes her entrance," the guest greets his welcoming host when she comes back from the bathroom, "namely, when King Solomon began building the House of the Lord in Jerusalem. But since the laborers were unable to cut the huge blocks of stone, and their tools broke one by one, Solomon had to resort to . . . —how would you translate палочка-выручалочка?[207]— . . . his magic wand, none other than God. At Yahve's suggestion, he commands hunters to catch a Rukh chick, which he places under a brass vessel, in such a way that its wings poke out from underneath. Meanwhile. the mother Rukh has returned to her nest and not finding her chick, she flies around the world until finally she finds it under the brass vessel, but isn't strong enough to break it. Desperate, she flies up into the firmament, to the Paradise of the Lord, east of Eden, where she finds a piece of wood that has been thrown there so that she will find it. She picks up the wood, brings it to Jerusalem and uses it to strike the brass vessel—by the power of the Lord, it breaks, releasing the chick. Witness to the miracle, Solomon and the children of Israel learn their lesson. The book later says: And straightaway King Solomon ordered the builders to take that piece of holy and blessed wood and, after marking and measuring the rock they wished to split, to place the wood on the marked spot. After they did so, by the power of the Lord, the rock split wherever they wished to split it . . ." "A bit like," she interjects, "*Cap-ra cal-că pia-tra. Pia-tra cra-pă-n pa-tru. Cră-pa-i-ar ca-pul cap-rei . . .*"[208] "Exactly, since the Queen of Sheba—the virgin queen!—had a goat's foot, for which reason she didn't want to marry any man. I'll pass over the Queen's journey to Jerusalem; here she is, then, at the gate of the Temple, whose courtyard has been filled with water, at the orders of Solomon, who wants to find out whether the rumors about the goat's leg are true. Since she cannot enter the House of the Lord on horseback, the Queen of Sheba dismounts and hitching up her skirt, she wades through the water, thereby revealing her leg without Solomon asking her to. But as soon as the Queen's goat leg touches the holy wood brought by the Rukh bird, with which they split the rock for the flagstones, and then paved the courtyard, the Power of the Lord revealed itself and the leg became like its pair. Listen to how wonderfully the Arabic text

---

[207] Children's game involving a wand (paločka) — Translator's note

[208] Romanian tongue twister, literally: The goat treads the rock. The rock cracks in four. May it crack the head of the goat — *Translator's note*

puts it: *And as soon as she realized the terrible power that had taken hold of her, great fear and trembling descended upon her.*" Caught in the spell of the myth, the girl learns of the Queen's sojourn at the court of King Solomon, and how he managed to get her between his sheets, after the poor woman almost died of thirst; she learns of how she became pregnant by him, how she returned to her own land, gave birth to a male child, whom she named David, after her grandfather; how the young man, when he grew up, wished to meet his father, despite the opposition of his mother, who told him: "I had to sully myself to make you!" (words to found a dynasty: "Speak and swear on heavenly Zion that you will never again make women queens and you will never again seat them on the throne of Ethiopia and that only the male line of David, son of Solomon, will reign over Ethiopia"), and undertakes a journey to Jerusalem, where King Solomon recognizes him and *straight away he put the crown of his father David on his head and seated him on the throne of David, his father, and the trumpets blew and the heralds cried, saying: "This is David, the son of Solomon, son of David, King of Israel*"; since on his departure he asked for the Tabernacle of the Covenant of the Lord and was refused by his father, he stole the Ark of the Law, and with it the glory of Israel, that the kingdom of David, moved from Jerusalem to Ethiopia, might be eternal . . . "Выходит, Пушкин потомок Царя Давида?"[209] the astonishment of the Russian girl, having appeared in the doorway out of the blue, is boundless, and so is theirs: "Want some tea?" and when the intruder nods, the girl's reply leaves her *bouche bée*: "How many eyelashes need to fall in a glass of water to make an infusion of *1001 Nights. Pure Ceylon tea?*"

To make a *tabula rasa* of this country merely to expose it—veronica of a messiah late in revealing himself—the whole thing is vanity of vanities. To employ the mold of Exodus in order to cast, in the naked form of a story that has come down to us only as its suspense, its legend, the only difference being that this

---

[209] Does that mean that Pushkin is a descendant of King David?

time, not the newcomers, but the aborigines leave their country of origin taking that country with them, each as much as he can carry. ("Duchess", that's what they called her behind her back, the old courtesan dressed in period clothes, after the fashion of ladies in the reign of Tsar Nicholas, who walked her grey poodle along Boulevard Dacia, at the same hour evening after evening, and who carried in her left hand a piece of white cardboard, inscribed in *encre de Chine*, visible from afar: "ВСТРЕТИМСЯ В АДУ!"[210] As punctual as Immanuel Kant and straight as a metal strand laid through a crisp new banknote, the woman had come to blend into the cityscape, with her daily round-trip walk between the Viaduct and the Gates of the City lending her the authenticity of an empire-period Ch—ău lost *à jamais*. But she was a nightmarish apparition to whomever saw her for the first time . . .) To daydream that everybody, young and old, *all at once*, crosses the frontier drawn in the soil by an index finger and, from the other side, crosses back—ah! the irresistible call of your origins; the voice of the blood: "*Torna, fratre, torna*"[211]—, for the toes of their boots to erase it from the face of the earth, but not before sticking their tongues out at it: "See if you can find any trace of it," in reply to the legitimate wonderment of the border guard: "Кто спиздил Родину, мать вашу?!"[212] But the infinitives lead nowhere: history isn't made while standing to attention. It would be like him nicking his cheek with the razor when the telephone rang, to know where he had got up to in his shaving. The writing notches the page of the form—you exist insofar as you advance from *NOM to Signature du demandeur;* the 25 shelves of the questionnaire constitute the ideal wardrobe for a gentleman, behind whose screen you change before stepping out; as many forms as there are families. As many family blazons as there are forms. By hand (a sure hand, trembling hand, nervous hand etc.), each stitches his biographical cadaver

---

[210] We'll meet in hell!

[211] *Torna, torna, fratre* (turn, turn, brother): the Vulgar Latin words of a soldier quoted in a Greek chronicle of the Byzantine period, dating from A.D. 587, but claimed by nationalist linguists to be the earliest recorded instance of the Romanian language — *Translator's note*

[212] Who swiped the Patria, your mother?!

into the cloth sack of the standard form in order to save his skin; the skill of the writing consists in pulling all the threads inside, without allowing the authorities to suspect that a mass breakout is being planned, operation *Patriam fugimus*, which means that you and the corpse in the sack are one, the narrative cloth on which has been printed: *Made in* . . . Where was he? At PAYS DE NAISSANCE. In other words, not USSR, not RM, not Moldavia, not even *Mal de Vie* . . . What then? then let its name be *I'LL THRASH YOU TO AN INCH OF YOUR LIFE*. In a word, *WEENIA*.

End

The *Last Wish* Columbarium[213]

"Life tied with string"

Beyond her powers
of comprehension
how it was that
the sister of mercy
was unable
to find her
vein in one go—
whereas she, eighty-
odd years old
even if she
had long since lost
her eyesight could still
thread a needle
unfailingly and without
anybody's help,
although she had to ask
her family to
tell her what
color the thread was.

The school of life

After his
"four years
of Romanian schooling"
my grandfather
needed
about 80 years
for his mind
to catch up
with Hamlet's
words,*
when on his
deathbed
he asked me
with a final
effort, enough
to make himself
understood, by
way of farewell:
"on the lips . . ."

* "Alas, poor Yorick! (…) Here hung those lips that I have kissed I know not how oft."

[213] to the persons mentioned, even if only mentally, in the pages of this book

Maternal octoechos

1. Feast day
In the summer of
forty-six,
mama boiled
and ate
her childhood
bran doll.

2. 22
The little
french
mama
spoke
will have been
enough
to give
birth to me
on june 22
along with
Nostalgia*
or perhaps
the future
romanian
teacher
will have had
the last
word
bringing me
into the world
of Our
language.**

3. Terzina
Mama of all people
to be missing from
the Holy Trinity?
But how, Lord?!!

4. The last sound
Diminished
by illness
even unto
her speech,
although
she had taught
the Romanian
tongue and
literature
a lifetime,
mama
bequeathed
with her
dying tongue
just four
words:

nothing
hurts
me
now

* the word "nostalgia" was coined on June 22, 1688 by Johannes Hofer, who, in his medical thesis Dissertatio medica de nostalgia, where he analyzes the illness affecting Swiss soldiers far from their mountains, combined the word nostos ("return") with algos ("pain").

** poem published by Alexie Mateevici on June 22, 1917 in Cuvînt moldovenesc.

5. Light from light
Melted away from
suffering
as she was,
when I lit
a candle
for her
on the evening
of march 8
the flame
turned
its face
to mama
and softly,
lest it
frighten
her sleep,
breathed
in her ear:
"Lights out"

6. Midnight service
Read in
the mirror
with orphan
eyes
verse
8:8 from
Ecclesiastes:
"There is no man
that
hath
power
over death"
seems to
have been
written
for Mama
on M
arch 8

7. Pietà
Now
all
I wish for
is
another 7
years of
life
and only
that I
might be
buried
in a
grave
with mama:
one in
the arms
of the other
awaiting
the resurrection
from the dead.

8. (∞.I.1943 — 2015.III. ∞)

Memento mori 2014

In its 44th
year
of posterity,
the poetry of
Paul Celan
(1920-1970)
increasingly
resembles
Romy
Schneider
(1938-1982)
shortly
before
she put an
end
to her
days.

Parallel lives/
serial deaths

Who for whom
had to put it in
who with whom
to take it out
—serially
or in parallel—
so that none
of the three:
Jimi Hendrix
(1942-1970)
Janis Joplin
(1943-1970)
Jim Morrison
(1943-1971)
—at least
out of respect
for the law
of communicating
vessels—
would not have died
of an overdose
all alone?

Jus vitae necisque

One birth
for every
(attempted)
suicide—
on departing
Sylvia Plath
(1932-1963)
owed nothing
to anybody.

Zippo

The flamboyant
                              body
of little englishwoman
Jane Birkin
bursting from the hands
of Serge Gainsbourg
(1928-1991)
long enough to light
une dernière cigarette.

"Ваше Сиятельство"

How sparkling
must have seemed
death
to the Grand Duchess
Anastasia Nikolaevna
(1901-1918)
dressed as she was
in her dress of diamonds
causing the bullets
of the firing squad
to ricochet
like fireworks
in the basement
of the Ipatiev house.

"Needle in the brain, thought"

To judge by
the size
of the gothic cathedral
of the icicle
that fell
on top of his head,
the man about whom
they said on the news:
"A person
unknown
died instantly . . ."
must have been
Immanuel Kant
(1724-1804)
at the very least.

"De la musique avant toute chose"

On piano—
Svyatoslav Richter
(1915-1997)
playing live
in fingerless gloves
in -10°C
and, from the ground—
nothing is too much
for the Father of Nations
(1879-1953)!—
a Stradivarius coffin.

CV = WC

. . . after they
beat him
till he
shat
blood
on himself, O.M.
(1891-1938)
flushed
and there flowed

     a
     n
     g
     e, 5 l—

blood is thicker
than water.

M.M.

In one palm
I clasp
the lifeline
in the other
a blade
placing (its)
sign
"="-ity
slantwise.
Guess in
which hand,
Madi Marin
(1956-2003)?

Wake

. . . now
even your eyes
Alexandru
Muşina
(1954-2013)
will enhance
the blue
of Voroneţ

Mutatis mutandis

Now that's
professional
solidarity—
in his final years
Eugen Cioclea
(1948-2013)
always asked
for food
and was given
from time
to time
drink.

Dead drunk

1.
Is it not so,
blood brother
Ioan Flora
(1950-2005)
that morning
dew settles
the stomach?

2.
Seven years—
and here it is,
Gheorghe Crăciun
(1950-2007)
it turns
your graveyard
dog's
stomach!

Sozzled diptych

1.
                    . . . without
Alexandru Vlad
(1950-2015)
this REALLY
isn't a pipe!

2.
A man of life
death knocked
him back—
now Al. Vlad
takes incense
snuff
and smokes
censer tobacco.

Golden section

1.
... and if
his mother
had given
birth to him
by cesarian
section,
would
Yukio Mishima
(1925-1970)
still have
committed
seppuku?

2.
... when
the wisdom
of old age
told him
that
being elderly
was shameful,
Yasunari Kawabata
(1899-1972)
washed away
the shame
with blood.

3.
... brothers
in sword
during life,
death
came
to them both
by the
(same)
samurai
sword belt—
in the form of
wakizashi,* Mishima
& katana,** Kawabata.

---

* wakizashi（脇差）— short-bladed japanese sword, measuring between 30 and 61 cm, worn on the same belt as the katana.

** katana（刀）— long-bladed japanese sword, measuring more than 60cm, worn by the samurai on the same belt as the wakizashi.

Parting with Goethe (1749-1832)

If I seek
death
with a candle
it is still
so that I might make
light
more light

Said and done

God
made the world
in seven days
Ludwig Wittgenstein
(1889-1951)
defined it in
7 sentences.

Heads or tails

1.
The final
orchid
from
the buttonhole of
Oscar Wilde
(1854-1900)
before he
exchanged
his dandy's
smoking jacket
for a prisoner's
striped uniform—
like a cockerel
fired from a
gun
aimed at his
　　e
　　a
　　r
　　t

2.
Every
orchid
threaded
through a
frock coat
buttonhole
is transformed
into a clitoris,
and only
the orchid of
Marcel Proust
(1871-1922)
into a prostate.

Runes

It was back when
the impatience
to grow up
was expressed as
notches on
the doorframe
at 4, 5, 6, 7 years
(happy birthday!)—
now you're dead set
on leaving behind
Edgar Allan Poe
(1809-1849)
Aleksandr Blok
(1880-1921)
Cesare Pavese
(1908-1950)
Ilarie Voronca
(1903-1946
Antoine de
Saint-Exupéry
(1900-1944)
Yukio Mishima
(1925-1970)
Oscar Wilde
(1854-1900)
Osip Mandelstam
(19891-1938)
Khalid Gibran
(1833-1931)
Jacques Brel
(1929-1978)
still with your eyes on
the cape of good hope
Paul Celan
(1920-1970)

TABULA GRATULATORIA

Readers who liked this book are invited
to add their names to the list below

Readers who did not like this book
should make it a

TABULA RASA.